The Grand Duchess of Nowhere

Laurie Graham

Quercus

First published in Great Britain in 2014 by Quercus Publishing Ltd
This paperback edition published in Great Britain in 2015 by

Quercus Publishing Ltd
Carmelite House
50 Victoria Embankment
London EC4Y 0DZ

An Hachette UK Company

PB ISBN 978 1 78206 973 7
EBOOK ISBN 978 1 78206 972 0

10 9 8 7 6 5 4 3 2 1

Printed and bound in Great Britain by Clays Ltd, St Ives plc

Typeset in Bembo by CC Book Production

Praise for Laurie Graham

'Why is Laurie Graham not carried on people's shoulders
through cheering crowds? Her books are brilliant!'
Marian Keyes

'A delightfully smart and sophisticated historical novelist'
Sunday Times

'She has an uncanny ability to conjure up worlds . . . and
just when you are laughing most, she brings you to tears. A
remarkable novelist'
Libby Purves

'A tour de force where nothing is quite as it seems, with
characters that breathe life and energy ... will have you
laughing and crying in equal measure'
Daily Mail

'Laurie Graham, what a find!'
Wendy Holden

'Funny, fascinating and profoundly moving.
I savoured every sentence'
Freya North

'Graham has a knack for bringing alive the sights,
sounds and smells of yesteryear. Perfect for fans of
Katherine Webb and Deborah Moggach'
We Love This Book

'Empathetic and entertaining'
Independent

'Thoroughly enjoyable'
Woman and Home

Also by Laurie Graham

To Ernest Pig,
Gloucester Old Spot *sans pareil*,
and to his humans

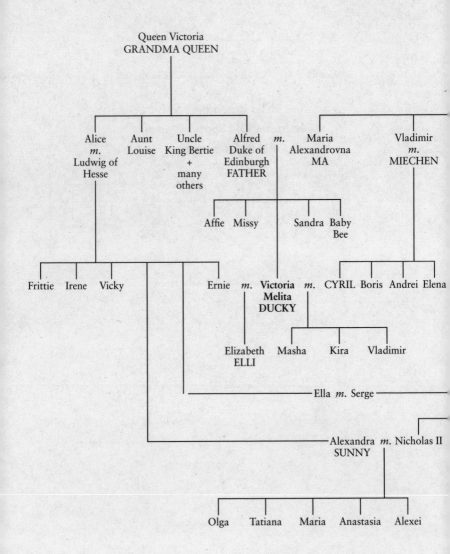

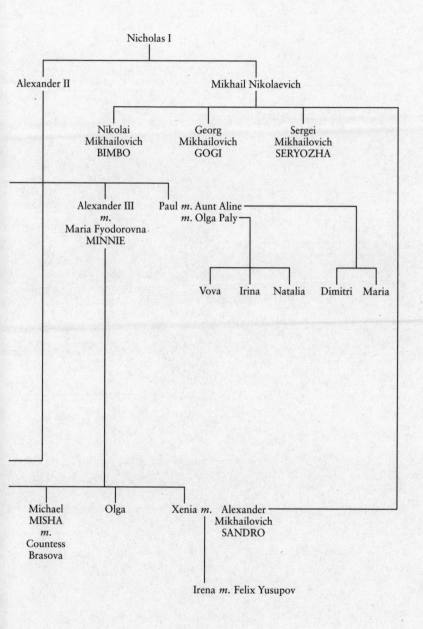

1

I can't say I remember the first time I saw Cyril Vladimirovich. Somehow he's always been around, just one of our many cousins. But I do know the first time I noticed him. It was at Aunt Aline's funeral. That was 1891, so we were both nearly fifteen and he was dressed in his new midshipman's uniform, back straight, eyes front.

It was a long way to travel, from Coburg to Russia, for the funeral of an aunt we'd hardly known, but Mother had her reasons. My sister Missy was sixteen so it was time for her to enter the parade ring and catch the eye of a good husband and, as Mother said, everyone who was anyone would be in Petersburg for Aunt Aline's obsequies. We're supposed to call it Petrograd now, not Petersburg. Too German-sounding, you see, now we're at war. Petrograd. I don't think I shall ever get accustomed to that.

Aunt Aline had died in childbirth. After childbirth, to be quite accurate. She was safely delivered of her second child, a baby boy, and then she just fell asleep and didn't wake up. Grand Duke Uncle Paul was beside himself with grief, left alone with two little ones to raise.

I was so innocent then, about babies and husbands and the facts of life, but my sister Missy thought she knew how it all worked.

She said, 'Ducky, it's too horrendous. The baby comes out of your BTM and if it's a very big baby, you just go pop.'

So I went to Aunt Aline's funeral rather under the impression that she might have burst, like a rubber balloon, but when I saw her in her casket she looked perfectly lovely and peaceful and not at all deflated. Grand Duke Uncle Paul cried and cried and seemed to want to jump into the grave and join her until Mother took him by the elbow and gave him A Talking To. She saw it as her duty. Mother was Uncle Paul's big sister.

After the tragedy of Aunt Aline, Missy swore she was never going to have babies. I must remind her of that next time I see her. If I ever see her again. As I recall things, at the time I was more interested in how the baby got *in* than how it got out.

Missy said, 'Oh, that's disgusting too. The man does The Thing. He makes a pee pee inside you and it turns into a baby. But first you have to have a wedding.'

It all sounded improbable to me but Missy insisted she had it from no lesser authority than one of our daily maids when we lived in England, at Devonport. Pa was in the Navy then, in the years before he had to be a Grand Duke and rule Coburg. But what ignoramuses Missy and I were. Mother thought it was better that way, to enter marriage unburdened by gruesome information. Why lose sleep, after all, over the unavoidable?

Aunt Aline's funeral wasn't the first time we'd been to Russia. Mother took us as often as she could, usually just Missy and me. Our baby sisters stayed at home with their nurses. Mother wished us to grow up knowing our Russian relatives even though she seemed not to like many of them. She never shrank from unpleasant duties. I think, though, the principal reason she took us to Russia so frequently was to annoy Grandma Queen, who had the lowest possible opinion of the Romanovs and all things Russian.

Some ladies like to press flowers or do crewelwork. Mother's favourite pastime was infuriating Grandma Queen. Whenever we were obliged to go to Windsor or to Osborne House she brought extra supplies of her black cigarettes, so as always to be seen smoking, and she'd pile on her jewels, far too many and too brilliant for a simple English house party, but she loved to remind Grandma of her rank and her superior jewellery. Mother, you see, is the daughter of a Russian Emperor. Grandma Queen was merely the daughter of a Duke of Kent. The more I think of it, the more certain I am the only reason Grandma had herself declared Empress of India was to try and overhaul Mother. They never actually quarrelled. Well, hardly ever. It was more a silent battle of wills and rank, and I will say Mother could out-scowl Grandma Queen any day.

I adored our visits to Russia even when they were supposed to be sad occasions. We seemed to attend more funerals than weddings, but even a Russian funeral was superior to anything in grey old England or stodgy old Coburg. Gold was golder and red seemed redder in Russia. Emperor Uncle Sasha rumbled about like a friendly bear and Empress Aunt Minnie was quicker and prettier and better dressed than any of our English aunts.

So, as I said, I began to notice Cyril at Aunt Aline's funeral and he certainly noticed me. I could tell by the way he made such a display of ignoring me. Mother got wind of my interest though and soon trampled on my dreams.

'You can forget Cyril Vladimirovich,' she said. 'Romanovs do not marry their first cousins.'

That was a sly dig at Grandma Queen who thought it the most sensible thing in the world for cousins to marry. She believed that it somehow enriched the blood and she clung to the idea long after the evidence seemed to indicate quite the opposite. We're hardly the healthiest family. We have the bleeding disease for one thing. I don't know of any other family that has it.

3

So Cyril Vladimirovich, who was turning out to be tall and broad-shouldered and rather handsome, was not even to be considered as a future husband and, in any event, the question of a husband for me wasn't uppermost in Mother's mind. Missy had to be matched first and Grandma Queen was promoting the cause of another cousin, Georgie Wales. Grandma Queen spent many happy hours studying our family tree and designing matches between her grandchildren.

Georgie Wales was a second-born son so just like Pa he wasn't likely to be required for the succession. He'd been allowed to join the Navy.

'And what could be more fitting,' Grandma said, 'than for a Royal sailor to marry a Royal sailor's daughter?'

We actually knew Georgie Wales quite well. He'd served under Pa's command when we were stationed in Malta. Missy had no particular objection to him, but Mother wouldn't countenance the match. She knew what it was to be a Navy wife, posted here, there and everywhere. She said it would be a terrible waste of Missy's great beauty. I think she rather held Georgie's stamp collecting against him too, though I'm sure there are worse vices in a husband.

Mother had her heart set on a German Crown Prince for Missy and after going through the *Almanach* very thoroughly she settled on Nando Hohenzollern. He seemed pleasant enough, though very bashful. How mistaken first impressions can be. Everyone said Nando was very keen on Missy but you would never have known it. His eyes were always directed at the floor. The only point Missy found against him was the unfortunate size and set of his ears but that was trumped by the fact that he was his Uncle Carol's heir. Romania had a rather threadbare line of succession and had had to call in Hohenzollern reinforcements. If Missy married Nando, it meant she'd be Queen of Romania someday. Of course as things turned out Eddie Wales expired quite unexpectedly which bumped Georgie up the succession. So if Missy had married him, she'd have ended up Queen of England. One simply never knows.

Anyway, Nando bid for Missy's hand and won it. Grandma Queen said if Missy must make such a mistaken match she had better at least be *properly* married at Windsor. Mother said, over her dead body. Missy would be married in Coburg. And then, after a start had been made on preparations, Nando's family announced that we couldn't possibly expect a Hohenzollern to traipse all the way to Coburg to be married. The bride must go to them. And so we struggled through snowdrifts to Sigmaringen, Missy and Nando were married in the Hohenzollern chapel, so cold you could see their breath as they made their vows, and then they left at once for Romania.

Missy and I had never been apart before. Even when we had scarlatina or the measles, we'd always done it together. Parting from her was too awful. We all went to the station to wave them off. Missy looked pale but very beautiful in her new fox collar, Nando's considerable ears were bright red and Mother cried, which I thought was pretty galling. The whole affair was of her creation, after all.

And the last thing Missy whispered to me was, 'You're next.'

2

We are a vast tribe. One winter afternoon I tried to count my first cousins, living and dead. I got to forty-seven and then someone brought in tea, so I gave up.

Mother was the only girl in a large family of Romanov boys. Pa was Prince Alfred, number three in Grandma Queen's brood of nine. He was Duke of Edinburgh, Admiral of the Fleet and Commander in Chief at Plymouth until one of his uncles died of an unmentionable condition and we were obliged to go to Coburg so Pa could become its new Grand Duke. It wasn't a job he'd particularly expected and I believe he'd have much preferred to remain in the Navy.

Mother and Pa had five children. Affie was the only boy. I'll tell you about him presently. After Affie came Missy, then me, then Sandra and Baby Bee. Some fathers enjoy life in a houseful of petticoats, but not Pa. He was perpetually cross. Mother's way was to ignore it – even when he threw her copy of *Washington Square* at the cat – or to leave the room with more gaiety than was natural in the circumstances, which made him crosser than ever. I have some experience of husbands now myself. I could never emulate Mother. Any husband who throws a book at my cat may expect a cigar box by return of serve.

So, with Missy settled, it came my turn to be found a husband,

and Grandma Queen and Mother, in agreement for probably the first time in their lives, had already decided who it should be. Ernie Hesse. I was rather surprised. First of all, he was just as much my cousin as Cyril Vladimirovich.

Mother said, 'Don't quibble with me, Ducky.'

I suppose you may wonder at my name. By baptism, I'm Victoria Melita but everyone calls me Ducky. They always have. No one can remember why. Pa swore that Mother started it and Mother denies all responsibility. I don't care. I'm perfectly happy to be Ducky.

So Ernie Hesse was proposed as a possible husband, in spite of being a first cousin.

Mother said, 'There are other considerations.'

She had her eye on his Grand Duchy.

The idea of Ernie for a husband wasn't an unpleasant one. Not at all. He was the greatest japester and terrifically good-looking, handsomer even than Cyril Vladimirovich. But I'd never thought of Ernie as husband material. If I'd thought of him at all, it was as a mad cousin who refused to grow up.

I said, 'Has Ernie asked for me?'

Mother said, 'Asked for you? What are you, a salt cellar? He doesn't yet have permission to ask for you.'

'Will he be given permission?'

'That is for me to decide and your father to give. You ask too many questions. It isn't becoming and you'd do well to break yourself of the habit before you marry. No husband likes to be quizzed.'

A kind of balance sheet was being drawn up. Ernie had just succeeded as Grand Duke of Hesse. He had a decent palace in Darmstadt and several country houses, all with good parks. On the other hand, the Hesses were not thought to have any jewels except perhaps some mediocre diamonds parsed out among Ernie's sisters. They didn't enter into Mother's calculations.

7

She said, 'Whomever you marry, you can always depend on Mother for your diamonds.'

We were summoned to Osborne House, directly after Easter. Ernie had already arrived.

'Hello, Ducky, dear,' he said. 'I'm under orders from GQ. I have to behave sensibly, act my age and converse with you soberly.'

He had ravishing blue eyes.

He said, 'Under no circumstances am I to act the fool, play pranks or by any means amuse you.'

Then he squirted me with water from the joke daisy he was wearing in his lapel.

We went for a walk, the first of many, many walks that week though it rained every day. Grandma Queen encouraged it. She thought every stroll must bring us closer to an announcement. She also liked us to sit with her for an hour each afternoon – 'my handsomest grandchildren', she called us. Those afternoons were a terrible strain because Ernie would do everything in his power to make me laugh.

The problem was Beppo, Grandma's white Pomeranian. Beppo was reputed to suffer from digestive disorders but Ernie planted the idea that Beppo might not always be to blame for those soft little explosions and the rich smell that followed.

'Observation,' he said. 'Beppo seems a civil enough mutt to me. The kind of doggie chap who'd have the decency to step out of the room. I'm afraid I think GQ may be exercising a bit of Royal licence here.'

Ever after that, when the smell occurred, he'd look at me, then at Grandma, then at Beppo, and raise an eyebrow, and I would have to bite hard on the inside of my cheek.

We did talk about marriage, in a roundabout way.

He said, 'I realise I have to do it one of these days. Keep the Hesse line going and so forth. I just don't think I'm quite ready.'

He was twenty-four.

He said, 'Don't take it personally, Ducky. You're a terrific girl. But you're not even seventeen, so I reckon we can drag it out a bit, don't you?'

It suited me. I really had other things on my mind. Missy had allowed Nando to do The Thing and she was expecting a baby. I was terrified that she'd die, like Aunt Aline. Mother assured me she would go all the way to Romania and take some proper German doctors with her too, to stay by Missy's side and prevent any such tragedy.

Missy's condition also distracted Mother from the question of Ernie, for a while.

All she said was, 'He doesn't seem very ardent. I hope you haven't said anything to discourage him?'

I said we were good friends. Well, we were.

'Friends?' she said. 'Friends! What a caution you are. Well, if Ernie doesn't put in a little more effort I shall look for someone else, when I get back from Romania.'

Ernie was given another chance to declare himself that September, at Balmoral. Pa was going there to shoot grouse and I was to go with him.

'Now, Ducky,' Mother said, before I left for Scotland, 'if you're offered a saddle horse there's to be no galloping madly about. A gentle hack is more conducive to conversation. And please, no sitting with your nose in a book either. There'll be time enough for reading when you're married and have your confinements. Your job now is to give Ernie a little encouragement. But only a little.'

Ernie actually came to Ballater station to meet us which everyone mistakenly thought was a sign of his blossoming ardour.

'Welcome to Midge Heaven,' he said.

'You should smoke Navy Cut,' Pa said. 'Navy Cut keeps the

buggers at bay. Forget those pansy foreign cigarettes. How's the shooting? Decent bags?'

Ernie couldn't say. He hadn't been out with the guns. He was eager to tell me about a new game he'd devised. It was called Tartan Nightmare and the aim was to design ever more hideous Balmoral accommodations.

'I'll start,' he said. 'A cosy wee nook, north-facing. The walls are covered in Stuart Dress Jaundice, and the upholstery is in Hunting McPuke with bile tassels. I thought it might do nicely for Mr Gladstone. Your turn.'

It was a game without winners. Pa didn't understand it at all.

'Not been out with the guns!' he kept saying. 'How very peculiar.'

There was quite a family gathering, though not everyone was staying at Balmoral. The Uncle Bertie Waleses were down the road at Mar Lodge. Georgie Wales and his new bride, dear May Teck, were at Abergeldie. There was plenty of company. But May Teck informed me that they'd all been warned not to monopolise my time, to give Ernie every courtship opportunity. It became quite embarrassing, worse with every day that passed. Ernie didn't avoid me, not at all. He just didn't ask me to marry him.

I began to think there must be something wrong with me. I studied myself in a hand mirror and found quite a number of imperfections. My face is rather long. My complexion has a slightly sallow cast. Then Aunt Louise arrived and weighed up the situation at once.

She said, 'You're not the problem, darling. You're stunning and Ernie needs to grow up.'

Aunt Louise was Pa's sister. We were supposed not to approve of her and I'm sure if Mother had known she'd be in the Balmoral party, I wouldn't have been allowed to attend. The charge against

Aunt Louise was that she was over-endowed with an artistic temperament that marriage had done nothing to tame. It can happen in the best of families.

'No regard for the proprieties,' Mother said.

We'd been denied any further explanation but Missy's guess was that Aunt Louise misbehaved with men. After all, if the problem were one of insanity she would have been put away. And being artistic wasn't in itself a bad thing. We were all encouraged to produce a watercolour or two. We were forced to the conclusion that our aunt received gentlemen callers when her husband wasn't at home. Missy grew quite excited at the thought of an aunt behaving so outrageously. I just loved the way Aunt Louise narrowed her eyes when she thought someone was talking tosh. Even Grandma Queen.

Aunt Louise was alone at the breakfast table one morning when I went in.

'Good,' she said. 'Just the girl I want to talk to. Tell me about the Ernie situation.'

I told her how things stood. Grandma Queen wanted it. Mother wanted it. Ernie wasn't against it. It just never seemed to progress.

'And what do you want?' she said.

Really, I just wanted to go home. I wanted people to stop discussing me.

'Quite right,' she said. 'You're still so young. What's the hurry? Where are you in the succession? Absolutely nowhere. Pass the butter dish.'

I said, 'Ernie's very nice.'

'Yes?' she said. I wasn't sure she was agreeing with me.

'The main thing, Ducky,' she said, 'is to marry someone you can rub along with. I did. Look, the sky didn't fall on my head. The ravens haven't left the Tower.'

Aunt Louise was married to Lorne. He was just a Marquess in those days. Later on he became Duke of Argyll. Now he's dead.

She was playing with the butter, shaping it into a little human head.

She said, 'What do you want to do with your life?'

It was a question I'd never considered. Surely we all did what we were ordained to do. The army, in the case of my brother, Affie. Marry suitably, in the case of myself and my sisters.

She said, 'You're a bright girl, healthy and able. What are your dreams? What do you hope to achieve?'

Dreams, hopes, achievements. One began to see why Mother avoided Aunt Louise. But there was no escape. It was just me, my aunt and two inscrutable footmen stationed at either end of the sideboard. I felt an obligation to give some kind of answer, and quickly. I told her I hoped to get my three-year-old jumping over poles by the end of the year.

She narrowed her eyes but I believe she was just judging her sculpture.

'Well, that's something,' she said. 'But you don't yearn to write books or cross the Sahara desert?'

These were not options I had realised might be open to me, as Aunt Louise understood from my gaping mouth.

'Those are merely examples I plucked out of the air,' she said. 'When I was your age, I'd already decided to be an artist.'

My breakfast kipper lay cooling on the plate. I felt I was a disappointment to my aunt.

'Some people know at once what they want to do,' she said. 'Others take longer. And some, of course, never want to do anything. The main thing is not to tie yourself to a husband before you know. Imagine discovering you have a passion to explore the

Amazon rainforests but you can't because you've previously agreed to be Queen of Romania.'

Which, if nothing else, demonstrated that Aunt Louise was impractical and also, possibly, slightly bonkers. Missy, in a rainforest!

'And who knows?' she said. 'You may end up marrying Ernie anyway. As you say, he's agreeable company.'

I said, 'I don't at all mind waiting. The problem is he hasn't even asked me.'

'Heavens, Ducky,' she said. 'If he's the one you want, why don't you ask him? So? What do you think?'

It was Grandma Queen, to the life, fashioned from best Deeside butter.

I didn't ask Ernie to marry me. Mother would never have forgiven me. And what if I'd asked him and he'd turned me down? It would have been too humiliating. I decided to try and enjoy what was left of my time at Balmoral and we did have some larks. Ernie wrote a little skit called *Dinnae Gang on the Moor* and we performed it for the tenantry before supper at the Tenants' Ball. Ernie played the hapless traveller, the Henry Prussias were cast as the innkeeper and his wife, and I was Ghoulish Noises Off. May Teck was supposed to operate the rainbox but Grandma Queen developed a fancy to do that herself and poor May had to content herself with the drumming of coconut-shell hooves. Everyone said it was a triumph.

There was one day when I thought Ernie really was about to propose. He asked me to walk with him down to his mother's memorial. It was a granite cross, quite overrun with ivy. **Princess Alice, Grand Duchess of Hesse. Her name shall live though now she is no more.**

Ernie was only ten when she died, although he was no stranger to death. His elder brother had already passed away. The bleeding

13

disease. That was why it had fallen to Ernie to become Grand Duke of Hesse.

I asked him what his mother was like.

'Very lovely,' he said. 'Kind and lovely and always busy doing good works. Actually, I hardly remember. But I'm sure she was. Everyone says so.'

We sat for a while listening to the sound of the river and then we both felt chilled and walked on and the moment passed.

He said, 'You're very quiet today, Miss Duckydoo. I hope you're not going all pensive on me. "Pensive" isn't permitted at Balmoral, don't you know? Not done at all. It would be like going out to the grouse butts wearing one's tailcoat.'

Once a week, Ernie and I would go into Ballater to buy butterscotch and packets of Gayetty's medicated papers for the littlest room – at Balmoral one was only ever given squares of the *Aberdeen Journal* and they were terribly harsh – but one could never just go on an ordinary errand with Ernie. He was always looking for ways to make life more fun. He wore a straw bonnet one time, which looked very puzzling because Ernie had such a splendid moustache, and the next time he dared me to drive the wagonette wearing a pair of his duck trousers and a monocle. His naughtiest jape though was the song he'd composed, a little ditty which he fitted to the tune of *Ode to Joy*.

> *Geeraffes, llamas and alpacas,*
> *Camels too, have necks quite tall.*
> *But, the saddest fluke of Nature,*
> *Grandma has no neck at all.*

Eventually he didn't need to sing the words. In sight of Grandma Queen, he'd simply whistle the tune. It was agony not to laugh and then Grandma would take me to one side and ask me if I was quite well.

'Is it women's troubles, dear?' she'd murmur. 'You'll find things get easier after you've had your first child.'

I will say she always treated me with kindness, even when I failed to become engaged. She recognised it was Ernie who was dragging things out. Mother was in a less forgiving mood. Just as Pa and I got back to Coburg, she was about to leave for Romania, to be with Missy for her confinement. We practically crossed on the doorstep.

She said, 'What a waste of my time and effort. Are you sure you're not discouraging him? I hope you're not still thinking of Cyril Vladimirovich, young lady, because he's quite out of the question.'

I promised her I'd never given a thought for Cyril, which wasn't strictly true. I also omitted to mention my conversation with Aunt Louise.

'Well,' she said, 'Ernie Hesse has had his last chance. As soon as Missy is well enough to spare me I shall come home and reconsider the Bourbons.'

Pa never talked about husbands. He usually left that side of things to Mother, but the very moment she'd left he sent for me.

He said, 'No flim-flam, Ducky. A straight yes or no. If Ernie Hesse asks for you, will you have him?'

I said I would.

Pa said, 'Then I'm going to write to your grandmamma and seal the affair, once and for all. If I don't, your mother will have you spliced to one of those Spanish buffoons and I'll never see you again. Bad enough business about Missy. Bloody Romania.'

It was the first time my father had ever hinted that he'd mind not seeing me if marriage took me far away. I began to cry.

'Now, now,' he said. 'No need for any of that nonsense. Hesse

15

seems a bit of a lightweight to me but he has many points in his favour. Raised by English nurses, so he should be pretty sound. He has a nice establishment in Darmstadt. Comfortable, plain. Not filled with silly drapery. And I've heard he has excellent shooting at Wolfsgarten, though from what one observed of him at Balmoral it may be rather wasted on him. But whatever, this stalling cannot continue. It makes your mother irritable and whatever discommodes her discommodes me. It seems someone has to put some resolve into the little pansy and the person to do it is Her Majesty.'

And that was how it happened. Pa wrote to Grandma Queen, she wrote to Ernie and Ernie came to Coburg for my seventeenth birthday. He brought me a Cairngorm pin, to remind me of the fun we'd had at Balmoral.

He said, 'I'll try not to make you unhappy, Ducky.'

3

Mother was jolly cross when she found everything had been settled in her absence.

I said, 'But I thought you wanted me to marry Ernie?'

'I did,' she said, 'but not if he had to be dragooned into it by that interfering old woman. Your father had no business meddling. I had everything in hand. And a Cairngorm brooch! What kind of an engagement token is that? Such an unattractive stone, especially for someone with your colouring. He should have given you amethysts, at the very least.'

It wasn't an auspicious start. Mother was begrudging, Ernie was glum and Grandma Queen was at her most bullying. The wedding must be in April, she said. Not inconsiderately in the middle of winter, as Missy's had been, and not in the summer when the heat of Coburg would certainly kill her. She would arrive on 16th April and we should therefore have the wedding three days later, after she'd had time to recover from her journey. That was how our wedding date was set.

Mother had given me diamonds and pearls, but then Emperor Uncle Sasha and Aunt Minnie sent an emerald pendant, so Mother, never one to be outdone, added an emerald diadem to my wedding jewels. Then Ernie said he'd very much like me to wear his dear, departed mother's veil and I of course agreed and walked into my first conflict with his sister, Alexandra. Sunny.

She said, 'You might have asked me before you presumed.'

I said, 'But I didn't presume. It was Ernie's wish, that's all. I really couldn't care less what veil I wear. It's just a piece of lace, and I'm only borrowing it for an hour.'

She said, 'It's not just a piece of lace. It's the finest Honiton and it was our dear mother's. I do hope you'll take proper care of it.'

What did she think? That I was going to tear it up for a jelly bag?

'Taking it all the way to Coburg,' she said. 'It poses such a risk.'

The family call her Sunny. I've never understood why. Frosty would suit her better. Or Cloudy.

Ernie had three darling sisters, Vicky, Irene and Ella, all long married, all perfectly sweet and welcoming to me. And then there was Sunny, the baby of the family, not yet settled and as cross as two sticks that I was about to displace her as First Lady of Darmstadt. People reckon her marriage to Nicky has been a great love match but I still say she only did what she did when she did so as to steal my thunder.

Missy and Nando were the first to arrive for the wedding, good and early as I'd begged her to because I had a million things I needed to ask her. It was worth getting married to have Missy's company for a while. I found her changed though. She fussed endlessly over baby Carol and expected me to adore him, which I found impossible because he smelled of cheese. It's different when the child is your own.

I said, 'You know what I need to ask you.'

'Yes,' she said. 'But Mother has asked me not to say too much.'

All she would say was that The Thing wasn't so bad because it only took about a minute, but childbirth was hell. She was expecting again, already.

She said, 'Getting the baby out takes days. I quite thought I'd die. Mother says it gets easier after the first one but I'd rather hoped not to find out. At least, not so soon.'

She'd taken up douching after Carol was born but Nando sometimes came back for seconds.

'Often, actually,' she said. 'He's quite insatiable.'

And that was probably how she'd been caught. Between douches.

'But this will be positively the last time it happens,' she said. 'Mother's going to have a word. She's going to suggest to Nando that he get himself a little ballerina.'

The other guests began to arrive. Aunt Louise sent her regrets, to Mother's great relief, but practically everyone else came. The Battenbergs, the Connaughts, the Henry Prussias, the Kaiser Wilhelms, Uncle Bertie Wales, Grandma Queen and, of course, Mother's people: Grand Duke Uncle Paul, Grand Duke Uncle Serge and Ernie's sister Ella, and Cyril's parents, Grand Duke Uncle Vladimir and Aunt Miechen. Not Cyril though, and I was glad. Better not to see him. I'd cast my die. Actually very few of the Russian cousins came, with the notable exception of Nicky and he had his own selfish reasons that were nothing at all to do with gracing my wedding.

I was never pretty. Missy was dealt that card. 'Striking' was the word they used when a compliment was required for me. I'm too tall to be doted on and my skin was always too dark to compete with the porcelain dolls. Mother always predicted I'd ruin my complexion, haring about in the midday sun and turning the colour of a Hindoostani, and I fear she was right. But I wasn't such a fool as to be jealous of prettier girls. I was a better rider than any of them. It would have been nice though, on my wedding day, to be the cynosure for just five minutes.

We had the civil ceremony first, as soon as Grandma Queen was up and dressed. Ernst Ludwig Karl Albrecht Wilhelm and Victoria Melita. It was strange to hear our names read out like that. We'd always been, always will be, Ernie and Ducky.

Grandma Queen said, 'Such a pity you couldn't be married at Windsor, but at least you chose Coburg. Grandpa in Heaven would be so happy. I'm sure he's smiling down on you.'

As soon as the civil ceremony was over and we were married in the eyes of the Duchy, everyone went down to the chapel to take their seats and see us married in the eyes of God. I was left alone with my bridesmaids. Even Pa abandoned me. It was his job to offer Grandma Queen his arm.

I had planned to have just two bridesmaids, my younger sisters, Baby Bee and Sandra, but Mother said an odd number looked better in procession and the next thing I knew Poor Cousin Dora had been foisted upon me.

It was Dora who burbled out the news, as we sat in Mother's dressing room waiting to go down.

She said, 'Isn't it thrilling, about Ernie's sister?'

I said, 'What's thrilling? Which sister?'

'Why, Sunny, of course,' she said. 'Haven't you've heard? Nicky has asked her to marry him and Sunny said yes.'

I didn't pay too much attention to it at the time, what with trying to quell my nervous stomach and the remark having been made by Dora. It was widely known that Poor Cousin Dora wasn't quite all there. And Tsesarevich Nicky had been pursuing Sunny for years but she'd always refused him because of the church thing. Someday Nicky would be Tsar of Russia and his wife would have to be Orthodox but Sunny couldn't bear the thought of converting. So there was no reason on earth why Sunny should suddenly have said yes, and on my wedding day.

But it turned out that Poor Cousin Dora was right. At the

wedding breakfast, my new sister-in-law's forthcoming engagement was the talk of the room and Cousin Nicky was flushed and
beaming like a loon. The official announcement was to be made
the next day. I suppose that was their feeble idea of good manners.

When it came time for Ernie and me to leave, I felt the crowd
that gathered to wave us off was rather going through the motions.
Their minds were already on the next wedding. And what a
wedding it would be. A Romanov wedding! The Tsesarevich's
wedding. Only Aunt Miechen whispered a kindness to me as Ernie
and I made our way to the carriage.

'Don't mind Sunny,' she said. 'If the Russians can make an
Empress of her, it will be a miracle. But you, dear girl, look every
inch the Grand Duchess.'

Even Ernie was caught up in the excitement about Sunny and
Nicky. We took the train from Coburg to Darmstadt and then
drove in a little park drag to Wolfsgarten for our wedding night
and he never once told me how lovely I looked or what a splendid
girl I was. All he could talk about was Sunny.

'Bloody fine match,' he kept saying. 'I used to think Nicky was a
bit of a nitwit but he's handled Sunny very well. He's been patient,
been persistent. Slowly reeled her in. Think of it, Ducky. Someday
you'll be sister-in-law to the Empress of Russia.'

We played rummy and Mansion of Bliss until midnight. Then
Ernie said, 'Well, Ducky, dear, I don't think we can put it off any
longer.'

We went to bed. And yet again my sister proved to have been
an unreliable tutor. Far from being over in a minute, The Thing
seemed to take forever and when Ernie fell asleep I was by no means
certain whether it had concluded satisfactorily or was to be resumed
after an intermission, like Act II of an operetta.

4

It had never been discussed how things would be arranged between Sunny and me. She was accustomed to running Ernie's household and she regarded me as a child. She'd told me so. But heavens, *I* wasn't the one who still consulted my nanny on everything, and anyway, Ernie had made me his wife and his Duchess and I was determined Sunny shouldn't trespass on my territory. As Missy said, 'Let her go off and marry little Nicky, if she wants to play House.'

I rather hoped Sunny would move out to one of the shooting lodges for the duration of her engagement and leave us in peace, but then something even better was decided. She was to go to England, to stay with her sister, Vicky Battenberg. Vicky would instruct her in the rudiments of Married Life, and Grandma Queen would advise her on how to conduct herself as a future Empress. She was gone for three blissful months and by August, when she returned, I had quite established myself with the people of Hesse. They cheered and took off their hats when they saw my carriage. I even started a fashion for wearing mauve.

But back Sunny did come, and as stony-faced as ever. Worse still, everyone was predicting a long engagement because she was still digging in her heels about converting to the Orthodox Church.

Ernie said, 'She knows she'll have to do it, so she might just as well get on with it. The Russians won't tolerate a Lutheran Empress. Ella did it when she married Serge and I don't remember her making such a fuss.'

But Sunny continued weeping and trembling and wringing her hands. It was all too boring. Anyone would really have thought the Romanovs were asking her to sacrifice a goat.

For weeks, the three of us played a variation of Musical Chairs. Musical Residences. When Ernie and I were in Darmstadt, Sunny stayed in the country and whenever we went out to Schloss Wolfsgarten she would come to town. On one occasion our carriages actually crossed on the road. It was the best we could manage. Ernie, of course, didn't care to hear a word of criticism of Sunny from me. He reserved that privilege for himself.

'She's a thoroughly sweet girl,' he'd say. 'A bit nervy, that's all. You're just not seeing her at her best.'

To add to my burden, I had, somewhat amazingly, fallen pregnant. I was as sick as a dog and whilst I didn't mind Ernie giving up all pretence of sharing my bed, I'd have appreciated a little husbandly tenderness.

'Splendid work, Ducky,' was all he said. 'How terribly clever of us to hit the bull's-eye, first try practically.'

I thought it was because of me, you see? The way Ernie had to work so hard to get to the point, the way he came to our bed looking like a man who's about to have a tooth pulled. Missy said Nando came back for seconds. Ernie just seemed relieved when it was over.

I did ask him, once, if there was something I did wrong.

'Not at all,' he said. 'Not at all. Perfect wife. Couldn't ask for better.' For a while I thought perhaps Missy was to blame for my expectations. I should have liked to ask someone else, but who? There was no one. One could hardly ask one's maid.

Ernie and I still did other things together: received well-wishers, cut ribbons, decided where to place the many vases we'd been given. We didn't quarrel and we generally dined together. But if we didn't have company, Ernie would go out directly after dessert and always to somewhere wives weren't invited. The sketching club, the glee club, the Three Thistles club. I threatened to set up my own club, strictly for girls, and Ernie said, 'I hardly think that would be a success, Ducky. Girls don't go in for chumming.'

The evenings dragged. I used to wander along the passages, opening doors that didn't particularly interest me, listening to ticking clocks that were eating up the minutes of my life. I longed for a visit from Missy but there was no hope of that. She was unimaginably far away and had just given birth to another child. Mother said I should apply myself to embroidering my own baby's layette and writing thank-you letters for our wedding presents but I just couldn't summon the will. I was seventeen and it seemed my life was over.

But then in October, when my spirits were low at the prospect of the winter that stretched before me, a crisis broke the monotony. Emperor Uncle Sasha became so ill that Tsesarevich Nicky wrote to Sunny and begged her to come to Russia at once, to be his comfort and support.

Ernie said, 'The chap's in a perfect funk. He writes, "If the Tsar should die". Well of course he's going to die. His kidneys are in ruins. And it's not as though someone just sprung this on Nicky. It was only ever a matter of time until he succeeded. Sometimes I wonder if he's made of the right stuff to be Emperor.'

Sunny and her beloved Nanny Orchard left immediately for Simferopol, in the Crimea. They were to be met at the station there and taken on by carriage to Livadia, where the Imperial family was gathered. Every morning Ernie looked for news and Sunny's first letter was quite cheerful. Far from being on his death bed, Emperor

Uncle Sasha had been up and dressed when she arrived. He'd come out to the front step to greet her and kiss her hand.

Ernie said, 'So typical of Nicky, panicking like a mouse in a cat's paw.'

I said, 'You've changed your tune. You told me Uncle Sasha was certainly dying.'

'We're all dying, Ducky,' he said. 'But Sasha's a strong man. He could come through this, live a little longer. However, as Sunny has travelled all that way they may as well have the wedding while she's there, don't you think? No sense trundling to and fro, and it seems Nicky desperately needs her at his side. She'll put some spine into him.'

Emperor Uncle Sasha may have been up and dressed when Sunny arrived, but it was his last great effort. Ten days later he was dead and Tsar Nicholas II was in pieces. He'd never wanted to be Emperor, he didn't know how to be Emperor. In sum, he was a blubbing wreck. This I had from Mother whose report came from her brother, Uncle Vladimir. He and the other uncles were all at Livadia, trying to make a man of Tsar Nicky.

Sunny's version of things, in her letter to Ernie, was rather different. Emperor Uncle Sasha's doctors hadn't kept Nicky properly informed, the government ministers ignored him in a most disrespectful way, and the uncles were now intimidating him. Furthermore, Dowager Empress Aunt Minnie was being horrid to her, aloof, and not welcoming at all.

As Ernie pointed out in his reply, the Dowager Empress perhaps had more important things on her mind, such as burying her beloved husband. He advised Sunny to be mindful of Aunt Minnie's grief, to put an end to her wavering and be received into the Orthodox Church. Above all, to stay in Russia and be married to Nicky as soon as possible.

I'll come to you there, he wrote, *never fear. You may always depend on me, but you must now be brave, grow up and help Nicky to face his destiny. I very much doubt he can be a resolute Tsar without your help.*

It was rather comical to see Ernie lecturing others on the need to grow up, but it was a good letter. I did have something of a hand in its composition. And by the time Sunny received it she had anticipated Ernie's advice and converted. Princess Alexandra of Hesse became Grand Duchess Alexandra Fyodorovna and the wedding was fixed to take place one week after Uncle Sasha's funeral.

Ernie's trunk was packed in haste. We agreed it was best if I didn't make the long journey to Petersburg, given my condition, and so I spent my eighteenth birthday alone, rattling around in Schloss Darmstadt, eating too much cake and trying different, slenderising styles of pinning up my hair. My consolation was that Russia was very distant and its Empresses travel very little. The thorn of Sunny had been removed from my side, permanently. Or so I thought.

5

Our little daughter, Elisabeth, was born on 11th March 1895. All the church bells in Darmstadt rang out to greet her and if she had been a boy I'm sure they could not have rung louder. Ernie was in and out of the nursery all day long, lifting her out of her cradle and driving the nurses to distraction. Mother said she'd never seen a man so devoted. She hinted that I was luckier than Missy. That Ernie was considerate, unlike Nando who showed no interest in his children and grew quite resentful when a confinement put Missy *hors de combat* in the bedroom.

'You see?' she said to me. 'It wasn't so very bad, was it? And things have worked out perfectly well with Ernie, just as I said they would. If only you'd give the child a different name. It's going to be so confusing.'

Mother's objection was that she now had two granddaughters named Elisabeth and, as Missy had used the name first, that Ernie and I should be the ones to back down and choose something else.

'Marie's a pretty name,' she suggested. 'Or Vicky, or Alice.'

We compromised. Our Elisabeth Marie Alice Victoria would be known as Elli, to distinguish her from any other Elisabeths in the family.

Mother said, 'And you'll have a boy next. I feel it in my bones.

It's no bad thing for a boy to have an older sister. I've often thought Affie would have done better if he hadn't been my first.'

My brother, Affie, was a puzzle. Around us girls he was quite the little lord of creation, but in anyone else's company he'd grow sly and wary, like a dog that had been beaten. I don't think he had been beaten, certainly no more than any other boy. At one point he was supposed to be engaged to one of the Württemburg girls but nothing ever came of it. Mother believed he suffered from extreme nervous debility of unknown provenance. She thought a spell at Baden-Baden would do him good. Pa said, bugger Baden-Baden. What Affie needed was a kick up the BTM.

Elli was a very pretty baby. She fed well and thrived and her first summer was bliss. I took her to England to show her to Grandma Queen and Missy, who by some miracle wasn't expecting again, took advantage of the fact and joined us there with her two little ones. Ernie elected to stay at home.

Missy and I rendezvoused in London first and did heaps of shopping. Marshall and Snelgrove, Gamages, Swan and Edgar. Gowns, shoes, hats, unmentionables, all ready-made. It was jolly hard work but much more fun than endless fittings and waiting for dressmakers. We used to pause at three o'clock and go to Lyons for tea and buns which was the greatest adventure, to feel one was out and about with the ordinary people. After tea, we'd do more shopping. Missy could be rather a slave-driver, but I could see it was essential. The poor dear couldn't get anything in Bucharest. As she said, childbearing had ruined her line so her trousseau was good for nothing and she was dressed practically in flour sacks. Not that Darmstadt was much better. There was so little choice there, unless one settled for cloth that looked like the cover for an old couch.

After London, our next stop was Windsor. We were there in time for Ascot Week which gave us a splendid opportunity to wear some of our new togs. Missy had a good eye for the difference an extra feather would make, or louder buttons, and we easily outshone the rest of the party. I'm sure that was why certain people took against us. I'm sure that's why we were accused of 'unbecoming behaviour'.

It was too silly. All Missy did was nudge Uncle Bertie Wales's topper off his head with the tip of her parasol. He didn't mind. He enjoyed the joke. But everyone else put on their lemon lips and said the man in the street didn't come to Ascot to see the future Queen of Romania and the Grand Duchess of Hesse behaving like children. Which was true, though not as they meant it. It seemed to me the man in the street came to Ascot to have a rare holiday from his work and to see the finest horse flesh in action. I must say Missy and I were quite unrepentant. We were married women, not infants. What were they going to do? Send us to bed without supper?

From Windsor, Missy and I moved on to Osborne House and had the most heavenly time. The whole month of July. Our sister Sandra joined us for a week. Pa had reluctantly agreed to her engagement to Ernst Hohenlohe-Langenberg so she was eager for information about Married Life. There was to be another Ernie in the family.

'Bit of a non-entity' was Pa's opinion of him, but that was because Ernst Hohenlohe was actually something of an intellectual. It was a quality Pa always mistrusted in a man.

Missy, Sandra and I were put up in the Albert Cottage at Osborne, so that the noise of the children shouldn't disturb the peace of Grandma Queen. But she loved to see them every afternoon, for twenty minutes or so, and she remembered their names and the exact dates they were born. Great-grandchildren! What must that feel like? Grandma was so ancient. Seventy-six. And yet she seemed never to have changed, within our memory at least, unlike Uncle Bertie Wales who had aged hugely. And what must that feel like? To watch your own child grow old? We felt sorry for Uncle Bertie, hanging about like the Twelfth Man all those years of waiting to be king, pads strapped on but not sure of ever being called to the crease.

I didn't want that month to end. The thought of going back to Darmstadt, to Ernie who dandled Elli all day and then stayed out all night and never, ever came to my bed, was more than I could bear. Missy could have been more sympathetic.

She said, 'I do miss you, obviously, but I rather like Romania, now I'm accustomed to it. You'll love it too when you come to visit. And things are a lot better since Mother had a word with Nando. He's made his own arrangements and, you know, I'll probably do the same, in a year or two.'

Missy was planning to have affairs. I was so shocked.

'Well, why not?' she said. 'I've done my duty. And I might even do it again, if I could be sure of having another boy, so as to give them a spare, you know? But I'm sure I'm entitled to a little adventure now. You too. Well, perhaps you'd better give Ernie a son first. But after that.'

That was when I told her about Ernie. How he seemed positively to dislike doing The Thing and actually had stopped doing it at all since Elli was born. Then it was her turn to be shocked.

'Gosh,' she said. 'And he's so very handsome. How disappointing. Did you do something to put him off his stride, Ducky? Did you scream in pain or make a terrible fuss?'

I said, 'Absolutely not. And he says I'm a perfect wife.'

'Really?' she said. 'How very odd. Generally speaking husbands don't say such things. Do you suppose he's a pansy? Pa always called him one.'

Pa called a lot of people 'pansy'.

She said, 'You're sure you've done everything you can to encourage him?'

I did wonder, obviously, if there were something more I should be doing. Missy said, 'Remember that gelding we had when we lived at Devonport? All the coaxing we had to do to get him to take the saddle? Rewards. Apples and humbugs. We got there in the end, and once we'd convinced him he became an absolute enthusiast. First into the yard every time, looking for his humbug.'

I didn't see how the apple and humbug method could be adapted to Ernie's case. Missy said I could be very obtuse.

She said, 'Well, he's your husband. I'd say it's your job to find out what he wants. It's not a problem I ever had with Nando. He'd just leap aboard and gallop to the winning post. And now he has his ballerina he hardly troubles me at all. So, you know, sauce for the gander and all that?'

Missy said she had plenty of admirers. She said Romania was full of divinely good-looking men.

I said, 'But what if you fall pregnant?'

'I shall be careful not to,' she said. 'Mainly, I'll just allow them to kiss my neck and bring me roses. Now who can we find to bring you roses? Darmstadt's so tame. We may have to look a little further afield. If you could only come to stay with me. I'd find you a lover in five minutes. What's your type, would you say?'

I didn't tell her about Cyril until we were lying in the dark. She got up at once and re-lit the lamp. She said she had to see my face, to know if I could possibly be serious.

'Cousin Cyril?' she said. 'Cyril Vladimirovich? It's a joke. Tell me it's a joke. I mean, I know you had a little pash for him when we were younger, but he's such a stuffed-shirt. Ernie's much more fun.'

That's what everyone said. Ernie is such fun.

31

As soon as I'd told Missy about my feelings for Cyril I regretted it. I swore her to secrecy, especially from Mother.

'Mother?' she said. 'Of course I won't tell Mother. She'd have a fit. After all the trouble she went to getting you Ernie.'

July ended and Missy and I started our homeward journeys. She came back with me to Darmstadt for a few days.

'Honestly, Ducky,' she kept saying. 'I'm sure Ernie doesn't mean to neglect you. One has to look at the positives. He's such a stitch, and he's so good with Elli. Could it be a case of low vitality? Maybe he needs an iron tonic?'

No one understood, not even my sister. I began to wish she'd stop patronising me and go home, and then when it was time for her to go, I wished she could stay. Any company was better than none. The best Missy and I could hope for was to meet up again in Russia, at Nicky and Sunny's coronation, but that was nearly a year off.

'Chin up, darling,' she said. 'Ernie may just be a slow starter. I predict he's going to become much more attentive. And don't worry about the Cyril thing. My lips are sealed. Absolutely.'

But Missy's lips were never entirely sealed. How else did Cyril get wind of my feelings?

6

My sister Sandra was married to Ernst Hohenlohe in the spring of '96. Mother seemed a good deal more satisfied with the match than Pa did.

'Ernst will do very well,' she said. 'And so will Sandra. She has such a steady, contented nature.'

That was said for my benefit.

After Sandra's wedding Mother seemed to relax. With three of us married and a few years before she needed to worry about a husband for Baby Bee, she became quite gay and girlish. She bought new gowns and wraps and slippers for our great excursion to Russia and when Pa complained about the expenditure she just laughed. Mother had Romanov money. She didn't need to cheese-pare like the Saxe-Coburgs.

Even from a great distance, my sister-in-law's life cast a shadow over mine. We were absolutely obliged to attend Nicky and Sunny's coronation but I, who had always loved going to Russia, suddenly dreaded the prospect. I didn't want to see Cyril – I imagined him dancing with one divinely pretty girl after another – and I certainly didn't want him to see me, a dull, married woman with a child and a neglectful husband. I longed for another confinement, to excuse me from travelling, but there was no chance at all of that. Ernie had quite forgotten the way to my bedroom.

My brother, Affie, tried to wriggle out of going to Moscow too but Mother was a most efficient whipper-in. We were half-Romanov and even half-Romanovs didn't shirk their duty. And so we boarded the train for three days of Pa's grumbling, Affie's dead-eyed vacancy and lectures from Mother on the correct way to raise my child.

Ernie and I stayed with his older sister, Grand Duchess Ella. Her husband, Grand Duke Uncle Serge, was Governor-General of Moscow and they lived in his official residence, on Tverskaya. I'd worried about bringing the noise and clutter of a baby into Uncle Serge's immaculate house. He and Aunt Ella had no children of their own. But dear Ella said it was their pleasure to have us there. That Uncle Serge loved to have little ones around. Indeed Grand Duke Uncle Paul would be staying there too, with his poor motherless darlings. His little Marie must have been about six then, and Dmitri a year younger.

'Plenty of room for nurses and governesses,' Ella said. 'We shall be quite a kindergarten. This house is far too big for us anyway.'

Missy and Nando stayed with the Yusupovs who had opened up their Moscow house for the Coronation. Mother and Pa and Baby Bee stayed with Grand Duke Uncle Vladimir and Aunt Miechen, Cyril's parents. The day after our arrival Aunt Miechen gave a luncheon party. I feigned a headache. I knew I was bound to see Cyril sooner or later but since I'd confided in Missy I felt as though I were walking around with a sign pinned to my gown. SAD CASE. CRUSH ON COUSIN CYRIL.

'Headache?' Ernie said. 'You never get headaches. Poor show, Ducky. They're your bally relatives after all. And frankly, your Uncle Vladimir turns my bowels to water. I was looking to you to sweeten his opinion of me.'

Aunt Ella told him to go and leave me in peace. I felt terribly guilty fibbing to her about my head. I don't believe Ella ever told a lie in her life. Ernie, after all his complaints, came home tipsy and very well lunched.

'How head?' he asked.

'Slightly better. How bowels?'

'Bowels in good order. Actually your Uncle Vladimir was damned cordial.'

'Everyone there?'

'Everyone.'

The entire city was *en fête* for the Coronation and more crowded than I had ever seen it. Pavilions and archways had been set up, everything had been given a fresh coat of paint and every house was decorated with flags and lilac boughs and laurel garlands.

We had no sighting of Nicky and Sunny until five days before their crowning. They were following tradition, staying out of town at the Petrovsky Palace, praying and fasting and contemplating their duties until the time came for them to make a grand entrance. They had Baby Olga and her nurses there with them too. Aunt Ella said they couldn't bear to be parted from the child for even one night.

The ceremonials got underway at last on the Friday morning. A cannon was fired from the Tainitskaya Tower in the Kremlin and that was the signal that the Emperor was on his way into the city. Then the bells started. There's no sound on earth like Russian church bells. There's a scheme to English bells, like the steps of a quadrille, and a German carillon makes a pretty sound. But the intention of Russian bells seems to be to rock the earth off its axis.

The Governor-General's house was right there, on the processional route. We had the best view ever. Uncle Paul's children watched with us. Marie had a new party dress for the occasion, with a pink sash, and Dmitri Pavlovich was dressed like a miniature

Pavlovsky grenadier. He held my hand, my right hand. His own right hand, he explained to me solemnly, had to be kept free for saluting.

Ernie put Elli on his shoulders but she fell asleep and didn't wake even when the cornets and drums passed beneath us playing the Imperial March.

The Cossacks came first, in their scarlet coats and fleece caps, the foot soldiers and then the cavalry on steppe horses, Russian Dons, bays and blacks. Some of the Cossacks had their little sons, or their grandsons, in the saddle with them, so that one day they'd be able to say, 'I was there.'

The Chevalier Guards came next, and then the lone figure of Tsar Nicholas in a plain green army tunic. Little Nicky. It was hard to think of him as Emperor of All the Russias. They'd put him on a good mount though, a grey, half-Westphalian, a mare but she stood fifteen hands at least.

The Imperial Suite and the Grand Dukes followed a few paces behind him. Uncle Paul glanced up at our window. He told me afterwards he'd had to do it so hastily that he hadn't really seen Marie and Dmitri, but they certainly saw him and they knew he was thinking of them. Uncle Vladimir's boys rode directly behind him. Cyril, Boris and Andrei. They were all wearing hussar regimentals, even Cyril who was in the Navy, but I knew him at once by the way he sat his horse. I talked to Aunt Ella about the weather prospects until he'd ridden out of sight.

The gold coaches brought up the rear. Dowager Empress Aunt Minnie was in the first. She looked up at us and waved. It must have been such a bittersweet day for her, proud of Nicky but sad for poor departed Uncle Sasha. Sunny's coach followed immediately behind. The soon-to-be-crowned Empress Alexandra Fyodorovna.

I will say she did look very like an Empress, perfectly still and *posée*, glittering like a snow queen. So tight-lipped though.

Ernie called out, 'Come on, Sunny, give us a smile.'

Aunt Ella said, 'She's nervous, poor darling. She's been so afraid she'll faint.'

The procession crossed Okhotniy and paused for Nicky to dismount and go into the Iversky Chapel to venerate the icon. Then on they went through the Resurrection Gate into Red Square and out of sight again. They stayed closeted in the Kremlin Palace from then until the day of the Coronation. Tuesday.

We had to be seated in the Ouspensky cathedral by nine o'clock though nothing was likely to happen before eleven. It was such a trial, with the heat and the fog of incense and the way they said the same prayers over and over. The crowning and the anointing took forever and then there was still Divine Liturgy to endure. The Orthodox do go on so.

Paki, paki, mirom Gospodu pomolimsya. Again and again in peace let us pray to the Lord.

Again and again, indeed. I began to understand why Sunny had been so reluctant to convert. I felt sorry for her actually.

Six hours. I thought I'd die.

Ernie said, 'I warned you not to have that second cup of tea. And think of us poor men. You ladies can at least hide a little potty under your skirts. You did bring a little potty?'

And then we had to join the crush for dinner. Ernie was longing to loosen his collar, my shoes pinched, my gown clung to me. And they served hot turtle soup, and pheasant, in May! I ate nothing. I remember asking Missy if I was flushed.

She said, 'We're all flushed, except for the Empress Ice Maiden. Look at her. How does she do it?'

Nicky and Sunny were on a dais, at a table for two, pretending to peck at their food. Not wishing to stray an inch from tradition, Nicky had kept his crown on until dinner was over. It was too big for him and had slipped down so you couldn't see his eyebrows.

Ernie said, 'Observation: when they stand side by side, Sunny is taller than Nicky but when they're seated they're the same height. Conclusion: the Emperor of All the Russias has very short legs.'

It was while they were serving dessert. I happened to look up and see Cyril Vladimirovich. He'd been watching me. I could tell because he looked away immediately. That was when I knew Missy had blabbed.

I said, 'You promised.'

'Really, Ducky,' she said, 'I don't know what you're talking about. If Cyril turned away I imagine it's because he has better things to look at than a red-faced, boring old cousin.'

But that was precisely my point. We were family. He should just have acknowledged me, not looked away in haste. I ate two ices and didn't taste a thing. We went to powder our noses.

Missy said, 'But do you still like him? Now you've seen him again?'

I said it was all just too stupid. I was a married woman.

'Yes,' she said, 'but are Things any better with Ernie?'

Of course they weren't. We lived as brother and maidenly sister, but I was in no mood to discuss anything so personal with my loose-lipped sister. I returned to the subject of Sunny's pallor.

Missy said, 'She's probably expecting again. Those dark circles under her eyes. I can always tell. Well, she may as well get on with it. She has to give them a boy, however many times it takes. But don't change the subject. Has Ernie paid you any attention?'

I said I wished I'd worn a lighter gown. I was soaked in perspiration.

'I'll take that as a No,' she said. 'Well then, this week is your

38

chance, Ducky. I'm trying to help you here. Cyril's not attached to anyone so I expect to see you dancing with him every evening. It doesn't sound as though Ernie will mind and, if he does, so much the better. A little jealousy might give him some pep.'

I said, 'How do you know Cyril's not attached?'

'Baby Bee said. Aunt Miechen told her.'

'Why? Is Cyril interested in Baby Bee?'

It was something that had never occurred to me. What if he married my little sister? It wasn't out of the question. She was thirteen. Another three years and she'd be marriageable. I felt quite sick at the thought.

But Missy said, 'No, you silly creature. I told Baby Bee to find out.'

'Why don't you just place a notice in the newspapers and make sure the whole world knows?'

'Ducky,' she said, 'one may as well be in possession of the facts. No sense in your hankering after Cyril if he's already spoken for. But he's not. And of course, Aunt Miechen adores you. You were always her favourite. She would have loved to have you as a daughter-in-law.'

'So you did say something.'

'Not really. Aunt Miechen quizzed me. After Baby Bee asked about Cyril. But honestly, Ducky, I hardly needed to tell her anything. She wasn't at all surprised about Ernie. In fact she said she'd always felt in her bones that he wasn't good marriage material. So you see?'

I didn't see. What was there to see? It was too late.

Missy said, 'Oh for heaven's sake, must I spell it out? Cyril's here, you're here. Have a little flirtation. Where's the harm? A six-hour Coronation. I'm sure we're all entitled to a little pleasure after that ordeal.'

I hardly slept, but no one slept much in Moscow that night. The Kremlin was lit up with the new electric lights and carts were on the move well before dawn. Some people were starting their long journey home, but many of them were going to Khodynka Meadow for free beer and gingerbread and souvenir Coronation cups.

I lay awake thinking of Cyril. There was to be one party after another that week. I was bound to be in his company again. I could have borne it, just seeing him. I could have carried it off. But Missy had ruined everything. She meant well, but the trouble with Missy was she was a stranger to embarrassment. She couldn't begin to imagine how mortified I felt.

The household was on the move early. Servants' voices, footsteps, doors slamming, and then I heard a carriage going off at speed. I dozed until nine, then Aunt Ella came in with my breakfast tray. Her hair was down and she'd been crying. There had been a terrible accident, she said. A crush of people out at Khodynka, pushing to be near the front when the beer was given out. Some had died. Uncle Serge had gone there as soon as he heard the news.

'Poor Serge,' she kept saying. 'And after everything went off so well yesterday.'

Aunt Ella was worried that Uncle Serge would be blamed for the accident, and with good reason. When arrangements go perfectly to plan no one asks who should be thanked, but when things go wrong they must have someone to blame. That was what a Governor-General was for. Uncle Serge came back from Khodynka Meadow and shut himself away in his study. All morning the telephone rang and people came and went, grave-faced. The news got worse by the hour. Fifty dead. Two hundred. Five hundred. That was when Uncle Serge went to see Emperor Nicky.

There was the urgent question of the Coronation celebrations.

40

Should everything be cancelled? The French ambassador was meant to be giving a ball that evening. He needed to know what to do. Uncle Serge thought the main thing was for Nicky and Sunny to visit the injured and meet the bereaved, to offer their condolences. After that they should make a brief appearance at the ball. Uncle Paul agreed that the ball should go ahead but he felt that Nicky and his suite should stay away, out of respect for the dead. Uncle Vladimir said it was madness to think of anyone giving or attending a ball when the dead were stacked up like so many log piles. Emperor Nicky didn't know what he thought. He was discussing it with his wife and his mother.

Aunt Ella said, 'If it's left to Sunny all the festivities will certainly be cancelled. She hates these occasions at the happiest of times.'

The day wore on. Eight hundred dead, we heard. Ernie went out to the Alexander Gardens with Elli and little Marie Pavlovna and came back with a number of different opinions he'd heard expressed by other families' governesses and nursery maids.

1. The tragedy at Khodynka was the fault of the authorities who had failed to keep order.
2. No. It was the fault of the peasants who'd trample their own mother underfoot for a free drink.
3. It was an omen. A reign that starts with a tragedy was sure to end badly.
4. The Emperor should go to the ball but look solemn and not dance.
5. The Emperor should go to a monastery.
6. The food for the ball supper should be distributed among the bereaved.
7. Bereaved persons have no appetite. They should be given money.

We never did know for sure how many had died. More than a thousand, anyway. They were to be buried quickly, because of the heat, but not in a mass grave. After a day of doing nothing, Emperor Nicky finally announced that he would pay for coffins, and give a pension to any child who'd been orphaned. Then we went to the French ball.

It was a grim evening. Dowager Empress Aunt Minnie made clear her disapproval and stayed away. So did Uncle Vladimir and Aunt Miechen and, because they didn't come, neither did any of their family or friends.

Missy was very put out. A ball without the Vladimirovichi was like soup without salt. She also had Cyril's brother Boris in her sights, for a little Coronation Week flirtation. His absence meant a wasted evening. I was relieved though. At least I didn't have to face Cyril.

Missy said, 'You are an oddity. Just when you might have had the opportunity to dance with him. Well, Aunt Miechen won't miss every event. They'll certainly be on parade later in the week so I hope you're not going to be stand-offish with Cyril and make me look like a perfect fool.'

We were at the Yusupovs' ball. It was unthinkable to miss it. Zinaida Yusupov's family own half of Russia. Perhaps I should now say *owned*. And unlike many wealthy people, the Yusupovs were never slow to spend their money. Their ball was bound to be splendid. It was four days after the Coronation, three days after the Khodynka tragedy. By eleven o'clock the only dance I'd had was the opening polonaise, and Ernie had disappeared to the card tables. People were going in to supper. My brother, Affie, offered me his arm. We turned into the corridor where the second buffet was set out and suddenly there was Cyril.

'Ducky! Affie!' he called. 'I just got here. Big brouhaha at home. Father thinks there should be no dancing at a time of national mourning. Mother thinks life must go on. Mother won. Have you two eaten?'

I'd been hungry but suddenly I wasn't.

Cyril said, 'A lemonade, then?'

Affie muttered, 'Something stronger,' loosed my arm and was gone. My brother was always looking for escape routes.

Cyril said, 'I see a pair of seats. Shall we grab them?'

Once I'd forced myself to look at him I found my nervousness disappeared. Cyril made it easy. He did all the talking, until I found my tongue. He'd just passed his Navy examinations and was off to the Baltic for the summer, on training exercises. Petty Officer Romanov. He wasn't the handsomest of my cousins. His brother Boris was certainly better-favoured. But I loved his face. I could have studied it for ever. He asked if my baby was thriving. He asked about my horses. And when he'd skirted around all permissible topics we sat in silence for a while. It became unbearable. I was cursing Missy's indiscretion. And then I thought it would be better just to have it out, to say it and be done, like poor Tatiana with Onegin. I'd look foolish for five minutes, Cyril would go off to his ship and I'd go back to Darmstadt and that would be that.

I said, 'I know Missy has been making mischief.'

He cut me off.

He said, 'I hardly know your husband. Ernie doesn't seem the vicious type.'

I agreed.

He said, 'Perhaps just not suited to marriage?'

I did pretty well. I kept my composure, until he asked me if I was dreadfully unhappy, and then I couldn't stop the tears. He gave me his handkerchief. People were looking. Not many, but it only required a few. Gossip works on the principle of compound interest.

I said, 'Now I've embarrassed you.'

'Hardly,' he said. 'Anyone asks, I'll say you twisted your ankle.'

He took my hand. We were in shadow.

He said, 'The thing is, Ducky, there's really nothing I can do. You have to go home to Darmstadt and I have to report for duty, and who can say when we shall ever see each other again? But I want you to know that I wish things might have worked out differently. Do you understand?'

How a mood can change in a few seconds. I remember thinking that if Cyril cared for me, even a little, it made everything else bearable.

I said, 'I've always liked you.'

'And I you,' he said. 'How silly that we only just got round to admitting it.'

I said, 'Perhaps we can write? I'd like to know where you are.'

He said I'd find him an erratic correspondent but he'd certainly try. And then the dancing started up again and he partnered me for the mazurka and a waltz. He was a superb dancer. It's been too long since we danced.

He said, 'I long to kiss you, Ducky, darling. I can't, of course, but I just wanted you to know.'

That was when I really knew that Things weren't right with Ernie. He'd never, ever said anything so delicious.

It was dawn when we drove the short way back to the Governor's house. The streets were empty and the shops were still shuttered although you could smell that the bakers were already at work. Ernie was tipsy. I was on air. I imagined I could still feel the press of Cyril's hand on my back.

Ernie said, 'Bloody excellent people, the Yusupovs. Bloody fine party. We should give parties like that.'

There were lamps burning in the library. Ernie made a terrible racket stumbling and crashing up the stairs and Uncle Serge came out and told him off. Aunt Ella had been home for hours and was asleep. Uncle Serge had little prospect of going to bed himself. At Khodynka there were still unburied dead. Emperor Nicky's gesture was all very well, but it wasn't so easy for Uncle Serge to find so many pine coffins at short notice.

'Sleep well,' he said.

And I did, a very contented sleep till late in the morning, but when I woke I found things didn't look as rosy as they had the night before. Cyril Vladimirovich was nineteen years old and just starting out on his naval career. He'd see the world, meet beautiful women, and eventually he'd marry. More than likely I'd be expected to attend his wedding. And all the silliness of the night before, all the talk of 'if only' and of forbidden kisses, was absolutely meaningless because I was stuck with Ernie and Darmstadt. I was in a hateful mood all day.

Ernie said, 'You're always disagreeable when you've been drinking champagne.'

He went out with the nurses again, when they took the children to the Gardens. He was a child himself, really. That was the day he came home with the idea of building a waterslide, at Wolfsgarten.

I was called to the telephone. Missy.

'Well?' she said. 'I've been waiting all morning to hear from you. Can you talk? Just answer yes or no. Did Cyril declare himself?'

'Yes.'

'I knew he would! Was it divine dancing with him?'

'Yes.'

'Are you happy?'

'No.'

Missy felt I had the wrong attitude to men.

'You take it all too seriously,' she'd say. 'It's nothing to do with marriage and babies and all that. Marriage is the sago pudding we're obliged to eat. Now you need a little jam.'

Missy enjoyed flirtations. She began them and the very moment they started to pall she looked around for the next one.

She said, 'By the by, did Cyril happen to say anything about me? In relation to Boris? I believe I've taken his fancy.'

I said, 'Missy, you're here with your husband and your children.'

'So?' she said. 'I'm only talking about a little holiday diversion. I do hope Boris will be coming out to Arkhangelskoe.'

When the Coronation celebrations were finished and the last of the Khodynka dead had been buried, we were all going to the country estates. Ernie and I were to stay with Aunt Ella and Uncle Serge at Ilyinskoe. Missy and Nando would be put up by the Yusupovs at Arkhangelskoe. There was to be no summer in the country for Cyril though. He was leaving to join his ship at Kronstadt.

I said, 'I hardly think Boris is the type for a country house party full of marrieds and their children. And anyway, doesn't he keep a ballerina?'

Missy said, 'Of course he keeps a ballerina. What's that to do with the price of tea in China?'

We set off for Ilyinskoe the first week of June. Ernie and me and Elli, Mother and Pa, brother Affie, and Uncle Paul's children. Uncle Paul liked Marie and Dmitri to enjoy the good air and freedom of Ilyinskoe but it was the place where Aunt Aline died and I imagine he couldn't bear to take them there himself. Aunt Ella said he had business to attend to anyway, in St Petersburg.

Missy said, 'Aunt Ella must think we were born yesterday. There's only one kind of business men rush off to in the middle of summer. Good old Uncle Paul! Who would have thought it!'

To reach Ilyinskoe, you go by train as far as Odintsevo and then on by carriage. The drive takes about an hour, first through a pine forest, and then out onto meadowland. You can see the roof of the house long before you reach it. There's a little wooden bridge that sways alarmingly under the weight of the troika, and then the great gates and an avenue of lime trees. Such a pleasant place. I wonder if we shall ever see it again. I wonder if any of us will ever go back to Russia, even when this war ends? They say it will certainly end this year. But everything has changed.

We stayed at Ilyinskoe for the rest of June and the whole month of July. All the neighbouring dachas were filled with parties too.

The Yusupovs, the Golitsyns, the Scherbatovs. Everyone had deserted Moscow. The sun shone, we ate our meals on the verandah and we swam in the river every day. Elli was in heaven with so many children to entertain her. Most days Missy drove over with her children, and sometimes the Yusupov boys came too. That was when I first remember Felix Yusupov. How old could he have been then? Eight, nine? He never did care very much for climbing trees or building rafts but he was endlessly patient with the little ones, making them fairy tea parties and forgiving them if they ruined his careful work.

I was so happy at Ilyinskoe. There was plenty of company if I wanted it and when I didn't, when I wanted to sit alone and think of Cyril, there were plenty of diversions for Ernie. We didn't quarrel at all. Then one morning a black cloud appeared. Aunt Ella announced that Emperor Nicky and Sunny and Baby Olga would soon be joining us. I suppose I wasn't very gracious about it.

Ernie said, 'You might try not thinking of yourself for a change. Consider poor Sunny, how her life has changed. I'm sure she's quite desperate to take a holiday from Empressing.'

The Imperials arrived in time for the great patronal feast on St Elijah's Day. Aunt Ella and I were near the roadside gathering white currants when we heard the sound of a carriage and a cry went up from some of the villagers, '*Batyushka idyot!*' Little Father was coming. They all made deep bows. Well, not quite all. There were one or two younger men who made no obeisance, nor even took off their hats. They just watched Nicky and Sunny go rattling past.

'*Nyemka!*' one of them said. 'The German Woman.' And he spat on the ground to show what he thought of his new German Empress.

I'd dreaded their coming and was sure Sunny would ruin my holiday, but she was all cordiality. A little dull, but apparently disposed to be my friend. She liked nothing better than to sit in the shade and discuss teething and colic and cradle cap. But Missy's diagnosis of her pale face and her tired eyes was incorrect. Sunny wasn't expecting again.

'Not yet,' she said. 'But very soon, I'm sure. We are trying.'

And as she said it she cast a shockingly doting eye on Emperor Nicky who was limbering up like a jumping-jack, preparing to play tennis with Ernie.

Behind her, quite out of her line of sight, Missy made a horribly realistic mime of vomiting.

Then Sunny said, 'But, Ducky, it's high time you and Ernie had another one,' and Missy leaped in at once and said, 'Ha! Tell that to Ernie.'

Sunny looked quite puzzled.

Ernie beat Nicky, two sets to one.

'Observation,' he said to me, later. 'If His Imperial Majesty rules All the Russias the way he plays tennis he'll make a sorry mess of it. He runs around far too much, like a spaniel. An untrained spaniel. And then he dithers and dabs at the ball as though it might bite him. I only allowed him to win a few games so as not to discourage him.'

In the middle of those lazy, comfortable days we had one moment of high drama. Missy almost drowned. There had been heavy rain in the night so the river was a little swollen. She went down to bathe, perhaps too soon after luncheon, and was swept off her feet by the current. We did hear her call, but then, one was rarely out of range of Missy's voice, and we were all well fed and dozing. I don't know how long it was before her cries became insistent enough for us to wake up and realise she was in difficulties. Hours, Missy says.

By the time we were all on our feet she was already some distance downstream. Nando flapped about on the river bank shouting helpful things like, 'Don't swallow any water!' and 'For heaven's sake, Missy!' Ernie began to take off his trousers and Aunt Ella ran for a long birch branch, but brother Affie overtook them all, plunged in, fully clothed, and dragged Missy to safety. None of us had ever seen him move so energetically.

He was the toast of the house, of course. Whether he enjoyed it, it was difficult to say. He smiled bashfully for the first hour or so of compliments and he saw off two good snorts of Uncle Serge's best cognac, but then he slipped back into his usual distant, cud-chewing habit and it was as if nothing had happened.

Nando said, 'Not quite the thing, is he, your brother?'

The ingrate!

I said, 'If it weren't for Affie, you'd have been widowed this afternoon.'

'Nonsense,' he said. 'Missy was just making an unnecessary fuss, as usual.'

8

We took the Nord Express to go home. It was such a depressing journey. Affie parted from us at Berlin, with rather tactless enthusiasm, I thought. He had his man get the bags ready the absolute moment we passed Konigsberg. Mother fretted, as though he were still a tiny child, and Pa growled at her about a boy needing to cut loose once in a while.

Mother said, 'But Berlin, in the middle of August? What can he possibly hope to do there? No one will be in town.'

Ernie mischievously suggested it would be an ideal time to visit the Altes Museum.

'No crowds,' he said. 'And Affie does so love those decorated Greek vases. He'll be able to study them in comfort.'

Pa chuckled.

'Greek vases, eh?' he said. 'Saucy, are they?'

'Athletic,' Ernie said, and Mother said she'd never heard Affie express the least interest in vases.

Mother and Pa's personal coupé was uncoupled at Hanover but we stayed on the Pullman as far as Cologne.

Mother whispered, 'We've all had such a lovely summer. Now do try to settle down, Ducky.'

I looked at her.

'I'm not a complete fool,' she said.

I opened my mouth to protest.

'And neither is your husband,' she whispered. 'Now do be a good girl. I have quite enough to worry about with Missy.'

There was no reason she should have known what had passed between me and Cyril but then, mothers know a surprising number of things when they choose to.

I was resolved anyway. I didn't need a lecture from Mother. Cyril and I had a delicious secret and, apart from the bedroom problem, Ernie was good fun, so I was determined to make the best of things. Ernie had plans too. He'd been bowled over by the parties we'd been to in Moscow. Aunt Miechen always gave wonderful dinners, even in a borrowed house, and the Yusupovs were like a lavish travelling circus. No one could ever tell me where their wealth came from so I can only imagine they owned a very large gold mine. Ernie wanted us to be the Yusupovs of Darmstadt,but we didn't have Yusupov money and Hesse wasn't Russia. Hessians are careful, sober people. As hard as we tried to be sociable and gay, it was uphill work. We acquired a hot-air balloon and a fleet of bicycles for our guests, and one of the ponds at Wolfsgarten was cleaned and excavated to accommodate Ernie's longed-for water-slide. He was still bored. He'd look at our guests' feeble efforts at dressing for a costume party and say, 'Not exactly Babylon, is it?'

My best friends in Darmstadt in those days were George and Georgie Buchanan. Sir George was the British chargé d'affaires and if he thought Ernie and I were madcap he never showed it. He had the diplomat's touch and that British easiness. I've often been advised, since the war with Germany started and then the other, Russian troubles, to emphasise my Britishness. I found the advice unnecessary. It is my natural plumage. They say scratch the skin of a British Royal and you'll find a German but my German blood runs very thin. As for Russia, which I thought I loved, I find it has become a stranger.

Ernie and I aimed always to have at least three guests staying with us. It kept us from futile conversations and arguments. He had his projects and I had mine. He built a play house for Elli, complete in every domestic detail, and then he began something far more ambitious: a proper Orthodox chapel in Darmstadt. He proposed the idea to Emperor Nicky who took it up with great enthusiasm. It would be somewhere suitable for Sunny to worship when she visited Darmstadt.

I said, 'But how often do you think that will be?'

'I hope very often,' Ernie said. 'I miss her dreadfully. You miss your sister so I think I may be allowed to miss mine.'

Sunny's chapel wasn't to be simply a church in the Orthodox style. It was to be a little patch of Russia in Sunny's childhood home. Trainloads of Russian soil and Russian granite began to arrive. Ernie was to oversee the project and design its interior. It kept him very happily occupied. Practically every day he'd disappear with a roll of drawings under his arm.

In his absence, I shopped for horses. I acquired two Lippizaners, a hunter from Kildare – chestnut with white socks and a blaze – and a Welsh pony, ready for Elli to begin her riding lessons. And every day I looked out for letters from Cyril.

He did write, but not often, and of course his letters betrayed nothing of our secret. They were just a rather dull recital of his travels such as a dutiful child might write. He was docked at Reval, which made sense, and at Danzig, but then he wrote that he was in Paris, which seemed a strange destination for a serving naval officer. Then Baby Bee wrote that she and Mother had seen him in Cannes and I was in agonies to know what he was doing there. Did he have a sweetheart? A beautiful, unmarried French sweetheart. I could hardly ask.

I always shared Cyril's letters with Ernie, to forestall any suspicions or accusations, but after the first few he stopped reading them.

'Leave them on my night stand,' he said. 'I'll use them instead of my Sydenham's Drops when I can't sleep. Honestly, Ducky, only Cyril Vladimirovich could make Paris sound boring. I wonder why he bothers writing?'

Ernie and I had never had a servant problem. We kept a happy household. But then suddenly people began to give notice, or rather not give notice but simply announce that they were leaving at once, very inconsiderately leaving one in a fix. An under-gardener went, then two footmen in rapid succession and then Seidel, the very best of our grooms, which vexed me enormously. Seidel wouldn't say where he was going or why he was in such haste.

I said, 'Won't you at least wait until after foaling?'

He was especially fond of my mare, Moonbeam. Still he said he could not stay.

I asked Gusenbauer if he knew the reason. Gusenbauer was my coachman. He was the fatherly kind of man a lad like Seidel might have confided in. When I pressed him, he said there might have been a slight altercation. He couldn't swear to it but His Royal Highness might have spoken to Seidel sharply and Seidel might perhaps have taken it too much to heart.

'Boys,' he said. 'They come and they go. Whoever knows what goes on in their heads? Sometimes they don't recognise a good position until they've given it up.'

Ernie was up at Kranichstein laying out new rose beds so he couldn't be asked and by the time he came home Seidel had already gone.

'Load of nonsense,' Ernie said. 'I'm sure I never reprimanded anyone. Seidel? Which one was he?'

Then I knew he was fibbing. Everyone knew Seidel.

A new groom was found. Hubert. Ernie made it his personal responsibility to find someone suitable, seeing how upset I was at losing Seidel. Hubert was young but very able and my horses accepted him, though I believe Moonbeam still looked out of her box every day, hoping to see Seidel again. She foaled, a good-looking colt that promised well but never made much progress. I sold him as a yearling.

I was supposed to take Elli up to Schleswig-Holstein, to meet her new cousin. Ernie's sister Irene had had another baby boy, Sigismund.

I liked Irene well enough. She was a bit dull, but pleasant. Ernie's sisters are all such homebodies. I've often wondered where his great appetite for limelight and drum roll sprang from. Perhaps every family must have its showman. But I confess my chief reason for accepting Irene's invitation to visit was that I thought she meant for me to stay with her at Schloss Kiel. Her husband, Heinrich, was based at Kiel and it was the kind of port where a ship of the Russian Imperial Fleet might put in with a certain Romanov cousin on board. It was only after I was committed to the visit that Irene explained we'd be staying out in the country, at Hemmelmark.

'So much better for the little ones,' she said. 'There's no point in being in Kiel. Heinrich will be at sea, on exercises.'

I cancelled. Ernie was furious. He said if I couldn't be friends with Sunny I should at least make an effort with his other sisters.

I said, 'I don't need to make an effort. I get on very well with Irene, and with Aunt Ella.'

'Everyone gets on with Ella,' he said. 'And you know Irene must be going through an anxious time.'

Waldemar, her firstborn, has the bleeding disease, so Irene was watching anxiously over the new baby. He was only six months old, but the signs can appear quite early and it always seems to be the boys. As things have turned out, Sigismund has escaped it, but others in the family haven't been so lucky. Ernie's brother, Frittie, had it. Always the boys.

I said, 'Irene's your sister. If you think she needs company, *you* go to Hemmelmark.'

He didn't, of course. He said he was far too busy. But as he was in such a quarrelsome mood I decided to take a little holiday anyway. I took Elli to Coburg to visit Mother and Pa. It was while I was there that I heard a piece of St Petersburg gossip. It concerned Mother's brother, Grand Duke Uncle Paul. We'd all guessed that he was courting someone. We just didn't know who it was. Uncle Paul is a very private person. Little by little the facts were revealed. He was seeing Olga Pistohlkors. Not only was she a commoner, she was a *married* commoner. She was about to leave her lawful husband.

'Not only that,' Baby Bee whispered to me, 'but she's expecting a baby. Imagine!'

I'm sure I was never allowed to know about such things at her age.

Mother confirmed the story, and added to it. Empress Sunny was so scandalised she wanted Uncle Paul banished from her Imperial sight.

Mother said, 'The Empress should mind her own business.'

Uncle Paul was Mother's youngest brother. Whatever he did she'd defend him.

'Your uncle has been alone quite long enough,' she said. 'Men aren't suited to widowhood. They need a woman to tell them what to do.'

Pa sucked his teeth.

I'd planned to stay a week at least in Coburg but first Baby Bee and then Mother developed a fever and a fearful headache.

'Take Elli home,' Mother said. 'I'd never forgive myself if our little angel fell ill.'

So I sent word ahead and Elli and I set off for Darmstadt the next morning. Gusenbauer met us at the station with the sociable. He said Ernie wasn't in town. Up at Wolfsgarten, he thought, seeing the steward.

I said, 'Then let's go up there and surprise him,' and Gusenbauer said was I quite sure I didn't want to go home first, to wash off the smuts and allow the little one to rest? But Elli wanted to see her Papa more than anything.

I said, 'No, no. I can wash just as well in the country as in town. Let's go directly.'

You see, I should have guessed, from the way Gusenbauer dawdled. First he said he didn't care for the way one of our horses was travelling, that it seemed to be sparing its nearside fore and he feared it was lame. But I knew there was nothing wrong with that horse. It always did bob its head excessively. Then he halted the carriage to show Elli some rabbits sunning themselves on a grass bank. It was all very well, but they were just rabbits. Anything, though, to delay our arrival at Wolfsgarten. Poor Gusenbauer. He knew Ernie had company up there. I suppose everyone knew, except me.

The only blessing was that Elli didn't see what I saw. I had Gusenbauer to thank for that. He stopped at the front door just long enough for me to get down, then he drove off very smartly to the stable yard. Two of the hounds had had puppies and Gusenbauer lured Elli away with the promise of petting them while I went ahead into the house. The door stood open. It was wonderfully cool inside. I took off my shoes to feel the cold marble through my stockings. The doorman's chair was empty. I called out and no footmen or maids came running. The house seemed deserted. I thought Ernie must be out, somewhere about the estate. It was the middle of the afternoon. His bedroom was the very last place I looked. It was the creak of the door that woke him.

'*Raus!*' he called. 'Out! How many times have I told you! Do not come in here unless I ring for you. Now get out and stay out!'

He thought I was a servant. At first he was groggy. Then he was wide awake and furious.

'Hellfire,' he kept saying. 'Hellfire and damnation. Why aren't you in Coburg?'

As though *I* were the one at fault.

I couldn't see who was in bed beside him but I knew, sort of.

He said, 'Where's Elli?'

I said, 'Do you want her to see this?'

He groaned and got up, as though it were the most tiresome thing to have to do. Funny, I'd never seen him naked before. He was always a lamps-off-nightshirt-on husband in my bedroom.

He said, 'I hope you're not going to make a scene.'

Then he pulled the covers off the bed and said, 'Up, boy! The party's over.'

And there lay Hubert.

9

I don't know what men do together. I don't want to know.

Ernie and I took turns to be angry about what I'd seen. He went first, because I'd robbed him of his secret.

He said, 'What possessed you to drive out here and surprise me? You know I hate surprises.'

Which wasn't true at all.

Then he said, 'We were perfectly all right, you and I. Now you've gone and upset everything.'

He made it my fault. So then it was my turn to be angry.

I said, 'We weren't perfectly all right. You haven't shared my bed since Elli was born.'

He said a good many wives would be grateful. That I'd always known his heart wasn't in the marriage business and surely we'd agreed just to be chums. Chums!

I said, 'But you've had Hubert, and I suppose you had Seidel and others too. Who do I have?'

He seemed astonished.

He said, 'You have Elli. And someday we'll have another child. But no rush, surely?'

I told him it was nothing to do with having another child. I hardly even thought of it. I wanted to be cherished. I wanted a lover. Then he was even more astonished, as though I were troubling him with something that was none of his concern.

'A lover?' he said. 'Then bloody well take one. When have I ever stopped you doing anything? Why do we need even to talk about this?'

I said we must end the marriage, as soon as possible. We were going to England for Grandma Queen's Diamond Jubilee. I said we must take that opportunity. We'd explain our incompatibilities to her, as delicately as possible, and ask her blessing for us to part. He laughed.

'Are you mad?' he said. 'I believe you are. Involve GQ? I absolutely forbid it.'

I'd made him nervous. Later, when the heat had gone out of that particular evening's argument, he was more conciliatory.

He said, 'Look here, Ducky, one can't involve grannies in cases of this kind. It simply isn't appropriate.'

I said, 'Except that Granny Queen was the person who threw us together in the first place. She does bear some responsibility for our misery.'

'Misery?' he said. 'I'm certainly not miserable and I think you rather overstate the case. If you take this to Granny Queen it will certainly kill her. Are you prepared to have that on your conscience?'

Ernie didn't at all see why we couldn't just carry on as before. He would have Hubert, or whomever, I could take a lover and eventually, perhaps in a year or two, we'd try to have another child. He made it sound so easy.

He said, 'As long as you're discreet. No dallying in town, that's all I ask. You can use one of the shooting boxes, or the lodge at Dianaburg. You're a fine-looking woman, Ducky. Men will fall over themselves. I'm not sure how ladies go about these things but

I imagine Missy will be able to advise you. From what I hear her boudoir door is never still.'

That did it. In my rage a Meissen cherub got broken, a window was cracked and Ernie sustained a small contusion to his right temple. Later, when we were both calmer, he said he'd always been jolly fond of me.

'Just not *that* way,' he said. 'I thought you knew that.'

That was 1897. Grandma Queen's Diamond Jubilee was in June. Clarence House was made available for Mother and Pa and we were to stay with them. Missy couldn't come because Nando was still recovering from a bout of typhoid and if he was obliged to stay at home so was she. Nicky and Sunny couldn't attend either because Sunny had just been confined. Another girl, Tatiana. Aunt Ella and Uncle Serge came as Emperor Nicky's representatives, and Ella brought news that made my heart race.

She said, 'Cyril Vladimirovich hopes to get here in time for the celebrations. His boat is due to dock at Devonport tomorrow. It's very sweet of him to make the effort.'

I believe I looked perfectly composed.

Ernie said, 'Cyril? I feel my eyelids drooping already.'

I said, 'Well, I think it's splendid. Cyril's quite the nicest of my cousins.'

Later Ernie said, 'You can't really think Cyril's the nicest. Boris is much more fun. Don't you find Cyril rather pompous? Don't you find him a little unbending? That ramrod back.'

I said, 'All my cousins have good posture. Cyril particularly. You're the only one who slumps.'

He caught something in my look. You never knew with Ernie.

Sometimes he could be so obtuse, sometimes he'd notice the flicker of an eyelash.

'Golly, Ducky,' he said. 'You don't have a secret pash for Cyril, do you?'

And then I really lost my head.

I said, 'More to the point, Cyril has a pash for me.'

'No!' he said. 'Does he really? But how would one ever know? He always has his nose in the air. He always looks as though he's on the parade ground.'

There was no stopping me.

I said, 'I know because he told me so.'

'Gosh,' Ernie said. 'The unsuspected rascal! I shall now look at him with different eyes. But, darling, he's not much use to you. You're in Darmstadt and he's God knows where, playing battle-ships. How can there be any future in that?'

That's how easy it was to tell him. Ernie didn't take anything seriously.

On the Monday afternoon Grandma Queen came into town from Windsor. Cyril's train was delayed because Her Majesty's arrival brought everything at Paddington Station to a halt but he arrived just in time to dress for dinner. I wore grey silk and my amethysts, Cyril greeted me in an impeccably cousin-like way and I kept my poise in spite of Ernie's beastly efforts at unsettling me with his imitations of Cyril's military bearing.

'He's like a heron,' he said. 'A heron in a tailcoat. Having recently swallowed a bad fish.'

The next day was a public holiday to celebrate the Jubilee. There was a carriage procession to St Paul's. Pa and Cyril and Ernie were all part of the mounted escort, and brother Affie too, though he didn't look at all well. 'Costive,' Mother said. 'He needs Syrup of Figs.'

62

She and I were consigned to one of the rearmost landaus. Mother swore she really couldn't have cared less.

'Call that a procession?' she said. 'Her Majesty's Lord Chamberlain should go to Russia to see how a procession should be done.'

Because of Grandma Queen's great age, the Te Deum was sung outside the cathedral, to save her the effort of climbing all those steps. She was still possessed of a sharp mind but at seventy-eight, which of us wouldn't be relieved to be able to stay in the comfort of our carriage?

There was a luncheon afterwards, at Buckingham Palace. That was when I first got the chance of a quiet word with Cyril.

I said, 'Ernie knows.'

'Knows what?' he said. 'There's nothing for him to know.'

That wasn't what he was supposed to say.

I said, 'What I mean is, I told him that you and I have feelings for each other and he doesn't mind in the least. As long as he can carry on as he pleases he doesn't care what I do.'

Cyril said, 'Doesn't care? The bounder. But I care, Ducky. *Bozhe moy*, another man's wife! I mean to say, it's unthinkable. You'd be ruined.'

I said, 'But I'm already ruined. I'm a laughing stock. Ernie goes with boys and the whole household knows about it.'

'Even so,' he said. 'If word of this were to go any further. Our names linked. It could be damned awkward.'

It was a sickening moment. Cyril thought I was about to faint. He helped me to a chair.

He said, 'I suppose this is my fault. I shouldn't have confessed my feelings. It's unsettled you. But you must see, it's a futile case. Best to forget we ever spoke. Put it behind us. Not that there ever was anything.'

I said, 'But what if someday I were free?'

He turned rather pale.

He said, 'Ducky, much as I adore you, I'm not prepared to fight a duel over you.'

I managed a laugh.

I said, 'No one fights duels any more, you noodle.'

He said, 'Then what can you mean by "free"? Is Ernie unwell? He looks perfectly healthy.'

I said, 'It's very simple. I'm going to talk to Grandma Queen. I'm going to ask her permission for Ernie and me to divorce.'

Then I thought *he* might faint.

'No, Ducky,' he said. 'Never, never. Our kind of people don't divorce.'

Our kind of people.

I said, 'So if I did get a divorce, you wouldn't marry me?'

He groaned.

'And if I'm divorced and you marry someone else, I'll be the kind of woman you won't allow your wife to meet. So whatever I do I'm doomed to wretchedness. And you don't care, so long as I don't create a scandal.'

'Ducky, Ducky,' he said. He touched my hair. He began to walk away, then he came back.

'Please stop and think,' he said. 'If you have any regard for Her Majesty, don't trouble her with this. It will kill her.'

I said, 'That was Ernie's excuse for doing nothing too, but I imagine he just doesn't want her to know about his stable-boys.'

'And quite right too,' he said. 'Ernie may be an invert but he at least understands that a frail old lady shouldn't be exposed to such an abomination.'

Anyone would have thought it was *his* granny. And anyway, I didn't believe Grandma Queen was frail.

Aunt Louise was at hand. I consulted her. I knew she wouldn't have an attack of the vapours.

I said, 'I have to divorce Ernie. What should I do?'

'Oh Lord!' she said. 'Do you really? But you were quite keen on him. What went wrong?'

I was getting accustomed to telling people about Ernie and his boys. It used to embarrass me, but one can get used to anything.

'Ah,' she said, 'I see. Well, dearest girl, you're not the first wife this has happened to and you won't be the last. But you know accommodations can be made, if a wife and husband are compatible in other respects? Lorne and I, for instance, have come to a comfortable arrangement. That's to say separate arrangements. You understand? As long as one is discreet it can work very well.'

Exactly what Ernie had said.

'And Ernie has given you that darling child,' she said. 'So he has made something of an effort.'

Ernie never wanted for supporters.

I said, 'But I don't want a discreet arrangement. I want a proper marriage.'

She sighed.

'Well, divorce isn't the way to go about things. Heavens, you'll never be invited anywhere. If you're divorced you'll never meet anyone remotely suitable for a "proper" marriage, as you call it. Just have affairs, darling. Honestly, it's much easier.'

I said, 'But I've already met someone.'

'You astonish me,' she said. 'What kind of man would encourage you in this folly? No, please don't tell me his name. Does your mother know about any of this? Of course she doesn't. Ducky, do take care. I'd hate to see you walled up in a convent. Write to me, visit me, but please, please don't do anything mad.'

Aunt Louise was right. It was a kind of madness. I so admired her and I had confided in her, and yet I ignored what she advised. When Grandma Queen went back to Windsor the next day I followed her. I left Elli with Ernie.

He said, 'I know what you're up to. Well, I'll have no part in it. You're the one who wants a divorce, not me.'

Grandma Queen was so pleased I'd gone to visit her. Quite gay, actually. Some old ladies diminish towards the end of their lives but Grandma seemed to grow rounder. I suppose she had long since lost sight of her feet. Her gowns never changed though. Perhaps she just had them made wider and wider. Always black, always bombazine.

'But where's your dear little one?' she asked. 'You should have brought her with you. I see you all far too rarely.'

She pinched my cheeks and told me I looked tired.

'Not your usual energetic self at all,' she said. 'Am I right in thinking we can soon look forward to another happy event?'

She thought I'd gone to Windsor to tell her I was expecting another baby. Of course she did.

I said, 'No, Grandma, there won't be any more babies.'

'Oh,' she said. 'Oh?'

'There won't be any more babies because Ernie never shares my bed.'

I believe I saw her hand start to move towards her bell, but I wasn't going to be cut off before I'd said my piece.

I said, 'And the reason is, he prefers boys. He always did.'

She was very pale. Her lips had no colour at all. I did wonder for a moment if she were going to die on me, as Ernie had predicted. But Grandma wasn't dying. She was mastering her feelings. She said nothing for a while. Then she asked me if I was being an affectionate and encouraging wife.

66

She said, 'Ernie has always required strong direction. That's why I chose you for him.'

Chosen, to give him strong direction! It wasn't to be borne.

I said, 'So if Ernie doesn't do what normal husbands do, it's my fault? That's hardly fair. And do you know what he tells me to do? He advises me to take a lover. What do you think of that?'

If the shock killed her, I thought, so be it. She'd had a long life. She was always maundering over Grandpa, her beloved Albert, in Heaven. Dear Albert this, dear Albert that. Let her go to him.

But the shock didn't kill her. She didn't even flinch.

'Boys,' she said. 'It's a phase some men go through and quite to be deplored. The church is very clear on that. No one knows the cause of it. But you know a helpful wife can set a husband back on the correct path. And you already have your little Elisabeth so there's proof that Ernie is willing to change. You must be patient with him, Ducky.'

I said, 'I've been patient. I've tried and tried but I won't stand for any more of it. I must have a divorce.'

Grandma Queen's eyes were grey-blue and watery when she spoke of places she loved, or the dear departed, but let someone utter an unmentionable word and they became as hard and beady as boot buttons.

'Never say that word again,' she said. 'We will not hear it. Marriage is sacred. Happiness is irrelevant.'

Then she did ring her little bell and Lady Ampthill came in and tutted at me for overtiring Her Majesty. But Grandma Queen put on her pleasant face again and said, 'You must all come to Osborne House this summer. So much healthier than Darmstadt for the little one. And I shall talk to Ernie. All will be well, Ducky. You'll see.'

10

By the time I got back to London, Cyril had already left for Devonport. He had orders for Malta and then on to India. Perhaps our trains had crossed. I'd so hoped to see him again, to reassure him that I hadn't killed Grandma Queen. I had it all planned. I'd tell him I'd never give up and he'd promise to wait for me until every obstacle had been overcome. Then we'd kiss and perhaps exchange locks of hair. It would have kept me going until we could be together again.

But Cyril was gone, and I was in trouble. Grandma's report of what had passed between us had travelled faster than my train. She had sent a wire to Pa and the cat was out of the bag.

When I got to Clarence House, Mother was waiting to pounce.

'So!' she said. 'This was your idea of a pleasant visit to your grandmamma? Now we have telegrams arriving every five minutes and one of them I was not even permitted to read. Why? One dreads to think. Has Her Majesty criticised me? Your father seems very ready to. Why? Am I the one demanding to undo vows made before God? Where am I to blame?'

I said, 'You were the one who chose Ernie for me.'

'No,' she said, 'I saw it would never work. It was clear from the way Ernie delayed and dragged his feet that he didn't want you, but your father would interfere. He would go behind my back. Well, now let him deal with this unpleasantness. He's in the library. He wishes to speak to you.'

Of course Pa didn't at all wish to speak to me but he was under instructions from Mother to bring me to my senses. Poor Pa, squeezed between his mother and Queen, and his wife. It was a little early for a sundowner but there was a distinct smell of brandy about him so I think he'd taken a stiffener or two while he waited for my return.

He had Grandma Queen's messages before him and, not being sure how to begin, he just quoted from them at random.

Greatly distressed. Marriage sacred. Duty before happiness. Death would be preferable.

I said, 'I wonder whose death she means? Grandma Queen is seventy-eight and I'm nearly twenty-one, so I'll just make sure to outlive her. Once Uncle Bertie Wales is King, I'll be able to have my divorce. I don't think he'll prevent it.'

Pa made a noise. It was difficult to be sure but I interpreted it as a bronchitic concession that there was truth in what I said.

I said, 'And it's really such a farce. Do you know what I learned just this week? That Grandpa in Heaven's mama was divorced. I wish I'd thought to mention that to Grandma.'

'Long ago now, of course,' Pa said. 'All dead and gone. Still, least said the better. Who told you about that?'

'Aunt Louise.'

'Ah,' Pa said. 'Louise. Always a stirrer. I suppose she's been egging you on.'

I said, 'Not at all. She's worried I'll be sent to a convent. But Pa, the thing is, Grandpa in Heaven's mother's divorce wasn't the end of the world. Coburg still prospered. Grandma still married Grandpa. It sounds to me as though the only person who suffered was Grandpa's mother, not being permitted to see her children ever again. But I know Ernie would never be so cruel. He'll always let me see Elli.'

I wasn't sure if our conversation was over. I sensed not, but Pa's eye kept wandering in the direction of the decanter so I poured him a generous measure and myself a smaller one. He cleared his throat.

'Your mother,' he said, 'has brought to my notice the name of Cyril Vladimirovich.'

I said, 'Yes. I love him. I always did. And he loves me.'

'He's declared himself?'

'Yes. He just doesn't wish to be the cause of any difficulties.'

'Bit late for that. We're now beset by difficulties. What's to be done? Her Majesty is very disappointed in you. Your esteemed mother is disappointed in both of us. I'm to blame, apparently. Buggered if I know why. If it rains tomorrow that will no doubt be my fault too.'

I said, 'Are you disappointed in me?'

'Not at all,' he said. 'Champion girl. One is simply rather feeling the heat of female fury. Cyril Vladimirovich. Hardly know the fellow myself but he always seems rather pleased with himself. Stand-offish. What kind of man is he? Does he sail?'

'He's in the Navy.'

'That's something. Russian Navy, of course, but still. Is he a good shot?'

'I don't know.'

'Pretty basic information, Ducky. I mean, are you quite sure about this? Now, his brother one could understand. Boris. Very well-favoured, so the ladies seem to think. Good value over the port too. He can tell a joke.'

Everyone said that. Boris was handsomer, Boris was funnier. As though one chose a husband like a pair of shoes. Oh, but these have a bow, these have a prettier heel.

I said, 'Ernie's well-favoured and funny. It doesn't make him a good husband.'

'No,' Pa said. 'Well, the material point is this: Her Majesty has spoken. There can be no question of a divorce so you must, how can I put this? You must wait on future events. Wait for the watch to change, hmm? In the meanwhile, make the best of a bad job, as have many before you. And you know, with time your feelings may change. Ernie might surprise you.'

I said, 'Ernie has already surprised me.'

Pa flushed and said there was no need to go into All That.

'Damned shame too,' he said. 'It's handy having you in Darmstadt. Bloody Russia. I shouldn't like to think of you ever going so far away.'

He had tears in his eyes, but as it turned out Pa didn't have to endure my going to Bloody Russia. I didn't see Cyril again for two whole years, but he wrote to me and little by little his letters grew warmer and more daring. He knew Ernie couldn't have cared less. I paid a price though for having declared my feelings. Mother ran a very thorough campaign to keep Cyril from me. He wasn't invited to any family gathering that I was likely to attend and I received no invitations to Vladimirovichi events. But there was a limit to Mother's powers. She might prevent me from seeing Cyril but not from hearing about him. When the family gathered to celebrate Pa and Mother's silver wedding anniversary, there were certain people she was obliged to invite. Cyril's parents, for instance. Grand Duke Uncle Vladimir and Aunt Miechen.

The very moment they arrived in Coburg, Aunt Miechen made a point of taking me to one side to give me news of Cyril. He was on exercises in the Black Sea, he was very well, and he always mentioned me in his letters.

'Darling Ducky,' she said. 'What a horrid mess this is. And I should so have loved to have you as a daughter-in-law.'

She brought other news too. Sunny was expecting again.

'She hardly leaves her bedroom,' Aunt Miechen said. 'Quite the invalid. It's too boring. There's no Court life at all. We're all praying she has a boy this time, then we can look forward to a decent Imperial ball or two.'

Sunny's indisposition may have spared her from hosting Imperial balls but it wasn't preventing her from testing other powers. Her campaign to have Grand Duke Uncle Paul banished looked likely to succeed. Olga Pistohlkors had had his baby and Uncle Paul had therefore crossed a line too far. He was being urged to leave Russia quietly before Emperor Nicky actually banished him.

Aunt Miechen said, 'Sunny's only being so shrewish about it because Paul's new child is a boy. It's sheer jealousy. After all the sadness he's endured, I'm sure nobody thinks any the worse of him for taking happiness where he finds it. Where's Paul in the succession? Nowhere to speak of. He should be allowed to marry Olga and left in peace. If Pistohlkors is willing to let his wife go, what business is it of Sunny's?'

I said, 'It doesn't augur well for me and Cyril, does it?'

'Never worry about Cyril,' she said. 'When the time comes he'll do what he wants to do. No son of mine will be intimidated by that sourpuss.'

My aunt has quite often been proved wrong.

Mother said, 'I saw your tête-à-tête with Miechen. I hope she hasn't been encouraging you in your silliness.'

Pa and Mother's wedding anniversary celebrations were held at Schloss Friedenstein in Gotha. The guest accommodations there were better than those at Coburg. When Ernie and I arrived, Missy and Nando were already installed. Missy was waiting for us in the front hall.

'Thank heavens you're here,' she said. 'Affie's not at all well.'

Those were her first words to me.

'Too much hock,' Mother said. 'He should go for a good brisk walk. But no one ever listens to me.'

Missy rolled her eyes. I followed her upstairs and went to see Affie at once.

He had the curtains closed. There was deep snow outside and the light hurt his eyes. He was up and dressed but just sitting like a lump, doing nothing.

'Hello, sis,' he said. 'Excuse me if I don't get up. Bit of an off day. Can't seem to get going.'

The doctors had prescribed bed rest and milk puddings and absolutely no strong drink. The official diagnosis was nervous debility. Pa thought he'd been Overdoing It. In Pa's world there were only two conditions men suffered from. Overdoing It and Being in Need of a Strong Dose.

More guests arrived. A buffet supper was served, a string quartet sawed its way dutifully through an hour of Haydn, and Missy smuggled a half bottle of Sekt into the sickroom. Early the following morning Affie shot himself. He slightly missed his aim. As in life, so in death. What did I know about my brother? He went to school in Potsdam, at the Military Academy. I suppose he had friends there but he never brought any of them home. He was meant to marry Elsa Württemburg, but she changed her mind and Affie appeared not to care one way or the other. He rode well, he was a hopeless dancer, he enjoyed a drink, he had no conversation. That's all I can say. Did he mind being the only boy, did he mind having four sisters? Not especially. I don't think Affie ever thought about that, or anything else. Missy thinks he went with girls who showed him a good time. I hope she's right.

Pa asked the menfolk to assemble quietly in the billiard room. Affie's doctor wished to address them.

Missy said, 'Why just the men? I don't see what this is to do with Ernie and Nando? Ducky and I want to hear what the doctor has to say. Affie is our brother.'

Mother said, 'What did I ever do to deserve such disobedient children? If Dr Moller says this is for men's ears only who are you to argue with him? I dare say anyway he'd have expected my daughters to be busily attending to *my* needs. And as for your brother, this is so typical of his thoughtlessness. Of all the days to have a mishap with a gun. It's far too late to cancel tonight's dinner.'

Ernie came back from the billiard room quite shaken.

He said, 'Things are pretty bad, Ducky. According to Moller Affie's rather botched things. Better really if you don't see him.'

Missy and I went in anyway. His head was entirely bandaged. He couldn't speak. I think his jaw was shot away. We told him we loved him. We told him to buck up.

Chairs, candelabra and floral arrangements were being carried in ready for the anniversary dinner. Mother and Pa weren't speaking. Mother had told Dr Moller to take Affie away, to Merano, for a water cure. Dr Moller advised that Affie shouldn't be moved. Pa slumped in a wing chair all day smoking and declaring it to be a hopeless case. At the time we thought he meant Affie's head wound but looking back I think he meant himself too, and life in general.

Mother had her way. The anniversary dinner was eaten, followed by an hour or two of joyless dancing, and Affie was spirited away to Merano. Within a week he was dead. We were required to say that he had lost a long and valiant fight against consumption though it was generally known that the instrument of his death was a Rast-Gasser service revolver. He was twenty-four years old. It was all too stupid.

They brought him back to Coburg to be buried. I never saw Pa so broken and grey. Mother too, though I felt less sympathy for her. Affie hadn't been right for years but Mother would never have it. It was simply a matter of too much hock. Nothing that fresh air wouldn't cure. And then to send him to Merano, jolting over those mountain roads when he had a bullet lodged in his brain.

What had his life amounted to? He'd never seemed particularly unhappy, but not happy either. Elli once found a frozen chrysalis in the garden at Dianaburg, a grub that would never turn into a moth and flutter out into the world. That was my brother, Affie.

Pa took his grief north to Mecklenburg, to sail. The sea was his consolation. Mother and I took Elli to England, to stay with Grandma Queen at Osborne House.

'So you may mend some of the fences you've broken,' Mother said. 'I can't stay in this house anyway. I keep thinking I hear Affie's footsteps.'

But at Osborne the broken fences had disappeared and Grandma Queen was all sunshine. Affie's death wasn't mentioned and neither was my marriage to Ernie. Elli was declared to be the most beautiful of the great-grandchildren, which was certainly true, and a likely future bride for Georgie and May Wales's son, David. Grandma Queen just couldn't leave off her matchmaking.

When Her Majesty moved on to Balmoral in August it was expected we should all go with her, but I couldn't face it. I asked Grandma Queen to excuse me.

'Of course,' she said. 'You've been too long away from dear

Ernie. I understand. You see, Ducky? You're learning. Marriage requires *application*.'

Elli and I were about to begin our long journey home when I received a telegram. Ernie was sick. It was almost certainly smallpox and he was being nursed in strict isolation. Elli had been vaccinated, I hadn't. We set off anyway and when we reached Darmstadt the house was like a mortuary. Everyone spoke in whispers and moved about on muffled feet. A doctor met me at the door and told me Ernie lay at the very brink of the grave.

If Ernie had died it would have changed everything. A widow may certainly remarry, after a decent pause. Even Grandma Queen would have allowed that. And yet I prayed for Ernie to survive. Isn't that odd? Perhaps I did it for Elli's sake. And when I was eventually allowed to see him again, when the crisis was over and the risk of contagion had passed, I cried with relief. He was so thin and weak.

'Observation,' he said. 'I'm told I came as close to death as damn it but I heard no angelic voices and I had no visions of Paradise. Not even a quick peek through the gates. Do you think I'm destined for the other place?'

His convalescence was slow but by September he was making plans. He wanted to have a party, a lavish and wonderful party to signal to the world that Ernie Hesse was alive and well. The occasion, the official occasion, was to be the consecration of Emperor Nicky's little patch of Russia-in-Darmstadt, the Orthodox church of St Mary Magdalene. I encouraged him. I thought if he did it soon enough Nicky and Sunny were unlikely to attend. Sunny was still recovering from her latest confinement. Another girl. Maria. Aunt Ella and Uncle Serge would surely be sent to represent the Imperials.

But word came that Emperor Nicky and his Empress would definitely attend.

'Don't be a grump,' Ernie said. 'Of course Sunny's coming. The place has been built for her. Besides, I'm Lazarus, back from the dead. I'm going to invite every Orthodox I know.'

Not every Orthodox. Not Cyril, of course. Ernie was aware that Mother had her opera glasses trained on our marriage and he never liked to engage in hand-to-hand combat with her. He found her rather frightening. Many people did. But he cleverly did something I shall always thank him for. He invited Cyril's brother, Boris, and when Boris said that he'd have liked to accept but had a prior commitment to keep Cyril company while he was on shore leave, Ernie replied by return that Cyril would of course be welcome too. So when Mother descended upon him in a fury he was able to say, in all honesty, 'But I didn't invite Cyril. I'm simply doing Boris a courtesy.'

Mother had many troubles that year. First Affie. Then Pa's health began to fail. She'd had twenty-five years of him snarling and banging doors and going off to sail or shoot for weeks on end and suddenly he was at home all the time, under her feet and coughing day and night. And then there was Missy. As threatened, she had had an adventure and been left with a little souvenir. At first Nando insisted he wasn't the father but his Uncle King said, 'You damned well *are* the father and let's hear no more about it.'

One did feel rather for Nando. Missy changed her story every minute. Zizi Cantacuzene might be the father. No, it was Cyril's brother, Boris. Well, actually, it was Nando, after all. I think the truth was she really didn't know. But the one thing everyone agreed on was that it would be best if she went home to Mother to have the baby, to be away from the Romanian gossips and attended by good Coburg doctors.

So Missy was put privily away and didn't come to Ernie's great celebration. She was starting to show.

I didn't sleep the night before Cyril and Boris were expected. I was suddenly full of fears and doubts. What if Cyril didn't adore me any more? All those girls he must have seen on his travels. And what if I'd grown old and undesirable without even realising it? Ernie was so nonchalant about it all, so amused at my nervousness, I began to hate him for inviting them. And then when they did arrive it was earlier than they'd said, and with a dozen other guests, so there was no time to make a pretty speech or compose myself in a flattering attitude. We just greeted each other as cousins do and afterwards Ernie whispered to me that I had the stain of a coffee drip on my chin.

Sunny, for once, lived up to her name. She was very happy to be home. She loved the church, 'her church', she called it, she approved the changes we'd made to the kitchen garden, and she was relieved to see how fit and well Ernie was looking. That's what she said. She took my hand and thanked me for nursing him back to health.

'Our treasure,' she called him.

She said, 'I do love my new life, but I miss Ernie most dreadfully. You must come to Russia as often as possible. Every year without fail.'

Of course Ernie had no intention of going to Russia.

'Ridiculous language, filthy climate,' he'd say. 'And as for the people, well they're just not like us.'

And having topped out Sunny's Orthodox church he felt even less of an obligation.

'Let her come here,' he said. 'We can now offer her everything she requires and without the risk of frostbite.'

Cyril and I still hadn't talked. It wasn't that he was avoiding me. We were constantly part of the same huge, jolly gathering. Ernie had so many jaunts and activities arranged that there was never a quiet moment. But then one morning when the men were going out to a horse sale, Cyril pleaded an earache and an urgent letter to write and Ernie advised him against going out in an east wind.

'Stay indoors, old boy,' Ernie said. 'Write your letter. Ducky will provide you with everything you need.'

Cyril came and found me in my drawing room.

'Can't believe I'm doing this,' he said. 'It feels like shockingly bad form.'

He hugged me anyway.

He said, 'Is it my imagination or is Ernie trying to throw us together?'

I said, 'He's trying to be nice to me. He's still enjoying a resurrection glow. He nearly died, you know? So now he's being everything considerate, to show his gratitude. Health restored, second chances and all that.'

'Still,' Cyril said, 'it's a pretty rum way for a husband to carry on. Has he . . . you know?'

Ernie's resurrection glow had actually brought him to my bed, twice. He needed a son. But on both occasions he'd presented himself like a man awaiting execution.

Cyril said, 'What a terrible affliction he has. It really defies comprehension. How can he resist you?'

Then we wrapped ourselves in each other and a velvet curtain and stayed there, out of sight and pressed against each other for I don't know how long, until someone came in to put wood on the fire and must have been surprised to hear the curtain sneeze. And so, when Cyril and Boris left, to go to Paris, I was in a state of bliss. We were promised to each other. One day, whatever the price, however long the wait, Cyril and I would be together.

Ernie said, 'Observation: you've been uncommonly gay since the morning Cousin Cyril faked earache and availed himself of your escritoire. Did you let him dip his pen in your inkpot?'

I threw a hairbrush at him.

'Ah!' he said. 'You're cross. Does that mean he did or he didn't? Didn't, I'll wager. So punctilious, our Cyril. Not like Boris. I don't think there's a woman born that Boris wouldn't oblige. Well, you can't say I didn't give you the opportunity. I think I was rather generous. Under my own roof and so forth.'

It was Ernie's way of telling me that he was going to continue his resurrection celebrations in his own, private, special way. We spent Christmas apart. I went to Coburg to be with Mother and Pa and Missy. Ernie spent it with a dragoon called Dieter.

11

Missy was near her time. Under the circumstances – paternity of the child shrouded in winter fog – one really might have expected her to be in Mother's bad books but instead *I* was the one who received a telling off. Mother was angry about Cyril's visit to Darmstadt.

'After all the advice I've given you,' she said. 'The way to avoid temptation, young lady, is not to invite it into your house.'

I said, 'I didn't invite him. He came with Boris and Boris was Ernie's guest. Besides, I haven't done anything wrong. What about Missy's mess?'

That was Nando's fault, Mother said.

'When a wife gets into a muddle, it's her husband's job to correct her.'

Missy herself was entirely unrepentant.

'Why such a fuss?' she said. 'Babies all look alike anyway.'

Not if they have Nando Hohenzollern's ears they don't. Missy was just cross at having missed Ernie's big party.

She said, 'Boris Vladimirovich must have been so disappointed not to see me.'

I allowed her to enjoy this fantasy though I'm sure Boris had never given her a thought.

'And what about Sunny?' she said. 'I hear she's consulting some special French doctor. He's supposed to guarantee you get a boy, though heaven knows how. Smuggles one in in a warming pan, probably. Why doesn't Sunny do that anyway? It'd be a lot cheaper than paying a doctor.'

I said, 'Never mind about Sunny, what about you? What are you going to do?'

'Do?' she said. 'What do you think I'm going to do? Have this damned baby and go back to Romania.'

She said Nando didn't make fusses or study the features of new babies.

'He just does whatever Uncle King Carol tells him to do. When one has waited for a throne one doesn't do anything to mess up one's prospects.'

I said, 'But are you happy?'

'Happy?' she said. 'No idea. I never think about it.'

Missy's baby was born at the beginning of January. A girl, Marie, but to be called Mignon to distinguish her from all the other Maries in the family. I saw no particular resemblance to Boris Vladimirovich but neither did the child have Nando's ears so God is good. Encouraged by Mother, Missy lingered at Coburg until March when Nando came to take her home.

'Hey ho,' she said.

By June Nando was back in Coburg and so was I. Pa was dying. But Missy had been forbidden to travel by King Carol. He wanted her where his courtiers could watch her closely. I don't suppose it occurred to King Carol that Missy didn't need to travel to find adventures, nor that she was perhaps taking life gently so soon after childbirth. It was a particularly unkind punishment, the price Missy paid for the Mignon muddle, not to be allowed to see Pa one last time, but even the approach of death doesn't necessarily bring out the best in people. While he was still able to speak, Pa gave instructions that Mother was not to be admitted to his bedside.

After twenty-five years of marriage, after five children, he refused to see her.

At first Mother said it was a misunderstanding. Pa's speech had become indistinct. The doctor had misheard.

'Royal Highness,' he said, 'I am not deaf.'

Mother cried a little. Then she said, 'Your father means to spare me. That's what it is. He doesn't want me to see him suffer. Ach! What a good man he is.'

I'd never heard Mother speak so lovingly of Pa.

I said, 'You know, sometimes cancers wander. Perhaps Pa's has gone to his brain and makes him say things he doesn't really mean.'

'Yes!' she said. 'Of course that's it. How clever you are, Ducky. I'm so glad you're here with me. Such a comfort.'

During Pa's last days, Mother and I grew closer than we had ever been. Mother, who was accustomed to being obeyed, seemed quite cowed by Pa's doctors, but I promised her that she would be with Pa at the end. I'd make sure of that.

Pa had asked to be taken up to Rosenau where the air was cool and fresh. The only company he seemed to want was a silent doctor and a good supply of Herr Merck's morphine. Nando was allowed to enter the sickroom. Heaven knows why. Pa didn't even like him.

Mother reminisced about Pa. So handsome! So dashing! It was funny to imagine my stout, growling father as a dashing suitor.

'Penniless, of course,' she said. 'But I knew he was the husband for me.'

Then came the day Pa's physician said we might be allowed to visit.

'See,' Mother said. 'His mind has cleared. I knew it would.'

What a shocking sight Pa was, shrunken and grey. I heard Baby Bee catch her breath. We took turns at his side.

I told him I loved him, which was true, and that Missy was on her way, which wasn't. I showed him a picture of an elephant and a sailing ship that Elli had drawn for him. And Mother told him his colour was much improved and he might even be well enough to sail at Cowes if he'd only get out of bed and go for a walk. Then she spoke to him very quietly, in Russian. I don't know what she said, but he managed a little smile. He died that evening while we were at dinner. Nando was the first to be told.

I said, 'We should have been sent for.'

'The death struggle,' Dr Moller said. 'Very distressing for the ladies. Better to see him now he's at peace.'

Perhaps. It's just that he didn't really seem like Pa any more. He didn't even smell of Navy Cut.

So Affie was gone, which left a small, sad space, and Pa was gone, which made me ache to hear him rumble, 'Needs a Good Strong Dose' one more time, but Grandma Queen hung on and on. A wire was despatched to inform Her Majesty that she had outlived yet another of her children.

Letters from Ernie's sister, Vicky Battenberg, were our main source of information from England. Vicky said Pa's death had quite knocked the stuffing out of Her Majesty. She had lost interest in life and yet somehow couldn't let go of it. Ernie predicted another winter would finish her, and in our letters Cyril and I began to speak of future plans. Grandma Queen would die and Uncle Bertie Wales would become King. After a decent period of family and Court mourning, I would be granted a divorce. There would then follow a period out of the public eye, appropriate to a fallen woman who hopes to make good her reputation. Then Cyril would marry me.

It was all so frustratingly far in the future. *Be patient, darling*, Cyril used to write. *We're still young. This is the way it has to be. Let no one ever say we haven't been considerate and discreet.*

Mother made the surprising decision to go to England for Christmas. After twenty-five years of gentle bickering, she found she missed Pa terribly. She couldn't bear to stay in Coburg without him and Nice seemed to have lost its usual attraction. United in grief over Pa's death she and Grandma Queen had buried the hatchet. Mother took Baby Bee with her. Poor Bee. She was seventeen, so in Mother's eyes the matter of a husband was becoming quite urgent, and if there was one activity likely to restore Grandma's appetite for life, it was a little matchmaking.

As Ernie said, it sounded like the Christmas from hell. Osborne House, in winter, with duelling mourners.

Ernie had his own Christmas torture to get through. After much pleading from Sunny we were going to Russia.

'Oh God,' he groaned. 'Those endless church services. And they can't even get the date right. Christmas in January? What a benighted country.'

We stayed out at Tsarskoe Selo in Uncle Paul's recently vacated house. Sunny had had her way. When Uncle Paul asked for permission to marry Olga Pistohlkors, Emperor Nicky had refused to countenance it and so they had gone quietly away, Uncle Paul, Olga and their baby, Vova, to Paris where a Russian Grand Duke could live as he pleased. What a price Uncle Paul paid though. He left behind his older children. All the years he'd been a widower he'd farmed out Dmitri and Marie. They'd lived in Moscow with Aunt Ella and Uncle Serge. Occasionally they'd gone to St Petersburg to stay with Sunny and Nicky. They were growing up. Marie was ten, Dmitri was nine. Better not to disrupt the life they'd become accustomed to. Better not to expect them to fit in with a step-mother. Especially a divorcee. Everyone said so.

Ernie and I saw the Imperials almost every day. We had snow fights and went sledding with Emperor Nicky and his three little daughters. Sunny just watched us, bundled up in furs. She was expecting again and in the very gayest of moods. She was confident she was carrying a boy. Her French doctor had assured her the signs were auspicious.

I asked her about it.

'I ate lots of red meat,' she said. 'And I douched with soda water. Do you see how low I'm carrying? That's a sure sign it's a boy. Are you and Ernie still trying?'

'Sort of,' I said. 'No hurry.'

The New Year came in and Mother still lingered at Osborne, dragging Grandma Queen out for little carriage rides every day and poring over the *Almanach de Gotha* every evening, trying to raise her spirits. Vicky Battenberg wrote, *If Ducky's Mama has anything to do with it, Her Majesty will live to be a hundred. What an unlikely pair they are!*

On 18th January, we received the news that Grandma Queen had suffered a seizure, brief and nothing too serious. SITTING UP. TAKING BROTH, according to Mother's telegram.

On the 23rd, I heard Ernie's valet go in to him very early. It was a hunt day and I was already up and dressed. I thought perhaps Ernie had decided to ride out after all. But a few minutes later he appeared in the doorway to my room, huddled in his dressing gown, hair standing on end.

'Sad news, Ducky,' he said. 'GQ's gone. In her sleep. Sunny just telephoned. She's in pieces. So, no hunting today.'

I felt nothing. After all those conversations I'd had with myself that began, 'When Grandma Queen dies . . .' the fact of it fell very flat. It wasn't the end of my wait. Only the beginning of the end. Sunny, though, was inconsolable.

'Darling Gran-Gran,' she kept saying. 'She was like a mother to us and now we shall never see her again. How shall we manage without her, Ernie?'

Ernie wore his most compassionate face all day though I could see his patience was wearing thin. Emperor Nicky hovered around Sunny wondering what to offer: hot, sweet tea? Cool compresses for her temples? Tender words? Poor Nicky. He must have been worried that grief would cause Sunny to miscarry the son for which she had so carefully douched.

Of course I knew perfectly well how I should manage without Grandma Queen, but there was no one I could say that to. Cyril was far away, on exercises in the Black Sea. When I saw Aunt Miechen she did give me a significant look, but neither of us said anything.

Just when I should have been feeling optimistic, I was forced to take to my bed. My tonsils were inflamed and I ran a high fever. Emperor Nicky felt unwell too. So it was decided that he would be represented at the Queen's funeral by his brother, Grand Duke Misha. Ernie and Misha set off the next morning and travelled together to Windsor. And that was the start of a new headache for Mother though none of us foresaw it. Baby Bee fell for Grand Duke Misha, but Misha didn't fall for Baby Bee.

I stayed on at Tsarskoe Selo until my fever subsided and I was well enough to go home.

'We'll be company for each other,' Sunny said. 'We'll help each other through this sad time. You know it was always my wish that we should be better friends.'

I saw then Sunny's strange and lonely life. She disliked the Winter Palace and stayed in the country whenever possible, but even there her world was bleak. The Alexander Palace was no place to make a home. Sunny had made great efforts at cosiness – her sitting room, the children's playroom, Nicky's study – but they were tiny islands of comfort in an ocean of marble and gilt. I gave her many opportunities to complain about her lot but she never took them up. Russia, Nicky, babies, everything was wonderful. She would have liked to go to England for the funeral but her duty was to the health of her unborn child.

'The next Tsar,' she said. 'That's what matters above all. Dear Gran-Gran would have understood.'

Sunny and Ernie had known a different Grandma Queen than I had. She'd always been gentle with them, because they'd been so young when their mother passed away. They hadn't seen her hard face as I had.

'Marriage is sacred. Happiness is irrelevant.'

12

When I returned to Darmstadt, there was a letter waiting for me from Cyril. His ship would be putting in at Toulon in February and he expected to get some shore leave. Was my mother likely to be taking her usual winter rest in Nice? And if so was there the remotest chance I could join her there? In fact Mother had gone to the South of France directly from Grandma Queen's funeral and had taken Baby Bee with her in the hope of distracting her from her crush on Grand Duke Misha. I told Ernie I thought I might visit them there. He guessed the reason at once.

'I suppose the good ship Cyril Vladimirovich will be in port,' he said. 'Well, please yourself. But you may not take Elli with you. She's to stay here with me.'

Ernie had changed. With Grandma Queen gone he ceased pretending that we could get along. Every evening, as soon as he had read Elli a bedtime story, he went out and left me alone. And when he went to the country he insisted on going alone, no matter how many Meissen figurines I threw. I called him a beastly invert. He called me a sulking child. Windows rattled. It made no difference. He always went off and did as he pleased.

All of Darmstadt knew about our frightful rows and of course I was held responsible. It was one thing for the servants to know, but something else entirely when people talked about it in the street.

Even the George Buchanans had heard, and they'd left Hesse by then and were living in Rome. Some thoughtful friend had written to tell them that Grand Duchess Ducky had hurled an antique French spear at Grand Duke Ernie and almost killed him, which was completely inaccurate. It was a German halberd and Ernie was already through the door when it struck. My aim was good but my timing was slow.

It was bliss to get away to France. Cyril stayed at an hotel in Cannes and motored over to see me every day for a week. Mother never received him. She contrived always to be out or resting when he called for me.

'Nothing happened. And anyway I didn't see it.' That was Mother's way of being both disapproving and a little lenient.

Cyril and I were simply cousins who both happened to be wintering in France. That was the position Mother had decided to take, and she made sure we had no opportunity to become lovers by insisting that I take Baby Bee with me wherever I went. Darling Bee. For the price of an ice cream she'd make herself scarce for half an hour so Cyril and I could park somewhere secluded and kiss. It was exquisite agony.

'Steady on, old thing,' he'd say. 'One's desperately trying to be a gentleman.'

I asked him once if he was a virgin.

'Ducky!' he said. 'What kind of a question is that?'

I took the answer to be No. Well, these things are different for men.

There was so much to talk about. Uncle Bertie's coronation wasn't to take place for another year and a half. We decided we couldn't possibly wait so long and if I knew Uncle Bertie he wouldn't expect us to. In a family as enormous as ours there would always be some reason the timing was inappropriate. Someone would die and there'd be Court mourning. Or there'd be a wedding that mustn't be overshadowed. No, we must just get on with it.

I was to ask Ernie for a divorce towards the end of the year. Cyril was concerned that he might refuse, that he might insist on holding on to me until I'd given him an heir.

I said, 'But Ernie knows where babies come from. He never makes the least effort to make one. I think he's given up on Hesse. When he reaches the end of his days they'll just have to scrape the barrel for a successor.'

I believed it could all be managed very discreetly. Uncle Bertie would be amenable, Ernie would be a gentleman and Cyril and I would be married, quietly. We'd live in St Petersburg, to be near Cyril's base at Kronstadt, and Elli would go to Darmstadt each summer for three months, to see Ernie. What a child I was, thinking all these things would come to pass, just because I wished it.

In June of that year Empress Sunny gave birth to another girl. Anastasia.

So much for the French doctor, wrote Aunt Miechen. *He's been dismissed. One does begin to feel sorry for Sunny. An heir is really the very least we ask of her.*

In August Cyril received orders for the Pacific Squadron. I saw the hand of Sunny in his sudden transfer. I was sure Ernie must have written to her, to warn her that Cyril and I were determined to be married. He didn't deny it. He just laughed.

He said, 'How very self-absorbed you've become, Ducky. Do you really think Sunny has any power over where the Russian Navy sends its men? And do you really think she could care less about you and Sailor Cyril?'

I said, 'I know Sunny would move heaven and earth if she thought it would make you happy.'

91

'Make me happy?' he said. 'I'm completely indifferent to Cyril Vladimirovich's movements and so had you better be if you insist on pursuing this idiotic pash. That's the life a Navy wife must expect.'

Cyril was transferred to the battleship *Peresvet* and sailed for Port Arthur, Manchuria, immediately. It would be a year, at least a year, he said, before he'd see me again and I must be brave and patient. Well, I managed two months of patience and bravery and then I did the only thing I could think of. I went home to Mother.

Ernie didn't ask how long I expected to be away. Perhaps he guessed I wasn't coming back. If I'd taken Elli with me he'd have wanted to know every particular of my plans, but I didn't. I left her in Darmstadt until I was sure of my next step. I anticipated there would be a great deal of shouting and weeping when I got to Coburg and told Mother my intentions. It would be no scene for a six-year-old to witness.

Mother went on the attack at once. I was twenty-four years old. I had a husband, a child and a Duchy to consider. Why must I be so selfish and infantile? What had she ever done to deserve two such silly daughters as Missy and me? And then the sharpest barb of all: if I had really left my husband why hadn't I brought my child with me?

She said, 'What kind of mother are you?'

That broke me. I'd been nursing that pain all the way from Elli's nursery door to Mother's drawing room. It was a fair question. What kind of mother leaves her child? I cried so noisily that Mother held her fire and sat in stunned silence.

When my cries had subsided to silent sobs a cup of chocolate was rung for. Mother went to the door and waited for it to be brought from the kitchens. She was determined that no servants should witness the state I was in.

I said, 'I have to tell you something. It's something I couldn't allow Elli to hear.'

'That was no reason not to bring her here,' she said. 'She could have been taken out for a walk in the park. And I hope this isn't about Cyril Vladimirovich.'

I said, 'No, it's about Ernie's perversion. He prefers to have relations with men.'

Then she listened.

I told her about the scene I'd stumbled on that afternoon at Wolfsgarten, about Hubert and Dieter and heaven knows how many other boys, and how I could count on the fingers of one hand the number of times Ernie had shared my bed since Elli was born.

She said nothing for the longest time. When I looked at her, to try and gauge her mood, I thought how very old she looked. Eventually she said, 'I seem to have made a bad job of choosing husbands for my daughters.'

I said, 'Sandra seems happy.'

Mother said, 'Sandra chose her own husband.'

I was exhausted.

She said, 'If only your father had lived, or dear Affie. They'd have given Ernie Hesse the thrashing he deserves.'

The idea of my brother giving anyone a thrashing introduced a welcome note of comedy to that grim afternoon. Mother took my hand. Her skin was so thin and papery.

'My poor child,' she said. 'One hears of such things, of course. But in Russia we don't have it, and I don't think Germans suffer from it either, not real Germans. Is it an English disease? I think it must be. Well now, don't worry. Mother will see to everything. There must be an annulment, of course, not the other thing. An annulment is so much more elegant. But the first thing you must do is send for Elli. Think what she might witness if she spends another moment in that house of depravity. Her nurse must bring her here at once. You and she shall always, always find a home in Coburg.'

Later she said, 'I suppose you still have thoughts of Cyril Vladimirovich?'

I told her that Cyril loved me and when my marriage to Ernie was dissolved I intended to marry him. She sighed.

'Well,' she said, 'at least he won't run around with boys. But I must warn you, Ducky, Romanov men don't always make devoted husbands. They can be very hot-tempered. And they will spend money on their ballerinas. Apartments, furs.'

I said, 'Emperor Nicky doesn't.'

'Perhaps not now,' she said. 'But only because Sunny keeps him on a short tether. I'm sure he'd still go to that Kschessinskaya creature twice a week if he could.'

I was astonished. Mathilde Kschessinskaya was one of those women whose name was linked to several Grand Dukes. But Nicky! He'd always been so ardent for Sunny. I could only think he'd gone to La Kschessinskaya to learn the ropes, so to speak. I'd never seen her. I don't know if she was a great beauty or just very obliging, but she seemed to be a kind of shared Romanov utility. Like a good tailor.

Mother recovered very quickly from the grenade I'd tossed into her life.

She said, 'Of course if you do marry Cyril Vladimirovich, you'll make your home in Coburg. You could have Schloss Rosenau.'

I said, 'No. We'll live in St Petersburg.'

'Darling,' she said, 'don't be silly. Do you really think Sunny will have you there after you've exposed her brother? She'll defend him, you'll see, and she'll make sure she never has to see you. You'll be just another Navy wife, always on the move. You'll be posted to

Vladivostock, and then I shall never see you, never see my grand-child. No, if you're determined to have Cyril he'll have to leave the Russian Navy and settle here. We can find something for him to do. Does he shoot?'

Everything Mother said made sense. An annulment, not a divorce. People would be so much kinder about that. And then a home in Germany where Elli's occasional visits to Darmstadt would be easy to arrange. I slept very well that night and felt so full of energy when I woke the next morning. I wrote to Ernie. My tone, I thought, was practical and reasonable.

A week passed and I'd had no reply. I began to think my letter hadn't reached him.

Mother said, 'Of course it reached him. He's up to something. He's scheming how to make you the villain in all this. Your name will be mud in Hesse.'

I said, 'But the people there love me.'

'Do you really think so?' she said. 'Just see how quickly they'll forget you.'

On the tenth day Ernie's reply came. A cold, scornful letter. An annulment? On what grounds? Was I completely out of my wits? Divorce was the only option and it must be made clear to the world that I was the instigator of the suit. His terms were that Elli must spend at least half of every year with him in Darmstadt and return to live there permanently when she came of age. That was it. No sorrow, no regret. Mother said his demands were ridiculous. What did a man know about raising a daughter? Particularly a man with Ernie's tendencies. A little girl needed to be with her mother, not a succession of catamites.

I said, 'What if Elli doesn't want to live with me? She's such a daddy's girl.'

Mother said, 'Want? She's a child. What she *wants* isn't the point.

You must stop being so feeble, Ducky. Think! What if Ernie marries again? He probably will. He'll find some dupe. Are you going to allow another woman to raise your child for six months of the year? No, it's quite unacceptable. Elli must live here, with you. Ernie can visit.'

Ernie's note signalled the start of open season on my reputation. Letters flew between England and Russia and Germany. Aunts and in-laws and cousins and second cousins. The men kept quiet on the whole, perhaps anxious to keep the lid on their own little peccadilloes, but the womenfolk had plenty to say. Baby Bee became my listening post.

'General opinion seems to be that you've lost your mind. Aunt Ella hopes time will heal. Irene finds it all most perplexing and Empress Sunny wishes you were dead. I must say, Ducky, I hope all this isn't going to ruin things for me.'

'Did Sunny actually say she wished I were dead?'

'Not actually. She said it would have been better for Ernie to be widowed than be dragged through the horror of the D thing. Amounts to the same thing though, doesn't it?'

Better death than divorce. Grandma Queen's opinion precisely. Perhaps when one is Empress it comes naturally to move untidy lives and inconveniences around like pieces on a chess board.

Others, who at least didn't wish for my early death, suggested the only course of action was for me to take the veil, to go into some closed order and never be spoken of again. Ernie's sister, dear Vicky Battenberg, wrote that she would always remember me fondly, which made me feel that perhaps I was dead. Aunt Louise sent a postcard with the single word *Coraggio!*

One good thing happened. The more the world raged against me the more staunch Mother was in my defence. She vowed never, ever to have me put away. I'd always known she loved me but it was the first time in my life I felt the warmth of her love. Cyril's mother, Aunt Miechen, stayed wisely but very unusually silent.

The grounds for an annulment were problematical. Not impossible, but likely to proceed at a snail's pace. There was the little matter of Elli. Clearly our marriage had been consummated. Even Mother conceded that I'd be an old woman before an annulment freed me to marry Cyril.

My marriage to Ernie ended on 21st December 1901. We were granted a divorce on the grounds of invincible mutual antipathy. It was a bleak phrase that ignored what good friends we'd been and what good times we'd had before we were laced into marriage, but it saved the public washing of any soiled linen.

Ernie and Elli spent Christmas in Kiel with Irene and her children, then Ernie brought her to Coburg, to spend a month with me.

'But I don't want to stay here,' Elli said, even when I told her about the new pony. She glowered at me and clung to Ernie's leg.

'I don't want a new pony,' she grizzled. 'I want to go home with Pappi. Mamma's cross with me.'

I said, 'I'm not cross with you at all.'

'Well, you look cross,' she said. 'Always.'

People said that. Missy always looked gay and I always looked stern. It was so unfair.

Mother suggested that Ernie stay on for a few days, to help Elli settle in.

'Not sure I care to,' he said. 'I suppose Sailor Cyril's in town?'

I said, 'He's in the Pacific.'

'Really?' he said. 'Gosh. Poor old Ducky. All divorced and nowhere to go.'

I said, 'Cyril was nothing to do with our divorce.'

He sniggered.

He said, 'Honestly, who do you imagine you're fooling? Everyone knows about you and Cyril. When will his tour finish?'

I didn't know.

'Oh, Ducky,' he said. 'You don't know? I do hope Cyril Vladimirovich hasn't taken fright now you're a free woman. I do hope you haven't thrown out the baby with the bath water.'

Ernie stayed on in Coburg for three ghastly days, with Elli constantly begging to go home. So I let them go. What was the point of making the child miserable? Mother said this was a grave error, that I should have forced Elli to spend more time with me until she grew accustomed to our new situation. I don't know. I only ever wanted her to be happy. I did tell her so.

I said, 'And you know you may come to me as often as you like. You have your own room here and no one else shall ever sleep in it.'

'I don't much like that room,' she said. 'I like my room at home.'

I said, 'Then we'll change it to your liking. You can draw me a picture of how you'd like it to be. Pappi will put it in the post for you.'

She said, 'Why are you crying?'

I said, 'I'm going to miss you.'

'Then why are you staying here?' she said. 'Why don't you just come home with me and Pappi?'

Which made it all the harder. I could have gone back to Darmstadt. I'm sure Ernie would have agreed to it. But I needed Cyril more. That's what I chose.

The last thing Ernie said to me was, 'By the by, once you're a Navy wife, don't imagine I'm going to let you spirit Elli off to Manchuria or wherever for years on end. Not bally likely. She'll stay with me.'

13

I waited four years for Cyril Vladimirovich. Four years of looking out for letters and listening to the ticking of the clock. The Grand Duchess of Hesse was reduced to being Ducky, living under her mother's roof again, like a child. Elli gradually thawed enough to visit me – she still asked me when I'd be going home – but her life was elsewhere and Ernie was its centre. I suppose I became more like an aunt than a mother. I over-indulged her, anything to be liked. I didn't see that clearly until later, until I was a proper mother again.

Why didn't Cyril come galloping up to the gates of Rosenau and carry me off at once? Because Cyril is Cyril. There's nothing impetuous about him. Everything he does: accounts, morning toilette, affairs of the heart, they are all attended to carefully and methodically. I never doubted his love for me, only his judgement, sometimes.

The first time he got shore leave after my divorce he went to see Emperor Nicky, to talk to him man to man. We had agreed that it would be far better to marry with Nicky's blessing than without it. I thought the outcome of their meeting was ambiguous but Cyril put a positive gloss on it. *Nicky*, he wrote, *expressed every hope that with time things will straighten themselves out. So hold fast, my love! We'll do things correctly and all will be well.*

With time things will straighten themselves out. Cyril took this to mean that Sunny might eventually accept the fact of my divorce.

Mother said, 'It doesn't mean that at all. It means that Nicky hopes if he drags it out for long enough Cyril will forget about you and marry someone more acceptable. Which he may well do.'

Sometimes, when a week passed without a letter, I feared Mother was right. Other times, like the summer of 1903 when Cyril was on furlough and rushed to be with me, my hopes were raised. We bought a Richard-Brasier and went on a little motoring holiday. That was when I taught myself to drive. We stayed in *pensions* as Mr and Mrs Brown and if anyone suspected we were lovers, no one showed it. The French don't get so excited about such things.

How do men learn to please women? I didn't know Cyril's history or what he did when he was away from me and I didn't want to know, but he seemed quite confident. And so enthusiastic. Cyril didn't waste time cracking jokes or horsing around as Ernie always had. At last, a man who couldn't wait for me to slide between the sheets. Of course Cyril wasn't the type to murmur endearments. He's a military man, after all. But I felt adored and sometimes, I will admit, rather wild. I began to understand Missy's taste for adventurettes, if that was how a man could make one feel.

It was such a happy summer, but it came to an end and we were still no further forward. Cyril went back to Kronstadt to await his next posting and I went back to Coburg, the divorced daughter, the absent mother. So much for patience and doing things correctly. Before he left Cyril promised me he'd speak to Nicky again.

'Soon,' he said. 'The very moment the time seems right.'

I remember saying, 'We could just do it. We could be married tomorrow, before you leave. Once it's done Nicky can't unmarry us.'

'True,' he said, 'but he could make things pretty unpleasant for us. Better to wait for his blessing. I'm confident our patience will be rewarded.'

And off he went. I had no idea when I'd see him again, and when my very great hour of need came I wasn't even certain where in the world he was.

The first telegram arrived as Mother and I were sitting at breakfast.

ELLI SICK. DON'T WORRY, BUT SUGGEST COME. ERNIE.

He'd taken Elli to Poland, to the Skierniewice hunting lodge for a holiday with Nicky and Sunny and their girls. Mother and I were still at table, discussing train times when a second wire was delivered.

FEVER WORSE. COME AT ONCE.

I couldn't think what I needed to take with me or how, precisely, I was going to get to Skierniewice. I ran about, achieving nothing. Mother was perfectly calm.

'Sit down and collect yourself,' she said. 'Amsel will pack your bags. That's what maids are for. And Kuster will go with you. You can't travel all that way without protection. Anything might happen.'

Kuster was Mother's steward. A mountain of a man who only spoke when spoken to. I was glad to think I could leave the particulars of the journey to him. From Coburg we had to go to Leipzig, from Leipzig to Dresden, then to Breslau and finally to Lodz. So many trains. At Breslau Kuster was to wire Ernie to tell him what time to meet us.

Amsel was already in the carriage and Kuster was strapping on the last bag when another telegram arrived. I don't remember reading it. I suppose I must have. Mother collapsed. She had her prayer book in her hand.

'No,' she said. 'No, no, no.'

There was no point in travelling to Skierniewice. Elli was already on her way home to Darmstadt, in a silver coffin.

Typhoid, they said. Perhaps from the water, they said. But why my child and not one of Sunny's and Nicky's girls? They must all have drunk from the same well. I found I went over every event, every fork in the road that might have changed things. If Ernie and I hadn't divorced, would Elli have gone to Skierniewice? Probably not. The idea of being cooped up in a small lodge in the middle of Poland with Sunny and Nicky wouldn't have appealed to me. But then, if we had gone and if I had been there, would Elli have clung more fiercely to life? No. She was always Ernie's girl. If she could have lived she would have done, for his sake.

I travelled to Darmstadt in a kind of fog. People's voices seemed muffled, their questions seemed idiotic. Did I want tea? Did I want a blanket? I wanted nothing, except for everyone to go away, but the more I said that the more they crowded around me. What did they think? That I'd throw myself from the train?

The thing I dreaded most was seeing Ernie. I thought he'd rage at me, I don't know why. But Ernie was too broken to rage.

'The sun's gone out,' he said. 'My life's over.'

Which has turned out not to be entirely the case because he remarried two years later and forced himself to carry out the disagreeable chore of fathering two sons. But in that first week it really seemed that he might die of grief. He wandered about the house and lay on Elli's bed.

'Sunny's taken this terribly hard,' he said to me one evening. 'You know how she is. She feels everything so.'

Sunny! I didn't see what business it was of hers to suffer. She had four healthy daughters and mine was dead.

Elli would be twenty-three now, had she lived. I wonder what ill-advised marriage Mother might have canvassed for her? Or has she learned her lesson. This war has changed everything. Half of those cousins are on the wrong side now.

We took Elli to the mausoleum at Rosenhohe, to be buried with all the other Hesses. Mother urged me to go in and look at her before the casket was closed. She said it would help me to accept. It didn't, not at all. But I did put my Hesse medallion into her cold little hands. After all, I wasn't their Grand Duchess any more, and I hoped, I hope never to see Darmstadt again as long as I live.

She looked like a wax doll. Only her black curls seemed real. One little drink of water. What a stupid, stupid waste.

Cyril wrote to me but he didn't rush to my side. He was in Palermo.

Tricky situation, he wrote, *with regard to Ernie. I don't wish to intrude at such a sad time, but, darling, I do think of you every waking minute.*

I don't know how one calculates the decent period to stay away from a bereaved lover. Cyril left it two months. Then he came to Coburg and asked if he might stay for Christmas. Baby Bee persuaded Mother to allow it.

She said, 'Ducky's had such a sad year. And how is Cyril ever to propose if he never sees her for more than five minutes?'

Mother said, 'Cyril Vladimirovich has had ample opportunity to propose. He may stay in the Callenberg shooting box. If he desires the greater comfort of my house he knows what he must do.'

Cyril didn't take the hint. Marriage wasn't mentioned. Not once. He says now that it wouldn't have been proper, during a time of mourning. I disagree. I wasn't looking for the fuss of a betrothal and a public announcement. I just wanted Cyril's reassurance. I wanted a private pledge and a date. Missy said I should give him an ultimatum. Her letters were full of advice but I'd grown to see that Missy wasn't particularly brilliant at managing her own affairs, let alone telling others what to do.

Do you know whom I have to thank for the wedding ring on my hand? Admiral Togo of the Japanese Imperial Navy.

The Japanese attacked the Russian fleet at Port Arthur and war was declared. Cyril was still at Rosenau when we heard the news. He said he should leave for Petersburg at once, to report for duty. I think I cried more that night than I did when Elli died. Well, they were a different kind of tears. When a child dies a worm of pain buries itself in your heart and never goes away. It sits there and every day, without fail, it flexes its hateful little body and gives you an aching reminder. But when a man goes away to war without leaving you the promise of a firm wedding date, the tears are fierce and angry.

Mother said I should forget Cyril.

She said, 'I regret to say it of my own people but Russians have no sense of urgency. "Tomorrow will do," they say. But tomorrow never comes.'

Cyril was posted to Port Arthur. Manchuria. It's the other side of the world. His letters took weeks to arrive and by the time I heard that the *Petropavlovsk* had sunk, he was already back in Petersburg, recovering from his injuries. It was the beginning of May 1904. Aunt Miechen wrote to Mother. Cyril needed a place to recuperate. Would Mother consent to his coming to Rosenau? Mother sniffed and put Aunt Miechen's letter aside. Then, after a calculated period of silence for which only she knew the formula, she agreed. She said that as Cyril clearly had no intention of marrying me I might as well help nurse him. He was my cousin, after all. And it would help prepare me for the life of lonely spinsterhood and good works that was now clearly my destiny.

Baby Bee and I went to the station to meet him. At first sight he seemed unchanged. It was only when he moved that it was obvious he was in pain. His back was burned, but it was healing well. His mind had a different kind of injury that couldn't be dressed. He suffered from nightmares when everything came back to him in terrifying detail. He told me about it, eventually.

His boat had been on a night sortie. Port Arthur had been blockaded by the Japanese Navy so every night a convoy of Russian destroyers ventured out to report on any change in the Japanese positions.

'It was almost dawn,' he said. 'We were heading back into Port Arthur. I was on the bridge with Captain Yakovlev. It was snowing.'

The *Petropavlovsk* had hit a mine. Cyril remembers being thrown into the air.

'And then I came back down, with a thump. Yakovlev was dead. He was cut almost in two. I couldn't hear a thing. Ears refused to function. Eyes still working though. Just as well. We were sinking fast. So I went overboard. Water was bloody freezing. Took my breath away. Then I thought best to pull myself together and move away from the wreck sharpish. Vessel that size goes down, Ducky, it can drag you with it. There were men in the water. I told them to swim for it. Don't know if they heard me. Then down she went.'

That's the worst part of his nightmare, being under the water and powerless to rise to the surface. But he did get to the surface.

'God tossed me back up,' he says. 'And thoughtfully provided me with a piece of flotsam to keep me afloat.'

He was nearly dead from the cold when a Russian torpedo boat plucked him out of the water.

'Extraordinary thing,' he told me. 'Brother Boris witnessed the whole incident. He was inspecting a battery on the ridge above the harbour, saw the explosion, felt sorry for the poor buggers who'd caught it, never realising I was one of them.'

Cyril stayed with us at Rosenau all through that summer. His burns healed and he began to be active again. Only the nightmares persisted. One day, a perfect summer's day, we were sitting by the Princes' Pond watching the swallows drinking on the wing and he said, 'That's exactly like death. It felt like something brushing over me, when I was in the water. Like a bird's wing. But then it passed on. So I suppose it wasn't my time.'

I said, 'Doesn't that make life seem doubly precious?'

'Absolutely,' he said, and he took my hand. 'That's why nothing will prevent me from marrying you.'

It was what I'd longed to hear, of course. I suggested we do it immediately, while he was in Coburg, but Cyril's moment of poetry, birds' wings and all that, had passed.

'Inauspicious time, darling,' he said. 'What with Elli's death, and the war. Wedding during a time of mourning. Not quite the thing. But as soon as this damned war's over.'

That's Cyril all over. Not yet. Not quite the thing. As for the war, I was perfectly prepared to be a war bride. Lots of girls did it. Then, in the middle of August we received wonderful news. Empress Sunny had at last produced a baby boy. Alexis. It meant that Cyril and his brothers were pushed reassuringly down the line of succession. Tsesarevich Alexis would succeed after Nicky, so who Cyril married was really no longer of any concern. We were free to do as we pleased.

Aunt Miechen wrote that Emperor Nicky was like a little dog with two tails and Sunny, boy produced and duty done, had retired to a day bed.

When Cyril went back to Petersburg, to re-enter the war effort, it seemed the perfect time to inform Nicky of our plans. We could ride on his wave of joy at fathering an heir. Furthermore, Cyril was a war hero, wounded but returning to do his patriotic duty. Nicky could not possibly raise any objections. Cyril, though, let the moment slip. He spent the rest of the year as Nicky's aide. He dined with him almost every night, but he never brought up his wish to marry me. Missy told me I was a perfect fool. Aunt Miechen wrote that Cyril never was one to be chivvied, even as a child; he got there but in his own good time.

Then the year turned, and so did Emperor Nicky's mood. Port Arthur surrendered to the Japanese. The war was going against Russia, so many lives lost and what had they gained? The factory owners were richer, that was all. Workers' strikes were called. Aunt Ella wrote to Mother that Uncle Serge was struggling to keep order in Moscow and thought of resigning and handing over to an abler man. In St Petersburg men were milling about on the streets, gathering around anyone who chose to stand on a box and speak. Then a march was got up, the Sunday after the Blessing of the Waters, to go to the Winter Palace and petition the Emperor. And what did the marchers want from him? Everything, according to Aunt Miechen. Higher wages, a vote for every man, free education.

Mother said, 'Russians are like children at a birthday party. Give them everything they ask for and they'll make themselves sick. Trust me, I know what I'm talking about.'

The Sunday march ended badly. Some of the marchers were shot, to prevent them from getting too close to the Winter Palace. I don't know why. Emperor Nicky wasn't even at the Palace. He was at Tsarskoe Selo building a snowman for his daughters. Some people say fifty marchers died, some say thousands. I still don't know what to believe. But I do know that it was the start of a run of bad things. Three weeks later, in Moscow, Grand Duke Uncle Serge was killed.

He and Aunt Ella had just had lunch and he was on his way back to his office. She heard the windows rattle and she guessed that it was an explosion. She said she knew at once that Uncle Serge was dead. A bomb had been tossed into his coupé. Uncle Paul's Dmitri and Marie were in the house and Aunt Ella's first thought was that they shouldn't see anything of the carnage. She ran down to the street herself, to cover what was left of Uncle Serge with blankets. His driver was still breathing, though he died later too. The assassin survived long enough to be hanged.

'Just like they did to our dear father,' Mother said. 'Russians. They always kill the good men.'

Uncle Serge was one of Mother's baby brothers. Grandpa Emperor Alexander had been killed by a bomb too. I know that now but when it happened it wasn't spoken of in our nursery. We were told only that he had passed away. Missy claims to remember him. She says he was seven feet tall.

After Uncle Serge's murder, Aunt Ella was very concerned for the safety of Grand Duke Uncle Paul's children. Dmitri Pavlovich was nearly fourteen and quite old enough, as Mother said, for those lawless savages to harm him too. So he and Marie were sent to St Petersburg, to live with Emperor Nicky and enjoy the greater protection of the Imperial Guard. If you ask me they should have been sent to Paris to live with their father, or better still, Grand Duke Uncle Paul should have been allowed to go home to Russia and make a proper home for those poor children, but nobody asked my opinion.

Mother mourned Uncle Serge's death in a quiet, stoic way. I never saw her weep for him. But she did greet me one morning with a grim face and a letter in her hand.

'So,' she said, 'Ernie Hesse has pipped you to the post. He got married last week. He didn't waste much time, did he? When I think how he dragged his heels asking for your hand, it's pretty infuriating.'

I said, 'He needs an heir.'

'Pah!' she said. 'He could have had an heir of you if he'd only *concentrated*.'

It wasn't that I minded. I just thought Ernie might have warned me. And actually he did try but his letter was misdirected and didn't arrive until several days later. His bride was Onor Solms-Hohensolms. Missy used to call her The Tongue-Twister. I remembered her well from Darmstadt, a dull, stocky little creature with thin lips. Her family must have despaired of ever getting her off their hands. But she'd landed Grand Duke Ernie, no less. Well, in a way it was a good match. Ernie was desperate for a son and the Tongue-Twister was just plain desperate.

In apple blossom time, when Cyril should have come to Coburg and married me, he accepted another posting to the Pacific. The Baltic Fleet were on their way east, to support the Pacific Squadron.

Mother said, 'I won't trouble to say what I think. I've already wasted enough breath on the subject.'

Missy wrote, 'Now will you concede that Cyril has no intention of marrying you? Come to Romania. I'll find you a dozen husbands.'

It was my lowest moment. Though I was too ashamed to say it, I thought I had made a mistake. Several, actually. I'd divorced Ernie and there was no turning back. My reputation was stained. And I'd allowed Cyril to share my bed though he delayed and delayed our marrying. I thought of disappearing. That would show him. But I didn't know how to go about it. I thought of Aunt Louise and her 'what do you want to do with your life?' I still had no idea. I'd allowed everything to depend on Cyril. I felt foolish and useless and took to my bed under the pretext of a chill. It was the dark hour before the dawn.

14

The war with Japan ended in May. Cyril didn't see any more action. While he was still on the train to Vladivostock, the Baltic Fleet had entered the Straits of Tsushima and found the Japanese lying in wait for them. Those ships that weren't sunk surrendered and for Russians it felt as though it had all been for nothing. The Japanese were the victors.

Cyril came to Coburg directly.

'Darling,' he said, 'name the day. We've waited quite long enough.'

I thought he must have talked to Emperor Nicky.

'No,' he said. 'It's not a good time. War lost. Strikes everywhere. Sailors mutinying. Poor Nicky has quite enough on his plate. Somehow it's never a good time. We'll just get married and then I'll tell him.'

I remember asking him if he was sure.

'Of course I'm sure, you muggins,' he said. 'You were always the girl for me.'

I was so happy. All my doubts disappeared, even when Mother seemed less than joyful at our news.

'Joyful?' she said. 'One has rather gone beyond that. Relieved, certainly. You'll be married discreetly, of course, and immediately.'

It wasn't so simple. There was the difficulty of finding a priest.

110

I'd have been happy for anyone to marry us, but Cyril said we must be married according to the rite of the Orthodox Church because he was still in the line of succession, albeit only fourth. But what Russian priest would marry us without the Tsar's permission? Mother saved the day.

She said, 'Father Arseny will do it.'

He was Mother's confessor.

'But how can he? What about Nicky's permission?'

'Father Arseny will do it,' Mother said, 'because I shall tell him to. And not here. Somewhere quieter. Bavaria is still pleasant at this time of autumn. Yes, Tegernsee would be perfect. We'll use the Adlerbergs' old house. There's no one in it. Neutral territory.'

Anyone would have thought we were signing the Treaty of Portsmouth, not celebrating a marriage.

Missy couldn't be there. Boris didn't even know of our plans. Nor did Aunt Miechen and Grand Duke Uncle Vladimir. Cyril was still being cautious and Mother understood why, but she didn't interfere. I think she just wanted us to get married and leave her in peace.

How very different from when I married Ernie. I didn't even buy a new gown. The ceremony was soon over, very short by Russian standards because it was abbreviated in view of my regrettable divorce. The light grew strangely yellow and snow began to fall, unseasonably early. We had a hasty wedding breakfast then our very few guests all left. Poor Father Arseny led the stampede.

Cyril said, 'Did someone give the order to abandon ship? Was it something we said?'

It all felt a bit flat. We'd waited so long to be married, and we were already lovers. But something strange occurred. I found I was more in love than ever. Not wildly, as before, but deeply. And we were beyond the reach of anyone's disapproval, or so I thought.

The snow melted, the sun came out and we spent our honeymoon motoring *around* the lake, rowing *on* the lake, and paddling our feet *in* the lake.

'Good morning, Wife,' Cyril would greet me.

'Good morning, Husband,' I'd reply. 'Is the lake still there?'

'Lake present and correct,' he'd say.

Missy sent a rather lukewarm message. Something along the lines of, she hoped my saintly patience would be rewarded and that marriage to Cyril would live up to my expectations. Aunt Louise sent a card. *And still the ravens haven't left the Tower!*

At the end of October, I went back to Coburg to begin packing for my new life and Cyril travelled on to St Petersburg to announce the news of our marriage.

He said, 'While I'm gone you must think what name you wish to go by in Russia. You can probably get away with "Victoria" but your patronymic is a problem. "Victoria Alfredovna" doesn't really work.'

Mother recommended 'Fyodorovna'. It was the patronymic Dowager Empress Minnie had taken when she went to Russia to be married, and Sunny too.

She said, 'Saint Fyodor's a perfectly respectable saint and look, Fyodorovna isn't so very different from Alfredovna. Quite similar at a glance.'

That was how I became the Grand Duchess Victoria Fyodorovna.

The plan was that Cyril would spend two weeks in St Petersburg, seeing family members and choosing a place for us to live. I would then follow on. We'd be together in Russia in time for Christmas. Cyril said not to buy any new furs, to wait until I got to Russia and he'd buy me a sable.

Three days after his arrival there I received a telegram from

Aunt Miechen. CYRIL VLADIMIROVICH RETURNING COBURG, it said. DISASTER.

My new husband seemed shorter and less dashing after his brief visit to Saint Petersburg. Half the man, I thought, when he walked back through the door at Rosenau. He had been reduced and humiliated and it showed. Here's what had happened.

Things had begun well enough. Aunt Miechen and Uncle Vladimir were very happy to hear about our marriage.

'Thrilled,' he said. 'But you know they always loved you.'

After he'd received their congratulations and they'd opened a bottle of champagne, Cyril arranged to go and see Emperor Nicky the next morning. But the reason for Cyril's arrival in St Petersburg reached Nicky's ears before bedtime. I suppose if you're the Emperor of All the Russias you had better know what everyone is up to. Emperor Nicky sent one of his courtiers, Count Fredericks, to deliver the blow. His Imperial Majesty would not receive Cyril the next morning, nor at any other hour. Cyril had contracted a marriage without his Emperor's consent and must pay the price. He had forty-eight hours to leave Russia, for ever.

Given an opening Aunt Miechen still talks about it, all these years later. 'Coming to a person's house on Court business at that time of night,' she says. 'Unheard of. Of course it wasn't poor old Fredericks's fault. One mustn't blame the messenger. It was Nicky's doing and not even entirely his. He'll have had Sunny urging him on.'

Cyril's parents were beside themselves, both at Cyril's punishment and at the way it was announced. Uncle Vladimir went out to Tsarskoe Selo the next morning to protest. He didn't have an appointment, or even wait to be admitted. He just marched right in to Emperor Nicky's study. Aunt Miechen told Mother that Nicky's knees were knocking – well, Uncle Vladimir did have a very considerable presence and an extremely loud voice – but Uncle Vladimir himself told a rather different story. That Nicky just continued smoking a cigarette and leafing through papers as though he'd no more noticed Uncle Vladimir's presence than he might a fly on the window pane. Better to accept Uncle Vladimir's version, I think. Aunt Miechen does tend to embellish. And Uncle Vladimir's actions speak for themselves. When there was no sign of Emperor Nicky reversing his order, Uncle resigned all his own positions in protest. It was a grand gesture but it made no difference to us. Cyril was stripped of his titles and honours, his allowance, his naval rank and decorations, and the right to live in Russia. I was the Grand Duchess of Nowhere and my husband was unemployed.

I said, 'Things will work out.'

'Just a setback,' Cyril said. 'We'll survive.'

Mother didn't utter a word. Her face said it all. 'Didn't I warn you?'

The news of our marriage reached Darmstadt via St Petersburg and I received a wire from Ernie. HOPE YOU'VE FOUND HAPPINESS AT LAST. I think he meant it sincerely.

Cyril, who had been accustomed to the Navy telling him what to do, seemed not to have a plan. He filled his days playing golf and his evenings smoking too much. As to where we should make our home now Russia was off the menu, he left that up to me. I chose Paris. Dear, banished Grand Duke Uncle Paul was already living there with his new wife, Olga, so it seemed like a fitting place for Cyril's exile. And his brothers, Boris and Alexei, both loved Paris. I knew they would visit us often. The only difficulty was money. I thought I'd try my hand at watercolours. Ernie had always said I painted quite well.

Mother said, 'You're going to paint watercolours? And sell them?'

I said, 'Just until Cyril can find something.'

Mother said, 'Find something?'

'Employment.'

'And what do you imagine he'll do? Drive a hansom? Don't be silly, Ducky. He's a Grand Duke.'

I said, 'Well, Pa was a Royal Highness and he had a naval command. That was employment.'

'Do you really think so, dear?' she said.

She sat and thought for a while and then she said, 'Well, before you starve to death I think I'd better buy you an apartment.'

She chose a property in Passy. As she said, the 16th arrondissement was a superior area and the apartment had a south-eastern aspect. It could only be a good investment. That was our first home together, small and simple, with only room for four servants. We were like children playing house.

'And what's on the cards for today?' Cyril would ask me every morning, even though we both knew perfectly well he was going to play golf while I shopped for cushions.

We saw a lot of Uncle Paul and Olga. They lived nearby and as they said, we banished ones had better stick together. Olga would have been happy to stay in Paris for ever but there was always a sadness about Uncle Paul. He longed to go back to Russia. Russians always do, no matter how badly Russia has treated them.

Olga used to say, 'Paul wants all his children to know each other. What could be more natural? But it won't happen, not as long as those stiff-necks are on the throne.'

Olga and Uncle Paul had three children by then. Vova was nine, Irina was three, Natalya was just a baby. They'd never even met their half-brother, Dmitri, or their half-sister, Marie. It was the spring of 1906 when we settled in Paris. Only eleven years ago and yet it seems like a lifetime. Marie has been married and divorced,

Dmitri is banished to Persia, and the last we heard of Vova, he was under house arrest. His pen got him into trouble, as we feared it might. I don't think Minister Kerensky has a highly developed sense of humour. Better anyway not to have put it to the test. But both such lovely boys, Vova and Dmitri Pavlovich. I hope they'll come through this all right.

Missy visited us the very minute we'd nested. She was pretty jealous.

'Paris!' she said. 'Well, your bread certainly landed butter side up. Mother never offered to buy *me* a place in Paris. But you always were her favourite.'

It wasn't true at all. Mother didn't have favourites. She just wasn't convinced that Cyril could keep me in fitting style, nor could she see the point in our paying rent to a stranger.

Brother-in-law Boris visited us too, and brought news from St Petersburg. The Tsesarevich wasn't thriving. We'd already heard something to that effect, though Aunt Miechen wasn't the most reliable of sources, but it seemed it was true. Tsesarevich Alexis had the bleeding disease. One of Pa's brothers had had it and Ernie's brother Frittie. Ernie's sister, Irene, had just lost her youngest son to it. And now Nicky and Sunny's precious Alyosha, who had been so long in coming, and on whom so much depended.

People said I shouldn't feel sorry for Sunny and Nicky, after what they'd done to Cyril, but I did feel sorry for them, particularly Sunny. After all, it was her main purpose in life, to give Nicky an heir. I thought she might try again, for another, healthier boy, but Aunt Miechen said she very much doubted it. Empress Sunny had withdrawn to her boudoir with sciatica and Emperor Nicky had other things on his mind. Since his defeat by Japan, the Russian people had begun to change. Some of them weren't so ready to look upon him as their wise and protecting father. They met in secret rooms and questioned whether Russia even needed an Emperor or Deputies or bosses of any kind.

Cyril's old friend Vice-Admiral Kuzmich was assassinated, stabbed in the back by his own port workers. Then there was an attempt on the life of the new Governor of Moscow. A monarchist meeting was attacked, some said by anarchists, some said by socialist revolutionaries. No one could explain to me what the difference was. Every week there was some new outrage, and Emperor Nicky's answer was always to be more severe, and with everyone, not just the perpetrators.

Cyril said, 'One can understand Nicky's thinking. Give troublemakers an inch, they'll take a mile. He's evidently decided the most efficient way to keep order is to use the big stick on everyone. Not sure he's right though. Beat a dog too harshly and it can go either way. It may learn to behave. Or it may just slink away and wait for the next opportunity to bite you. I wonder who's advising him?'

People were anxious. Aunt Miechen told us so in every letter. But it was hardly any of our concern. Cyril hadn't deserved to be exiled, and neither had Uncle Paul. It wasn't our fault if we were having a splendid time in Paris.

It's funny how things turn out. I was expecting our first child that autumn and feeling absolutely sick and fatigued, when I received a letter from Ernie. He and the Tongue-Twister had had a son, Georg.

Just wanted you to hear it from me, Ducky, he wrote. *Hope all's well with you*.

I did feel a pang. What was it? Not regret, that's for sure. Irritation, perhaps, that with dreary old Onor he'd forced himself to do what he'd resisted with me. I shall never understand Ernie as long as I live.

But his letter unsettled me and made me think of Elli and a lot of pointless What Ifs. What if she hadn't run about too much at Skierniewice and made herself so thirsty that she drank unboiled water? What if my new baby wasn't as pretty as she'd been? I found myself hoping the child I was carrying was a boy. It wasn't. Masha was born on 20th January 1907. I went back to Coburg for my confinement. Mother insisted. She said the French were all very well for gowns and wine but for childbirth there was nothing to beat a German doctor.

Masha wasn't as beautiful as Elli. She was different. And I felt she was mine in a way Elli never had been. Cyril was delighted with her but he wasn't the kind of father to look in on the nursery a dozen times a day and pick her up out of her cradle. We wondered whether Cyril's parents would be allowed to visit us, to see their little granddaughter. Emperor Nicky could easily have forbidden them to travel, but he didn't. Uncle Vladimir and Aunt Miechen came to stay with us in Passy. It was the first time I'd seen them since Cyril and I had married.

Aunt Miechen said, 'Ducky, we must settle on what you're going to call me. It seems silly to keep calling me Aunt but I don't want to be Ma-in-Law.'

We decided I should simply call her Miechen.

'And Masha can do the same,' she said, 'when she's old enough to talk. "Grandma" makes one sound so ancient.'

'Time that woman acted her age,' was Mother's verdict. In fact Miechen became Granny Miechen.

We had a riotous time. We went to the Bobino to hear the darkie singers and the Cirque d'Hiver to see the wrestling. Uncle Paul's Olga took us shopping for affordable hats. Miechen thought it the greatest adventure to go to Bon Marché and rub shoulders with ordinary people.

We dined together every night and sometimes at home, with just a cook and a maid. 'The Undesirables', we called ourselves. We joked, but Uncle Vladimir didn't really think it was funny that perfectly decent members of the family had been forced to live abroad.

'Nicky's out of his depth,' he said. 'But he won't ask for advice. Well, who can he go to? Serge is dead, Paul's banished and I'm on his blacklist since he chucked Cyril out. The only person he seems to listen to is his wife, heaven help Russia.'

Miechen had a tasty morsel to add.

'It's not just that Nicky goes running to Sunny every time he has to make a decision. It's who Sunny goes to for advice. She has a new medicine man. Every day he's there, in the inner sanctum, and they don't just talk about Sunny's aches and pains, let me tell you.'

Sunny had had many doctors. When she was desperate for a boy she'd try anyone.

Miechen said, 'No, not a doctor. This new man's a monk, can you believe?! She's brought him in because of Alexis's bleeding disease and he's a very strange fellow. Stana Nikolaevna discovered him. I don't know where she found him but she says he's quite a miracle-worker.'

Grand Duchess Stana was the wife of Cyril's great-uncle, Grand Duke Nikolasha. I knew nothing of her except that Mother disapproved of her.

'A Montenegrin!' she'd say, as though that explained everything. Miechen seemed to agree.

She said, 'Well, of course Stana is very odd herself. We never mix. All those séances! Not the thing at all. But this monk she's discovered apparently has bishops vouching for him, so what is one to think? I don't know whether he's done anything for the Tsesarevich, but they say Sunny won't move a finger now without his approval and of course Nicky won't do anything without Sunny's.'

Miechen said Sunny's monk was called Grigory Efimovich Rasputin.

'But he's not really a monk because he doesn't live in a monastery. He has a six-room apartment on Gorokhovaya. He's more of a holy man. A wandering holy man.'

'Wandering's about right,' Uncle Vladimir said. 'He wandered all the way from Siberia and into the Empress's private drawing room, if you please. And there you have it. Russia's heading for the rocks and we have a henpecked ninny at the helm and a quack monk navigating.'

Cyril said, 'So, can the Tsesarevich be cured?'

'Who knows?' Miechen said. 'But Isa Buxhoeveden is one of Sunny's bedchamber ladies now and she says this monk has a great calming effect on Alyosha. He sits with him, when he has an attack, and holds his hand and the crisis passes. And one time he wasn't even there.'

'What do you mean?'

'He was out of town but he sent word that he was with Alyosha in spirit and the pain and swelling subsided.'

Uncle Vladimir said it was nothing but mumbo-jumbo.

Miechen said, 'But, surely it can't hurt. Anything that restores calm. Alyosha's such a boisterous child. I'm sure it's because Sunny keeps him so swaddled. She won't allow him to do anything and then of course, the minute the nurse's back is turned he's clambering onto furniture and throwing himself about. Well, it's natural. Boys can't be kept indoors all the time with story books. I should know. I've raised three sons. Boys need to run about and climb trees.'

But not when they bleed.

Cyril said, 'How serious is it? Will the boy live?'

I knew what he was thinking, and so did his father.

Uncle Vladimir said, 'Serious enough. One bad knock and they could lose him. One feels sorry for them, of course. Damned tragic thing to see in a child. But how can he ever be Tsar if they daren't let him sit astride a horse? So I suppose we must hope for the best but prepare for the worst. Meanwhile we seem to have a magician beguiling our Emperor and Empress. Wandering miracle-worker indeed!'

As things stood, Cyril was fourth in the line of succession. Ahead of him were Tsesarevich Alexis, then Emperor Nicky's brother, Grand Duke Misha, and then Cyril's father, Uncle Vladimir. Uncle Paul was out of the running because of his double sin. Olga wasn't just divorced, she was a commoner too. What we didn't know at the time was that Grand Duke Misha was about to set out on his own road to exile. He'd just taken up with Natalya Wulfert, a married woman and highly unsuitable for the Emperor's brother. It was the absolute end of Baby Bee's dreams, and the start of another fine Romanov mess, but I'll tell you about that later.

Cyril was fourth in line so you might say that Russia's throne wasn't an impossible prospect but a distant enough one that I never really gave it any serious thought, even when Uncle Vladimir said, 'You can count me out of the running. I'm starting to feel my years.'

He was sixty and quite vigorous. He didn't seem terribly old. But that summer in Paris was the last time we saw him. Soon after they got back to Russia he began to suffer little attacks of apoplexy, each one worse than the one before and he was such a contrary man he ignored all medical opinion on principle. If he was told to drink less he'd send for another bottle. If he was advised to be calm and close his eyes to the shortcomings of Emperor Nicky, he ranted all the more.

He was fond of Nicky. He still regarded him as a boy, I suppose, and would have been very willing to offer him a guiding hand. But Nicky had decided that he didn't need guidance, only blind obedience. And the thing above all that drove Uncle Vladimir to distraction was the policy-making that apparently went on in Sunny's boudoir.

I hate telegrams. In my whole life I only ever received one that brought good news. I'll tell you about it. I was expecting Kira and getting quite near my time, so it must have been early in 1909. Cyril could tell you to the very minute. The wire was from Miechen. Just one sentence. All it said was, TA FEMME EST MAINTENANT DUCHESSE.

Cyril came running to find me.

'Nicky's relented,' he kept saying. 'We're on our way back, Ducky!'

Which wasn't quite true, but it was the first step. Emperor Nicky had been to visit Uncle Vladimir on his sickbed and been shocked by what he'd found.

'Shaken to the core,' Miechen said. 'It suddenly hit him that my Vladik's dying. Too late now to ask for his counsel. Nicky sat there weeping. Well I'm sorry but I don't care to see an Emperor blubbing. He said he'd never wished to quarrel with Vladimir and perhaps things had been blown out of proportion. Out of proportion! And then he asked me what he could do, to make amends, so I told him. Blow your nose and restore Cyril's title. And he did. Sunny won't like it, of course, but who cares about her. That title should never have been taken away. Now we must make him recall you to Russia and put an end to this nonsense.'

The next telegram was a more typical specimen of the beast.

122

Uncle Vladimir was dead. Cyril was permitted to go to St Petersburg for the funeral. Given my condition we didn't press for me to be allowed to go with him.

Miechen said, 'Stay home and rest, Ducky. We don't want you giving birth in some Polish railway siding. Time enough later for your grand entrance. When you do come we'll make a great fanfaronade of it and put Empress Sunny into an absolute fury. And have you heard the latest about Misha?'

Emperor Nicky's brother, Grand Duke Michael, had declined to behave like an Imperial heir. He'd refused to give up Natalya Wulfert, and even in the grief of her widowing Miechen was scheming.

She said, 'Nicky's had Misha sent to some God-forsaken posting, to try and keep him out of Mrs Wulfert's bed, but needless to say Misha's still going to Moscow to see her, every minute he can get away, and the husband is making the most enormous fuss, talking about a duel, threatening to take poison. No dignity at all. So this can only end badly, for Misha, I mean. Either Wulfert will demand satisfaction and put a bullet in him, or Emperor Nicky will banish him. You heard it from me. And in either case that will put Cyril next in line, if the worst should befall the Tsesarevich. I wish no one ill, of course. We all hope Alyosha will thrive. I'm merely pointing out how close you and Cyril have now drawn to the throne.'

15

So my husband had his title again. Grand Duke Cyril Vladimirovich – though to be honest, in Paris he had never stopped using it – and then he was given a job, as a Captain Lieutenant in the Baltic Fleet. It was good to think of him being occupied again. Golf is all well and good but on rainy days he was rather under my feet. But the Navy? I dreaded his going back to sea. I was the only person who knew how shattered his nerves still were.

Even pootling around on Tegernsee on our honeymoon I could see the water made him anxious. He still had his drowning night-mare. I'd hear him let out a strangled cry and see his arms reaching up and I'd have to wake him.

The problem was, I couldn't go to Russia, to at least be there at Kronstadt when he had shore leave. Emperor Nicky wasn't willing to restore all Cyril's privileges at once and my residence in Russia was the very last concession he made. I saw Sunny's hand in that. Though Ernie was settled with his new wife and was himself per-fectly civil with me, friendly even, Sunny has never forgiven my divorcing him. She has a resentful streak in her character. Well, perhaps her present misfortunes have softened her.

Ernie and Onor had another son. I got the usual scrawl from Ernie. *An heir and one to spare*, he wrote, *so all's well in Hesse. He's a dear little fellow. We've called him Louis. Somewhat envious of your Parisian exile however.*

I found I minded the arrival of Ernie's second son much more than his first. I knew it didn't necessarily signify that Onor's bedroom charms were greater than mine. More likely that Ernie's sense of urgency and duty to Hesse had grown stronger. But still I imagined all of Darmstadt saying, 'Two sons! Nothing wrong with Grand Duke Ernie. That first wife of his, what was her problem?'

Cyril was at sea and I was in Paris with a two-year-old and a new baby. Kira was born on 26th April 1909. Cyril said he didn't at all mind that we had another girl but I think he did, just a bit.

'And later on,' he'd say, 'when things are more settled, who knows? Perhaps we'll have another.'

When things are more settled. I wonder when that will be.

I went to Coburg that summer to see Baby Bee married to Alfonso. He was a rather dashing aviator who had quite taken Bee's mind off Grand Duke Misha, but he was also an Infante of the house of Orlean y Borbon and a Catholic which meant Baby Bee was supposed to convert. She didn't. She has now, but there was a fearful fuss at the time and Alfonso was stripped of his rank for a while. Bee didn't care. She was in love. But Mother cared very much.

'What is it about my daughters?' she said. 'Why must there always be complications?'

I said, 'Sandra hasn't had complications.'

'No,' she said. 'And thank goodness. It's disappointing enough that she only married a Hohenlohe.'

The final barrier to my settling in Russia was lowered just before Kira's first birthday. Emperor Nicky offered Cyril the use of a house at Tsarskoe Selo, 'if your wife cares to join you there'. I saw the letter. Nicky, who was a cousin, whichever way you cut it, and who had known me forever, couldn't quite bring himself to name me. *If your wife cares to join you.*

Mother said I mustn't appear too eager. She hated the idea that Nicky and Sunny had dominion over me and she was certain that if I went to St Petersburg, Sunny would never receive me, but I didn't care. I began packing at once. I wanted to be with Cyril and I wanted to be in Russia. Actually I'd wanted to be in Russia for as long as I could remember. I called at Coburg on my way. Baby Bee was there, expecting her honeymoon baby. She had a boy, Alvaro. My baby sister was a mother!

She said, 'You might have warned me.'

I said, 'What? About Married Life?'

'No,' she said. 'About childbirth.'

As soon as she was safely delivered I continued my journey to be with Cyril.

'Heaven knows when I shall see you again,' Mother said.

I said, 'But you'll visit. St Petersburg hasn't suddenly moved further away.'

'Yes, it has,' she said. 'That's what happens when you grow old.'

She'd just received the news that Uncle King Bertie had died.

'Another one gone,' she said. 'I'll soon be the last one standing.'

May was the loveliest time to arrive at Tsarskoe Selo. The lindens were in flower and the lilacs and the bird cherry and the air was still fresh. The house we'd been allocated was on Sadovaya Street, close to the manège, which rather pleased me, and to the horse cemetery, which fascinated Masha.

Miechen's little summer palace-ette was close by and so was brother-in-law Boris's rather over-rusticated cottage, but our nearest neighbour was Genya Botkin. He was physician to the Emperor's family, to all of them except the Tsesarevich. Alyosha has his own doctor, because of his particular condition, a Dr Derevenko who is reckoned to be an expert in the treatment of the bleeding disease. And of course in those days they had Sunny's monk in attendance too. Grigory Rasputin. I never heard Dr Botkin express any opinion of Rasputin. I imagine he might have been relieved that the responsibility for Alyosha's health and survival was someone else's. As it was, the poor man never had a minute to call his own, with Empress Sunny sending for him every time she had the slightest twinge.

Cyril always said Genya Botkin must have been resigned to his fate from the day he was born. His father had been physician to two Emperors so Botkin knew what was expected of him: to attend the Imperial Family every day, at whatever hour, and to agree politely with the Empress's own diagnoses. His life was not his own. Whether this had been the cause of Mrs Botkin's discontent I do not know. By the time we came to Sadovaya Street she'd run off with some penniless professor and left Botkin with four children to raise. Tanya is the eldest. I'm sure she'd be married by now if it weren't for this damned war. Gleb is the baby of the family and in between came Mitya and Yuri, both dear, lovely boys. Masha still asks about them. I haven't told her yet that they won't be coming home. For one thing it would rather raise the question, where is home now?

But Cyril was right, Genya Botkin is the consummate Court physician. I never heard him gossip or complain. When Nicky and Sunny go into exile I'm sure he'll go with them, to the ends of the earth.

The house on Sadovaya wasn't grand, but it was spacious enough for our needs and full of light. I liked it at once. There were no rugs and only one armoire but Cyril had prepared something of a welcome surprise. He'd bought a Don mare for me, a chestnut, fifteen hands, and a Shetland pony for Masha.

Miechen sent me an army of cleaners, followed by several wagon loads of furniture, some from the Vladimir Palace and some she'd borrowed on our behalf from the Bachelor Uncles.

'Not bad pieces but nothing special,' she said. 'Men know nothing about furniture. But the Uncles have more than they need. When do they ever give parties? So you may as well have the benefit, for the time being. We can't have you living like gypsies. And as soon as you have a moment, there's a town house I'd like you to look at. It's not perfect but you must have somewhere, at least for your first Season.'

That house in St Petersburg was on Glinka Street, something of a bargain for a quick sale and, though Miechen thought of it as a temporary arrangement until we found something grander, we never did move on. At least, not until now.

We summered at Tsarskoe Selo. It was the most heavenly time. Cyril had a desk job. He came home almost every evening. We were a family, and we were in Russia, where we belonged. Emperor Nicky and Sunny were out at Tsarskoe Selo too, in residence at the Alexander Palace, but the weeks went by and I didn't see anything of them except their children, occasionally, out walking. I call them children but Olga wasn't a child by then. She was fifteen and starting to look like a young woman. Tatiana was thirteen, Masha, *their* Masha, was eleven, Anastasia was nine. They'd wave to us but never stop to speak. Alexis was rarely with them and when we did see him he'd be in the arms of one of his boatman-nurses, though he was fully five years old by then. Masha, our Masha, used to ask me, 'Why is that boy carried about like a baby?'

Tsesarevich Alexis was small for his age, but he looked well enough. That's the thing about the bleeding disease. It does its damage in hidden places. I've heard people call it a family curse but surely every family has its troubles. Ernie and I lost Elli. Mother lost

128

our Affie. Grandma Queen buried three of her children. There's no particular reason the Emperor of All the Russias should be exempt.

We may have been living with borrowed chairs at Sadovaya Street but we had one great amenity: a telephone. I thought I should never get used to it and now I wonder how I ever managed without it. Miechen used to call me every day to see whether I'd been summoned yet by Sunny. She was longing for me to report back on Sunny's décor.

'From what I hear,' she said, 'she went through the Maples catalogue and ordered one of everything in chintz. For the Alexander Palace! The woman has no idea. She should have married some minor English Duke and gone to live in, where is it, Surreyshire? That's the place for chintz.'

It was a long, long time before I got to see whether Miechen was right about Sunny's crimes against Imperial elegance. No invitation arrived.

Miechen said, 'Never mind, darling. People say her teas are very poor affairs. Just bread and butter and a McVitie's Digestive if you're lucky.'

I did see Sunny, on the rare occasions she attended a gala or a sale of work. She was polite, always asked after Mother and my girls and I would reciprocate. But one wasn't to ask about Alyosha's health. I'd been warned of that. As though to ask if he were well was to suggest that he wasn't. The Tsesarevich's disease was a State secret that everyone knew about, but there was to be no idle speculation about the succession.

It must have cost Sunny a great effort to be pleasant to me in company. I knew what she really thought of me because a well-wisher once kindly passed on what she's heard from the Empress's lips.

'People like that will be the ruin of this family.'

'People like that' were women like me and Uncle Paul's Olga. Sirens who cast off unsatisfactory husbands like last year's neckline and seduced helpless Romanov men. And we weren't even the worst. Mathilde Kschessinskaya, 'that creature' as Mother always called her, occupied that position, unchallenged. Blatantly unmarried and parading her son around like a trophy. Who was the boy's father? Mother reckoned it was impossible to guess given Kschessinskaya's career, passed around the Romanov men like a plate of sugar biscuits. The field of possible fathers was a large and illustrious one.

That summer more fuel was thrown on the fires of Sunny's displeasure. Grand Duke Misha's sweetheart, Natalya Wulfert, gave birth to a baby boy. As Miechen said, it was going to be interesting to see how Emperor Nicky dealt with that. In the case of an unsuitable lover there's always the possibility that they can be silenced with a house and a pension, but a baby isn't so easily bought off. Not when the identity of his father is public knowledge. For one thing the child requires a name.

Miechen said, 'If our dear Emperor were to ask my advice, I'd suggest he let Paul come home and send Misha into exile. That would be a sensible exchange, don't you think? I'm sure Mrs Wulfert would love Paris. If it turns out a new heir is required,' Miechen lowered her powerful voice at this point, 'I mean if Sunny's holy man can't save Alyosha, they can always rely on Cyril for the succession. You know you'd make a much better Empress than Sunny.'

Miechen had everything worked out. But of course Emperor Nicky didn't ask for her advice. Instead he used a handy Imperial privilege and arranged for Natalya Wulfert's divorce to be backdated and then decreed that the former Mrs Wulfert should in future style herself Countess Brasova. That was his nod towards Grand Duke Michael's part in all this. Brasovo was one of Misha's estates, south of Moscow, miles from anywhere.

Perhaps Nicky thought a title would persuade Countess Brasova to stay quietly in the country, making jam. If so he quite misjudged the matter. Grand Duke Misha had no intention of giving up Natalya and his baby son or hiding them away and Natalya had no intention of being hidden. Misha brought them with him to St Petersburg and his only concession to protocol was to live out of town, in Gatchina. He perched in his official bachelor quarters at the Gatchina Palace and Natalya and the baby lived in a rented villa just down the road.

Miechen said, 'Misha will marry her, just see if he doesn't. One of these days he'll slip his leash.'

Cyril said, 'But they'll never find an Orthodox priest willing to do it. Look at the difficulty we had. Ducky's mother practically had to hold the poor man at gunpoint to get him to marry us and he was her tame chaplain.'

Miechen said, 'Then Misha will go abroad to do it, and he won't worry about the flavour of the priest. He'll go to France. Any mayor will marry you there. I'm telling you, Misha's determined.'

She was right, as has sometimes been the case, but it took a while. The Emperor's brother, you see, can't just jump aboard a train. He's required to say where he wishes to go and then ask if he may. Grand Duke Misha told Cyril he believed he was being followed, by disguised policemen. Cyril thought it might be true.

'Look at the situation,' he said. 'The Tsesarevich isn't strong. Misha's boy may have been born the wrong side of the blanket but he's healthy. The last thing Nicky wants is for Misha to marry Brasova. It would be a step towards regularising their child's standing. Sunny will be nagging him about it, you can be sure. Anything to keep Misha's boy out of the succession. If I were the Countess Brasova I'd watch my back and my child.'

I was never sure how much to believe in the lengths Nicky

might go to to keep Sunny happy. For all the years I'd known him Emperor Nicky was a mystery to me. He still is. A little man in a big man's boots. I could feel sorry for him. With a different roll of the dice, he'd have made a perfectly happy farmer. It's harder to summon up sympathy for Sunny. She may be frail and worn out and frantic for the health of her son but there's something at the heart of her that's as hard as flint.

Though Sunny hardly ever came into society she did have her own little circle, her Ladies. Anna Vyrubova, Nastinka Hendrikova, Isa Buxhoeveden. Sunny went nowhere without them. Vyrubova was her particular favourite. Practically like a sister, Miechen said.

'A sister, with slow glands. A devoted little heifer, mooing along in Sunny's shadow.'

St Petersburg wasn't like Darmstadt, where everyone dined politely with everyone else, whatever their real opinions of each other, and it wasn't like Paris, where everything was free and easy and no one dined with anyone unless they really wanted to. In St Petersburg there were social obligations but there were also undisguised opinions and factions and I had married into the faction that was the most feared and admired. Miechen's set were ruthless. If you didn't glitter, if you didn't dress fabulously and give wonderful parties you didn't belong. We were the Vladimirovichi and we outshone Empress Sunny's drab little coterie without even trying. It didn't come naturally to me. I hate changing my clothes three times a day. But I was finding my feet in St Petersburg and Miechen was not to be let down.

Cyril had been promised a command. He talked it up and put on a brave face but I knew he dreaded it. No matter how many times he went to sea, no matter how he tried to master his terrors, he's never overcome them. He still has his *Petropavlovsk* nightmare. Eventually they recognised the problem and found him a desk job at the Admiralty. Well, why not? He'd served his country. He'd volunteered to go back into action against the Japanese when he might easily have been declared an invalid. And we had a young family. I'm sure he had nothing to feel ashamed about.

Miechen took the house on Glinka Street for us, our city home for the Season 1910-1911, and directed its decoration. Furnishings don't much interest me. I like a comfortable chair and a bed to suit my long legs, but the finer points of gilding and marquetry escape me. I'd have borrowed again from the Bachelor Uncles but Miechen wouldn't allow it.

'Shabbiness can be charming in the country,' she said. 'But in town you must remember your position.'

It was Miechen's doing that Peach came to live with us too. She said I must get an English nanny for the girls. She'd already given us Nanya, who had been Cyril's old nurse, but Nanya was of great age and girth, more in need of being cared for herself than she was able to help me. Masha and Kira ran her ragged.

Miechen said, 'You must get someone from Norland. They're the absolute best. You want one in her thirties and plain. Any older than that, she'll be too set in her ways. Any younger, there's always the danger . . . Well, I don't need to spell it out. Cyril's pretty steady but no sense in inviting trouble.'

So it was actually Miechen who selected Ethel Peach from the list of applicants. She was a thirty-seven-year-old spinster – 'too old for any mischief', according to Miechen, and she came with excellent references from diplomatic families in Paris and Shanghai. Miechen felt that was also a sign in her favour. It meant Miss Peach was a restless soul who moved on. She wouldn't be hanging about our necks in her old age, expecting a pension and accommodations.

In fact Ethel Peach turned out to be quite personable for

thirty-seven, but she'd come all that way to St Petersburg so I didn't have the heart to send her back on the grounds that she had dimples. Anyway, Masha and Kira seemed to take to her and there is much to be said for a quiet life. They liked her name, of course. And when Masha discovered Peach had a sister, Ida, who was married to a man called William Notion, she fairly screamed for joy. So Peach stayed, in spite of Miechen's reservations.

'Feed her up,' Miechen said. 'You must get rid of that enviable little waist of hers before it causes any problems.'

It can be a difficult thing, to have a mother-in-law living just around the corner, and doubly so when she's your aunt, but I daren't complain too much.

I did warn you, Mother wrote. *Well, you must be firm. You must put your own mark on your household. Never forget, Miechen is only a Mecklenburg. You are a granddaughter of Queen Victoria.*

Fond as I was of Miechen, she did interfere. I must go to Druce's for my soap and to Treumann's to get my cards printed, and I must get Cyril's cloudberry jam from Yeliseev's and nowhere else. Her friends took me up too, Zinaida Yusupov and Betsy Trubetskoy. She instructed them to. It took me a while to widen my own little circle and dare to include people who weren't quite up to the Vladimirovichi mark of smartness. The Obolenskys, who lived at Tsarskoe Selo. The Nabokovs on Morskaya Street. Moritz and Henny Lenz who had a house on Vasilievsky and Gitta Radloss who lived Vyborg side. Best of all, I'd only been a year in Russia when the George Buchanans were posted to St Petersburg. Sir George and Lady Georgie had been dear friends in Darmstadt. They were such welcome, familiar faces. And then there were the Bachelor Uncles with their repository of spare couches and unimportant paintings.

Some of the people we call Uncle aren't really our uncles, and one of the Bachelor Uncles isn't strictly speaking a bachelor, but in the great sprawl of the Romanov family it's essential to have signposts of some kind.

The true bachelors are Uncle Bimbo, that is to say Grand Duke Uncle Nikolai Mikhailovich, and Uncle Seryozha, whose title is Grand Duke Sergei Mikhailovich. However, Seryozha is rumoured to have been one of the many who've sampled Mathilde Kschessinskaya's attractions so perhaps that places him in a special category. I once asked Cyril if he thought Uncle Seryozha could be the father of La Kschessinskaya's son. He smiled.

'One candidate in a very long line,' he said.

Uncle Gogi is in a special category too. He's been married, still is married I suppose, but his wife doesn't like him or Russia so she ran away, many years ago, and took their little girls with her, to England I believe. After they left Uncle Gogi moved himself and his coin collection into the Mikhailovsky Palace to live with Uncle Bimbo and Uncle Seryozha.

They're all tall and thin, the Bachelor Uncles. You'd know them at once for brothers. And the Mikhailovsky Palace always smells of their cigarettes. I like that. It reminds me of Mother and Pa. My sister Missy is convinced that smoking brought on Pa's bad throat and caused his death but his doctors had always recommended it. They said it invigorated the lungs.

The Bachelors rattle around the Mikhailovsky in their separate apartments. I'm surprised they never moved in together, in one wing. It would have been much cosier. Perhaps they'll have to now these Housing Allocation Committees are dictating how many rooms people can have.

Whenever we were in town, I used to call on the Uncles. First Uncle Bimbo, then he'd take Masha and Kira on the crossbar of his Raleigh bicycle and I'd trot along behind. They'd go wobbling off down the corridor to Uncle Gogi's apartments, to find out if he was at home and see whether he had any caramels in his pocket. Gogi has always been so kind to my girls. They must be a painful reminder of his own daughters but he never speaks of that. Perhaps he was like Ernie, not really cut out for marriage.

I wonder how they're all managing now? Bimbo, Seryozha, Gogi. I hope the Bolsheviks aren't being too hateful to them. Maybe they've left Russia too. We get no news. Perhaps if the war really does end this year letters will become easier.

16

By 1912 I was so settled it was as though I'd been in Russia all my life. Everything that had gone before seemed like a bad dream.

'Can you believe what we went through?' I'd say to Cyril.

'Told you it would work out,' he'd say. 'Our patience was rewarded.'

Here's how we parsed out our Russian year. We'd spend Christmas in the country. There was usually some good hunting to be had. Cyril gave me a young steppe borzoi for my first Russian birthday. Strela, which means 'arrow'. It was a fitting name for her.

Cyril said, 'A Don hunter and a borzoi. Now you're a real Russian Grand Duchess.'

The Imperial Hunt was based at Gatchina but one of our neighbours, Timofei Ivanov, kept a smaller establishment at Tsarskoe Selo so I boarded Strela in his kennels and rode out with his pack as often as I could, to train her.

I looked forward to hunt days. I loved the silence at the start, waiting for a wolf to run. Just the creak of the snow under the weight of the horses and the occasional gentle whinny. Strela whimpered the first time I took her out but I had two of Timofei Ivanov's old hounds on leashes either side of her and they soon taught her to wait in silence until the leash was slipped. I enjoyed the chase too. That's the best part. It was just the kill I didn't care for. I've no great love for wolves. We lost so many deer to them at Wolfsgarten. But it's still a sad thing to see so powerful a creature brought low. A wolf never admits defeat. He snarls and threatens even when his situation is quite hopeless. As I wrote those words I found the image of Nicky came to me. Not that there's anything of the wolf about him – Ernie Hesse used to characterise him as a spaniel – but he's certainly been brought low. The Emperor of All the Russias confined to walking in circles in a small patch of garden.

But I was telling you about the pattern of our year. From the middle of January we lived mainly in town. We'd take the girls for sleigh rides on the Neva and Peach helped them make an ice slide in our yard. The ball season began directly after the Blessing of the Waters and lasted until the beginning of Lent. We might go to two, even three, in a week and the fact that we had no ballroom of our own at Glinka Street didn't matter because Miechen flew the Vladimirovichi flag.

'She waves it all the more wildly since Father passed away,' Cyril used to say. 'Father dreaded his own ball. No escape, you see.'

Maslenitsa Week marked the end of the Season. We'd stay in town for the carousels and the bonfires and Uncle Bimbo's pancake party, and then, as soon as Lent began, we'd move back to Tsarskoe Selo, to live a quieter life. One was supposed to fast, of course. No meat, no cheese, no wine, but we only kept the fast for the first week and then for Holy Week. 'Part-timers', Aunt Ella called us. She'd become terribly pi, considering she was raised a Lutheran. So had Sunny. Mother said converts often went that way. I didn't.

We kept Easter, Paskha, as I learned to call it, at Tsarskoe Selo. Emperor Nicky was having a cathedral built for Sunny but it seemed to be an endless project. I preferred to go to Our Lady of the Sign and the Botkin children came with us sometimes, but not their father. Wherever the Imperial family celebrated Paskha,

Genya Botkin felt obliged to follow. All those hours standing in church. What if Empress Sunny had a fainting fit?

Peach wasn't a religious person, not at all. In fact she once announced that she thought it all so much rot, a new word Kira picked up with relish. But wherever Peach lived, she liked to follow the local traditions, just so long as it didn't involve making the sign of the cross. It was at her urging that we learned how to colour eggs with onion skins. It was Peach who took our girls to the Botkins' house, to watch Tanya Botkin and their cook make *kulich*.

Miechen said, 'Great heavens, what for? Doesn't she understand that they're Grand Duchesses? What does she think? That they're going to be domestics?'

But as Peach said, Masha and Kira were growing up in Russia. They should be familiar with its customs.

'And I don't think it hurts anyone to know how to cook,' she said. 'Not even a Grand Duchess.'

How those words have come back to me lately.

We'd close up Glinka Street entirely for the summer. No one stayed in town, except the Uncles, who seemed not to be troubled by the airless heat. Uncle Bimbo would come out quite often to Tsarskoe Selo though and dine with us. He always had some project in hand in the Imperial hothouses. A seedless tangerine was one of them.

Masha said, 'But if it has no seeds how will it grow more tangerines?'

'Aha,' he said, and tapped the side of his nose. Perhaps he didn't know the answer.

He used to take Peach and Masha and Kira butterflying in the Park, 'Hoping to see a Lesser Purple Emperor,' he'd say. 'And who knows, if we don't see a butterfly perhaps we'll catch ourselves a real Emperor instead. I hear our Imperial Majesty is at home.'

Uncle Bimbo loves our girls but I think he was a little sweet on Peach too, for a while.

Sometimes even Tsarskoe Selo was too stifling and we'd go away in search of fresh air. Cyril's favourite place was Lake Ladoga but the mosquitoes there tormented me, so after we got to know the von Etters we took up their invitation to stay with them here, at Haikko in Finland. We'd generally stay well into September, until we'd been mushroom picking at least once. And now here we are. Except this isn't a summer holiday and I don't know when the von Etters will ever be rid of us. When the Bolsheviks run out of steam? When Russia begs Misha to be its new Emperor and all us Romanovs can safely go home?

In October we'd return to St Petersburg, open up Glinka Street and take the dust sheets off the furniture. Miechen would begin her plans for the Season. There were gowns to be ordered or altered, furs to have brought out of storage, chandeliers to be cleaned and Christmas gifts to be bought. She kept it very simple. She'd choose one item for the women, perhaps a hat pin or a pill box, and one item for the men. Then she'd order a quantity of them from Cartier, by the dozen, just as one might buy breakfast rolls. As I recall, 1912 was the Christmas of lapis cufflinks and 1913 was enamelled cigarette cases with different-coloured tinder cords. That was a very special year, of course, an anniversary. Three hundred years of Romanovs ruling Russia. It was also the year Grand Duke Uncle Paul was allowed to come home.

It happened very suddenly.

Cyril said, 'There's to be no fuss. Just a discreet return. That is, if Paul chooses to come back. Olga always seemed very happy in Paris. He may just tell Emperor Nicky what to do with his largesse.'

Miechen said largesse was nothing to do with it. She was right. Grand Duke Misha was the reason the door had been opened for

Uncle Paul. In the space of just a few weeks the Imperials had suffered two crises. Misha had run off to Vienna and married Countess Brasova and Tsesarevich Alexis had had a bleeding episode so serious that they'd feared for his life. Emperor Nicky was starting to panic about the succession. He needed dear, steady Uncle Paul closer to hand.

The Imperials had been on their summer holidays at Spala in Poland when Alyosha's attack happened. A tumble, a knock, that's all it took. But Sunny's miracle-working monk wasn't with them. He was taking a holiday too, in Siberia. A wire was sent to him, a reply came by return that all would be well and sure enough Alyosha pulled back from the grave's edge. Can miracles be performed by telegram? Or was the poor boy already on the road to recovery? I once asked Genya Botkin his opinion but he wouldn't be drawn. If Empress Sunny believed Grigory Rasputin had saved Alyosha's life, she was not to be contradicted.

That autumn of 1912 there was a quiet change of the Romanov guard. Uncle Paul slipped back into Russia with his wife and children and Olga was granted a title. She was to be known as Princess Olga Paley and her children were to be Paleys too, to emphasise the distinction between them and Uncle Paul's older children, Dmitri and Marie, who had the Imperial seal of approval.

Miechen said, 'What a small mind our Emperor has. As if anyone cares what Paul's children call themselves.'

As Uncle Paul returned, Grand Duke Michael exited, or rather was forbidden to come home from a trip to France. He was banished for the unforgiveable crime of marrying the mother of his child. Just as Miechen had predicted, Misha had found a way. He'd petitioned Emperor Nicky to be allowed to go to Cannes for a holiday and after some hesitation Nicky had agreed. If he sent his secret police to follow Misha and make sure no wedding took place,

Misha and Natalya managed to outwit them. They pretended to be heading south, then jinked back to Vienna and were married before any Imperial snoops could catch up with them. Misha knew it would mean exile. He must love Natalya very much. Everyone thought they'd settle in Paris but in fact they chose England.

'Like the little weathermen on a barometer,' Cyril said. 'Paul comes in, Misha goes out.'

Uncle Paul's return made little difference to the line of succession. He could no more become Tsar, with his unapproved Paley wife and his inconvenient Paley children, than could Cyril. What we all watched to see was how things would be managed with regard to Dmitri. Would they all become one big happy family? Marie was out of the picture. She'd married one of the Swedish princes, Wilhelm. Not a happy match. But Dmitri was another matter. Empress Sunny was very attached to him, very proprietorial. She'd had a hand in raising him, after all. I thought she'd do everything she could to keep him away from the Paleys. If she tried, she failed. Dmitri Pavlovich and Vova Paley became more than half-brothers. They've become unlikely friends.

Dmitri loves a party. He's a night-owl. He and Felix Yusupov were practically part of the furniture at the Akvarium Café. When Uncle Paul came home to St Petersburg, Vova Paley was about fifteen, too young for strong drink and naked tableaux and, anyway, he was the kind of boy who preferred to stay quietly in his room and compose verses. Nevertheless he and Dmitri became very close. As for Uncle Paul's wife, I think Sunny simply pretended she didn't exist.

As Cyril said, 'Easy enough. It isn't as though she and Olga Paley are likely to bump into each other at the fishmonger's.'

17

Everyone predicted 1913 would be the best Season ever. The most lavish, the most glittering. A celebration of three hundred glorious years of Romanov rule.

Miechen said, 'It will be wonderful as long as we don't rely on our dear Empress to organise it. Sunny couldn't throw a good party if her life depended on it. It's up to us, Ducky.'

And so the Vladimirovichi led the way, and just as well because there was nothing much planned at the Winter Palace except dreary diplomatic receptions. Dr Botkin said Sunny was far from well. She was plagued with neuralgia and was in no condition for balls. Miechen said it would do her good to get off her couch and dance a few mazurkas.

'The more you do, the more you *can* do,' Miechen said. 'That has always been my experience.'

It was exactly the kind of thing Mother would say. Whatever their differences Miechen and Mother were of the old school of grit and duty. Neuralgia or no, you put on your corsets and a smile.

Sunny's indisposition didn't matter to us. We had entertainments enough without her. Dolly Sheremetskaya and Helen Bobrinsky both gave wonderful costume parties. Cyril and I dressed as the Grey Wolf and the Firebird. Felix Yusupov came to Dolly's as Snegurochka and then to Helen's as the Queen of the Night.

'Good God,' Cyril said. 'Yusupov's wearing a gown. What must his mother think?'

But I don't think Zinaida Yusupova minded at all. Her son made a rather beautiful Snow Maiden.

Miechen topped everything with a ball the week before Maslenitsa. Black, white and diamonds were the instructions.

She said, 'Ducky, this is probably a good moment for us to talk about jewels.'

She explained the terms of her will. Her diamonds would go to Cyril's sister, Elena, who was the only girl in the family. Elena was married to Greek Nicky who apparently had two thrones he might inherit, those of Greece and Denmark, but hardly a *sou* to his name.

The rest of Miechen's jewel collection was to be divided as follows: Boris would inherit the suite of emeralds, Andrei the rubies and Cyril would get the pearl parure, or rather I would.

'Though not the garland tiara,' Miechen said, 'because it has diamonds as well as pearls and I'm afraid, darling, that diamonds trump pearls. But do borrow it for my ball. Elena won't be here and anyway she wouldn't mind.'

I did borrow it too.

'Ravishing,' Cyril said. 'What a bloody lucky chap I am.'

That was the difference between Ernie and Cyril. Ernie would express very valuable opinions about what I should wear – he was the one who first got me to try lilac – but he'd never take me in his arms and tell me he wished we could miss the ball and go to bed.

The official celebrations of the tercentenary began at the end of February with a Divine Liturgy and a *molyeben* of Thanksgiving in the Kazan Cathedral. Another marathon of worship and we all had to be in our places at least half an hour before the Imperial suite arrived. The wait was enlivened for some by a little incident that

I regret to say I missed. One of my shoe buttons popped off and I was bent over, looking for it.

Cyril was laughing. 'See that?' he said.

I'd seen nothing.

'Sunny's holy man,' he said. 'Just got ejected. Must have helped himself to somebody's seat. Nicky's probably! Serve the bugger right.'

I looked and looked but I couldn't see any holy man. Of course I wasn't sure what I was looking for and Cyril couldn't even say what colour shirt he'd been wearing. He's hopeless at colours. I was so cross. I'd been dying to see this famous miracle-worker.

I often passed his house on Gorokhovaya Street. Women went there to ask for his advice or for healing. There were always cars lined up outside his building, with the drivers standing in huddles smoking, waiting for their ladies to come out. I suppose he had a waiting room, just like a doctor. And if you were important enough he made house calls. Grand Duke Uncle Nikolasha's wife, Stana, often had him round to meet her friends and cure their ills.

Miechen used to say, 'Miracles! In a drawing room! Can you imagine? Does one serve tea before or after, I wonder?' The word around St Petersburg was that even if you didn't require an actual miracle, if you just needed a little help say, for your son's career or your husband's preferment, Grigory Rasputin could open doors too. But that day I missed him. And I never found my shoe button.

The Imperial procession arrived, at long last. I thought how tired Nicky looked. I can't imagine why. He certainly hadn't been attending any parties. Sunny was wearing pale blue, a pretty shade but a mistake because it made her look stout especially when she stood beside Dowager Empress Minnie who still has the neatest waist. Tsesarevich Alexis was wearing his usual sailor suit and he was walking unaided, very proud, quite the little man. You would never have thought he'd been so very ill. Really you wouldn't have believed there was anything wrong with him at all.

The daughters were all in white. Olga wasn't really 'out' yet. Seventeen. Missy was married by that age. But the only suitors we'd heard mentioned for Grand Duchess Olga were Missy's son, Carol, or my brother-in-law, Boris. Both entirely unsuitable.

Prince Carol's suit was soon dismissed. He didn't like Olga's looks and she didn't like anything about him. Neither do I. He may be my nephew but I find there's something quite repellent about him. Missy has overindulged him. As for Boris, I'm afraid that was just another of Miechen's fantasies, that one of her sons would marry one of Nicky's daughters and burrow a tunnel closer to the throne. Boris was far too old and jaded for Olga Nikolaevna. She's twenty-two now and still she's not matched. The Imperials have more important things on their minds. Well, I hope she finds someone who'll be kind to her, and soon. If she's left on the shelf it could hold things up for her sisters.

St Petersburg was ablaze with parties that week but Nicky and Sunny only put in the briefest of appearances. She pleaded nervous fatigue and he didn't like to go anywhere without her. The Vladimirovichi were not impressed. They thought Sunny should behave like an Empress. They thought Nicky should insist.

'And if she'd only crack her face with a smile,' people said. That was the problem. They'd have been more sympathetic about her aches and pains and her worries over Alyosha if she didn't always look so cross.

'Doesn't she like us?' they said.

I confess I felt some sympathy for her when I heard that. Men aren't expected always to be smiling so why should we be? Sunny just has one of those faces. So do I.

There was a pause in the festivities during Lent, but directly after Paskha, Emperor Nicky and his family set off on a kind of Imperial progress, sailing along the Volga, from Nizhny Novgorod to Yaroslav and Kostroma and then by train to Moscow for the grand finale of the celebrations. There was a huge parade in Red Square and a service in the Arkhangelsky Cathedral. Aunt Ella said the city went wild, people lining the streets and cheering.

Such displays of affection and loyalty, she wrote. *It was very touching to see, after some of the troubles we've had. I believe we have turned a corner. If only my dear Serge had lived to see it.*

Grand Duke Sandro accompanied the Imperials on their tour. He's married to Nicky's sister Xenia.

Uncle Bimbo said, 'Had a chat with Sandro. Emperor Nicky's delighted with the success of the tour. Rolling up his sleeves to start the next three hundred years. But, between you and me, I don't like the look of the Tsesarevich. The poor lad's clearly an invalid. I can't see him lasting long enough to reign. And where will that leave us?'

Where indeed?

18

In the spring of 1914 Mother came to St Petersburg. It was the first time she'd seen me in my new home. She found several things to make her sigh – the country house smelled of horses, the town house had no ballroom and I allowed Uncle Bimbo to take my daughters and their governess tapping for birch juice.

'Like ragamuffins,' Mother said. 'And Bimbo is as mad as a brush. Always was.'

I said, 'But we're happy, Uncle Bimbo is a darling, and Cyril is a wonderful husband.'

'If you say so, dear,' she said.

The official reason for Mother's visit was to attend the wedding of the year, no, the wedding of the *century*. Uncle Sandro and Aunt Xenia's daughter, Irina, married Felix Yusupov. Xenia's only a year older than me, and to have a daughter married! It made me feel old, and sad, to think of my Elli's wasted little life. I remember Irina when she was a baby, and Felix when he was just a boy, playing with Elli in the garden at Ilyinskoe. And now they're married.

Some people, actually quite a lot of people, thought the marriage was doomed, though that didn't deter them from attending the wedding and enjoying the festivities. Felix had a certain reputation. He was no quiet stay-at-home. Uncle Sandro even hinted that Felix might suffer from the same tendencies as Ernie Hesse. He'd attended Oxford University, after all, a place famous for corrupting healthy young men.

Uncle Sandro said, 'But Rina insists on having him, so what am I to do about it?'

'Forbid it, you fool,' Mother said. 'That's what you must do. Prevent another tragedy before it's too late. Look at what happened to poor Ducky.'

But Miechen said, 'How can you speak of Ducky that way? She's quite recovered from the Ernie episode. My son has made sure of that. Poor Ducky indeed! And anyway, think of all that lovely Yusupov money Rina will have at her disposal. I'm sure that would help a wife live with any number of tendencies.'

Whatever anyone thought, Rina did marry Felix. They made the handsomest couple. Rina's gown was white satin, very slender and simple, *très moderne*. Her veil was antique French and Felix had commissioned her tiara from Cartier: platinum, rock crystal and diamonds. Lots of diamonds. Something old, something new.

Mother stayed with us until June, then she travelled on to Romania to inspect Missy's latest baby, a boy, Mircea. I asked if the child was Nando's.

'Of course he's Nando's,' Mother said. 'What *are* you suggesting?'

'I thought it might be another of Missy's muddles.'

'If your sister suffers from muddles, we certainly don't speak of them. But I pray this will be her last confinement. Six is more than enough. At Missy's age one never recovers one's silhouette.'

I promised to bring Kira and Masha to Coburg later in the summer.

'Yes,' Mother said. 'Please do. I'm not getting any younger, you know.'

For some reason we didn't come to Haikko that year. I don't remember why. Instead we cruised a little in the Baltic. All we did

149

was swim and walk and ride. Peach took the girls shrimping and built a fire on the beach, to boil their catch in a bailing bucket. The girls still talk about it.

The plan was that Cyril would go back to St Petersburg towards the end of August and I would take the girls on to Coburg. We made our way to Riga for a last few days together, and that's where we were when war was declared.

We'd known about Archduke Franz Ferdinand, of course. We'd heard the news of his murder before we left for our holiday, but it hadn't seemed any affair of ours. I'm sure he and his wife were perfectly sweet people, but we didn't know them. To think what it has led to. Cyril blames Cousin Kaiser Willie. He thinks Willie could have told the Hapsburgs to stop being so belligerent, then everything would have calmed down. But Cousin Willie was apparently in the mood for a fight too.

Cyril and I were at dinner when a man came into the restaurant and shouted, 'It's war!' Some people ordered champagne. Some left in a hurry. I thought we should leave too. I wanted to see if any trains were still running to Germany. Cyril called me a fool. Actually he called me a bloody fool.

'You won't be going to Coburg,' he said. 'Don't you understand? We're at war. Germany's the enemy now.'

He said we must go home immediately, which was easier said than done. We were obliged to take a public train and Peach had to stand almost all the way. It seemed as though the whole world was on the move and when we eventually got back to St Petersburg the streets were impassable because of the wagons and horses and soldiers heading to the railway stations. We took the girls straight out to Tsarskoe Selo and Cyril telephoned around for the latest news.

Felix and Rina Yusupov were away, still on their honeymoon

and believed to be somewhere in Germany. Grand Duke Misha had already booked passage on a ship out of Newcastle. Emperor Nicky had given him permission to come home, to do his patriotic duty.

Cyril said, 'If Misha's got any sense, he'll bring his wife and child with him. Make the most of the open door before Sunny kicks it shut again.'

Misha did just that. He and Natalya set up home again in Gatchina, just far enough out of town to be invisible to those who didn't wish to see them.

Nicky and Sunny went to Moscow to ask God's blessing on the war. Uncle Bimbo said it would perforce be a rather one-sided conversation but it was a Russian tradition that must be honoured. Meanwhile England pledged support for us, and so did France.

'It'll all be over in a month,' Cyril said.

Italy followed France and came in for Russia. Romania seemed not to have declared.

I said, 'If Missy has anything to do with it, they'll fight on our side.'

Cyril said, 'Missy? You don't imagine anyone listens to her, do you? Anyway, the old king there is as much German as any other breed. He's probably more German than Kaiser Willie, so if he's going to take any position I hardly think it'll be with us.'

It was all such a hateful mess. War with Japan had been one thing. Asiatics are a different, distant type of people. But Germans were our kind. Grandpa in Heaven was German. So were May Teck and Miechen. Empress Sunny was half German. And then there was Mother. I was very concerned for her, half Russian and living right in the enemy heart of Germany.

Cyril said, 'I wouldn't worry too much about your mother. She went native years ago.'

Miechen agreed with him.

She said, 'I'm more Russian than she is these days. But I'll tell you how we can end this war immediately. They should put your mother and the Kaiser in a small room and lock the door. A fight to the death. We all know who the victor would be. Marie will kill anyone who prevents her from travelling to Cannes for the winter.'

A good many conflicts might be resolved that way but no one ever consulted Miechen on the quickest path to peace.

When Emperor Nicky got back from talking to God in Moscow he did two extraordinary things. First, he banned the selling of vodka for the duration of the war.

Uncle Bimbo said, 'What a chump. Doesn't he realise how much money it brings in?'

Miechen was worried that the new law would have other consequences.

She said, 'Not for ourselves, you understand. We have plenty of champagne. But the ordinary people may grow rebellious again if they can't get their drink.'

But Uncle Bimbo said nothing would prevent a Russian from getting his vodka. If it couldn't be bought he'd simply make it himself.

'Even if he has to brew it from his own slippers,' he said.

The second thing Emperor Nicky did was much more profound. At least I thought so. He changed the name of the city. St Petersburg became Petrograd. Cyril thought it was no great matter but people like the Lenzes did. After the German Embassy was attacked they changed their name to Lensky and Gitta Radloss swapped her two Ss for a more Russian V.

'Better safe than sorry,' she said. 'I'm Gitta Radlova until you hear to the contrary.'

And then there was Empress Sunny. If you listened to her devoted coterie she was Russia's beloved Little Mother, their *matushka*.

According to Peach who wandered all over the city on her half-day, even as far as horrid, dirty streets like Ligovskaya, the Empress was now widely referred to as 'The German'. So what would people make of me, a mongrel mix of English, Russian and German? Cyril said I should always emphasise my Englishness.

'Everyone loves the English,' he said. 'Fair play, the straight bat and all that.'

My greatest fear, after war was declared, was that Cyril would get orders to go to sea. I knew his nerves would never survive it. He'd been tense enough cruising close to shore on our holidays. But when Grand Duke Uncle Nikolasha was made commander-in-chief he kindly asked for Cyril to be appointed to his naval staff. It was a planning job at headquarters, at the Stavka as we called it, at Baranovichi in Poland. Cyril had his valet pack his bags immediately.

He said, 'Now, darling, you know what you have to do?'

In times of war it was customary for Grand Duchesses to set up hospitals. Dowager Empress Minnie led the way at once and donated the Anichkov Palace. She was rarely there anyway. She preferred to live in Kiev. Empress Sunny ordered the Catherine Palace to be prepared to receive the wounded and for a wing of the Winter Palace to be equipped for surgery. Genya Botkin was despatched to the Crimea to set up a hospital there in her name. We all wondered how Sunny would manage without Botkin visiting her twice a day but of course she still had Grigory Rasputin and anyway she found, as many women did, that war made her feel stronger.

I could have gone into hospitalling. Our house on Glinka Street wasn't particularly suitable but Georgie Buchanan was searching for premises for what she called her English Hospital. I could have joined forces with her. But I doubted I had what it took to be a nurse or a counter of feeding cups and crutches. I remembered Aunt Louise's words.

What do you want to do with your life?

I decided to do what I liked best: driving. I'd form my own ambulance unit and take it to the battlefront. A few cars, perhaps a motorised van or two if someone were generous enough to donate them, and half a dozen drivers. We'd go as close to the action as we could get. Betsy Trubetskoy declared it was the maddest, most dangerous idea she had ever heard. I set about it at once.

I owned a Delaunay in those days, so that was the first vehicle in my fleet. Masha and Kira thought it hugely exciting that they'd have to ride around on the electric trams while my motor went to war. My second acquisition was Miechen's Pierce Arrow. I didn't press her to give up her Daimler too. It was enough for people to know she'd donated her touring car for the duration. Wherever Miechen led her friends generally followed. But it was the trades-people who were the most generous, the mill owners and boiler-makers who gave us the motorised wagons we really needed.

By the beginning of September I had five motor cars, three half-ton delivery lorries and ten volunteer drivers. Some of them had never been behind a steering wheel but as they soon realised, it was a good deal easier than riding or driving a cart. Unlike a horse or a donkey, a motor vehicle has no wicked designs or sly ambitions of its own.

Semyon Petrovich Malkov was the kind of Russian volunteer who stepped forward. He was one of the estate workers from Tsarskoe Selo, too old for the army, too young to sit at home and do nothing. Three strapping, cheerful English girls volunteered too. I'd have taken more if I could have found them but not every Petrograd family was willing to give up its English governess. I'd never realised how many English girls there were in town, and they all seemed to be acquainted with one another, from attending the English church. Peach, being a thorough sceptic, had never shown any interest in going there.

'If I wanted to sing hymns and go to cocoa socials,' she said, 'I'd have stayed in Somerset.'

She never asked to be released from her position either, not then at least. She never expressed any wish to do war work. On the day I left, I told the girls they must behave for Peach. She was in charge in my absence.

Kira said, 'But where are you going?'

'To Poland, to help our soldiers.'

'Will you get killed?'

'No.'

'How do you know?'

'I'll be careful.'

Masha said, 'Peach says there shouldn't even be a war. Peach says all it'll do is make a lot of people dead and a few people rich.'

19

We drove in convoy towards Galicia. Two of the English girls, Florrie Marsh and Lil Lanham, came with me in the Delaunay and we took turns at the wheel, all very jolly. You'd hardly have thought we were going to war. There was just the problem of my title. After a few hours of being Highness'd I could stand it no more. I asked them to call me 'Ducky'.

Florrie Marsh asked if I'd always been a Grand Duchess. I had to think. It was a complicated story.

I said, 'I was a Royal Highness to start with. Princess Victoria Melita. But when you're a child it doesn't really signify. It was just a name. Then I married Ernie, so I became Grand Duchess of Hesse and Darmstadt. Then I got divorced so I suppose I reverted to Princess, but no one invited me anywhere or talked about me so titles didn't matter. I was The Unmentionable. And then I married Cyril Vladimirovich, so I became an Imperial Grand Duchess.'

Florrie said, 'Is that a step up, then? Imperial Grand Duchess?'

I said, 'It depends on your point of view. But you know I was always Ducky. Even Grandma Queen used to call me that, and the funny thing is, no one can remember who started it or why.'

She whistled.

'Grandma Queen,' she said. 'Well, I'll go to the foot of our stairs.'

★

I was only on the road with my ambulances for two months and yet it seemed like a lifetime, another thrilling lifetime. Isn't that strange? As each day dawned we had no idea where we'd be going or what we'd be asked to do. There were no rules, no routines. Sometimes we transported the wounded from a Clearing Station to the Base Hospital or from hospital to a Red Cross train. Sometimes we went closer to the action and drove nurses to the Advance Dressing Stations. Very occasionally there were days when we weren't needed to drive anyone anywhere. That was when we slept.

Sleep became our great obsession, after we'd learned to stop thinking about food. Black bread, weak tea, a hardboiled egg if we were lucky. Florrie Marsh did come back from one night transport with a couple of dead rabbits.

'Ask me no questions and I'll tell ye no lies,' she said, and they went into the stew pot, but generally food became something to consume quickly, without longing or reflection. But sleep. I became a connoisseur of sleep. That autumn I slept in a potato field and a forest clearing and an apple orchard. I slept under canvas, under the stars, on tarpaulin, on borrowed wheat straw. Pine needles are the best. I'd happily spend another night beneath a pine tree. There were times when I felt I'd slept while I was driving but as I never did any worse damage than clip the wheel of a baggage cart, I think I must have imagined that.

The war was going to be over by Christmas. Everybody said so. Our army in the field was much bigger than Germany's. But Russia had another enemy: its own disorganised haste. When our troops pressed into Galicia no account had been taken of the terrain. Men may march over anything, as long as they have decent boots, but supply wagons must go by road and in many places there were no roads, just narrow, sandy tracks. So the wagons were left far behind, men went hungry and the horses weren't fed.

Florrie Marsh said, 'The top brass, they couldn't organise a Sunday school picnic. They should put you in charge, Ducky. Or me. Or even Lil Lanham. We couldn't do any worse. Well, you're the one who has the connections. You should tell them, the powers that be. Can you not write a letter? I would if the Tsar was my cousin. I'd soon tell him.'

It was a funny notion she had of our family, that she thought Nicky would even read a letter from me. The best I could do was talk to Cyril, to tell him about some of the sad, silly messes I'd witnessed. If I ever saw Cyril again.

When I set off for Poland, I hadn't had a plan. To take my ambulances to a place they could be useful, then go back to St Petersburg to organise more of the same, or to stay with my fleet? I suppose I thought things would become clear once I got there. They didn't. Once we got close to the ever-shifting Front I had little time to think. When I lay down to sleep I always prayed for Masha and Kira and Cyril to be kept safe but somehow I never stayed awake long enough to get to the end of my prayer. I knew I couldn't stay away from home indefinitely but the days raced by and for the first time in my life I felt I was doing something useful. I wished Aunt Louise could see me.

I had in mind to go back to Petrograd in December. Even if the war wasn't over, the fighting was sure to subside once the snows came. I'd go home in time for Christmas. Then a letter came, dog-eared and redirected. It had been to Krasnobród and Lublin before it found me at Młodych. Kira had the measles.

Peach wrote, *She's not in any danger, but I thought you'd want to know.*

There was no date on her letter.

I asked Semyon Petrovich to drive me to the railhead at Brest-Litovsk. Everyone kept saying, 'Of course you must go, but don't fret. Children are stronger than you think. A pound to a penny she'll be over the worst by the time you get there.'

But they didn't know I'd already buried one daughter.

The roads were crowded, even at night. Troops were moving towards the Front and villagers were hurrying away from it. Once we were at a complete standstill while a battalion of infantry came through. Sometimes the road was quite blocked with slow-moving refugees. Even when Semyon sounded our horn they hardly moved. Perhaps they were sleep-walking.

The things people take with them, the things they choose when they realise they had better run. I saw a girl, not much bigger than Masha, carrying a basket of hens, and an old man with a bible the size of a doorstep. There was a family sitting by the roadside with a harmonium. Their horse, all skin and bone, lay dead and their cart was on its side in the ditch but there they lingered, as if they couldn't bring themselves to leave behind that one piece of home. I wonder what became of them and their harmonium. I've often thought of that scene these recent weeks.

At Brest-Litovsk the trains were impossible.

'There is a war on, you know?' they said.

They said I'd have a better chance starting out from Warsaw but our fuel tank was running low and petrol was impossible too. A telephone call to Petrograd? Out of the question. So was sending a wire.

Semyon Petrovich said, 'This here is the Grand Duchess Victoria Fyodorovna.'

'Oh, yes?' said the telegraph clerk. 'And I'm Kaiser Wilhelm.'

I couldn't really blame the man. In my leathers and my sheepskin soul-warmer I didn't look like anyone's idea of a Grand Duchess. And then there was my hair, cut off in mortal fear of catching lice. Lil Lanham had done it with her nail scissors.

She'd said, 'I'm no stylist but never mind, it'll grow back right enough. Just don't look in any pocket mirrors.'

I had peeped, of course. I couldn't resist. And I'd discovered that I looked like one of those Black Orpington hens Mother used to keep when we lived in Devonport. A Black Orpington halfway through its moult, claiming to be a Grand Duchess. I suppose I must count myself lucky that the *sanitar*s weren't sent for to escort me to an institution for the insane. If I'd mentioned that my sister was the Queen of Romania I'm sure I'd have been taken to one at once.

After two desperate days when no trains came in, through or out of Brest-Litovsk, there was a sudden flurry of Red Cross activity and I managed to squeeze onto a hospital train bound for Petrograd via Riga. Trying to climb aboard seemed a hopeless exercise but then I was pushed up from behind by an old man who had made pushing people onto trains his war work. He was rather good at it. If he deemed you worthy of his help he would put his all into getting you aboard a train, and your chances were particularly good if you had a female derrière.

It was after midnight when we reached Petrograd. There were no trains running to Tsarskoe Selo. I took a droshky. The driver was a woman. I asked her if her husband was in the army. She shook her head.

'*V balnitse*,' she said. 'In the hospital. Fell off a tram. *Tak, nyet deneg*. No money coming in.'

I told her my daughter had measles. *Korevoy*.

'*Bozhe moy*,' she said, and she crossed herself.

The house lights were burning. It seemed a good sign. Cyril's terrier, Krot, worked itself into a frenzy of barking even when I took off my scarves so it could see my face and hear my voice. It never was the brightest of dogs. Peach was in her dressing gown.

160

I said, 'I came the minute I got your note. How is she?'

'Kira's over it,' she said. 'Masha's got it now, much worse.'

The infection had gone to Masha's chest. I could hear the rattle of her breathing even from outside her bedroom door. Miechen had sent a Dr Lukin to treat her.

'Waste of money,' Peach said. 'Steam inhalations and her room kept dark. I could have told him that.'

I sent Peach to bed. She looked all in.

She said, 'What happened to your hair?'

'Cut it off. Practicalities.'

'You should keep it that way. It takes years off you.'

I believe I've always looked older than my true age, but Peach was the first person to hint that I was ageing. She also failed to call me Madam, I noticed. Something had shifted between us.

I sat by Masha and dozed, on and off. She was burning hot. At one point she clung to my arm though I'm not sure she knew me. Half awake, I saw a little girl in a nightgown standing in the doorway and I spoke to her. She sneezed. Then I was properly awake.

She said, 'Why did you call me Elli?'

It was Kira.

I said, 'I was dreaming. Come here and let me kiss you.'

She hung back.

She said, 'Why is your face so dirty?'

'I came on a train.'

'Are you going away again?'

'No, never. I missed you. Did you miss me?'

You can depend on children for the truth.

'Not terribly,' she said. 'Granny Miechen bought us new dresses and Uncle Bimbo took us mushrooming. Is Masha going to die?'

'No,' I said, although I knew she might. 'Show me your new dress.'

She came back wearing it over her nightclothes. Blue velveteen, shirred bodice, bishop sleeves and a ribbon sash. Very Miechen.

'Masha's is red,' she said. 'But I like mine better. I did miss you, really.'

Masha's fever broke the following night. She slept peacefully for an hour then she sat up and scowled at me.

'I didn't know you were here,' she said. 'You shouldn't creep up on a person.'

I was still wearing my ambulance breeches. Underneath them my skin looked grey. All those weeks of washing in splashes of pump water, or not washing at all. I sat in a hip bath and had Nanya pour hot water over me until the grey turned to pink. Then I put on a gown, ate two slices of soft, white bread with butter, and fell asleep.

Miechen telephoned. She was in Livadia.

I said, 'Masha's out of danger. She'll be fine now.'

'Oh, I knew she would be,' she said. 'Dr Lukin is the absolute best. And is Cyril home yet?'

Miechen had written to Uncle Nikolasha and told him Cyril must be allowed home at once, to see his sick children.

'Especially,' she said, 'considering the heroic work *you've* been doing.'

I could imagine Grand Duke Nikolasha snorting at the word 'heroic'.

I said, 'Cyril isn't here. I don't think his movements are up to Uncle Nikolasha.'

'Of course they are,' she said. 'What's the point of having the Commander-in-Chief in the family if he can't manage a little courtesy like that for you? If Cyril doesn't arrive this week, I shall telephone the Emperor. When I think of what my family has done for this country.'

I said, 'Miechen, please don't. Anyway Nicky doesn't receive telephone calls, you know that.'

'Then I shall plague him day and night until he does,' she said. 'Great heavens, even Dowager Minnie isn't afraid of the telephone.'

Cyril didn't come home, not even for Christmas. It was altogether a rather dismal time. There was no opera, no ballet. A performance of Bach's Christmas Oratorio was cancelled. 'Inappropriate,' they said. 'Too German.' And of course even the Yusupovs didn't dare to give a party. Actually, particularly the Yusupovs. Like everyone with a wing to spare, they'd offered part of their palace for use as a military hospital but Felix was still in bad odour. He'd pleaded 'only son' exemption from active service and snagged himself a safe little job at the Peter Paul Fortress, as a map librarian or some such. Rina was expecting so it was nice for her to know Felix wasn't in any danger, but still rather shaming to have him come home to dine every evening when all the other men were away, doing their duty.

Cyril's brothers, Boris and Andrei, both had commands. Uncle Bimbo was in Kiev, as a kind of Imperial inspector of hospitals, Uncle Seryozha was in the far north inspecting munitions factories and Uncle Gogi was about to go east, to confer with the Japanese. That was the stupidity of war. One could almost understand Peach's point of view. Japan, which had been our mortal enemy just a few years before, Japan which cost us so much, not least my husband's health, was now our ally.

Peach and I did what we could to give Kira and Masha a gay time. We had our own little party and the girls wore their Miechen dresses. I suggested they put on a little display for me, to show me what they'd been learning at their ballet class, but Peach had prepared something else. They were to act out the story of someone called Stenka Razin. The name meant nothing to me.

Masha said, 'Gosh, but everyone knows about Stenka Razin.'

163

Peach said, 'Russia's Robin Hood.'

She didn't trouble to hide her disdain at my ignorance.

'Yes,' said Kira. 'He helped the poor people because the rich people were so beastly and selfish.'

'Not all of them, I'm sure,' I said.

Masha said, 'I hope you're not going to spoil our play.'

We made treacle toffee to send to Cyril and built a magnificent snow hill. We were outside, sledding, when I saw an express-letter delivery go to Genya Botkin's house. I guessed at once what it was. In wartime no one with a family member at the Front wants to receive an urgent letter and I knew only Tanya was at home. It was the hour when Botkin made his daily call on Empress Sunny. I went in to Tanya. The dear girl was as white as a bone and she hadn't even opened the envelope.

'Should I, do you think?' she said. 'I would normally. Since Mama went away I deal with everything. I just don't like the look of this.'

We opened it together. It was as I'd feared. I telephoned the Alexander Palace but the switchboard couldn't connect me to either of Their Imperial Majesties, or wouldn't. I told the Botkins' *sloozhanka* to give Tanya strong, sweet tea and then I set off on Tanya's bicycle. The Imperial Guard gave me no difficulty. I always waved to them when I rode past the gates so they knew me well. Chief Steward Taneyev was a different matter. Perhaps it was the sight of my jodhpurs that flustered him. But when I whispered my reason for being there he agreed to take me to Nicky directly.

He was in the playroom with Alyosha. Marie was there too and Anastasia. How those girls studied me. The aunt who had abandoned their darling Uncle Ernie.

The Emperor of All the Russias was sitting at the top of a wooden slide. He was wearing an army undress tunic.

'Ducky,' he said. 'What a pleasant surprise.'

And slid down onto the pile of cushions.

He enquired after my health, and Cyril's.

I said, 'Cyril Vladimirovich is at the Stavka. I think he's well. I hope he is. You'd know more than I do.'

'Ah yes,' he said. 'Of course.'

But he offered me no news. I told him why I was there. That young Mitya Botkin had been killed in action at Limanowa and Tanya needed her father to go home to her at once.

Nicky rang a bell and lit a cigarette. I took one from his case while it was open. Marie and Anastasia were still examining me. I felt like an interesting exhibit in a zoological garden. Warning: this animal may bite. So I was rather pleased to be able to give them a talking point to take to Empress Sunny. Not only is Aunt Ducky divorced, but she wears men's trousers and smokes too. Actually I rather needed that cigarette.

'Sad business,' Nicky said. 'Botkin's other boys? Are they . . . ?'

Yuri Botkin had just gone off for basic training, Gleb was too young for the army but raring to follow his brothers. I made the observation that there'd be many families learning to dread the sound of the postman at the door. I think I also mentioned that there was no Mrs Botkin at home, just Tanya and the servants. I don't remember.

Alyosha was studying me. He's still very small for his age, but he knows how to play his part.

He said, 'I'm the Tsesarevich.'

I said, 'I know. And I'm your Aunt Ducky.'

'No,' he said. 'I don't think so.'

I suppose no one corrects your manners when you're the Heir. Well, I'm afraid those Bolsheviks will soon put him in his place. They don't give a fig for any person's bloodline.

Then he asked me, 'Do you have any boys?'

He wasn't a likeable child, but was it any wonder? There was little that was normal in his life, watched over every minute, cooped up with Sunny and all those fussing sisters and doctors. No one to play with but his sailor-nurses and Emperor Nicky. He needed his corners smoothed.

I said, 'No boys. I have two girls, but they're younger than you. Five and seven.'

Did they have bicycles, he wanted to know. They did, of course.

'You see, Papa?' he said. 'This person's children are younger than me and they're allowed bicycles.'

I'd rather hoped Nicky would go straight to Sunny's suite to break the news to Botkin in private but instead he had him sent for and then stood about discussing the prospect of more snow and puffing lightly on his cigarette.

I said, 'Should I stay? When Botkin comes?'

'As you wish.'

'Perhaps somewhere less public?'

'Public?'

'The children?'

'Ah, yes, I see what you mean.'

Too late. The door opened and Genya Botkin walked in, so genial and unsuspecting. I wished myself a thousand miles away. And then Nicky muffed things even further. Instead of going straight to the point he asked first about Sunny's health and I had to listen to a long reassuring rigmarole about the workings of the Empress's nervous system, all the while waiting for that terrible blow to be dealt. And in a room full of toys. It was too awful.

Poor, poor Botkin. He remained perfectly composed. Apologetic even, for having to cut short Sunny's consultation.

Nicky said, 'The Empress will understand perfectly. Sad day. No

166

greater sacrifice. You have the nation's gratitude, Botkin. Won't keep you. You must be wishing to get off.'

I thought he might order a car to take Botkin home but he didn't. He just lit another cigarette and turned away. The interview was over.

I wheeled Tanya's bicycle and Botkin and I walked together. It's not a great distance but it seemed to go on for ever. I suppose that's why I talked to him about losing Elli, to fill the silence. To put myself on a certain footing with him, that I knew what it was to lose a child.

'I'm so sorry,' he said. 'I never knew.'

Then he said, 'My wife, my former wife, will have to be told about Mitya, but I'm not entirely sure where she is. So many things I don't know.'

20

There was an accident on the line just north of Tsarskoe Selo. The Petrograd train halted at a signal and was shunted by another train coming up from Pavlovsk. It jumped the rails into the path of the down train. There were dead and injured. Anna Vyrubova was among them. Lyubov Obolenskaya was the first to tell me. She said Vyrubova had been killed.

An hour later the news had changed. Anna Vyrubova was alive but only just. She'd been carried to her house and a priest had been sent for. Tsarskoe Selo was the village of unreliable information. Uncle Paul's Olga brought me the revised version the following day. It wasn't a priest that had gone to Anna but Grigory Rasputin. He'd stood by her bedside and told her to get up and walk.

'And she did,' Olga said. 'The Empress's monk really seems to have performed a miracle.'

'Just like Jesus,' said Kira, who was not supposed to be listening.

Anna Vyrubova did recover, though not completely. On good days she walks with crutches, on bad days she uses a merlin chair. It was after the accident that she closed up her house and moved into rooms at the Alexander Palace. Sunny's orders. What Anna's husband thought of his house being given up, I don't know. Vyrubov was away with the Pacific Fleet and I don't ever recall seeing him. Perhaps he made his own arrangements.

It was April. Cyril's idiot dog was celebrating the thaw by digging his way to the centre of the earth, when he suddenly left off this important work to start yipping and squealing. I thought he must be injured and ran to the window, but Krot was barking with joy not pain. A car had pulled up and his master had climbed down from it. Cyril was home on leave.

The girls came running but then, when they actually saw him, were a little shy of him for a minute. Then they joined Krot in his frenzy of doggy happiness. I had to wait in line for my kiss.

'At last,' he said. 'I thought I'd never get here.'

Kira said, 'Why is Daddy kissing you so much?'

Cyril said, 'Because I've missed your lovely mama so very much.'

'Even so,' she said.

He looked tired but he'd put on weight. Whatever else might be going wrong on the Polish Front they dined well at Headquarters. He had things to tell me too, after the children were in bed. In particular about Sunny and her holy man. After a few glasses Uncle Nikolasha apparently grew very free with his opinions.

'According to Nikolasha', were the opening words of several delicious pieces of gossip. In ascending order of outrage they were: that Grigory Rasputin wasn't a miracle-worker at all, but a fake; that he was plotting against Uncle Nikolasha, to have him removed from command; that he was an insatiable satyr who cured women's ailments by driving them to excesses of ecstasy and that Empress Sunny sometimes received him wearing nothing but her nightgown and shawl.

Cyril agreed with me that the last charge was utterly fanciful. Sunny would never do anything so improper. I thought Nikolasha's fears for his position sounded a little mad too, but Cyril wasn't so sure.

He said, 'They had a set-to, you know, quite some time ago?

'Nikolasha came right out with it, called the Holy One a fraud. Told him he saw straight through him. Rasputin went running to Sunny and Sunny was in an absolute fury with Nikolasha, for upsetting her ju-ju man.'

'But that was before the war. Nicky needs Uncle Nikolasha now. Even Sunny must understand that. Who else could run the war?'

'Oh, but it gets worse. You know what Nikolasha's like. He doesn't care for anyone's good opinion. Rasputin wrote to him, acted all conciliatory. He offered to come out to the Stavka to bless the chapel and lead the officers in prayer. And do you know how Nikolasha replied? "Yes, come, you reptile. I'll string you up." And now there's talk of Nikolasha being replaced. It's just a rumour, but these things come from somewhere. There's talk of Nicky taking command himself.'

'Would that be a bad thing?'

'Bad? It'd be a bloody disaster.'

'Have you ever seen Rasputin?'

'Only that time in the Kazan Cathedral. Got chucked out of the ADC's seat, remember? Well, he certainly seems to have enchanted everyone now. You'd think it was the Second Coming.'

The Russians do love their Holy Men. I was always reluctant to say anything for or against Grigory Rasputin. I didn't know him, and if he'd truly stopped Alyosha's bleeding when he was sick, what mother could blame Sunny for believing in him and keeping him close at hand? I will only observe that the women who flocked to his apartment and invited him into their own drawing rooms were, without exception, reckoned to be St Petersburg's silliest.

Cyril brought news of Missy too. Nando's old Uncle King had died and Nando had succeeded him, so my sister now truly was the Queen of Romania. They still hadn't come into the war though.

170

Cyril said, 'Nor will they, unless the war reaches their own doorstep and they're forced to declare. Nando prefers a quiet life.'

I said, 'He may do, but Missy doesn't. I'm sure she's raring for Romania to come in on our side.'

He laughed.

'Missy, the Warrior Queen?' he said. 'I'm not sure about that. Mightn't it rather ruin her hair?'

I said, 'Is that what you think of us? Don't you think Missy will want to do her bit?'

He said, 'It was just a joke.'

But I didn't find it very amusing. He underestimated Missy and he underestimated me. He never asked me anything about my time in Galicia, about the things I'd seen.

'*Pas devant les enfants*,' he'd say. 'Sterling work, Ducky, I'm sure, but you should never have gone to the Front. I'd never have permitted it. Your place is here, with the girls. Offer Sunny a hand at one of her hospitals if you feel you must do more. She'd appreciate that. Might even improve relations.'

It came time for Cyril to return to the Stavka. It hung over us those last few days.

I said, 'I dread getting a letter, like Botkin did.'

He said, 'I'm not in any danger. You were far more likely to be killed, going off with those damned ambulances. Promise me you won't go back.'

I promised.

He said, 'I waited long enough for you. I couldn't bear to lose you now.'

I was very teary his last day at home. He had his valet pack his dress coat, to be ready for a victory parade.

He said, 'Chin up, darling. I reckon we'll be in Berlin by October.'

The Germans had turned their attention to the west, so Russia had breathing space, to build up her lines, to train her men and equip them properly. But Russia isn't like Germany. Things don't happen in a timely, orderly way. Sometimes they don't happen at all. Supplies are despatched but somehow they never reach their destination.

'Well,' people say, 'it *is* a very big country.'

Of course we weren't in Berlin by October. On the contrary, we were in retreat. Cyril hates to recall that time.

'Sheer bloody incompetence,' he says. 'Defeat snatched from the jaws of victory.'

Towns that we'd captured were lost again. And while our units and munitions went missing or arrived in the wrong place the Germans regrouped, very quietly, and then hit us hard, first at Gorlice and then all along our southern lines. They took back Lviv, they took back Przemyśl, and our infantry turned and ran. It's been said that they threw away their weapons. Cyril grows very angry when anyone repeats that.

'What weapons?' he says. 'Half of them had nothing but broom handles, poor buggers.'

But in May of 1915, when he went back to Headquarters he was still full of optimism.

'Next year,' he said to the girls, 'when the war's over, we'll go up to Haikko and have a lovely holiday.'

War quite altered St Petersburg. Petrograd. I must remember to call it Petrograd. Many familiar faces were missing but there were plenty of new arrivals. There were the press men, like Dr Williams who was terrifically brainy and had a rather fierce-looking Russian wife, and Mr Walpole, whose eyes were too weak for the army to have him. Then there were the military bods, like General Alf Knox who worked out of the British Embassy, and Sam Hoare who set up the British Mission at the Astoria Hotel. And then there was Bertie Stopford who was neither one thing nor the other.

I first met Bertie at Miechen's lunch table in the summer of 1915. He was English but he often lapsed into French. His age was difficult to guess. By his skin, certainly over fifty, by his deportment he could have passed for thirty-five. He wore no uniform and he had no credentials, but he seemed to know everyone. Miechen said Felix Yusupov had 'discovered' him when he was in London and added him to his collection, but I have the feeling Mr Stopford was the one doing the collecting.

Cyril's brother, Andrei Vladimirovich, was at that lunch party, home on leave.

He said, 'Who's the exquisite, Ma?'

Miechen said, 'Bertie Stopford is a great expert on Cartier. He also dances like an angel. There's no one better to lead off a cotillion.'

As Andrei said, a good dancer is a useful type to have around when there's a war on. I've grown to like Bertie Stopford though. Some people think he's a dangerous tittle-tattler but I've found his gossip to be entirely reliable. He has courage too. One wouldn't think it to look at him but he's jolly plucky, in that quiet English way.

The summer heat settled over us like a damp horse blanket. Even riding our bicycles seemed like too much of an effort. Masha and Kira ran around barefoot and Miechen predicted the end of civilisation. I longed to go back to Galicia, to defy Cyril and try to find my lovely ambulances, but our kitchen boy had chickenpox and then Peach broke out in shingles and was wretchedly ill, so that put paid to any such plans. I did get news of my unit though. Florrie Marsh had broken her arm trying to crank-start the Talbot and been sent home, back to the Kudrin family who had kindly donated her services. I went to call on her, over Vyborg side. The Kudrins were tradespeople, manufacturers of rope. They had a very fine house. Funny, one never thinks where rope comes from and yet there are people who've made great fortunes out of it.

I'd hardly have recognised Florrie. She'd lost a great deal of weight.

'Not only me,' she said. 'We all have. We've been living off our blubber. The Boche have had us on the run and we've never had a minute's rest. You've no sooner put your head down and there's orders to retreat. At this rate we'll all be speaking German by next year.'

She said the worst part of retreating was leaving the wounded behind.

'You can't take them all with you,' she said, 'it stands to reason. You just have to hope the Boche will treat them right. I don't know. If it was the Germans who shot them to pieces in the first place why should they treat them kindly once they find them in a hospital cot? Doesn't make any sense. But that was the order. The able-bodied were to retreat and regroup. I've had men spit at me for walking away from them and I can't say I blamed them. It haunts me, it really does.'

My lovely Delaunay had leaked oil from a cracked seal and died on the road to Włodawa.

'Pity,' she said, 'it was a very nice motor. I suppose some German brass'll have his eye on that, whatever's left of it. The last time I saw it a pair of milch cows were having a taste of its canvas hood.'

She didn't know whether she'd be going back into the war.

'I wouldn't mind,' she said. 'But I reckon it might be over by the time this arm's mended.'

Uncle Bimbo telephoned.

'Just back in town,' he said. 'Thought I might motor over.'

I told him we were a plague house but he said he'd come anyway. He brought flowers for me and calves' foot jelly for Peach.

'You may not have heard,' he said. 'Nikolasha's out. He's been relieved of his duties. Nicky's declared himself Commander-in-Chief.'

It was as Cyril had feared.

Uncle Bimbo said, 'It's a regrettable step. I'm no great admirer of Nikolasha. He can be very quarrelsome. Always was a scratchy individual. But he's a damned fine soldier. God help us now he's gone. Our Imperial Majesty is a decent enough man, but what does he understand of warfare? Nothing at all. As you may imagine I thought it best not to say any of this on the telephone.'

Uncle Bimbo was quite convinced that our telephone conversations could be overheard. I didn't really see how, but one didn't wish to argue with him. He understands how all kinds of machines work.

He said, 'The general feeling is that this is Rasputin's work. He's been campaigning against Nikolasha for months.'

Also as Cyril had thought.

I said, 'But why? He's a monk. What does it matter to him who's in charge of the army?'

'Monk, my eye!' Bimbo said. 'Monks don't go out carousing till all hours. I'll tell you what he wants. Emperor Nicky out of town. He already has Sunny in the palm of his grubby hand. Our beloved Empress doesn't wipe her nose without his approval. And with Nicky at the Stavka who'll be running the shop here? Sunny. That's Rasputin's game. We'll have that German dumpling as Regent and an unwashed schemer as her right-hand man. That I've lived to see this day!'

I said, 'But Sunny won't have any real power. She mayn't do anything without consulting Nicky first.'

'Consult Nicky?' he said. 'As well ask the man in the moon for a decision. He won't even use the telephone. He'll sit at the Stavka chewing his pencil while Rasputin tells Sunny what to do. You'll see. Then all his friends and relations will start getting positions and contracts. They'll be swarming in, under the doors and up the water pipes.'

Uncle Bimbo got quite worked up, and I'm afraid I laughed at him, even later on when, true enough, Grigory Rasputin's friends did start to profit from his influence. There was the wonder-working flame-thrower that turned out not to be worth a kopeck let alone the considerable sum Rasputin's friend had been paid for it. I have apologised to Uncle Bimbo since.

He said, 'Never blamed you, Ducky. What sane person would have believed it? After three hundred years, our great house pulled down by a stinking faker and a foolish woman.'

One afternoon, when she came in from her piano lesson, Kira asked me, 'Who's the *Nyemka*?'

I said I didn't know.

'I do,' said Masha. 'It's the Empress and no one likes her because she's German.'

I told her not to repeat such things.

I said, 'Granny Miechen is German too. Granny Edinburgh is half German. You should mind your tongue.'

Kira said, 'And anyway, Peach says the Germans are really our brothers and we shouldn't be fighting them.'

Aunt Ella wrote to ask me if I would talk to Sunny. In Moscow, she said, wherever a crowd gathered they shouted for the Empress to stop interfering in Russia's affairs and take the veil.

It's so very unfair, Aunt Ella wrote. *We can none of us help our blood or our upbringing and I'm sure Sunny has done everything she can to become a good Russian but if they take axes to Bechstein pianos, what might they do to*

176

a German Empress if she continues to provoke them? The children too. She should take them to a convent for safety. If Nicky must stay at the Front he should appoint Misha to be his Regent. Sunny has to understand her limits.

To which I could only reply that Sunny had never been my friend so I was the last person on earth she would listen to. And the very idea of Grand Duke Misha being Regent seemed too ridiculous. Emperor Nicky had only allowed him to return because of the war. If Misha reigned in Nicky's absence, people would have to start receiving his wife. And then, what if Tsesarevich Alyosha were to have a bleeding episode and die while Misha was Regent? Wouldn't that make Misha's little son the obvious next heir? It was unthinkable. Besides, in Petrograd there was another slogan going around. Grand Duke Nikolasha for Tsar!

Warsaw fell in August 1915. My ambulances returned to Russian soil and the Stavka pulled back from Baranovichi to Mogilev. I offered my services to Georgie Buchanan at her hospital on Vasilievsky Island. I drove for her, as required, and when I wasn't needed as a driver I helped in the laundry. I loved the steam and the soapy smell and the endless, mindless nature of the work. I'd always thought I was strong until I had to haul wet sheets. But my strength improved and so, by all accounts, did Empress Sunny's. Her neuralgia disappeared, her headaches stopped and daily visits from Dr Botkin were no longer required. Suddenly she was well enough to jump out of bed at first light. She put on a kind of nurse's uniform and learned how to dress wounds.

I saw her one evening at the train station and she greeted me like I was her dearest cousin in the world.

'Ducky,' she said. 'What do we both look like! Look at your hair. Look at the state of my boots.'

I'd never seen her so gay.

She said, 'You'll never guess what I've been learning today. The administration of ether. Isn't that splendid? One has to be very attentive to the surgeon's instructions. Quite nervous-making really, but so much more satisfying than going to receptions.'

I felt a little envious of her. To be assisting a surgeon sounded much more thrilling than washing sheets but of course they'd only allowed her to try her hand at it because she was Empress.

'Come to tea on Sunday,' she said. 'We can compare war stories!'

Sunny and I have been family and we've been neighbours but in all those years she'd never invited me into her life. It took a war for her to open her drawing-room door to me. And that was how I met Grigory Rasputin.

21

He was sitting with Anna Vyrubova. He didn't stand when I walked in, or even look up. Countess Hendrikova was in attendance too, helping Sunny perform her Russian tea ceremony. I love to see a samovar and hear its hot water murmuring but honestly, if you want a cup of tea why not put some of Mr Twining's leaves in a china pot and be done with it?

His presence made me nervous. Some of the stories I'd heard about him were enough to make a trooper blush. But several times I found myself taking a quick peep in his direction, in spite of myself. He continued deep in conversation with Vyrubova, his head bent close to hers.

We talked of the satisfactions of war work – Sunny's two oldest girls were helping out in the Catherine Palace hospital – and I was encouraged to admire the cosiness of the drawing room. I do like mauve. In moderation.

Sunny said, 'I think Gran-Gran Queen would have liked it, don't you?'

I think she would have.

Suddenly Rasputin said, '*Matushka*, your guest is nervous of me. Please put her mind at rest.'

Sunny said, 'I don't think Grand Duchess Victoria is nervous of anything. She's been to the Front, you know.'

'You know best, Little Mother,' he said. 'Well then, perhaps she peeps at me because she would like me to be her friend.'

He got up from his seat and approached me. His shirt was peasant-style, a *kosovorotka*, but made of crimson silk. There was a sour smell about him. Unwashed hair, and who could say what might be caught in the great tangle of his beard. He drew a chair up to mine. I clung to my cup and saucer. I was determined he shouldn't take my hand.

'Such a strong face,' he said. 'But I see you have suffered. A child, was it? Yes, a little one. A daughter, I think.'

Sunny said, 'Oh, don't speak of it. It was too awful. I was there, you know? We were at Skierniewice. Ernie had brought her there for a holiday and she must have drunk some bad water.'

'Hush, Little Mother,' he said. 'Hush now. I'm speaking to Grand Duchess Victoria.'

And Sunny shut up, like a chastened child.

'Vika,' he said. No one ever, *ever* calls me Vika. 'Vika, why do you hide your face behind your cup? There's no tea left in it.'

He gestured to Hendrikova. 'More tea for Grand Duchess Victoria,' he said.

Then very quietly, smooth as silk, he said, 'Don't be afraid, Vichka. Let me fill your empty cup.'

You will have heard about Rasputin's eyes. Everyone who had ever consulted him talked about his gentle, grey, all-seeing eyes.

'Your little one is with you,' he said. 'Whenever you think of her she's as close to you as I am now. *Dushenka s taboy.*'

Taboy. He'd *tutoyered* me. The ultimate impertinence.

Sunny said, 'I don't know if she understands you. Her Russian isn't very good.'

'*Matushka!*' he said. 'Please! The Grand Duchess understands me, in her soul.'

I did too, though not as he meant it. I felt him working on me, touching what was buried. He had no business going there. I was close to tears but I was angry too, that he'd try his conjuring tricks on me in Sunny's drawing room. We were never a pious family but Mother once said to me, 'If God speaks to you, you'll know. If it doesn't feel like God it isn't. It's the Evil One.' Those words came back to me and I mastered my tears.

I said, 'I know where my daughter is. Why do you intrude?'

'Ah,' he said. 'The door locked against grief. Well, well, I understand. But some day you must open it, or it will destroy your health. I see you clearly.'

'And I you.'

'Your heart is pounding,' he said.

How did he know? Was a vein throbbing in my temple?

'Such passion,' he said. 'I know it when I meet it. I too am a passionate person. Come to Gorokhovaya Street. I can help you, Vichenka. I have the key to that locked door.'

I said, 'Leave me alone. I came here for tea. You have no right.'

Then I saw his other eyes, pale and cold as ice. Was he Mother's Evil One or just a thwarted showman? If I'd looked at them a little longer I might have known for sure but Sunny interrupted him again, very cross at his attention to me.

'Grishka!' she said, and she rapped her fan on the arm of her chair. He went to her at once.

Then I understood the gossip. Empress Sunny didn't call him 'Father Grigory' or 'Grigory Efimovich'. She called him 'Grishka' as one might a child or a brother.

He was taking his leave. I was glad. I'd feared if I were the first to leave he might follow me. He kissed Sunny's hand, then Vyrubova's, then Hendrikova's. Not mine.

'Dear ladies,' he said. 'Until tomorrow, if God spares us.'

181

When he'd gone, Anna Vyrubova said, 'Grand Duchess Ducky doesn't approve.'

Sunny picked up her knitting. An army sock.

She said, 'Sceptics don't trouble our Dear Friend. He's greater than that. He gives his back to the smiters.'

Vyrubova said, 'Very true. Is that from the Bible?'

'Book of Isaiah,' Hendrikova said.

'Yes,' said Sunny. 'And his cheeks to them that pluckèd off his hair.'

'Except no one has pluckèd off our Dear Friend's beard!' said Vyrubova.

Hendrikova said, 'It can be understood metaphorically, Anna.'

'Can it?' she said. 'How clever you are.'

Sunny said, 'But wasn't it astonishing how he went straight to the matter of Ducky's sad loss? So powerful.'

I said, 'Sunny, how can you bear the smell of him?'

'It's the smell of sanctity,' she said.

I looked at Countess Hendrikova. She seemed the likeliest person in the room still to be in possession of her wits. Nothing.

I said, 'It's the smell of a man who never bathes.'

'That,' said Sunny, 'is because you don't believe. But you will. When you've seen what I've seen, you'll find he smells of frank-incense and myrrh.'

'And anyway,' said Vyrubova, 'I'm sure I remember him saying he'd been to the *banya*.'

When I left the Alexander Palace, I found myself looking back over my shoulder all the way home. I was cross with myself but I couldn't shake off the idea that Grigory Rasputin was following me.

I hadn't been in the house more than five minutes when Miechen telephoned.

'Well?' she said. 'What's her drawing room like?'

'The holy man was there. He stinks.'

'So I've heard. Did he go into a trance?'

'No, but he talked about Elli. I suppose Sunny must have told him about that. She calls him "Grishka".'

'No!'

'Yes. And he addressed me as *tu*, without so much as a by your leave. He made my skin crawl. And now I can't get him out of my mind. He invited me to go to Gorokhovaya Street. He said he'd fill my empty cup, or unlock my door, or some such disgusting talk.'

'The beast. He means to ravish you.'

'Of course I made it clear I saw what he was up to. That annoyed him. So then he left. But now I feel as if he's haunting me. Those eyes.'

'Oh, Ducky,' Miechen said, 'how terrifying. You must get a priest in at once. Have him slosh holy water all over you. Now tell me about Sunny's décor.'

'Mauve, lilac, mahogany.'

'Just as I'd heard. What did she serve?'

'Olivier salad sandwiches.'

'Cake?'

'Iced gems.'

'And they told me at Yeliseev's they couldn't get them. Because of the war.'

'Sunny is the Empress.'

'I'm sure I spend far more at Yeliseev's than she does. Well, darling, thank you for the gossip. But do get a priest in, to put your mind at rest. Get a good one. Get a bishop.'

I didn't get a priest in. I couldn't bear the thought of the children's questions and Peach's scorn. But whenever I thought of Grigory

Rasputin or remembered his eyes I said the Our Father, and after a few days he faded from my mind. Even when Uncle Bimbo called on me and brought up his name, I felt calm.

Uncle Bimbo's main topic was Grand Duke Nikolasha. As Emperor Nicky had taken command of the army, Uncle Nikolasha was being sent to the Caucasus, to be Governor-General.

'Kicked upstairs,' Uncle Bimbo said. 'And far enough away not to disoblige Sunny and her witch-doctor. I hear he's still slithering around her feet.'

I said, 'He is. I met him, at last.'

'Did you, by Jove? And what did you make of him?'

'Clever. I could see how he draws people in. Sunny's besotted.'

'Oh, I know,' he said. 'He has her transfixed. She thinks he holds the boy's life in his hands. But how did you come to be invited? Has our dear Empress decided to be your friend after all?'

I said, 'I think Sunny's manner has improved. I think getting out of the palace and doing a little war work could be the making of her. And you know Olga and Tatiana are nursing too? People will like that. Wounded men love any nurse, and to be nursed by one of the Tsar's daughters no less. That will be something for a man to tell his children.'

He said, 'I hope you're right, Ducky. That would be good news indeed. If we could just get rid of the reptile she might make a decent Empress yet. If only he'd fall under a tram.'

If we could just get rid of him. That was the first time I heard those words, but not the last.

Uncle Bimbo said, 'And perhaps we may console ourselves that Nicky can't do too much harm. He has some good men advising him, and the Germans have pushed us back so far they've probably lost interest in us anyway.'

The autumn fogs began, filthy and yellow. Miechen was trying to gauge the city's atmosphere and decide whether she dared to plan a party.

She said, 'Nothing unsuitable, you understand. But a little dancing and cards would lift everyone's spirits.'

I said, 'How can you have dancing? All the men are either at the Front or waiting to be fitted with a wooden leg.'

'Nonsense,' she said. 'There are plenty of men. There's Bertie Stopford for one. And what about all those lovely officers at the British Mission? I'm sure they'd adore a walk-around and some pleasant female company.'

The British Mission occupied a suite of rooms at the Astoria but its officers were often out and about. I'd met some of them at Georgie Buchanan's afternoon teas. They were strange types, not quite soldiers, not quite deskmen. One could hardly ask them what they did all day – in time of war we're all supposed to keep our eyes open and our mouths shut – but the Mission men seemed to spend a great deal of time sitting in the Winter Garden pretending to read newspapers, watching the comings and goings. Some of them travelled out of town – one mustn't ask where – and would be gone for weeks. Then suddenly they'd reappear.

There was Captain Alley, for instance. He seemed to have a passe-partout, perhaps because he spoke Russian, not careful, precise Russian as Cyril or Uncle Bimbo did, but rough, slurred Russian, like an old *dvornik*. Captain Alley was billeted with Lieutenant Rayner and they made a very odd couple. Alley usually looked as though he'd slept on a train and Oswald Rayner seemed always to have stepped that very minute out of Trumper's, freshly shaved. Rayner knew Felix Yusupov from Oxford and one could see why they'd been friends, both so elegant and composed. Their uniforms fitted when no one else's did. Cuddy Thornhill was another figure from the British Mission. I knew him by sight, though we hardly conversed. Actually Thornhill rarely conversed with anyone. He'd just fade into the background and gaze at his glass or his tea cup. Ex-Indian Army, according to Georgie Buchanan.

'Been everywhere,' she said. 'Speaks languages no one else ever heard of. And he's such a good listener.'

I couldn't at all imagine him turkey-trotting around Miechen's reduced wartime drawing room. But she was determined to throw a party and so many came, it was ladies we lacked, not men. I danced every dance.

'You see?' Miechen said. 'Now sit and take a glass of fruit cup with General Knox. He wishes to quiz you.'

Dear Alf Knox. He seemed to think I was the person to ask about Empress Sunny.

I said, 'But I hardly ever see her.'

He said, 'But you're family, and neighbours?'

Of course he had no reason to be fully acquainted with my history.

I said, 'I was married to her brother. Then I was divorced from her brother. And we're only neighbours in the loosest sense. We don't call on each other if we run out of sugar.'

'The Empress must find her situation difficult,' he said. 'With the Emperor away and a family to care for. You'd think she might be relieved to have someone else appointed Regent.'

I said, 'You mean Grand Duke Misha?'

'Yes, Grand Duke Michael,' he said. 'Or even your husband. A purely temporary arrangement, for the duration of the war. I just wondered whether the Empress has expressed an opinion.'

'Certainly not to me,' I said, 'but I can tell you she'd never give up the Regency to Cyril. As a matter of fact, I can't think of anyone in the family she trusts. She and the Emperor are a tight little love knot, you know. No one else gets close to them. Apart from Grigory Rasputin. Perhaps you should canvass him.'

'Ah yes,' he said. 'The monk. I don't think so. I'm afraid he might propose himself as Regent.'

So even then, in 1915, people were worried that Nicky and Sunny were their own worst enemies.

'What a pair,' Cyril says. 'Too wrapped up in each other to notice what's going on in the world. Too busy standing on their dignity to listen to advice. And now look at what they've brought down on all our heads.'

He thinks they'll go to England. King George and Queen May will surely find them a house.

'Bloody Sandringham,' he says. 'That's where they'll end up. Some drafty lodge house in Norfolk. Serve them right.'

We hear nothing. Maybe they're there already.

But back then we were all still hoping that our Emperor would wake up and acquaint his wife with some home truths.

'Someone must talk to Sunny.' That was what everyone said.

Aunt Ella suggested Dowager Empress Minnie should do it. A mother-in-law carries a certain weight of authority, after all, but she was in Kiev, and anyway she and Sunny had always padded about each other like cats preparing for a fight. Clearly it was Nicky's job. He should have given command of the army back to Uncle Nikolasha, gone home to Petrograd and confined Sunny to her boudoir. At the very least he should have sent Grigory Rasputin on his way.

Cyril got no leave for the rest of the year and his letters were written in a kind of code.

We feel the heat of the Sun, even here. Has it wandered from its ordained orbit?

Mrs Nicholas and her pet monkey seem to have taken up playing with toy soldiers.

Cyril now says that Empress Sunny had sight of every order, every map, every military decision that was committed to paper.

And whatever Sunny saw, Rasputin undoubtedly saw too. Cyril isn't given to exaggeration. He swears everyone at the Stavka knew Nicky was leaking like a sieve but when anyone tried to raise it with him he'd go off in an Imperial huff, shut himself away in his railway carriage and write another billet-doux to Sunny.

All I knew was what was happening in Petrograd. In February 1916 half of the Council of Ministers resigned. The news was sent to Nicky and his rather comical reply was that they needed his permission to resign and permission was denied. Sunny made matters worse. She said the Council of Ministers were traitors, every one. Not only must their attempted resignations be ignored, but they must be sacked immediately and replaced with better, loyal men. It would be no trouble at all because she already had a list of suitable candidates.

After that it became rather like a dangerous party game. Whenever the music stopped yet another of Rasputin's recommendations was to be found wearing a ministerial hat. Sturmer became Prime Minister. He was a famous mediocrity but Rasputin recommended him. Then Polivanov was removed as War Minister. Miechen heard it from Bertie Stopford and called me immediately.

She said, 'Polivanov is replaced by Shuvayev! Can you believe it? He must be a hundred if he's a day.'

Actually Shuvayev wasn't quite that old but everyone knew it wasn't a wise change. He was just a faithful old dog. He should have been left to sleep in his basket. A War Minister needs teeth.

There was worse to come. Protopopov was promoted as new Minister of the Interior. It wasn't that he was incompetent. He was perhaps out of his depth but those in power often are. The real problem with Protopopov was that he tried to be all things to all men. He'd always appeared to be a reformer but suddenly he abhorred any talk of reform. He'd deplored Rasputin, but then he became Rasputin's friend and Sunny's man, willing to do whatever made her happy, whatever would keep the throne safe for Nicky and then for Alyosha.

Things began to unravel. Nothing was ever where it should have been. An army needs munitions but factories can't make them if they run out of fuel and metal. People must be fed but they won't be if the railways are clogged with trains going nowhere. Russia was too big to be run from Sunny's mauve couch.

Cyril returned to Petrograd in the autumn of 1916. His new posting was to the Kronstadt garrison so he was often able to come home and see the girls before their bedtime even if he couldn't stay to dine. He was horrendously busy. Quite often he'd have a late meeting and have to go back to the base rather than sleep at home, but it seemed to suit him. I'd never seen him looking so well. Miechen noticed it too.

She said, 'I suppose he's got a girl.'

I'm afraid Miechen had no concept of how busy a senior naval officer is in time of war.

She said, 'Don't look at me like that. It's only normal, after all. How long have you been married?'

Then she slid the knife between my ribs.

She said, 'If only your complexion had held up better. You are using Pond's, I hope?'

I didn't mind her criticism. Well, I did, a bit.

'You know how it is,' she said. 'Men can grow jowls and nose hairs but if they've got a bit of jingle to spend the girls will still go for them. But the first wrinkle and we're finished. But never mind. Cyril's discreet, just as his father was. I'm sure he'll never bring any trouble under your roof.'

I laughed at her. I knew women like Miechen and Mother took their husbands' carryings-on for granted but Cyril and I were a different case entirely. We were kept apart for too long for either of us to have any appetite for love affairs. Cyril kept himself vigorous for me, not for some silly soubrette. Or so I thought.

22

I'm afraid to say it often didn't feel as though we were at war. So many of our menfolk were back in town, especially towards the end of 1916. Miechen entertained, on a suitably restrained scale, and there was almost a full programme at the Mariinsky. That's not to say things were completely normal. There were days when one couldn't get proper *kalach* for breakfast, even from Filippov's. There were days when it was difficult to find petrol. But the war wasn't thrilling any more. People were bored and restless. That was when Peach started to be so contrary and at times quite rude.

'Is that your greatest problem?' she said to me one morning. 'That you have to eat yesterday's bread?'

I was shocked. A Russian servant would never be so rude to one's face.

Then Masha said, 'When is Peach leaving?'

'She isn't.'

'Well, when she made Kira do her seven-times table over and over and Kira told her she didn't like her she said "you'll miss me when I'm gone".'

'It's just a thing governesses say.'

Nevertheless I sent for Peach.

I said, 'The girls have the impression you're thinking of leaving us.'

'Not immediately,' she said. 'But nothing lasts forever.'

'Well, you won't be able to sail for England till after the thaw, and even then it'll be fearfully dangerous. Look what happened to poor Herbert Kitchener.'

'I don't intend going to England,' she said. 'I mean to stay in Russia and see what happens.'

See what happens. It sounded slightly batty at the time, like those people who carry boards, THE END IS NIGH. But Peach saw it coming, I suppose because of the neighbourhoods she ventured into on her half-day. She never went for a walk with the other English governesses. She seemed to prefer her own company, but as her Russian improved, and to be truthful it overtook mine in no time, she began mixing with certain types.

I said, 'Then if you intend staying in Russia, why leave a perfectly good position? Has another family made you an offer?'

'No,' she said. 'As a matter of fact, I'm rather tired of governessing. It's very tying. Half a day a week isn't much time off. And I don't even get that if it isn't convenient to you.'

'But I make it up to you.'

'No, you don't. You forget.'

I said, 'So, what do you intend to do? How will you live? Do you have an income?'

I knew she didn't.

With friends, she said. She'd live with Russian friends. And when I asked her what she'd do for money she laughed.

'Money?' she said. 'That'll soon be a thing of the past. It'll be fair shares for all.'

I'd never heard anything like it. I called Miechen.

She said, 'It sounds to me as though she's losing her mind. Perhaps she's going through the climacteric? You had better get rid of her at once.'

191

She said she'd find me a replacement. With half the Vladimir Palace given up for a hospital she had far more servants than she needed.

I said, 'But a maid's no use to me. Even if Masha goes to the Smolny next year, I'll still need a proper governess for Kira.'

'Well, Ducky,' she said, 'we must all make sacrifices. There is a war on, you know.'

So there was discontent in our schoolroom and discontent, so we heard, on the streets. Political meetings were the great new fashion. They were held in upper rooms and back rooms, and on any evening you might choose from half a dozen of them. What did they discuss? Change, according to Cyril. But what changes exactly?

'That depends which meeting you go to,' he said.

All through December there was a procession of senior Romanovs, anxious to talk to Emperor Nicky and acquaint him with the mood of the people. There must be an elected government, sooner rather than later, and it must be willing and able to make reforms. The days of a Tsar having the power of life and death over all of Russia were disappearing. Petrograd wouldn't stand for it any more and where Petrograd led the rest of the country would soon follow.

Uncle Bimbo was the first to see Nicky. He went all the way to the Stavka to give him a paper he'd written, a kind of essay on the state of the nation.

'Thought it best to put it in writing,' Uncle Bimbo said. 'To avoid any misunderstandings. Poor blighter looked dead on his feet. I told him to read my report when he wasn't so tired. Nothing in it he doesn't know in his heart, I'm sure. Things have to change. For a start Sunny must be deprived of the Regency and Rasputin must be sent back down the hole he crawled from.'

But Nicky didn't read Uncle Bimbo's report. He just sent it on to

Sunny in the next Imperial bag and after she'd read it she allowed her fury to be widely known. Uncle Bimbo, she said, was guilty of treasonous sentiments. She wanted him punished. We were worried for him but he appeared not to care. Instead of leaving town as everyone advised he went out to Tsarskoe Selo every day to potter around his hothouses and be right under Sunny's nose.

He said, 'If she wants my guts for garters, let her come and get them. Personally I'm not afraid of her. I only fear her for Russia's sake. If Nicky doesn't listen to older, wiser heads we're liable to end up with troubles far worse than Empress Nincompoop.'

Uncle Paul was the next to try. He waited till Nicky was back at Tsarskoe Selo for a few days. That was a mistake. At the Alexander Palace no one saw the Emperor on official business without Sunny sitting in or listening through an open door.

Sweet, reasonable Uncle Paul. If anyone could have persuaded Nicky to stop and think, to make some concessions before the matter was taken out of his hands, surely he was the one to manage it, but Sunny interrupted and countered every suggestion he made.

'Paul Alexandrovich,' she said to him, 'you seem to forget, the Emperor has a sacred duty to pass the throne to his son, not to give half of it away.'

But it was Uncle Paul's criticism of Rasputin that tipped her into an absolute rage. How dare he! Grigory Rasputin was the Imperial Family's beloved friend. He'd saved the Tsesarevich's life on several occasions and would continue to do so. He wanted nothing for himself. Only the well-being of his Emperor and Empress and their children.

Uncle Paul said, 'Beloved friend! Can you imagine? She calls that fleabag their beloved friend! And all the time she was berating me, Nicky just sat there, puffing on a *papirosa*. Never said a word.'

Cyril said all we could hope was that Rasputin would be his

own undoing, that he'd overstep some invisible mark laid down by Nicky and be banished.

He said, 'If you ask me, Paul and Bimbo have only made things worse. We'd do well to keep our opinions to ourselves. We just have to hope Sunny gives her Beloved Friend enough rope to hang himself.'

But there was one last attempt made to bring Nicky and Sunny to their senses. Aunt Ella came, all the way from Moscow. She'd taken the veil after Uncle Serge was killed and I must say she looked quite lovely. She'd designed her own habit. Dove grey and white. Very sensible and flattering. Black can look so draining as one gets older.

Cyril had warned her it was likely to be a wasted journey because Sunny was deaf to all advice. Ella said nevertheless she must try. Sunny might be the Empress of All the Russias, but she was also her baby sister and she would never forgive herself if she didn't try to pull her back from the edge of calamity. In Moscow, she said, there was a new slogan being paraded quite openly.

Doloy Sashe. Down with Sasha! Which was both treasonous and disrespectful, to refer to Empress Alexandra as Sasha. Imagine if Grandma Queen's subjects had gone about calling her 'Vicky'.

Aunt Ella lunched with us before she went to see Sunny. I walked her as far as the Children's Pond before I turned for home. She was back in my drawing room within the hour. I believe she'd been crying.

'Hopeless,' she said.

She and Sunny hadn't exactly quarrelled but she'd quite failed to persuade her of the gravity of the situation and they'd parted in icy silence.

Aunt Ella said, 'I suppose my timing wasn't the best. Nicky left for the Stavka this morning. When he's gone she must feel terribly lonely.'

All the more reason then to welcome a rare visit from a dear sister.

Cyril said, 'Was Sunny quite alone? The serpent wasn't coiled at her feet?'

Aunt Ella crossed herself. 'Please, Cyril,' she said, 'don't judge the monk Grigory. Leave that to God.'

'So was he there?'

'I didn't see him. But I had the strongest feeling he was there somewhere, listening. What does it matter? They say Sunny tells him everything anyway. Perhaps he was outside the door.'

It was very much what George Buchanan had said.

'In conversation with the Tsar, one has the distinct feeling a feminine ear is pressed to the keyhole, and when one talks to the Tsarina, one detects a whiff of sulphur from the next room.'

Sunny had told Aunt Ella she would hear no criticism of Grigory Rasputin. Not only had he saved Alyosha's life but he also came highly recommended by at least two bishops and she thought Ella would concede that a bishop's opinion always carries more weight than that of a nun, particularly a nun who didn't even submit to the authority of an abbess. Ella managed to smile at that jibe. But when she'd offered to leave, Sunny had said it would be best.

Aunt Ella said, 'We didn't even kiss goodbye.'

I tried to cheer her up.

I said, 'Sunny's never good face to face. You know that. When you get back to Moscow write her a letter. Just tell her you love her.'

'Yes,' she said. 'Of course I will. But, Ducky, I have the most awful feeling I'll never see her again.'

We had a good birchwood fire burning but I still felt a chill when she said that. Cyril said it was just Aunt Ella having one of her mystical moments.

He said, 'Of course they'll see each other again. If Nicky carries on the way he's going we'll all end up in bloody Norfolk. Better start sewing your diamonds into your drawers, darling.'

I said, 'I don't have many diamonds.'

'Nevertheless,' he said. 'And your emeralds.'

The first proper snow came. Big, slow-falling flakes. Kira and Masha liked to stand outside and catch them on their tongues. It was the day before Miechen's Christmas bazaar so I went into town and stayed at Glinka Street. Cyril was going to a party at the Akvarium.

I said, 'Why don't I come with you?'

We'd seen so little of each other lately in spite of his home posting.

He said, 'I don't think so, darling. Not tonight. It's not that kind of party.'

Just men letting off steam, he said. I called the Yusupov palace. If it was that kind of party Felix was sure to be going. I thought Rina and I might have tea and exchange magazines. But Rina was away from home. She'd taken the baby south, to escape the Petrograd winter.

Cyril came in extremely late but rather frisky. I know they sometimes have tableaux at the Akvarium. Girls without corsets, or even in the altogether, though not in December one imagines. I heard him go to the drawer where he kept his rubber goods. I heard him whisper, 'Damnation.'

It was the coldest night of the year. I was glad to have him to warm my feet on.

The telephone woke us. It was still completely dark. I expected Cyril to ring for shaving water at once but he came back to bed.

I said, 'Is there a flap on? Do you have to go in?'

'Not yet,' he said. 'That was Bimbo.'

Before he could say any more the telephone rang again, and again. I got up.

I said, 'What's going on? Did someone die?'

'No,' he said. 'But Sunny's ju-ju man is missing.'

It seemed rather early in the day for anyone to be reported missing. I'm sure there were plenty of men still weaving their way home with sore heads. But Uncle Bimbo had it from Betsy Trubetskoy and Betsy had it from three different sources, though she couldn't quite remember where they had it from. Grigory Rasputin had gone out for the evening and never returned home.

I said, 'I wouldn't depend on Betsy for information.'

'I agree,' he said. 'But George Buchanan thinks there's something afoot.'

Miechen telephoned at eight thirty. I'd never known her to be up so early.

Cyril kept saying, 'Ma, please, do *not* start calling everyone in your book. It's just a rumour.'

He came back to the breakfast table.

He said, 'My mother will get us all into trouble one of these days. Rasputin may well be the Devil incarnate and Sunny is certainly a dangerous fool, but she's still our Empress. One must be careful.'

Uncle Bimbo came to the house. Cyril said they'd better talk in his study. Man talk.

I said, 'You might at least tell me what you're going to talk about. I have to go to your mother's wretched Christmas bazaar.'

Cyril said, 'All the more reason to tell you nothing. What you don't know you can't repeat.'

So infuriating. Uncle Bimbo winked at me.

He said, 'Don't fret, Ducky. It's all something and nothing, I'm sure. Rasputin's probably asleep under a table somewhere, like the dog he is. Fine thing.'

Grigory Rasputin was all anyone talked about at the Sale of Work. Actually it was rather good for business because people shopped mindlessly. They threw money at us and filled their bags with spectacle cases and doilies and crocheted angels the quicker to get back to discussing the exciting question of the day: where was the Empress's miracle-worker?

Miechen asked me to stay to luncheon.

'Just you,' she said. 'And Bertie Stopford. If there's any news, Bertie will have it.'

He came late, but he brought an armful of Crimean tuberoses and plenty of information for us to chew on. Rasputin was still missing. His daughters were accustomed to his late hours but said he always came home, eventually. His bed had not been slept in. As to where he'd spent the evening, the stories varied. He'd been at Villa Rhode all evening. He'd left in a troika, with two gypsy girls, at around midnight. No, no, he'd dined at Kubat, then gone off in a motor. Possibly a Delage. Destination unknown.

Rasputin's daughters swore he hadn't dined anywhere. He'd been feeling unwell and had planned to stay at home all evening, but then Felix Yusupov had persuaded him, quite pressed him, to go to a little soirée he and Rina were giving at Moika Street. Told him Rina wanted most particularly to seek his advice on something.

I said, 'Well, that's certainly not true because Rina's not even in town.'

Stopford said, 'Precisely. And as if she'd want that creature in her house anyway. But the police have been to see Felix. They wanted to know what company he had last night. Names and addresses. He says they're only doing their job but he's quite shaken. It was just a few friends, for cards and supper.'

Miechen wanted to know which friends, precisely. Stopford said he didn't have the full guest list, it was only an impromptu card evening, after all, but he believed Vladimir Purishkevich had been present.

Miechen said, 'Purishkevich? That old thunderer? How extraordinary. Are he and Felix friends? No, you must be mistaken. Russian names can be so confusing.'

Vladimir Purishkevich had been a member of the Duma, a staunch supporter of the Emperor, a man who thought all reformers should be shot at dawn. He did sound like an unlikely playmate for dear Felix.

Stopford saved the juiciest morsel till last.

He said, 'Well, whoever was there, it's rather rotten luck that shots were heard during the course of their card party. Questions are bound to be asked.'

A night watchman on the Moika had reported hearing gunfire, very late and apparently coming from the Yusupov Palace. The police were summoned and Felix explained what had happened. A street dog had got inside the Yusupov courtyard and when the *dvornik* tried to shoo it back onto the embankment it had bared its teeth, as though to savage him. He'd cried out for help and Felix and his guests had rushed outside and shot the creature.

Miechen said, 'Good. It's the only thing to do when a dog runs mad. Who fired the shot?'

That was one question Bertie Stopford couldn't answer. It wouldn't have been Felix, I'm sure. And who on earth takes a loaded gun to an evening of cards?

Stopford said, 'Whoever it was, they showed great presence of mind. And a steady hand too, after a glass or three of champagne. Oh, Dmitri Pavlovich was present too, by the way. Did I mention that? I expect you'll get the full story from him. Felix was very piano. Well, no one likes a visit from the police.'

Dmitri Pavlovich. He was a much more likely guest at one of

Felix's soirées. I thought Miechen would rush to telephone him immediately but she didn't. She was unusually quiet.

I remember saying, 'Presumably Felix showed the body to the police?' Miechen and Stopford both looked at me rather absently.

Stopford said, 'The body?'

I said, 'The dog?'

'Ah,' he said. 'Yes, the dog. Indeed. Well, no. Unfortunately its body had already been disposed of.'

Of course. Thrown into the canal.

Then Stopford said, 'But we've strayed from the more interesting topic of the missing monk. Where can he be? Perhaps he's decided to make a pilgrimage. Perhaps he's walking to Jerusalem.'

Miechen said, 'A pilgrimage under the Empress's skirts, more like.'

Which caused Bertie Stopford almost to choke on his tea.

'Naughty Grand Duchess,' he said, 'what a horrid image. They say you could grow potatoes in the dirt under his fingernails.'

'Ask Ducky,' Miechen said. 'He offered to unlock something or other for her. And he *tutoyer*ed her.'

I didn't see Cyril till evening.

'Nothing new to report,' he said. 'Isn't it amazing? This morning everyone was asking "where's Rasputin?" Now all they're concerned about is can they get a table at Donon's. The fickleness of people.'

He'd seen Georgie Buchanan in the street but she wouldn't be drawn into gossip. Yes, the British Embassy was aware of the rumours but it was none of their affair. The British Mission was almost deserted. Cuddy Thornhill was in Moscow and not expected back for several days. Alf Knox was away at the Stavka. No one could say where Oswald Rayner was.

I said, 'I suppose you heard about Felix?'

'Yes,' he said. 'A mad dog destroyed. How thrilling. And the Moika used to be such a dull place to live.'

'Stopford says Dmitri Pavlovich was there.'

Cyril looked at me.

He said, 'We don't know, do we, Ducky? We really know nothing at all. Therefore best to say nothing.'

I travelled back to Tsarskoe Selo the next morning. I wondered whether I should telephone Sunny when I got home, whether I should extend the hand of friendship. Her Beloved Grishka was missing and Emperor Nicky was at HQ. He'd taken Alyosha with him, to show the troops their young Tsesarevich and boost their morale. She'd be feeling lonely and anxious. I was still debating whether to make that call when my train pulled in to Tsarskoe Selo and who should I see on the platform but Dr Botkin.

You know, I was so full of my own thoughts I didn't at all take in his mood at first. How was the Empress? Bearing up. Was there any news of Rasputin? He believed not. Then I noticed the catch in his voice, the fatigue in his face.

'My boy,' he said. 'Yuri. Killed in action. I've lost two sons now, Highness. Two.'

He cried, but somehow there were no tears. Genya Botkin was a considerable figure. It was much harder than seeing a woman cry.

I tried to find some words. That it wasn't fair, or something equally stupid. As though bullets and shells consult a book of rules. I took his hand and rubbed it, like you would a child's grazed knee. What can one say?

It had become a little too easy for me to forget about the war. Cyril had a desk job. I knew he was safe. And, away from the hospitals, Petrograd was hardly any different. But to lose two sons?

I hoped Botkin could remember exactly why we were at war and find some consolation in it because I couldn't. But through all his troubles and losses he was so staunch for Nicky and Sunny and our war effort. He still is.

'Our *Batyushka* will lead us to victory,' he said. 'God save the Tsar!'

On Sunday morning our doorman Kuzma and the kitchen boy carried a small spruce into our yard so Peach and the girls could make a kind of Christmas tree for the birds. They hung it with bacon rinds and suet balls and then watched from a window for their favourite wren and greenfinches to come and feast. It ended in tears. A cock robin saw off every other bird, including another robin, and Kira was inconsolable.

'Children have to learn,' Peach said. 'Life isn't a story book.'

Peach was getting quite above herself. She made a great display of speaking to Kuzma in Russian and laughing gaily at his remarks.

Cyril telephoned just after lunch.

I said, 'I think I may give Peach notice. She's threatened to leave anyway. And now she keeps chattering to the *shveytsar* in Russian. They could be saying anything.'

He said, 'Probably discussing the weather. Don't trouble me with domestics, Ducky. Rasputin's been found.'

A workman had noticed it first, downstream of the Petrovsky Bridge. He'd thought it was the body of a wolfhound, trapped just beneath the ice, but it turned out to be a long-haired man in a fur coat and one felt boot. It was Grigory Rasputin and he had a bullet hole in his head.

23

I believe everything began to change from that moment. Even though the excitement over Rasputin soon subsided, now I look back, his murder was the beginning of the end of our lovely life. When Cyril told me the news I wanted to go back into town where I could hear every theory at first hand.

But he said, 'Why? Are you a detective all of a sudden? No, stay where you are and don't gossip. Particularly not about a certain young relative of ours.'

'You mean Dmitri?'

'I'm serious, Ducky. This could get very unpleasant.'

It was all over Petrograd. The mad dog that had been shot in the courtyard of the Yusupov Palace was none other than the Empress's beloved friend, and Felix was now talking about it quite openly. He seemed to think he and his friends had done the Emperor a great service.

Two things happened almost immediately. Special policemen went to Rasputin's apartment and searched it. Ransacked it, his neighbours said. One had to feel sorry for his daughters. He may have been an unpleasant character but to lose one's father and then to have one's home turned upside down, it seemed terribly unfeeling.

Uncle Bimbo said they'd be looking for anything that might embarrass Sunny. Letters, gifts, anything that had her crest on it. And while that was going on a great gathering of the Romanov men took place at Glinka Street. Cyril, brother-in-law Boris, Uncle Bimbo, Uncle Paul. Even Grand Duke Uncle Sandro rushed back from Kiev. Rasputin's death had become a family matter. Felix Yusupov was Uncle Sandro's son-in-law. And he'd now named those who'd been with him that evening and helped him despatch Rasputin. He saw no reason not to. He imagined Russia would thank them for it. Purishkevich was named, so Bertie Stopford had been right about that. And most worrying for us, Uncle Paul's son, Dmitri Pavlovich.

You know, I still thought of Dmitri as a child though he must have been twenty-four or twenty-five by then. He'd seen active service. He'd been awarded the Cross of St George. And yet when the finger was pointed at him my first thought was to defend him, to say it was impossible for him to have been party to a murder. Dmitri himself made no pretence. He never denied his part in it. He was just surprised Rasputin's body had been found so quickly. I suppose they'd all imagined the ice would keep their secret, that nothing would be discovered until the spring thaw.

When the body was found Dmitri wanted to go immediately to Sunny, to confess to his part in the killing and to explain himself.

'She loves me. She'll forgive me, with time,' he said. 'I was present but I have no actual blood on my hands. Eventually she'll understand why it had to be done.'

Sunny was certainly fond of Dmitri. She and Aunt Ella had been special, kindly aunts to him, a dear little boy growing up without a mother. He was convinced he was the one who could make Empress Sunny see that Rasputin had been killed out of pure concern for her good name. But wiser heads prevailed. Uncle Paul ordered Dmitri to stay at home and speak to no one.

Sunny had shut herself away with Anna Vyrubova and her other ladies. We guessed she must be in a state of hysterical collapse.

Genya Botkin was in attendance but no one wanted to trouble him for information. Our chief concern anyway wasn't that Sunny's heart would break but what the aftermath might bring, when her hysteria subsided and she began plotting her revenge. A man had been murdered, after all. And then, what about the next time the Tsesarevich had a bleed?

Uncle Bimbo said, 'Well, I suppose that's when we'll discover whether Rasputin really was a miracle-worker.'

Cyril felt everything depended on Nicky's reaction. He might be quietly relieved to be rid of Rasputin. Perhaps he'd find a way to be lenient with those who'd done the dirty work. But Sunny didn't wait to hear from Nicky. She ordered Dmitri and Felix to be placed under immediate house arrest and when Uncle Paul tried to talk to her, to plead their cause, she refused even to see him.

There were a hundred versions of what had happened on the night Rasputin died. Betsy Trubetskoy told Miechen that Felix had tried to poison him first, with cake. Bertie Stopford said that was nonsense. Rasputin preferred candy to cake, as any intending poisoner would surely have troubled to check. Gitta Radlova's version was that he'd received a shot through the heart but then had risen from the dead and pursued his assassins through the Yusupov Palace, eyes blazing, unearthly howls issuing from his throat, until someone brought out a pistol loaded with silver bullets and felled him with one shot. Gitta was ever a great romancer.

There were stories about his body too. It had been taken to a police morgue and then to a secret address out of town but to listen to the talk around Petrograd you'd have thought the whole world and his wife had been allowed to inspect it. It was riddled with bullets. It was run through with a sabre. It didn't have a mark upon it.

Uncle Sandro was more concerned about where the body was to be buried. He went to see someone he knew at the Prefecture.

'All taken care of,' he told Cyril. 'It's on a train already, going back whence it crawled into our lives.'

I said, 'But Sunny won't stand for that. She'll want him buried here, so she can visit his grave.'

'Precisely,' Cyril said. 'All the more reason to send him back to Siberia. It's just a pity it's winter. I hope they'll be able to dig a deep enough hole. We don't want a resurrection.'

Again and again we underestimated Sunny. Rasputin's body wasn't on its way to Siberia at all. A grave was being prepared for him at Tsarskoe Selo and Emperor Nicky was on his way home from the Stavka, coming to support his grieving wife and pay his respects. They buried him quickly and quietly, early one morning, before it was light. Dr Botkin said the entire family walked to the burial place through the snow. The Empress had wept a little, as was to be expected, but she'd been calm. She believed the spirit of her Grishka was at her side and would be for all eternity. He'd gone to a place where the likes of Felix Yusupov and Dmitri Pavlovich could do nothing more to harm him.

Cyril wasn't happy.

He said, 'So much for Sandro squaring everything away. Knowing Sunny she'll be visiting the grave every day. She'll make a shrine of it. In fact she'll probably build another damned cathedral over it.'

Well, he was wrong about that. Rasputin didn't rest there long enough even for a stone to be laid.

Nicky went back to the Stavka but before he left he dealt with Dmitri Pavlovich, privately. The crime was heinous, and all the more so for a family member being involved, but there was no sense in making the matter public. There would be no police investigation, no murder trial. Dmitri was banished, posted to Persia, to a Cossack Brigade, with no one but an orderly for company. He was to go immediately and not see or talk to anyone.

Felix had already defied his house arrest and slipped away to Crimea to join Rina and their baby. Purishkevich had returned quietly to his desk at the Red Cross and Oswald Rayner, whose name came up from time to time in connection with steady hands and skilled marksmanship, went blithely about his usual business, whatever that was.

As Cyril said, 'Rayner's with the British Mission. Even if he was in on it, Nicky can't touch him.'

Uncle Paul was obedient to Emperor Nicky's orders not to speak to Dmitri though it must have broken his heart to let his boy go off without seeing him. Persia. I'm not even sure where that is. Uncle Bimbo and Uncle Sandro were not so compliant to the Emperor's order. They went to the station with Dmitri and stayed with him until the train pulled out.

Uncle Bimbo said, 'Of course I went. What's Nicky going to do about it? Have me hanged for seeing a lad off to war?'

I had wondered if Cyril might feel a pang and go to the station himself.

'No,' he said. 'I see no point in all of us defying Nicky. We need to make him listen and he won't do that if he feels the whole family is against him. We have to ride this out, Ducky. We have to coax Nicky into a more reasonable attitude, because the alternative is very worrying. If Nicky falls he might take us all down with him.'

I didn't catch his meaning at first. If Nicky falls.

I said, 'How can a Tsar fall?'

He said, 'In Nicky's case, rather easily. Look at him. He has one foot at the Stavka, one foot in Petrograd, his head's in the sand and he has Sunny's considerable weight perched on his little shoulders. I'd say it wouldn't take much of a push. And then what? George Buchanan went to see him, you know? Told him straight, he needs to regain the confidence of the people and quickly. Damned plucky of Buchanan. Know what Nicky said? "It's not *I* who need to regain their confidence. *They* need to regain mine!'"

Cyril said the best we could hope for was that Nicky would retire, 'abdicate' is actually the word he used.

'And then?'

'Misha could take over. Until Alexis is of age.'

'Misha! With Natalya Brasova as Empress?'

'Don't be ridiculous. He'd have to reign without a consort.'

'They might ask you instead. Promise you won't. I don't want to be Empress.'

He laughed.

He said, 'Don't worry, they'd no more have you than they would Brasova. A divorcée? No darling, you're perfectly safe.'

'Who else does that leave? If Nicky goes and Misha doesn't want the throne?'

'Plenty of candidates,' he said. 'The question is rather what if Russia doesn't want any of us?'

We went to the Mariinsky to see *Sleeping Beauty* and then had dinner at the Europa. There was a blizzard raging when we came out but Cyril said he had to go to the base. Urgent naval business. He wanted to drop me at Glinka Street but I preferred to walk. It was no distance at all and I love the snow when it's still clean and powdery.

I didn't sleep well. I tried running through the names of all the Grand Dukes, trying to find someone who was qualified to be Tsar, but it wasn't like counting sheep. The exercise left me even further from sleep, with the worry of how unsuitable we all were. Uncle Paul was doubly damned, in disgrace because of Dmitri and the Rasputin affair, and resented for having run off and married Olga Paley. Cyril's brothers, Boris and Andrei, liked their freedom too much. Uncle Bimbo wanted a quiet life. Uncle

Gogi had the problem of an estranged wife. The only possibilities seemed to be Uncle Nikolasha, who was old and had no heir, or Uncle Sandro. He was the one. In fact the more I thought about it the more obvious it was.

Grand Duke Uncle Sandro was ideal. He was married to Nicky's sister, Xenia, so she'd know how to conduct herself as Empress. She'd learned it at her mother's knee. Also, she and Sandro had a whole palace full of heirs. Half a dozen sons at least. After I'd settled that, I was able to sleep, but the next morning I felt distinctly unwell. I thought perhaps it was the pickled herrings we'd had at the Europa. Miechen was supposed to come for lunch. I tried to put her off but she said she'd come anyway. She was never one to allow someone else's indisposition to ruin her plans.

'Just take a little clear soup, darling,' she said. 'But I must see you.'

Cyril had warned her to be careful what she said on the telephone. She needed to see me face to face, and no servants in the room or even outside the door.

'We must be very careful,' she said. 'Cyril believes we're being listened to.'

I said, 'Uncle Bimbo's thought so for a long time.'

'Oh, that old fool,' she said. 'Who'd eavesdrop on him? All he talks about is moths. And pollination. But we're a different matter. Sunny's always regarded me as a threat. So now, do you know what I do? If Betsy calls me or Bertie Stopford, we'll chat away and every so often I'll say, "What do you think about that, Sunny?" Just so she knows I know she's listening.'

We talked about Emperor Nicky, about who might replace him. If Nicky falls.

Miechen said, 'Well, of course it should be you and Cyril. You'd be perfect.'

I said, 'But obviously it won't be, because of my divorce. Plus, we don't have a son. I think Sandro and Xenia are the obvious couple.'

But Miechen wouldn't have that.

'No, no,' she said. 'That might have been true, once upon a time, but not now. They're tainted. Felix has seen to that.'

In my midnight calculations, I'd overlooked the Rasputin connection. Uncle Sandro's daughter Rina was married to Felix. Felix had lured Rasputin to his death. He'd conspired in a man's murder, even if he hadn't fired a shot. People might fête him for it. People might condemn him and everyone connected to him. With Russians you could never tell.

Miechen said, 'This *vinegret* is delicious. Remind me, did I give you your cook? Why aren't you eating anything?'

Then she looked at me.

She said, 'Great heavens, Ducky. I do believe you're expecting!'

24

It had truly not occurred to me. I was forty years old.

Miechen said, 'Have you been having a little adventure?'

I said, 'Absolutely not. I love my husband.'

She said, 'So you and Cyril still . . . ? Well, aren't you the devoted one?! I thought he was seeing someone at the Mariinsky these days. Karsavina or one of those girls.'

So then I couldn't even finish my mint tea.

She said, 'Don't look at me that way, Ducky. I'd be very suspicious of any husband who didn't keep a dancer or two. One has only to think of Ernie Hesse.'

I think I tried to change the subject. I think I said I was pretty sure I wasn't expecting. It was the herrings.

'Herrings!' she said. 'It's written all over your face now I look at you. And how absolutely perfect. You'll have a boy this time, so when Nicky gets pushed off the throne you and Cyril will be the ideal replacements.'

The world according to Miechen. She moved us all around the way she liked to rearrange the enamelled boxes on her little tables.

I said, 'You mustn't say anything to anyone. Certainly not Cyril. You may be quite wrong.'

'Darling,' she said, 'you can trust me. I won't say a word. Just do go and see someone at once. Dobratov. He's very good, and very discreet.'

I said, 'If I go to see Dr Dobratov, someone is sure to see me going into his consulting rooms or leaving them. I think I'll just wait. Time will soon tell.'

'No,' she said. 'Time won't soon tell. You might be going through the change. You might have a growth. Look what happened to poor Lida Guchkova.'

I didn't know or want to know what had happened to Lida Guchkova.

Miechen said, 'I'll give you a few days, Ducky. After that I'll simply burst if I don't tell someone.'

I didn't go to Dr Dobratov. One might as well walk up and down Nevsky Prospekt with a banner announcing one's condition. Instead I consulted a doctor working at Georgie Buchanan's hospital, a Welshman with a surgical boot. I suppose he thought I was mad. A strange woman whispering to him in a corridor. But he took me into a store room and closed the door.

He said, 'This isn't really my field, you understand? Fractures are more my line. Perhaps one of the nurses?'

I told him I needed discretion. All the nurses knew me by name.

'Discretion, is it?' he said. 'So long as we're clear, I don't do female procedures. I don't dispose of inconveniences, never have, never will.'

I told him all I could. He asked me a few questions.

'Well,' he said, 'you have certain indications. You have prior experience. If you think you're up the spout it's my considered clinical opinion you probably are.'

Cyril came in late. He'd already dined.

I said, 'I have something to tell you.'

'Do you?' he said. 'That's funny, I have something to tell you. Ladies first.'

He was very sweet about it. It was a feather for his cap, I suppose. Cyril Vladimirovich, greying at the temples but still siring children.

He said, 'Let's hope this bloody war is over by the time she's born. Let's hope we'll have reason to name her Victoria.'

I said, 'Miechen's decided it's a boy.'

'Good grief,' he said, 'you've told Ma? Why did you do that? The news will be in Vladivostock by tomorrow.'

Cyril's news wasn't so momentous as mine, nor was it welcome. He'd been posted to the Northern Fleet. Its sailors were feeling neglected and forgotten. Nicky had ordered Cyril to go to Murmansk and Arkhangelsk, to deliver some inspiring speeches and hand out a few gongs. A shore posting but still, he'd be gone for some time.

He said, 'It's just a got-up errand, of course. Nicky wants me out of the way. Bimbo's got orders too. He's off to Grushevka and not to come back until he's sent for. It's because of all this talk of plots to get rid of Nicky. There is no plot, of course. Only discontent. But Ma doesn't help matters with her silly gossiping. Sooner or later it all gets back to Sunny. So you can probably blame your mother-in-law for my being sent to the Arctic.'

I said, 'Speaking of Miechen, she tells me you're seeing a girl from the Mariinsky.'

I hadn't planned on saying it. It just came out. I was feeling raw, I suppose. Pregnant, old, husband going away. Cyril didn't miss a breath. No denial, no astonishment or indignation.

'As you very well know by now, Ducky,' he said, 'my mother lives in a fantastical world of her own. The moment life seems dull she makes up a scandal.'

He didn't look me in the eye though. He just busied himself with his preparations.

My mother lives in a fantastical world of her own. Now where's my sheepskin ushanka?

'So it isn't true?'

'Honestly, Ducky, I thought you had more sense. Is this really how you wish to spend what's left of my time at home?'

Therefore, as Cyril didn't take me in his arms and tell me he loved no one but me, I supposed it must be true. Karsavina was very pretty and very young. We'd seen her in *Le Corsaire*. I'd thought she was married. Perhaps I was mistaken. Or perhaps a husband made no difference if you caught the eye of a Grand Duke.

Had Cyril been keener to go to the ballet recently? I wasn't sure. But he had unaccountably run out of rubbers, which had led directly to my present condition. All husbands did it, sooner or later. Everyone said so. And I didn't wish to quarrel with him. He was leaving. There was a war going on, though it didn't feel much like it at Glinka Street. What if we parted on bad terms and he never came back? I made jolly sure not to cry until he'd left for the station.

Masha said, 'Don't be sad, Mummy. Daddy always comes home.'

So I was forced to dry my eyes and dredge up a little cheerfulness, but everything had gone sour. I'd never suspected. If only Miechen hadn't come to lunch, I might never have known. The less you know the better you sleep. Old Russian saying.

Maslenitsa fell in the middle of February this year. It was the coldest I ever remembered it. I brought Masha and Kira into town for the funfairs and we went for a sleigh ride on the Neva. The reindeer had frost on their antlers. Everywhere we went there was the smell of frying pancakes and hot butter. Maslenitsa is no time to be suffering from morning sickness. Peach gave up her half-day to take the girls to Ciniselli's Circus when she saw I wasn't well enough to do it

214

myself. It was considerate of her. I took it as a sign that her restless phase was over and confided in her about my condition. She didn't seem at all surprised.

'Yes,' she said. 'I'd noticed you were a little thicker around the waist.'

I said, 'You did talk of leaving us. I hope you'll think of staying, at least until after the baby is born.'

'Well,' she said. 'I'm a governess, not a nursery maid. And anyway, who knows what this year will bring?'

Who knows what this year will bring?

Was it really only February when she said that?

The trouble began directly after Maslenitsa. At first it was about bread. There was bread to be had, we certainly didn't go short, but the quality of it was very poor. Such things happen in a time of war. Supplies can get disrupted. I'm sure it was no reason for people to start milling about the streets and shouting slogans.

I saw Georgie Buchanan at the hospital and told her my news. She hugged me.

'What a happy prospect,' she said. 'Let's pray the war will be over before the child is born.'

The Buchanans were going up to Finland, to Lake Saimaa, for a short rest. Of all the postings they'd had she said Russia was the hardest. Sir George was frustrated with the Emperor. He wouldn't listen to reliable intelligence, nor to the fatherly advice of a seasoned diplomat. Frustration can be very fatiguing and Sir George wasn't a young man.

'Sometimes,' she said, 'I wish we could be back in stuffy old Darmstadt. Nothing ever happened there.'

Nothing at all. Except for the Grand Duke sleeping with stable-boys and the Grand Duchess going home to her mother.

'When we get back from Finland,' she said, 'we must have tea,

215

you and I. And of course you must stop your hospital work. You must take care of yourself, Ducky, carrying a child at your age.'

She didn't really need to say it. I already felt as old as Methuselah's first shirt. Miechen had given me a recipe for a mask to brighten the complexion, something made with baking soda and castor oil. I never tried it. But I did go to the Mariinsky to see *The Firebird*. I wanted to take a closer look at La Karsavina.

She wasn't pretty. She was beautiful. More curvaceous than some of those dancers but she had extraordinary flight, as though she weighed nothing. Dark eyes, dark hair, the same type as me, in a way, but so young and so limber. It gave me a strange, painful kind of pleasure to study her. Cyril is my husband, after all. She'll never be more than his passing fancy. She'll grow old too. They ruin their bodies, you know, those ballerinas?

I longed to be able to talk to Missy. She was the great expert on managing husbands, and on unplanned babies. She was thirty-eight when Mircea was born. But I couldn't talk to her. With this damned war she might as well have been living on the moon.

25

It was women who started it. Their factory had shut down, waiting for supplies of coal, so they came across from Vyborg side, looking for trouble, marching and calling for bread. I must say they didn't look as though they were starving. Quite heavy, I'd say. Peach begged to inform me that hunger can cause a person's belly to swell though I'm sure she had no expertise on the subject. I don't recall Peach ever missing any meals.

If the weather had continued cold, I believe those women would have tired of parading about and gone home, but there was a thaw overnight. They came back the next morning in even greater numbers and they called the men out to join them, first from a boiler factory and then from a big steel works. They began singing.

Vstavay, padimaisya, rabochny narod.

Arise, awake, working people! Or so it was translated by Peach, who went about humming its tune. Masha asked her why the working people needed waking up. Peach said they didn't because they were now wide awake and on the march.

Kira said, 'In that case, it's a rather silly song.'

The only word I could make out was *vpyeryod*. Forward! Forward! Like the beat of a drum.

Vpyeryod! Vpyeryod! Vpyeryod, vpyeryod, vpyeryod!
So annoying. I couldn't get it out of my head.

There were Cossacks posted on Nevsky Prospekt. Not crack Cossacks. They were at the Front. The Cossacks in Petrograd were just boys. The sight of them was supposed to reassure us but as soon as the troublemakers smashed the window at Filippov's, those boys didn't hesitate to fill their own pockets with sugar buns. Miechen said she had it on the highest authority that more cavalry were on their way. I don't know. Sometimes Miechen's idea of 'the highest authority' was Bertie Stopford. I didn't see any more cavalry. Only machine guns placed at the corner of Gorokhovaya and Admiralty.

I felt uneasy. I told Peach to take the girls back to Tsarskoe Selo. She opened her mouth, as though to object, but then said nothing. They left that afternoon, and just in time. The next morning there were no trams running, no trains and one couldn't buy petrol at any price.

It was Saturday. I was supposed to be going to the Alexandrinsky that evening with Miechen, to see *The Cherry Orchard*. I quite expected the theatre would be closed but Miechen was confident the play would go ahead and she was determined to attend. She said it was our duty to go about our normal lives and uphold civilised standards. Besides, she couldn't bear to sit at home listening to the noise from the rabble in the streets. Arise, working people! *Vpyeryod, vpyeryod, vpyeryod.*

The theatre was like an ice house. They had no fuel for the stoves and we had to keep our furs on. There were very few people in the audience. Mimi Vasnetsova, Henny Lensky, hardly anyone else that we knew and certainly no one of any note. At the end of Act II, Miechen looked around and said, 'Ridiculous people.'

I wasn't sure if she meant the few who'd gone to the play, the many who'd stayed away, or Chekhov's characters, standing around dithering while their world goes to ruin. We sent for Miechen's sled and left without seeing Act III. I know how it ends anyway. I never liked that play.

It's no distance at all from the Alexandrinsky to Glinka Street but our short journey home turned into an exercise in navigation because Miechen's *izvozchik* said we must avoid Nevsky Prospekt at all costs, and Gorokhovaya and Voznesensky. The main avenues were all blocked with crowds and banners. We made our way home along the Fontanka and then by the Kryukov Canal and all the way Miechen kept shouting to her driver not to hurry.

She said, 'Sit up straight, Ducky. Cover your pearls, but hold your head high. We must never allow these troublemakers to think the streets belong to them.'

Her defiance didn't last the night. The next morning she left, quite unexpectedly, for Kiev.

Everyone expected Emperor Nicky to come back to Petrograd when he heard about the trouble on the streets, but he didn't. With Cyril and Uncle Bimbo away, Uncle Paul became my only source of information. As far as he knew, Nicky had simply sent a wire ordering that the streets were to be cleared. Whatever was required.

Uncle Paul said, 'He means bringing in the army, of course, and armed police, but he forgets, we're dealing with our own people here, not with Germans or Turks. Will Russians be willing to fire at their brothers? I doubt it. Anyway, most of the troops in the Petrograd garrison are children. Not shaving yet, half of them.'

He recommended that I go home to Tsarskoe Selo.

'In your condition, Ducky,' he said. 'Cyril Vladimirovich wouldn't want you staying alone at Glinka Street when things are so uncertain.'

I promised to think about it. But the next day was Sunday,

not the best day to travel even in the most orderly of times. I decided Monday would be better, by which time everything would probably have blown over. And actually I rather wanted to stay in town, to see if anything happened. I got up early. The maids hadn't even lit the fires. I put on my least good cloth coat, wrapped myself in shawls and made my way to the British Embassy. Everywhere was deathly quiet. There was a policeman on the corner by Horse Guards, but he didn't even look at me. I'd adopted a plodding sort of walk, slightly stooped, the kind of gait one imagines a factory worker might have. It was rather fun, pretending to be someone else. Like taking part in a play. Georgie Buchanan hardly recognised me. She and Sir George were just back from Finland.

'Gracious, Ducky,' she said, 'you shouldn't be out on the streets. Didn't your doorman warn you? Today's going to be a very testing day.'

There was quite a gathering upstairs. Excited voices and people still wearing their coats. It was like the start of a parade. From the embassy windows there was the most extraordinary sight. Dawn was just breaking behind Vasilievky Island. The ice on the Neva was starting to colour pink and mauve and the bridges, the Troitsky and the Alexander, were so packed with marchers and banners that the spans themselves appeared to be moving.

The Governor could have had the bridges drawn up. Emperor Nicky's instruction was to restore order. *Whatever was required*. But as the young man standing beside me observed, drawing up the bridges would only have delayed the inevitable. People would just have marched across the ice instead.

'Winter's a good season for protesting, in Peter at any rate,' he said. 'And anyway, I expect the men who operate the bridges are marching with the rest of them.'

He called the city 'Peter', like its natives always do, not St Petersburg, and certainly not Petrograd. He was a recent addition to Alf Knox's unit, recruited on the strength of his fluent Russian.

'Born here,' he said. 'And I'll probably die here if this lot start stringing us up.'

I said, 'But you're an Englishman. They like us. We're their friends.'

'Well,' he said, 'let's not presume. Let's not forget the French Revolution. Once their blood is up, it'll be enough to be seen wearing a pair of spectacles or a good shirt.'

He offered me a cigarette.

He said, 'I notice you said, "*We're* their friends." So you regard yourself as English?'

I'd said it without thinking. I don't know. What am I? Not Russian. I don't feel even half Russian, though that's my mother's heritage. Pa was a British Royal, which is tantamount to being German, and if I were to count the years, I've probably lived more in Germany than anywhere else, but that's not me either. I'm the Grand Duchess of Nowhere.

I said, 'I'm Victoria Fyodorovna. Ducky, actually.'

'Yes,' he said. 'I know. Gerhardi. Second Lieutenant.'

On and on the crowds came. They poured off the bridges into the city and though Sir George said the troops had been called out we saw no sign of them. Georgie gave us soup for luncheon, then Cuddy Thornhill and Willie Gerhardi walked along the Lebyazhya Canal to see what was going on.

'Side streets deserted, Nevsky packed solid but everyone very good-humoured,' was their report.

They'd cut through the Engineers' Castle Gardens and gone as far as the Anichkov Bridge. No one had given them any trouble.

Georgie Buchanan kept suggesting I should make my way home, while it was still daylight, while the crowds were still friendly.

She said, 'You must be anxious about your little ones, Ducky.'

I wasn't at all anxious about them. They were out at Tsarskoe Selo, probably playing Go Fish with Peach.

There was then some discussion as to whether, in times of civil unrest, it was safer to be in the country or the city.

Bertie Stopford said, 'Oh, the city, every time. The trouble with the country is one never knows what's lurking in the forest. The Alexander Palace for instance. It's frightfully exposed. In my opinion the Empress should think of moving somewhere that's easier to guard.'

And someone, I don't know who, said very quietly, 'Yes. Germany sounds about right.'

Cuddy Thornhill escorted me home. I'm sure there was no necessity but Georgie Buchanan insisted on it. It was about four o'clock and starting to grow dark. As we walked along the Moika we heard a strange popping sound, like distant fireworks. Thornhill didn't say anything, but I noticed he slid his hand inside his greatcoat.

I said, 'Was that gunfire?'

'Mmm,' he said.

'And you're armed?'

'Webley.'

I was pretty good with a shotgun when I was a girl. Miles better than my brother. Pa used sometimes to let me use his second-best Purdey. But I've never even tried a handgun.

I said, 'Do you think we should all arm ourselves? I do. I think I may get a pistol. What do you recommend?'

'A little Derringer,' he said.

Cuddy Thornhill, a man of few words. It was the most I ever heard him say.

The telephone was ringing. None of the servants would ever answer the damned thing. They'd just look at it and look at it and wait for it to fall silent. It was Masha.

'When are you coming home?'

I said, 'Maybe tomorrow. If the trains are running. If it's safe to travel.'

'Why wouldn't it be safe?'

'Because some people are misbehaving and guns are being fired.'

'What kind of misbehaving? I want to come and see them.'

I said, 'That's a silly thing to say. Daddy would want you to stay out of harm's way. Let me speak to Peach.'

'She's not here. She's in the kitchen, talking to Kuzma.'

'Then how did you make this call if Peach wasn't there to help you?'

She said, 'Mummy, I'm ten. Besides, anyone can make a telephone call. Even Granny Miechen.'

Kira wished to speak to me.

'I don't like Peach any more.'

'Did you misbehave?'

'Definitely not. I've been as good as gold. What's a bloody revolution?'

26

That night wasn't like previous nights. The marchers didn't go home. Many of them stayed on to drink and sing and light fires. It was like a party. But there were some who could never go home because they lay dead in the street. The shots Cuddy Thornhill and I had heard had come from Nevsky Prospekt. Uncle Paul said it wasn't clear which regiment had done the shooting. The Pavlovsky and the Volinsky had both sent out companies but there was a rumour going about that they'd disobeyed the order to shoot, that they'd mutinied and shot their commanding officers instead. But marchers had been killed too. Someone had shot them.

Uncle Paul was very agitated. He said, 'Nicky should be here. He should come home at once and be seen to take charge. Well, perhaps he's on his way. They say he's being kept informed.'

Emperor Nicky wasn't on his way at all. He simply promised to send more troops, men who really were needed at the Front, who might arrive in two days, or two weeks, or never. He also issued an order that the Duma was to cease sitting until further notice.

Brother-in-law Boris dropped in. He was on his way to Betsy Trubetskoy's and thought I might like to go with him. Dinner and cards. But I didn't think it seemed right, to have a party when people were being shot.

'Ducky,' he said, 'those people had due warning. Disperse or face the consequences. So now they know we mean it. Everything'll be back to normal in the morning, you'll see.'

Still, I didn't go with him. Betsy always kept her rooms so dreadfully hot.

I slept fitfully. Every time I woke I got up to look out of the window but there was nothing to see. Glinka Street was deserted. I had in mind to go out to Tsarskoe Selo directly after breakfast, except when morning came there was no breakfast, only tea and jam. All the bakeries were closed. Neither were there any cabs to take me to the station, nor any trains leaving the station. I was cross. It seemed the excitement was all over but I was stuck in town for another day. In the country I could at least have gone for a ride.

But as it turned out, the excitement was far from over. Uncle Paul telephoned to say that under no circumstances should I venture out onto the street. The Petrograd garrison had deserted their post and joined the marchers. The Volinsky regiment had been the first to come out, then the Litovsky and the Izmailovsky.

I remember saying, 'But not the Preobrazhensky.'

'Yes,' he said. 'Even the Preobrazhensky.'

It was unthinkable. It was like the Household Cavalry deserting old Grandma Queen. On Liteiny Prospekt the Law Courts were burning, and so was the prison on Shpalernaya Street.

I said, 'Are there prisoners trapped inside?'

'No,' he said. 'The prisoners are out on the street. They're the ones who put the torch to it.'

It was a day of fires. Some were just street-corner braziers for people to warm themselves. Most were government buildings. Even with the windows closed the smell of scorched paper reached me. Georgie Buchanan said she could see smoke rising from Petrograd side too.

'But the flag's still flying over the Peter Paul Fortress,' she said.

'Sit tight, Ducky. We hear Grand Duke Michael is on his way in from Gatchina. Perhaps he'll take charge in the Tsar's absence.'

I said, 'But where is the Tsar?'

No one seemed to know. And what could Misha do? The people hardly knew him. The Emperor's brother who led an irregular life and was rarely mentioned. Why would anyone listen to him?

Georgie said, 'Of course it may be too late anyway. The city's in uproar. Have you spoken to your husband?'

'He's still in Murmansk, as far as I know.'

'Is he, dear?' she said. 'Shall I ask General Knox if he can send one of those nice English boys round to you, if you're feeling nervous?'

But I wasn't feeling nervous at all. I was cold and hungry and bored. I went down to the kitchen. There was no sign of Anna, nor of the girl who helped her. The only person I could find was Anna's old mother, leaning rather pointlessly against the unlit stove, groaning and nursing a swollen cheek.

'*Zoobnaya bol*,' was all I got out of her. '*Aiee, aiee, zoobnaya bol.*'

Toothache. As to the whereabouts of my kitchen staff, she just waved her hand. She was just one of those unavoidable presences in a Russian household. Whoever you employed, you had better be prepared to take in their mother and their grandmother and their second cousin once removed.

I poked around a little. Kitchens were a mystery to me then. Less so now. Since we've been in Haikko, I've learned to make meatballs and herrings with mashed potato. But that morning all I could find were mysterious items like cornflour and Liebig's Extract of Meat. There were cans of Crosse & Blackwell peas too. My mouth quite watered at that prospect, but I didn't know how to get them out of their tin and no amount of miming got me any help from the old groaner. So I breakfasted on piccalilli and a packet of malted baby rusks that must have been seven years old at the very least. Then I tried to make a call to the Alexander Palace.

In truth, I didn't expect to get through so I had no idea what I was going to say. I just had the strongest feeling that I wanted to make things all right between me and Sunny.

'Ducky!' she said. 'You just caught me. It's such a beautiful morning I'm going out for a little walk. I've been so cooped up.'

I said, 'You must be anxious.'

'I have been,' she said, 'but you know Botkin is an excellent doctor, and of course our Beloved Friend watches over us in spirit. Olga's a little better today, and Botkin thinks Alyosha is over the worst.'

We were quite at cross purposes. Her children had measles and she thought I'd called to see how they were getting on. Nothing was said of shootings or mutinies or burning buildings because Sunny appeared not to know what was going on in town. Well, I wasn't going to be the one to tell her.

'So kind of you to telephone,' she said. 'Is it true you're expecting another happy event?'

I was about to say that I worried about bringing another child into such an unsettled world but then I thought better of it. Her world wasn't unsettled that morning. The sun was shining, her children were recovering and she had reason to hope that Nicky was on his way home from the Stavka.

'We're lucky to have such loving husbands, Ducky,' she said.

Bertie Stopford came by later that morning. He'd brought me a packet of Peek Frean bourbons. Somehow Bertie always managed to obtain things. He always had news too though I sometimes felt he coloured in the gaps in his information with piquant inventions. Just so long as the story held one's attention.

He said the Duma had ignored the Tsar's order to suspend its business and was still sitting.

'And just as well,' he said. 'Because Protopopov's resigned. So that's the last of the Tsar's men gone. The Duma is all that remains. That and the hordes in the street. I wonder if Protopopov will shoot himself? Perhaps not. I think that kind of gesture has gone out of fashion.'

'So the Duma's in charge? They have things under control?'

He said, 'Highness Ducky, I don't think anyone's in control. There are machine guns on the Siniy Bridge but I couldn't work out who had charge of them. There were even women there. Fearsome-looking women.'

So by lunchtime the Duma was all that remained of any kind of authority in Petrograd. The law was what anyone cared to say it was, prisoners were walking free on the streets and still no one quite knew the whereabouts of Emperor Nicky.

Around four o'clock Georgie Buchanan telephoned again, not her usual calm self at all.

'It's gone, Ducky,' she said. 'The Imperial standard has gone. They've pulled it down and now there's a red flag flying over the Peter Paul Fortress. We can see it from here.'

At five I heard a commotion downstairs. Doors banging and a voice saying, 'Lock it and bolt it and bloody well keep it that way.'

I thought it must be Boris come by for the latest news and a drink, but it was Cyril. The Vladimirovichi men all sound the same. He was unshaven and grey with fatigue. He'd been travelling for more than a day without sleep.

'What in heaven's name are you thinking of?'

Those were his first words.

'I rush home, fearing for your safety and I find the street door wide open. You have lights blazing from every window. It looks for all the world like the Yusupovs' on New Year's Eve. And by the way, our doorman is drunk. Dead drunk.'

I said, 'This morning we didn't even have a doorman. Welcome home.'

My resolution had been to push La Karsavina from my mind. To give my husband the benefit of the doubt. Miechen was so often wrong. But his crossness brought everything back. He hadn't even greeted me with a kiss.

27

Whatever other faults he found, Cyril at least thought I'd done the right thing sending the girls out to Tsarskoe Selo while things were so unsettled in town.

I said, 'Bertie Stopford says we're terribly vulnerable out there. All that parkland and forest. If the people really turn against Nicky, the Alexander Palace would be easy to attack. We all would.'

'Stopford!' he said. 'What does that perfumed little jack-o-dandy know about ambushes? No, I'm perfectly satisfied the girls should stay in the country. And you should be with them. It won't be for long. This will soon be over.'

'You mean, like the war?'

'Don't be facetious. These marchers are just caught up in the moment. They'll come to their senses when there's no food to be had.'

'Speaking of which, our own cupboard is rather bare. Perhaps we could eat at Donon's tonight?'

'Yes,' he said, 'good idea,' and promptly fell asleep where he sat. He hadn't even taken off his Fleet overcoat. I sat still as death and let him sleep for an hour or so but the very moment I stood up he was wide awake.

'Donon's, then?' he said. 'I'm surprised they're open. What are they finding to serve these days? Grilled sparrows? Telephone still working?'

It was. First he called the girls. Kira asked him if he'd brought them anything. 'Yes,' he said, 'a bristly chin and a valise full of dirty socks.'

I said, 'I really think Peach will have to go.'

'Not that again,' he said. 'This is hardly the time.'

'Well, she's already reminded me she's a governess, not a nursery maid. And there are times when she's quite insolent. I think she actually sympathises with these people who're blocking the streets. We don't want her filling the girls' heads with silly ideas, do we? Also, she's always chatting to the other servants. Whenever I telephone, Masha says Peach is in the kitchen with Kuzma.'

He said, 'We should be thankful she isn't panicking and demanding to be shipped home to England.'

He also called Boris, who didn't answer, and Uncle Paul, who did. I heard a great deal of sighing. Also the name 'Kerensky'. It was a name I'd heard before though I couldn't place it.

'Well,' he said when he got off the telephone. 'It appears that Nicky's Imperial Cabinet are all hunkered down at the Tauride Palace wetting their breeches. Nicky himself may be on his way back to Petrograd. On the other hand, he may not.'

'Who's Kerensky?'

'Deputy in the Duma. Lawyer. Clever bugger.'

'Do we like him?'

'He's hard to gauge. He speaks very well, very persuasive. I'd say he could carry a meeting. He's in the Trudoviki Party, though anyone less like a toiler one can't imagine. Immaculate fingernails. So whether the unwashed will pay any heed to him remains to be seen.'

'What about Misha?'

'What about him?'

'He was supposed to come to Petrograd this morning, to take

charge of things until Nicky gets back. Uncle Paul said he might even replace Nicky as Emperor.'

'Fiddlesticks!' he said. 'No one's in the mood for a new Emperor. No Emperor at all is what they're talking about. The rule of the people. Kerensky's got Nicky's old ministers in one room and a bunch of mutineers in another. Factory workers, wet nurses, you name it. Convicted forgers too, I shouldn't be surprised. Suddenly everyone thinks they know how to rule Russia. If Kerensky can hold everything together something workable might come of it, but I suspect he's on a sled pulled by two-headed dogs.'

'Where does that leave us?'

'In the long run? Who can say? But presently, it leaves us without dinner. Chvanovsky's might be safer than Donon's though. More discreet. He'll give us a table in the back. But no finery, Ducky, no feathers. You must disguise yourself as a tired old washerwoman.'

I found I could do that without much difficulty.

I'd never been to Chvanovsky's. We took a long way round, along the Catherine Canal and then up a narrow alley that emerged on Kazanskaya Street. Cyril seemed to know exactly where he was going. We were challenged only once, as we crossed Voznesensky Prospekt. A group of men called out to us but they were so full of drink that they seemed not to notice Cyril's comical attempt at sounding like a labourer.

'*Doloy nyemka!*' they shouted. I could follow that much. I'd heard it often enough. 'Down with the German woman.'

And Cyril, to my great astonishment, laughed and bantered with them. They offered him a swig from their bottle but he declined. He said something and they roared and thumped him on the back.

I said, 'Translation, please.'

'Oh, nothing really,' he said.

'They meant Sunny. Down with Sunny. I got that much.'

'Yes.'

'You seemed to be agreeing with them?'

'One rather had to. One must be practical.'

'And what made them laugh so much, when you wouldn't drink from their bottle?'

'Told them I had the pox.'

I said, 'I suppose I should make more of an effort, to learn Russian.'

'Bit late now,' he said. 'Anyway, you'll never go far wrong with English.'

Chvanovsky's was open but there were very few people dining. The maître d' seemed to know Cyril awfully well.

I said, 'I suppose this is where you bring La Karsavina.'

'Ducky,' he said. 'Not that silliness again.'

Perhaps it was silliness. I couldn't be sure. I still can't.

It was a limited menu. We could have an omelette, with onions or without. There was no shortage of wine though. Cyril ordered an Haut-Brion.

'Might as well,' he said. 'I'd hate the rude mechanicals to get their hands on this little beauty.'

He was very quiet, preoccupied.

I said, 'What do you think is going to happen?'

'Impossible to say. It might fizzle out. Pity it's not a bit earlier in the year. A good blizzard would soon clear the streets. But Nicky's handled things very badly. I'm disappointed in him. I can't imagine who he's listening to. Actually, I don't think he's listening to anyone.'

He said he'd be going out to Kronstadt first thing in the morning, to talk to the ratings. Then he'd collect me from Glinka Street and we'd go out to Tsarskoe Selo.

'To see my girls,' he said. 'They're growing up far too fast.'

He hadn't once asked me how I was, even when I didn't finish my omelette.

I said, 'I wonder if we'll get a boy this time.'

'Oh God, Ducky,' he said. 'I'd completely forgotten. Fatigue. Worry. But still, unforgiveable. Utterly. How are you, old thing?'

'Old is right,' I said. 'Otherwise perfectly well.'

He took my hand across the table and a voice said, 'Look at you pair of lovebirds.'

It was brother-in-law Boris. He examined the empty wine bottle.

'Very nice,' he said. 'Shall we order another?'

Cyril said, 'Order what you like. I'm taking my wife home. She needs her rest.'

Boris said, 'Well, don't go along Sadovaya.'

'Trouble?'

'Trouble.'

I asked Boris if he'd heard from Miechen.

'No,' he said. 'Nor do I wish to. We must be thankful she left town. Leave it to Ma, she'll have us all in the first tumbril.'

We walked home very cautiously. On Grazhdanskaya Street there were people singing. The usual. *Vpyeryod, vpyeryod, vpyeryod!* I was getting tired of hearing it.

I said, 'That song. Tell me what the rest of it means.'

Cyril sighed.

'Arise working people. That kind of thing. It's the '*Marseillaise*', you realise, the tune they're singing. They've come up with their own words though.'

'What else, apart from "Arise"?'

'If you must know, they're calling Nicky a vampire. A bloodsucker.'

Later, in the dark, he said, 'Ducky, that thing I did earlier? Agreeing with those street ruffians about Sunny? I didn't mean it of course.

It's just that in dangerous circumstances one must adapt. You do understand?'

I did, of course.

I said, 'As a matter of fact I think Sunny should withdraw. Aunt Ella was right. She should go down to Kiev or somewhere, until things settle down, and there should be an official announcement made, so people know she's not giving orders and appointing ministers when Nicky's away. She's not an asset to Nicky at the moment, whatever he may think.'

'Still,' he said, 'better not to say as much, publicly. Probably best to say nothing at all. Just keep one's counsel and see how things turn out.'

He rose early, to go out to the Kronstadt base. It was Tuesday. Bertie Stopford called by on his daily progress and brought two pieces of news. The Winter Palace was still in the hands of troops loyal to the Tsar. 'Though one shudders to think,' he said, 'what they'll be doing to the furniture.' Also that the windows of the Astoria had been smashed.

'Idiots,' he said. 'A, don't they know the place is occupied entirely by the British and B, all they've achieved is to make a mess. Where is one going to find a glazier in a time like this?'

The city was quiet. There were no trams running on Voznesensky. I spent the morning playing house. Our staff seemed depleted but I couldn't work out quite who was missing. I just rounded up those I could find and we began to cover the furniture with dust sheets. There was no hot water and I didn't care to venture down to the kitchen again for fear of encountering the groaner. I lunched on half a box of rose creams I found in a drawer.

The noise started at about two o'clock. There seemed to be traffic on the move. Car horns were being sounded. It was as though the city was coming back to its proper life. I thought perhaps Emperor Nicky was back in town at last. I called Georgie Buchanan.

She said, 'I'd hoped you were out in the country by now, Ducky. We have vehicles racing up and down the Embankment flying red flags. We have men firing guns in the air. Alf Knox thinks the Winter Palace guard has deserted. Things are really looking rather bad.'

The plan was that when Cyril got back from Kronstadt we'd leave at once for Tsarskoe Selo. At four o'clock I thought I should find out whether any trains were running. The telephone line was dead.

I sat with my coat and hat on for two, three hours. I tried to read but every sound distracted me. For two pins I'd have gone to the British Embassy but then Cyril would have had to come and find me and he'd be cross.

Uncle Paul arrived. It was getting dark.

I said, 'Cyril's not back yet.'

'Ah,' he said. 'Beastly journey, I dare say. Roads impossible.'

He stayed but he wouldn't sit. Every moment he would be out of his chair and pacing about. Then Boris turned up looking ghastly.

'Any news?' he said, and I caught something in Uncle Paul's look.

I said, 'What's wrong? Did something happen?'

'No,' they said, in perfect unison. So then I knew they were keeping something from me.

Boris said, 'It's nothing, honestly, Ducky. They're saying there was a bit of a rumble out at Kronstadt this morning. But Cyril probably wasn't even there when it happened.'

'If indeed anything did occur,' said Uncle Paul. 'There are so many rumours flying about.'

I said, 'Is it true the Winter Palace has fallen?'

'Yes.'

'And what exactly is a bit of a rumble?'

'Discontented murmurings.'

'A few rotten apples in the barrel.'

'Was there a mutiny at Kronstadt?'

'Truly, Ducky, we don't know.'

They insisted on staying with me though I'd have preferred to sit alone and prepare myself for bad news. Uncle Paul kept telling me to stay away from the windows. Boris went downstairs to brave the kitchen and returned very cleverly with a tin of ham *and* an instrument for opening it. A tin opener. I'm now quite an expert.

He said, 'Who's the old groaner?'

'Cook's mother.'

He said, 'She's made considerable inroads into a bottle of rather good brandy. I'd have confiscated it but it had been in her mouth so I thought better not. What's the whisky situation?'

We were making the best of our strange little supper party when Cyril appeared. He looked all in. He'd walked from Finland Station.

Uncle Paul leaped up and fairly hugged him.

Boris said, 'You're a sight for sore eyes.'

I said, 'Is it true there's been a mutiny?'

Cyril just nodded. I poured him a generous measure of whisky. He touched my cheek and mouthed, 'Thank you, darling.'

Uncle Paul gestured towards the door. He said, 'Should we perhaps . . . ?'

He always thought men should talk in studies or libraries. Not in drawing rooms where ladies might overhear. Much as I love him he can be so annoyingly old-fashioned.

Cyril said, 'No need. Ducky's made of strong stuff.'

Boris said, 'So what's the damage?'

'Viren. Butakov. Stronsky. Nipenin.'

He listed those officers he knew for certain were dead. Many,

many names. They'd been taken out to Anchor Square and shot. It was all over by the time Cyril got to Kronstadt but he'd seen their blood on the snow.

After he'd told us, I realised my hands had begun to shake.

I said, 'Why did they spare you?'

Uncle Paul said, 'Because his men love him, that's why.'

Boris said, 'And because he's not an arrogant bastard like some of them.'

Cyril said, 'No. I don't know why. Actually they didn't even threaten me. I think they'd got it out of their system by the time I arrived. But I threw them a sop anyway.'

He hesitated.

Then he said, 'I've promised to break with Nicky. I'm going to the Tauride Palace in the morning, to pledge my allegiance to the Duma.'

Uncle Paul sagged in his chair. Boris made a long, low whistle.

Cyril said, 'I know, I know. But I've been loyal, right up to today. I've been patient, waiting for Nicky to come home and do the right thing, but where is he? No one seems to know. He's probably sitting in that bloody railway car writing love letters to Sunny. Well, I have a wife too, and children to consider. If Nicky has a death wish so be it, but I'm going to do my damnedest to get my family through this.'

My heart was flooded with love for him when he said that. My poor, exhausted husband. He opened his attaché case and brought out a Russian flag.

He said, 'And the first thing I'm going to do . . . Ducky, scissors please.'

And when I'd found scissors, he carefully cut away the blue and white stripes of the tricolour.

'This,' he said, holding up the red strip, 'will be flying from our house before daybreak.'

Uncle Paul said, 'No, not that. Do think, Cyril Vladimirovich. If you do that, there'll be no turning back.'

'Indeed,' Cyril said. 'But there can be no turning back anyway. I know it. You know it. The question is, does Nicky realise it? Has anyone tried to call him?'

I said, 'The telephones aren't working.'

'Of course not,' he said. 'Why would they be? Well, there are plenty of fires burning. Perhaps we could send him a smoke signal. Abandon ship.'

In bed he suddenly began to tremble. He said he was cold but even with my furs piled on top of him the shaking didn't stop until eventually he fell asleep. His men may have spared him from execution but there must have been a moment at Kronstadt when he wondered if he'd be the next to be taken out to die in the snow.

28

Cyril wasn't the only one to go to the Tauride Palace the next morning and surrender himself to the will of the Duma. The Tsar's Cossack cavalry led the way, followed by the Preobrazhensky regiment and the Semenovsky. Then the Marine Guard marched with Cyril at their head. It was all over very quickly. Very civilised, he said. He was shown into the chamber. Kerensky was present and Rodzianko, President of the Dunce and Sunny's old *bête noir*. They gave him a piece of paper to read from and he pledged his allegiance to the Provisional Government.

'So that's that,' he said. 'Scissors again, please, darling.'

He sat and snipped out the Imperial cipher from his epaulettes.

I said, 'Isn't that a bit premature?'

He shrugged.

'Badges are easily replaced,' he said. 'Lives aren't. And I have no intention of getting hanged or shot for the sake of a bit of gold thread. Now we must wait and see what happens. Nicky's only chance will be if he comes back at once and accepts the authority of the Duma. Then I think he'd better take Sunny to a convent, at least until the war's over. A convent with a big, strong gate.'

It felt awfully lonely. No one else in the family had declared their position. Boris had gone to ground. Grand Duke Misha was still out in Gatchina and keeping his opinions to himself. Uncle Paul was agonising. I wasn't exactly frightened, though I did rather wish we didn't have a red flag dangling so provocatively from our roof.

I said, 'Won't it attract attention? What if types come knocking at our door?'

Cyril laughed.

'Types!' he said. 'They may come anyway. And if they decide to hang the lot of us there's not much we can do about it. No harm in appearing to be sympathetic to their cause though. They're already roasting Nicky's eagles. The one over Brocard's door has gone, and Fabergé's and Nicholls' and Plincke's.'

On Nevsky Prospekt they were hauling the Imperial emblems down from shop fronts and tossing them on their bonfires.

Cyril wanted me to go to Tsarskoe Selo to be with the girls. He was going to stay in town until Emperor Nicky returned.

He said, 'Kerensky seems to think he's on his way so I may as well wait and see what happens. Face the music. But I'm sure if we asked Alf Knox he'd find a car to take you home. You must consider your condition, darling.'

I wanted to stay with him but he was right. There was no sense in both of us risking a bullet, either a stray one or a well-aimed one.

He said, 'I don't feel in any immediate danger. I'll tell you what I'm thinking of doing. I might put a sign on our front door that says PROPERTY OF THE PETROGRAD SOVIET. ADMITTANCE STRICTLY BY APPOINTMENT. That might make them pause before they break in looking for Sheraton firewood.'

Alf Knox very kindly sent Lieutenant Gerhardi to drive me. He was a very amusing young man. I'd even say he was flirtatious if it weren't such a ridiculous notion. He was born the same year as Elli. Imagine that. If Elli had lived it might have been her he was flirting with, not her deluded old mother. Except that Ernie Hesse would never have allowed me to bring her to Russia. She'd be back in Darmstadt, married to some cousin or other, and separated from me by this damned war.

The only problem with Willie Gerhardi was his driving. He seemed quite relieved when I suggested I take the wheel and was greatly impressed by my ability to talk and drive and smoke all at the same time.

He's the sort of man that pops up in one's life and then disappears just as suddenly, always on the move, not quite belonging anywhere. He was English by his manner, Prussian by his name, anything but Russian although he was St Petersburg born and bred. The Gerhardis have a house over Vyborg side, on the embankment, and some kind of manufactory. They were the sort of family we never met. Not our kind, as Miechen would say. Sometimes I feel we've missed knowing some perfectly nice people. Perhaps it'll be different from now on. They talk about The New Order. Perhaps we'll be the kind of people *they* never meet.

We drove out past the Ekaterinhof Vokzal, to avoid the city centre, but we were still flagged down at the corner of Moskovsky Prospekt. Two men came to our side window, red rags tied to their bayonets, but they were smiling.

'Britanski!' they greeted us.

'Yes,' I said. 'British Mission. Lieutenant Gerhardi is going to see General Guchkov.'

One of them stuck his head right inside the car. He had bad teeth.

'*Kto?*' he said. 'Keerharty?'

They consulted one another, then a head came back through the open window.

'This Keerharty?'

'Yes.'

'Hero of working peoples?'

Gerhardi leaned across.

242

'My father, actually,' he said.

'Father? You father? *Nepravda!*'

'No, *he* father, I son.'

'Ah! Son!'

The head retracted and a grimy hand replaced it. Gerhardi shook it.

'*Zdrastvuytye! Ochen rad!*'

Another hand appeared. He shook it. Then the message went along the line to the barricade, to clear the way for the son of Keerharty, hero of working peoples, and lady Britanski driver. We were waved through like Royalties. Although, come to think of it, not like Russian Royalties at all, not any more.

Gerhardi was laughing.

I said, 'Is your father really a hero of working peoples?'

'Of course not,' he said. 'He's a factory owner. He's one of those villains who employs people and pays them a wage. No, it was a case of mistaken identity but look, it worked in our favour so let's not quibble.'

'So, who did they think you were?'

'The son of Keir Hardie,' he said. 'Bloody Keir Hardie! Socialist. Land reformist. And who, by the way, is probably dead by now and if not he must be older than Moses. What a hoot. And funnily enough, it's not the first time this has worked to a Gerhardi's advantage. Back during the 1905 troubles my father had a close shave. A mob of workers bound him hand and foot, bundled him in a coal bag and were preparing to drown him when someone asked who he was and they mistook "Gerhardi" for "Keir Hardie", the same as this lot. Upon which, they let him go. And they apologised for putting him in a filthy sack. So I suppose on both occasions we should be grateful to the old Friend of Working Peoples.'

I liked Willie Gerhardi. He was supposed to have become an

accountant or a banker but the war had saved him from that fate. When peace comes, if it ever comes, he has no intention of surrendering to that destiny. He intends to write. Not just books. Scenarios for the cinematograph too. That's the coming thing, apparently, with good money to be made. Who knows, perhaps someday we'll hear of him.

I told him about my ambulance fleet. He told me about working for the British Mission.

'It's a jammy posting, really,' he said. 'Correspondence mainly. Writing reports, deciphering wires and so forth. I'm just grateful to be doing anything that doesn't involve sitting on a horse.'

He had had a brief, unhappy career in the Scots Greys.

I said, 'I suppose the wires you see are terrifically top secret?'

'Not all of them,' he said. 'Quite often they just say things like "Whereabouts flour consignment not clear".'

I said, 'Because, of course, what we're all wondering is, where is the Emperor? But I realise you're not likely to know.'

He said, 'I can tell you what little I do know. He left his HQ yesterday.'

'And he's coming to Petrograd?'

'One imagines.'

'So, he'll probably be here today?'

'Possibly. Except that there's some kind of problem on the line between here and Malaya Vishera so he might have to travel the rest of the way by road. Don't you hate the way we're supposed to call it Petrograd?'

'What kind of problem on the line?'

'Goodness knows. Snow, probably. Or perhaps someone's burned the sleepers to try and get warm. Roll on spring.'

I said, 'My husband thinks another snowfall would clear the streets.'

'Does he?' he said. 'I'm not sure I agree with him. I think people are having too much fun. But anyway, my guess is that the Tsar will try to go to Moscow if he can't get through this way. Or even go back to HQ. He can't just sit on a train that's going nowhere.'

In fact Emperor Nicky did precisely that. As we learned later, it wasn't snow that had blocked the line to Petrograd, it was soldiers with machine guns. Eventually, after a lot of discussion, it was decided to reverse the Imperial train and try to go west, as far as the command post at Pskov. From there the situation was to be reviewed. At Pskov, Nicky was told that even the Preobrazhensky Guard had deserted him. He also found out what Cyril had done.

I asked Gerhardi in for a cup of tea but vehicles were precious. He had to get the car back to the city as soon as possible. Masha and Kira watched him get behind the wheel and go juddering off down Sadovaya Street.

Kira said, 'I don't think that man knows how to drive.'

It was strange to be home, to hear birdsong instead of gunfire and smell hot food instead of scorching wood. Peach greeted me civilly. Had she shown the slightest hint of disrespect, I'd have sent her packing at once, trains or no trains, but she made no reference to the events in town. I even began to wonder if she was aware of them. She sent the girls to fetch their copybooks, to show me what they'd been doing.

She said, 'I'll take some of the time I'm owed tomorrow.'

She said she'd missed at least three of her half-days, two when I had morning sickness and the one she'd been obliged to work when I stayed in Petrograd, contrary to our arrangement.

I said, 'Well, you may take a half-day but you know circumstances have been very difficult. We're all having to make sacrifices.

And if you were hoping to go into the city, I think you'll be disappointed. There'll be very few trains until things settle down.'

'Oh,' she said, 'so you think things will settle down?'

I said, 'Mr Kerensky seems to be getting things under control. The city's already less tense. All we need now is for His Imperial Majesty to come. He's on his way. There are likely to be some changes, of course, but then life will get back to normal.'

'Do you think so?' she said. But she wasn't really asking me. She was challenging me.

It was bitterly cold. Fifteen degrees below, at least, Cyril said. He came home that night, very late, but the girls heard his voice and came running down to see him. I must say they never greet me so eagerly. He found them peppermints from his pocket and made them each a little bird out of notepaper. It was another hour before Peach got them settled again and Cyril and I could talk.

I had Sunny to thank for his coming home for the night. Minister Rodzianko was concerned for her safety so Cyril had been told to bring out a battalion of Marines to guard the Alexander Palace. A squadron of Cossacks was camped there too and a battery of foot artillery with field guns. Cyril had seen Sunny, briefly. She'd come out to thank the guards. He said she looked strained but had put on her best imperturbable Empress face.

'Asked if my men had everything they needed. Said she was very heartened to see us. Much comforted by our presence, etc. Very pleasant to me, actually. She clearly hasn't heard that I've jumped ship.'

'Is she really in danger, do you think?'

'Yes, I do. And I think Nicky has finally realised it. He's stuck in Pskov but he wired Rodzianko and said he understands the need to work with the Duma on certain concessions and will give the matter his attention when he gets back to Petrograd.'

'And what did Rodzianko say?'

'Too late.'

'Is it?'

'I'm afraid it is. The Duma and this self-appointed Soviet, they differ on a hundred and one points. They'll probably argue over where the sun rises. But if there's one thing they agree on it's that Nicky is finished. He has to go.'

'And how will that happen?'

'That's up to Nicky. He can go voluntarily. He should. He should go at once. Or he can wait to be removed. Knowing Nicky, he'll hesitate and hesitate until he feels the country's boot on his rear end.'

'What does "removed" mean?'

'I don't know. Siberia. Sandringham.'

29

Here is what happened next. Grand Duke Misha, Uncle Paul, Grand Duke Nikolasha, Uncle Bimbo, one by one, they stepped forward, spoke up and conceded that Nicky's opportunity to save his throne had passed. He must abdicate. Uncle Sandro disagreed.

'He should bring in more troops,' he said. 'Three hundred Romanov years down the drain just because of the price of bread? Just because of a few troublemakers? Nicky should stop wavering and remind Russia he's its anointed Emperor. He should give these revolutionaries a taste of cold steel.'

Uncle Sandro was in a minority of one. By the time the Imperial train reached Pskov, Nicky's abdication was unavoidable but his Chief of Staff had insisted that the news be kept from him until he'd had a night's rest. Nicky would have drunk to that. He was famous for leaving urgent telegrams unopened.

But I wonder if he did sleep? Could he possibly have believed that by morning the crisis would be over and we could all go back to our old lives? I asked Cyril who'd be the one to tell Nicky.

'Probably draw straws for it,' he said. 'Damned glad I'm not there. Nicky's been a fool, but still, one never likes to see a man broken.'

General Ruzsky was handed the cup of poison to deliver to his Emperor. He had telegrams from the generals at the Stavka and in the Caucasus. He had telegrams from the admirals in the Black Sea and the Baltic. Every one of them said Nicky must go.

They say he caved in very quickly. Just a few minutes of silence, one cigarette, and then he signed a declaration they put before him. He renounced the throne in favour of Tsesarevich Alexis. But of course it was so much nonsense. Alyosha couldn't reign, even if Russia were willing to accept another Emperor. Twelve years old and plagued with the bleeding disease.

As the day wore on, Nicky began anyway to regret what he'd done. Not the abdication, but the naming of Alyosha as his successor. He'd imagined that the whole family would be permitted to retire, perhaps down to the Crimea, until the boy came of age but then it dawned on him that it was very unlikely. Or perhaps General Ruzsky was sent in with more bad news. How could Nicky possibly be allowed to remain in Russia? What if he began campaigning to regain the throne? No, he'd have to leave the country, and the Tsesarevich would have to stay, perhaps with his Uncle Misha acting as his guardian and regent. Who could say when Nicky and Sunny would ever see their son again?

So then a new declaration was drafted, an abdication in favour of Grand Duke Misha. Nicky signed it and they varnished over his signature at once, to prevent any further change of heart. He signed letters too, his last act as Emperor. Uncle Nikolasha was reappointed as Commander-in-Chief and Prince Georgy Lvov was named as First Minister of a new Provisional Government.

So now I must cease referring to Nicky as Emperor. I don't know what we're supposed to call him. Cyril suggests 'Nikolai Alexandrovich' should be perfectly acceptable to everyone.

We heard gunfire during Thursday night. Just warning shots, according to Kuzma who went out to investigate. A crowd had broken into Velinsky's wine shop on Tserkovaya Street and gone mad with drink. There were casualties. Hundreds, some claimed, martyrs, driven to a moment's madness by hunger and desperation and shot down by troops still loyal to the Empress. Or was it more like half a dozen, who'd fallen into a deep, drunken sleep and died of the cold. It all depended on who you listened to. Everything depended on who you listened to.

That was the morning when confirmation of Nicky's abdication came to Petrograd. Uncle Paul went to the Alexander Palace to break the news to Sunny. In fact the news got there ahead of him, from servants who'd come in from town, but Sunny had disregarded it. She thought it was just another wild rumour.

Uncle Paul told us how it had gone.

'Anna Vyrubova was there,' he said. 'And Nastinka Hendrikova and Dr Botkin, I took the precaution of asking him to attend. I thought it very likely Sunny would faint. But she held herself together. No tears, no vapours, at least not in front of me. She conducted herself like an Empress, even if she's not one any more. If anything I'd say she was angry. Not with Nicky. With Russia.'

The papers with Nicky's signature were taken to the Tauride Palace, but it was several days before Nicky himself arrived. He was permitted to go to the Stavka first, to say farewell to the troops. I was about to write 'his troops' but of course they're not his any more. Everything belongs to The People now.

Cyril said, 'Stupid idea if you ask me, allowing him to go to HQ. Why draw out the agony with farewell speeches? And what if he tries appealing to the troops? What if he tries pulling on their heart strings and they start shouting "Long live the Tsar"? Then we could have a real mess on our hands.'

But Nicky did no such thing. He was well and truly finished. Cyril went into town as soon as the abdication was certain. He wanted to be there when Grand Duke Misha, Tsar Michael as we now thought, drove in from Gatchina. I asked him if he was going to pledge his allegiance to Misha.

'That rather depends,' he said. 'I don't think my allegiance will be the first thing on Misha's mind. There goes his nice quiet life. And anyway it's not entirely clear that Nicky had the right to hand him the succession. The lawyers will make a meal of that and you can see their point. Alexis was the heir. He still is, in a sense. If Nicky is allowed to pass the throne to anyone else, it makes a complete nonsense of the rules of succession. He could have passed the crown to his kennel man.'

I said, 'Or to you.'

'Please don't say that,' he said. 'It's going to be hard enough preventing Ma from scheming.'

I wanted to go with Cyril to Glinka Street but he insisted I stay in the country with the girls.

He said, 'We don't know how things are going to unfold. They may change very rapidly now, for better or for worse.'

But for two days it was almost as though nothing had happened. No bells were rung for Tsar Misha, no cannons were fired. Was he the new Emperor or was he not? There was a long meeting at the Tauride Palace. Kerensky was there, and Rodzianko, and at the end of the day there was still no clear decision. Misha hadn't claimed the throne but he hadn't declined it either. All he'd say was that it was up to the Provisional Government and the people to decide. Did they want him or did they not? Then he went home, or rather was sent home, with orders to go to Gatchina and stay put.

Cyril said, 'That's the Soviet's doing. They won't trust any Romanov. The Duma would probably have suggested that Misha go to the Front, to make a little speech of encouragement to the

251

troops. We are still at war after all. But this Soviet, they want him where they can control him.'

So we still had no Emperor. On Sunday morning I went to Divine Liturgy at Our Lady of the Sign. There was no prayer for Nicky and the Imperial Family, but there was no prayer for Misha either. There was just an awkward pause before the priest continued with the bit about seasonable weather and an abundance of the fruits of the earth.

Boris said, 'We must be thankful the telephones aren't working. Ma's no doubt in a spin, planning what to wear to Cyril's coronation.'

I feared he was right, but I did miss Miechen. Life seemed terribly dull without her and information was so much harder to get. If she'd been stuck out at Tsarskoe Selo, Bertie Stopford would have battled through all obstacles to bring her the latest news, but his attentions to me only extended as far as Glinka Street.

Everything I did hear was old news by the time it reached me. A letter came from Miechen. Dowager Empress Minnie had travelled to the Stavka to be with Nicky in his hour of humiliation.

Dearest, dearest Ducky, Miechen wrote, *we may see you Empress yet. Poor Minnie is destroyed of course. She blames Sunny entirely for what has happened, though I don't agree and I've told her so. An Emperor cannot hide behind his wife's skirts. But of course Minnie will never hear a word of criticism of her darling boy. I truly think this may kill her.*

It didn't. As far as we know Dowager Minnie is with us yet. She's a tough old bird.

Uncle Paul advised me to burn Miechen's letter at once. Brother-in-law Boris said stable doors and bolting horses came to mind. We were probably all being watched and listened to and spied on from dawn till dusk. A silly letter from Miechen was neither here nor there.

A new week began. On Monday nothing happened. I mean nothing. When an Emperor has been toppled, one rather expects thunderbolts to strike or the birds to behave in some odd way that makes old country folk run about crossing themselves. But nothing. On Tuesday some of the news sheets revived the rumour that Grigory Rasputin had been Sunny's lover.

Boris said, 'That's the press for you. When there's no news, rake up some old tittle-tattle.'

On Wednesday he and Uncle Sandro left for the Stavka. They were to be allowed to accompany Nicky back to Petrograd.

I said, 'Allowed? Why would you not be allowed? You're family.'

Boris said, 'Yes, but Nicky's still regarded as a bit of a hot potato. What if he's got a plan? Of course anyone who really knows Nicky knows the idea is laughable, but the Duma are taking no chances. They're sending their own escort too. They want to make sure he gets back safely and without incident.'

It all sounded rather heavy-handed to me.

Boris said, 'Not really. We're not bringing him back in chains, Ducky. Not actual chains.'

Cyril would not be in the escort party.

Boris said, 'Wouldn't be quite the thing, would it? Nicky knows Cyril was the first to abandon him. And, strictly speaking, Cyril's next in line, if Misha doesn't take the throne. It could make for a very long train ride if we had Cyril along. What would one talk about? It's going to be pretty hateful as it is.'

On Thursday Nicky began his journey home, but not to Petrograd. They brought him through Minsk and Vitebsk and then directly to Tsarskoe Selo. It was a long, circuitous journey but it saved the awkwardness of his arriving at the Baltic Station. What exactly is the protocol for greeting a former Emperor? And, as Cyril says, that way Nicky was at least spared the sight of the city streets.

The bill posters and the broken windows and the armoured cars parading red flags. Even the changes at Tsarskoe Selo must have given him a shock. There were soldiers all over the park and extra sentries at the Alexander Palace gates.

It was late on Friday morning when Nicky's train arrived. Cyril was in town, at meetings, but I had Uncle Bimbo for company. He'd grown tired of waiting to be released from his country exile and decided to come back anyway.

He said, 'Not much Sunny can do to me now, and I need to keep an eye on my hothouses. I hear these revolutionaries enjoy smashing glass. The needs of lemon trees are probably quite lost on them. I hope to educate them.'

My mind was on Nicky and Sunny. I felt I should go and see them at some point, much as one might call on a house in mourning. I should at least ask after Alyosha and the girls. I should at least enquire if there was anything they needed. Uncle Bimbo said better not to.

'Condolences on losing your Empire? Might sound a bit hollow, don't you think, Ducky? Particularly seeing that Cyril was the one who led the way? First rat off the ship?'

'Is that what you think? That Cyril behaved like a rat?'

'No, but I imagine it's Nicky's opinion. Anyway, I very much doubt you'd be able to visit them. When people are under house arrest, there are bound to be restrictions.'

House arrest. I had no idea what it might entail. Uncle Bimbo said they'd probably be permitted to walk in the garden. But they wouldn't be allowed any horses, or access to Nicky's motors.

'In case they try to make a dash for it, do you see?'

I said, 'Sunny won't mind so much. She never went anywhere even when she could. How long do you think they'll be kept like that?'

'Until there's a suitable transport, I imagine. There's a rumour the British are sending a cruiser to pick them up from Murmansk. There's also a rumour that they'll be evacuated through Vladivostock. Across to San Francisco and then, well, who knows where? But you can't depend on anything you're told these days.'

The last we heard, the whole family was being moved east so perhaps the Vladivostock rumour was true. But that was months ago. Perhaps they're already in America. That would be rather thrilling for their girls. Plenty of handsome husbands to be found there, I'm sure. And they'll still be able to style themselves Grand Duchess. The Americans like that kind of thing, in foreigners.

Uncle Paul went to the station, to be there when Nicky's train steamed in.

'Grey-faced,' he said. 'An old man. What is he? Not even fifty. He looks more like seventy.'

Nicky had been driven directly to the Alexander Palace. One of his adjutants, Valya Dolgoruky, was allowed to ride with him, and Uncle Paul too, as a courtesy. Boris and Uncle Sandro had stayed on the train until the sad procession had left.

Uncle Paul said, 'Can't say I blame them. It was a difficult moment and they'd already had the torture of the train journey. I shed a quiet tear when Nicky stepped down onto the platform, and so did Dolgoruky. Not Nicky though. He was dry-eyed. It was as though he were sleep-walking.'

They'd driven to the Alexander Palace in silence. When they reached the gates they'd been challenged by the sentry.

'So unnecessary,' Uncle Paul said. 'It was pure theatre. They just wanted to make Nicky identify himself. Humiliate him.'

'What name did he use?'

'Nikolai Alexandrovich Romanov. Then they made a great show of opening the gates as slowly as possible and glaring into

255

the car. You should see the state of those soldiers. Boots not polished, slouching at their posts, smoking on duty. Sunny came down to the door to meet him and they didn't even remove their caps. Disgraceful. I'd have said something but I didn't want to upset Nicky. He was so calm. In a world of his own. I don't think he even noticed that no one had saluted him.'

One might have thought Nicky would be left in peace for a few days, to rest with Sunny and the children after his ordeal, but apparently Kerensky arrived before they'd even finished luncheon. He just turned up with the officer who was to be in charge of their confinement. Colonel Korovichenko.

'A decent sort, from what I hear,' Uncle Paul said. 'Never met him myself.'

But Minister Kerensky and Colonel Korovichenko hadn't come for tea and introductions. Kerensky ordered a thorough search of the Alexander Palace before his man took over. A clean sweep with a new broom. Genya Botkin witnessed the whole thing. He told Uncle Bimbo about it.

'It was all a game,' Bimbo said. 'Everything's a game. Kerensky just wants to drive home the point that he's in charge now. I'm sure we all understand that. There was no need to march about opening cupboards. Certainly no need to disturb the Grand Duchesses when they're still recuperating.'

'What were they searching for?'

'Nothing. Anything. A tin of dentifrice with the Imperial crest on it. Who can say what goes through the minds of these idiots? And then there's that fool Vyrubova.'

Kerensky's men had caught Anna Vyrubova trying to burn papers.

Uncle Bimbo said, 'What was she thinking? If you have anything to hide, you get rid of it before Kerensky arrives. You don't start a fire when there's a search party in the house.'

Vyrubova had been arrested.

'Of course. She was just what Kerensky needed. Someone to make an example of in front of Nicky and Sunny.'

'But she's an invalid.'

'Oh, yes, she tried playing that card. She showed Kerensky her merlin chair. Kerensky asked Botkin for his clinical opinion. Poor Botkin. Can you imagine? Caught between a sobbing Vyrubova and Minister Kerensky.'

'What did Botkin say?'

'He perched on the fence to the best of his ability. He said that though Vyrubova was incapacitated by certain injuries, her life was in no immediate danger. So she was handed her crutches and driven away.'

'Where have they taken her?'

'To the Peter Paul Fortress presumably. The poor creature. That's a place that can destroy the strongest of constitutions. Maybe Cyril will be able to put in a word for her. If he deems it wise. He seems to be the Romanov flavour *du jour*.'

That was the family's latest opinion of Cyril. He'd taken a huge risk, but it appeared to have paid off. He'd be part of the New Order. He'd make sure the Romanovs were treated decently. Good old Cyril.

Tsarskoe Selo was usually quiet after dark, but not that night. Vehicles came and went and there were lights moving about in the park. I couldn't sleep and when I went downstairs for hot milk, Kuzma was just coming in, breath steaming in the cold air, eyes shining with excitement.

'*Magheela*,' he said, pretending to shovel. '*Magheela dyavola*.' The devil's grave.

A crowd had gathered, soldiers mainly, from an artillery battery, some students and a few workers from the estate. They were digging up Grigory Rasputin's body. Kuzma swore he'd had no part in it, but he hadn't tried to stop them either. He said they couldn't be stopped.

Why were they doing it? Did they think Rasputin might be about to rise from the dead to help Sunny and Nicky in their hour of need? And what were they going to do with his body? He'd been more than two months in the ground.

'*Dalyeko*,' Kuzma said. '*Ochen dalyeko. V Sibir, mozhet bit'*.'

They intended to take it far, far away, perhaps to Siberia. It seemed not to have occurred to them that distances don't mean anything to spirits and miracle-workers. Wasn't Rasputin supposed to have saved Alyosha's life when he was a thousand miles away?

Cyril heard a similar story about the grave diggers, but his version ended just beyond Vyborg, hardly any distance at all from Tsarskoe Selo and certainly not in Siberia.

'Bunch of idiots,' he said. 'Trying to transport a casket in the middle of the night. They ran into a road block, as they should have known they would. You can't go anywhere nowadays without answering to a crowd of jumped-up citizens with bayonets.'

'And then what?'

'They were made to open the box of course, to show they weren't making off with a coffin full of State treasures. Everything belongs to the State now, you know? Every teaspoon. I'd love to have seen their faces when they prised the lid off. No Imperial teaspoons. Just decomposing flesh. It must have been vile. From what I can gather, they all got into a complete flap and decided they'd better burn the body. More stupidity. Bodies aren't like autumn leaves. They don't just burn. It can take days. Further flapping. Can't you just see it? Pour on more gasoline! They ended up taking what was left of the body to the Polytechnic. It was the nearest place with a proper furnace. So Sunny's Beloved Friend is now reduced to bones and lard or he lives on in spirit, preparing to put Nicky back on the throne. Make what you will of it. I just hope the boilerman at the Polytechnic doesn't go into business selling relics.'

March, April. Cyril said things were quiet in town. The tram wires hadn't been repaired and weren't likely to be any day soon, but there were plenty of sleds to be hired or commandeered. We, or rather Cyril, even had a permit to use a motor, if he could find any fuel to put in its tank. Some bread shops had reopened. The Imperial family, the former Imperial family, were confined to quarters but the world hadn't stopped turning. Russia had a Government, of a patchwork kind. Also we still had a war to fight. Nearly three years on and it seemed no closer to ending.

I said, 'Are we over the worst?'

'At the Front?' Cyril said. 'I don't know. But here, yes, I'd like to think so.'

'But Misha won't be Emperor?'

'No.'

'And they won't ask you?'

'No. I'd say Russia's done with Emperors, for the time being. Maybe someday. People do enjoy a figurehead. Someone to pop up on certain occasions. Smile, wave, give the Crown Jewels an airing. Like Georgie and May. Otherwise to stay quietly in the country and mind one's pheasant shoots.'

'And you think we're safe. They won't be chopping off any heads?'

He said, 'This is Russia, darling. Russians can be very excitable one minute and then fall back into their old stupor. At the moment they're still like children on Christmas Eve. But I made a

259

pledge to this new government and I want to try and see it through. However, a little precautionary planning wouldn't go amiss. A little discreet packing.'

It was the first time he'd spoken of leaving, and just when it seemed things might be settling down.

I said, 'Where would we go? Not to Vladivostock with Nicky and Sunny? I couldn't bear it.'

He went to the drawing-room door, looked outside, then closed it firmly before he spoke. Rather melodramatic, I thought.

I said, 'Are we being listened to?'

'Listened to and watched,' he said. 'That journal you keep?'

'I hardly ever open it. There's really nothing in it.'

'Good. Get rid of it anyway. Also letters. Burn them, particularly any from my mother.'

I said, 'Is this Diamonds Sewn into Drawers time?'

Then I received a scolding.

He said, 'You're bloody flippant, Ducky. I hope your sense of humour won't desert you if things go badly. I hope you understand I'm walking on a high wire.'

30

Holy Week began. Any other year Sunny would have gone to services in the Fyodorovsky Cathedral every single day, but Sunny wasn't allowed to go even that short distance. The priest Afanasy went to the Alexander Palace instead. He took a deacon with him and some singers from the choir, but he was prevented from hearing confessions privately. We had it from Uncle Paul who had it from the adjutant, Dolgoruky.

'No private conversations permitted, even with God,' he said.

Uncle Bimbo had a good question. When the litanies were said, when it was customary to pray for the Sovereign Emperor and his family, what did Father Afanasy do? Stumbled, according to Uncle Paul. And then recovered himself and prayed for the Provisional Government.

Uncle Bimbo said, 'Well that makes sense. America has recognised it and the Allies have recognised it so God may as well fall into line.'

On Holy Thursday Minister Kerensky went back to the Alexander Palace to deliver a new blow. Sunny was to be 'investigated'.

What did it mean? Had she been charged with a crime? Was she on trial? Uncle Bimbo said it meant whatever the Provisional Government decided it meant. It was about her relationship with

Grigory Rasputin, and her decisions and actions, the appointments she'd made while Nicky was away at the Stavka. Also the unavoidable fact of her German birth. Her loyalty to Russia was to be examined. And until such time as the Court of Enquiry cleared her name she was to be separated from Nicky and the children.

I said, 'She may have been born in Germany but she's only half German. I was born in Malta. Does that make me Maltese?'

Uncle Bimbo said, 'Dear one, whatever they may say it's not really about Sunny's German blood. It's about her undue influence. And her Friend, of course. Shot, buried, incinerated and still he comes back to cause trouble.'

Uncle Paul said, 'That may be so but according to Dolgoruky something rather surprising happened. Nicky actually stood up to Kerensky. He said it was inhumane to talk of separating a mother from her children, especially when they were still weak from the measles. He said if there were to be any separation at all, he must be the one kept in isolation. Dolgoruky says he'd never seen Nicky so resolute. It seemed to catch Kerensky off his guard. He apparently didn't say anything for a few minutes. And then he agreed, just like that. Ignored whatever was written on his sheet of paper. Well, I dare say he'd written it anyway. But the main thing is, he backed down and agreed to do things Nicky's way. Does he have children of his own, do we know? I think perhaps he does. The human face of Kerensky.'

It was worth knowing.

There was no *kulich* baked in our house this year. We were short of flour. But on Holy Saturday the thaw began and three of our hens celebrated by laying. Masha rightly decreed that there was no point wasting eggs making a *paskha* if we had no *kulich* to spread it on, so the eggs were hard-boiled and their shells painted.

It was mild enough to open the windows. I had the strongest

urge to ride across the park, no hat, no gloves, no bulky coat, to see what flowers were peeping through. I thought I might even spot Nicky out with his dogs. It would have been nice to give him an encouraging wave. The Imperials, the ex-Imperials, were often on my mind since they'd been placed under house arrest. I sent word down to the stables for Fox to be saddled, just for a gentle hack. Then I felt the baby move.

After three children one recognises at once that first strange little flicker of life, like the popping of a bubble. It stopped me in my tracks. I'd hardly thought about this new child, with all the other things going on around us. Now I calculate it, my morning sickness disappeared the day Cyril insisted on flying that revolutionary rag from our roof. So that morning, Holy Saturday, with the drip of melting snow and the smell of spring, I was rather shocked to realise it was less than five months until this child would be born. I didn't ride.

I heard Kira wailing. Masha came to me, very solemn.

She said, 'Kira asked if we could take an egg to Tsesarevich Alyosha and Peach said we're not to call him the Tsesarevich any more. She said he's in prison and not allowed presents.'

'And that's why Kira is crying?'

'No, because she called Peach a fibber and Peach slapped her leg.'

I dealt with Kira first. I said it was true that Alyosha was no longer Tsesarevich. That Emperor Uncle Nicky had decided it was too big a name for a young boy so we should just call him Alexis Nikolaevich from now on. But he certainly wasn't in prison. Peach must have misunderstood.

The idea that Peach had been wrong seemed to cheer her up.

She said, 'So we can take him an egg.'

I said, 'No, I don't think we can. I believe he's still in quarantine.'

'Because of the weasels?'

'Yes.'

'But an Easter egg might make him feel better.'

'It's very kind of you. I didn't realise you liked Alyosha so much.'

'I don't. He's rather babyish for twelve. But Granny Miechen says either Masha or I had better marry him and Masha says she absolutely won't.'

I found Peach in the schoolroom. She was quite unrepentant.

I said, 'Masha and Kira don't need to know about the new arrangements at the Alexander Palace. Now we'll be having nightmares about dungeons.'

She said, 'Children should be told the truth.'

I said, 'Not always. And the Emperor's children aren't in prison.'

'Aren't they?' she said. 'Are they free to walk down to the Great Pond this lovely sunny morning? Can they go to Fyodorovsky Cathedral for Easter night? And anyway, they're not the Emperor's children. Russia's finished with all that.'

She just stood, four-square, and looked at me.

I said, 'Perhaps you'd better leave us, after all. I've thought so for some time.'

'Yes,' she said. 'So have I.'

I quite expected her to turn on her heel and go to pack her bags, but she stood with her arms folded, so self-assured. I should have summoned her to my drawing room. She wouldn't have been so insolent on my territory. But there we stood.

I asked her where she'd go.

'Me?' she said. 'Oh, never worry about me. I'm quite accustomed to changing circumstances. I've never been afraid to move on. More to the point, where do you think you'll go?'

I told Masha Peach would be leaving us.

I said, 'I need you to be brave.'

'Why?' she said. 'I don't need a governess. I'd rather go to the Smolny Institute. So would Kira.'

Kira certainly wasn't sad to see Peach go.

'Good,' she said. 'Is it because she fibbed about Alyosha? Or is it because of what she did with Kuzma?'

And Masha said, 'Shut up, squirt.'

Kira said, 'I don't see why I should shut up. I'll bet Mummy will be jolly glad if I tell her Peach and Kuzma have tickle fights. Because Kuzma's just a doorman. He shouldn't even come upstairs.'

Masha blushed and ran from the room. Poor child. Peach and Kuzma having tickle fights. Life is never the same after one has witnessed something like that. I remember the day Missy and I saw Uncle Bertie Wales playing jiggety-jig with a maid at Balmoral. One felt terribly ashamed even though Uncle Bertie was the one with his breeches unbuttoned. Missy said we must never tell anyone what we'd seen because no one would ever believe us and we'd get sent to bed without any supper. So we knew we'd seen something forbidden, even though we didn't quite know what. We avoided going past that linen cupboard for several days, and then a terrible itch of curiosity got the better of us and we tiptoed down the corridor again. But we never got a repeat performance. I imagine Uncle Bertie found all kinds of private places for jiggety-jig.

By the children's tea time, Peach was gone. She asked for wages she was owed, as though one could put one's hand on money so readily. I gave her what I had and she counted it in front of me. So vulgar. She didn't ask to say goodbye to the girls and just as well because I'm sure they would have refused.

I said, 'You understand I can't give you a character?'

'Oh, quite so,' she said. 'But it doesn't matter. A testimonial with a Romanov name on it wouldn't be worth anything anyway.'

Kuzma took her trunks on a hand cart, to the station I assumed. I watched them go. The street was a mess of mud and melting snow. Peach tied her skirt above her ankles and went striding off like some peasant woman. I think Russia rather went to her head.

Cyril came home for dinner.

He said, 'I gather we lost our doorman.'

I said, 'No, just a governess. I dismissed Peach. Kuzma's putting her on a train to Petrograd. Heaven knows what she thinks she's going to do there.'

'Darling,' he said, 'wherever Peach has gone, Kuzma's gone with her. Serafim has appointed himself our new *shveytsar* and he says he has a sister, very clean, knows how to read, if we're looking for a new nanny. Talk about jumping into a dead man's shoes!'

We accepted Serafim. One must have a doorman. As to replacing Peach, we decided not to decide, with the baby not due till the end of August. I thought if the war was over by then I might try another Norland, if only to keep Miechen happy.

Cyril said, 'Ah, yes, Miechen. You've just reminded me, I saw Stopford today. He's thinking of going to Kiev, to see how Ma's getting on. He wondered about suggesting to her that she head south. Perhaps take a water cure. It's a first-rate idea. Anything to keep her out of Petrograd while the Emperor question is unresolved. Good sort, Stopford. Useful.'

I said, 'You mean he's not such a perfumed little jack-o-dandy after all?'

I told Cyril what Peach had said as her parting shot. That a testimonial with a Romanov name on it would worthless.

'She might be right,' he said. 'There are those who'd like to see the whole lot of us shunted off to England. But you know Nikolasha's still quite respected and Uncle Paul's not entirely despised. On the whole I think we'll survive. The main thing is for Nicky and Sunny to make a quiet exit, and as soon as possible. Damned cheeky of Peach to take Kuzma with her though. What can she want with him? The man's barely educated.'

Cyril woke Masha and Kira to take them to the midnight vigil. I went to bed but I was still awake when they came home with their stumps of candle and their Easter kisses. I wish now I'd gone with them. I wonder if we'll ever see another Paskha in Russia.

Cyril and I talked till it was almost light.

'All things considered,' he said, 'I think perhaps we should move the girls back to Glinka Street. Kuzma deserting us. Bit of a shocker. I thought he could be relied on. It makes one wonder who might go next. Glinka Street will be easier to defend. I have Marine guards I can depend on. But out here, all this parkland, it's impossible to patrol.'

'Bertie Stopford's opinion.'

'Not that I think anything is going to happen. Not at all. It's just a sensible precaution, you understand?'

I told him what Kira had blurted out about Peach and Kuzma.

'Aha!' he said. 'So that's it. Funny age in women, the forties.'

'Funny?'

'Some go off the boil entirely. Some experience a surge. And you must agree, Peach was never your average governess. The way she threw herself into Russian-ness, for instance. Odd, but quite refreshing. And now I think of it she has had a certain look about her recently. The buttered bun. The late-in-the-day but neverthe-less lavishly buttered bun. Well, good luck to her. I suppose. It's still bloody annoying about Kuzma though.'

I said, 'And what about her revolutionary sentiments?'

'Revolutionary sentiments!' he said. 'A few days on cold *kasha* will cure her of those. No, the more I think of it, the more Kuzma is my concern. He knows every door and window of this house. Took a set of keys too, I shouldn't be surprised. Well, if his Red friends decide they want a Romanov sacrificed it's not going to be one from this household. We'll all shift to town as soon as possible. We'll take Nanya with us, and Serafim.'

'But we have Mefody on the door at Glinka Street.'

'Mefody's an old sot. He's asleep half the time. One of these days he won't wake up. Serafim can prepare to take over from him.'

So it was all settled.

I said, '*Christos voskrese*, dearest.'

He said, 'Now *you're* going all Russian on us! *Voistinoo voskrese*, darling! Christ is risen indeed! Absolutely.'

31

We were to leave Tsarskoe Selo without fuss and without great quantities of luggage.

Cyril said, 'If people ask, you're just going to town for a week or two. Nothing out of the ordinary.'

But everything I did felt like a true leave-taking. I walked across to the Catherine Palace hospital to find Tanya Botkin. She was working there as a nursing aide.

'I'm not surprised,' she said. 'But I'm so sad to say goodbye to you. You've been a kind neighbour.'

I said, 'It's not goodbye. It's just for a few weeks. Ethel Peach left us so we're sending Kira to the Annenschule. Once she's settled in I'm sure we'll be back.'

'Well,' she said, 'the thing is I'm not likely to be here much longer. When Their Majesties get away to England, Daddy plans to go with them. You know how the Empress depends on him. So my brother and I will go too. We have to stay together.'

She asked me what England is like.

I said, 'I'm no expert. I only lived there for a few years, and I was a child. All I remember are the horses we had there, and our lovely garden. You'll certainly find it calmer than here. The English don't go in much for revolutions. They did have one, but it never caught on.'

'Well,' she said, 'now it's been decided, I just wish they'd hurry up and send for us.'

Uncle Paul was my next stop. He promised, if anything should happen, if it should turn out that we didn't come back to Tsarskoe Selo, that he'd take Masha and Kira's ponies for his girls. Also my hunter.

He said, 'Are you closing the house completely? Permanently?'

I said, 'I'm supposed to say no.'

'Understood,' he said. 'But what about Cyril's little dog?'

There had been so much to think about Cyril and I hadn't discussed what should be done with Krot. We could hardly take him to Glinka Street. His sole mission in life was to dig and chew. Uncle Paul said he'd take him.

'Good little ratter, I imagine. I'll tell Olga I'm borrowing him, to deal with our vermin. But if you happen to see her before you go, please don't tell her you're leaving. She's jittery enough.'

I said, 'You don't plan on going?'

'Not yet,' he said. 'I feel I should stay and see Nicky and Sunny safely on their way. Olga does understand that. I wanted to send her and the children down to Kiev but she refuses to go anywhere without me.'

I went for a walk that last morning, by the Ponds, past the Catherine Palace and back along Dvortsovaya. It was so mild I only wore a short jacket and a headscarf. That scarf was my passport. I tied it Russian-style and no one gave me a second look. There was quite a crowd pressed against the Alexander Palace gates, some guards, some estate workers, shouting and laughing. I stopped to see what was amusing them. It was just the Imperial Family taking the air, going round and round their small permitted circuit. They were exhibits, amusing new arrivals in the People's zoological garden. Nicky was wheeling Sunny in an invalid carriage. She's grown very stout. Two of the girls were with them, Tatiana, I think, and Anastasia. I didn't linger to see if Alyosha and the other girls came out. It was too shaming to see them so reduced.

Serafim, very eager to make a good impression since his promotion, had everything ready for our departure. Old Nanya was nowhere to be found. When I'd told her she was going with us to Glinka Street, she'd made me her usual low bow and then slipped away. I suppose she preferred to stay in the country with her chickens. That was the Russian way. 'Yes, yes, yes,' they say, 'whatever the *barina* wishes,' when really they mean 'when pigs fly'.

So we set off, minus Nanya. I knew I mustn't look back. I concentrated on cultivating a mood of forced jollity, for the girls' sake. Eventually Masha said, 'Mummy, why do you keep saying "isn't this fun!"? We're only going to Glinka Street.'

And in town I found the atmosphere quite changed. People had ceased breaking windows and setting fires. The new fad was debating. Two men might be walking along and meet a third and, before you knew it, one of them would be standing on a fire hydrant delivering a speech.

As Cyril said, 'Wherever two or three are gathered together.'

Uncle Bimbo said they were being encouraged by various hotheads, agitators who'd been living in exile and now seized the opportunity to slip back into Petrograd.

'Just what we need!' he said. 'Clever types who don't know anything useful. The kind who can't tie their own bootlaces without consulting a book or conducting a debate.'

Still, it was a relief that people were doing nothing worse than talking. I began to feel we'd panicked unnecessarily, leaving Tsarskoe Selo. Cyril said better safe than sorry. He felt there were various phases we were obliged to go through and this was the latest. It was nothing to worry about. One of the armchair revolutionaries had tried to address the Assembly at the Tauride Palace and had to stop because of the jeering.

'You should have heard him. "Russian soldiers have no business fighting their German comrades. The true enemy is the bourgeoisie."'

'Who are the bourgeoisie?'

'Anyone who isn't a horny-handed son of toil. Rather comical really. According to Kerensky that particular buffoon never worked a day in his life. Still, I felt sorry for the chap in a way. He got such a barracking from the deputies and he's obviously not quite right in the head.'

That was Vladimir Lenin. We were soon hearing his name a lot. People said he was mad, he was a joke, he was a devil. He'd soon choke on his own tail and be gone. But he moved into Mathilde Kschessinskaya's abandoned palace and declared it his Headquarters, his Stavka. He was driven around in a purloined Talbot tourer with a red pennant flying, like some army bigwig.

'Straight out of a comic opera,' Cyril said. 'One of Mr Gilbert's creations if ever I saw one.'

Well, Vladimir Lenin doesn't seem like such a buffoon now.

Our telephone still wasn't working. As soon as we were settled at Glinka Street I walked round to the British Embassy to see the Buchanans. I wasn't shown upstairs. Georgie came down.

'Ducky,' she said. She looked at her feet. 'This is rather awkward.'

For a moment I misunderstood.

I said, 'Of course, you're busy. I just wanted you to know I'm back in town. Let's have tea soon.'

'No,' she said. 'It's not that. It's the situation, the diplomatic situation. Sir George is in a difficult position.'

I said, 'But Britain has recognised the new government.'

'Yes,' she said. 'It's not that. It's really more about George personally. Some of these new government people think he was too close to the Imperial family. Well, he did try terribly hard with the Tsar, you know, to make him see how things were going. Just in a fatherly way. But times have changed. People seem to put such mischievous interpretations on the most innocent things nowadays. So we're advised to avoid contact with all members of the Romanov family. For the time being. It's so silly, but I know you'll understand.'

I didn't understand. Not at all. I still don't. And it wasn't just Georgie Buchanan. I saw Henny Lensky in the street. She pretended not to see me at first.

I said, 'I have the children at Glinka Street. Would Tamara like to come and play?'

She looked horrified.

'After what your husband has done?' she said. 'Traitors!'

People were staring. It was too awful.

So some people wouldn't speak to us because Cyril had been the first to give up on Emperor Nicky, and others wouldn't speak to us because, when all was said and done, we were still Romanovs. We were pariahs. The only friendly words I heard that week were from Felix Yusupov. He was back in Petrograd 'lightly disguised' as he put it, as a friend of the Revolution. He was wearing a disgusting old coachman's coat and a red cockade but there was no mistaking his elegant walk. He, on the other hand, didn't recognise me.

'Christmas!' he said. 'Ducky, is that really you? I wouldn't have known you at all, dressed *à la citoyenne*.'

He asked me for drinks that evening.

'Best not to talk in the street,' he said. 'But come in through the back, through the garden. The gate's on Pirogova.'

I'd never even heard of Pirogova Lane, let alone walked along it. It was so dark and narrow. The whole point of any Yusupov palace was the glittering splendour of its front entrance but it felt quite thrilling to creep up to its garden entrance.

Felix was alone. Rina and Bébé had stayed in the south while he came to Petrograd to check on the state of the house.

'A cracked pane or two. Nothing serious,' he said. 'We've been lucky. I gather the Count Frederickses got practically burned to the ground.'

He said he'd seen Miechen who was safe and well but furious with Cyril for throwing in his lot with the new government.

'Incandescent actually,' he said, 'but, *entre nous*, I think anger is good for her health. The foolishness of others keeps the blood coursing furiously through her veins.'

I said, 'Do you think Cyril's been foolish?'

Felix just looked at me.

I said, 'They were shooting admirals out at Kronstadt, you know? And anyway, Miechen always said Nicky should step aside. She never had any confidence in him. She can hardly complain now it's happened.'

'I suppose,' he said, 'Miechen rather feels Cyril has lopped off the branch she was sitting on. And she isn't the only one who thinks so.'

He meant his father-in-law, Grand Duke Uncle Sandro.

I said, 'And there are some who feel Cyril did the only sensible thing. It's all very well for you people who weren't here. Cyril was on the spot. He had to be decisive. Most of the Grand Dukes are behind him now. As a matter of fact they're rather grateful he had the courage to lead the way.'

That told him.

'Well, anyhow,' he said, 'what's done is done. The aforementioned branch was creaking, I will admit. But tell me about the

Imperials? Are they still here? And what do we call them now? The Nicholas Egalités?'

I said, 'They're confined to the Alexander Palace. Waiting for a ship to England.'

'That'll be a come-down,' he said. 'From the Winter Palace to a little grace-and-favour at Windsor. But you know, it may suit them. I always found them terribly suburban, didn't you? Nicky'll be able to join one of those motoring clubs.'

Felix said he planned to leave Petrograd the next day.

'The very minute I've tidied up here. I have a little housekeeping to do. A few loose ends. One must work on the assumption that we won't be coming back.'

'What, ever?'

'Ever,' he said. 'It's all up for the likes of us, Ducky, you must surely see that. You and Cyril do have an exit plan?'

'Sort of. I keep a couple of bags packed.'

'That's the ticket,' he said. 'Are you all right for money?'

I had no idea. Cyril always had cash in the house but I didn't know how much or where he kept it.

Felix said, 'Not that it'll be worth anything once this new lot start printing treasury notes. Jewellery's worth taking, though. And anything else you can carry. Don't you have a rather nice little Corot etching?'

I said, 'You know we do. Your mother gave it to us as a wedding present.'

'Take it out of its frame,' he said. 'Seriously. Hide it between your nightgowns. I have our Rembrandts rolled up in my riding boots.'

I'd never been close to Felix. He was good fun but one never really knew him. A piece of froth. You couldn't quite catch hold of him. Even fatherhood doesn't seem to have changed him. But that evening, when it was time for me to leave, I felt so very sad, as though we were saying goodbye for ever. He felt it too. He hugged me in a most un-Felix-like way.

He said, 'Do watch out for yourself, Ducky, and for your girls. Cyril's taking a huge gamble but you don't have to stay for the next spin of the wheel. Come south. Everyone else has.'

32

I told Cyril what Felix's advice had been.

'Bloody typical,' he said. 'Directing operations from under the counterpane. What the hell does he know? He's been down at Livadia tending his roses.'

'So you don't think it's all up for us?'

'Ducky,' he said, 'do you really think we'd still be here if I did? This new government, they just need time and a bit of guidance. Kerensky's a sensible fellow. I believe I can work with him.'

'And what work will that be?'

'When I say "work", I mean assist him in establishing a proper government. But yes, afterwards he'll probably find something for me. Something in an advisory capacity, possibly. Naval, military. I'm sure he recognises my value.'

'But I thought the point of this new system is no more jobs for Romanovs.'

'Leave this to me, dear,' he said. 'It's more complex than you realise, but I have everything under control.'

That was the day a tiny voice whispered that I shouldn't necessarily accept everything Cyril said. Some people find it hard to admit they've made a mistake.

I said, 'Felix and Rina are hoping to settle in Paris when the war's over.'

'Paris!' he snorted. 'Yes, that's about Yusupov's mark. That's his kind of place. Well, good luck to them.'

I said, 'You and I were very happy in Paris.'

He looked at me. For a moment it was as though he'd forgotten.

'Yes,' he said, 'we were. And now we're happy here. Don't go all droopy on me, Ducky. I need you to be rock solid. I begin to wish you hadn't gone for drinks with him. Not to be depended upon, friend Felix. Not sound at all.'

I reminded him that Felix was the one who had rid us of Grigory Rasputin. He laughed.

'You don't really believe Felix fired a shot, do you? Honestly, Ducky, do think.'

'It happened in his house.'

'Mr Lincoln was shot in Ford's Theatre,' he said, 'but we know Mr Ford didn't have a hand in it. Darling, all Felix did was to provide the *mise-en-scène*. That's what he does. Everything's theatre for the Yusupovs and Felix always has to be on stage, even if he's only playing the butler.'

'So, do you think Dmitri did it?'

'I think,' he said, 'that provision was made for the deed to be done, to be finished off at least, by someone who could be trusted not to lose their nerve.'

'But who? Was it Oswald Rayner? I've heard that suggested.'

'I really don't know. Was he even in town? The only thing as sure as the dawn is that it wasn't Felix. Shoot a man? I'd say not. Too messy. I'll bet he had his good rugs taken up before the reptile arrived that night.'

In spite of Cyril's scorn for Felix's advice, I did take the Corot out of its frame. I packed it in a photograph album. My pearls I stuffed into the bone channels of an old corset, my emeralds I stitched into the hem of my hunting apron. I don't know if they'll be much help to us. They say the market is flooded with Romanov gems.

'Don't sell now,' people say. 'Wait for better times.'

All very well but when one has children to feed, waiting for better times may not be an option. Miechen might manage to hold on. There's actually a bit of a story about her jewels. She'd taken some of them with her when she went south, but only second-best pieces. There was no imperative to dazzle in Kiev and in Crimea she always dressed very simply. Three pearl strands at most. So her collection was mainly still in Petrograd though I'm sure Cyril hadn't given it a thought.

We were on our way to the Summer Gardens one afternoon, the girls and I, when Kira said, 'Here comes Uncle Boris. What *is* he wearing?'

Two grimy workmen were walking towards us, carrying tool bags, but Kira was quite right, one of them was Boris Vladimirovich. The other, astonishingly, was Bertie Stopford.

'Don't stop. Keep walking. You don't know us,' Boris said, as we drew close. 'We're going to clean the boilers at the Vladimir Palace. Which is now the property of the People.'

They turned down Mramorny Lane. Kira wanted to follow them. She thought they were going to a costume party. But Masha understood we should do as Boris said. She knew Petrograd had become a place where strange things happened and some of them ended badly.

She said, 'Kira, I think Uncle Boris is doing war work. Top secret. We have to pretend we didn't see him.'

We had a few more questions from Kira. Was cleaning boilers war work? Why wasn't Granny Miechen's boilerman doing it? And what did 'Property of the People' mean?'

Eventually she said, 'What fun to wear a disguise! How old do you have to be to do war work?'

Cyril knew nothing of what Boris might have been up to at Miechen's palace. He just held up his hands.

'Enough,' he said. 'Don't say another word. Why can't my family stay quietly below the parapet?'

Pretty priceless, I thought, from a man who'd been so quick to fly the red flag.

The next time I saw Bertie Stopford he was washed and recognisable. I'd planned anyway to call on him at the Europa, to see what he was up to, but then I saw him crossing Nevsky Prospekt.

'Tea?' he said. 'Or something stronger?'

We went to Demoute's.

I said, 'The strangest thing. I dreamed I saw you in the street, dressed in overalls, you and Boris Vladimirovich. You had soot on your faces and you were on your way to repair Miechen's boiler.'

'Extraordinary,' he said. 'Me in overalls! Dreams do throw up the strangest images.'

I said, 'I suppose Miechen asked you to drop by while you're in town? To pick up a few things she might need?'

'Indeed,' he said. 'She hadn't anticipated being away for so long. And her departure was rather hurried. There are always things one forgets. But Her Royal Highness is now thinking of the future.'

'Probably not here?'

'Probably not. Nice has been mentioned. Should the opportunity arise.'

'For which she'd require lighter coats, and parasols.'

'Quite so.'

'I hope you found what you were looking for.'

'We did, thanks to Boris Vladimirovich. He knew precisely

where to look. For parasols. His Imperial Highness knows every corridor.'

'And no one challenged you?'

'No one, thanks to our disguise. We make very convincing boilermen. It was rather thrilling now I look back on it, although at the time I was surprised the People's Militia didn't notice the sound of my heart pounding. It seemed to me to be loud enough to be heard in Moscow.'

He and Boris had gone right to Miechen's suite, opened her safe and emptied it of jewels. Then they'd taken everything to the boiler room, wrapped each piece in newspaper and stowed them in their tool bags. The only item they hadn't found was her Cartier *kokoshnik*. Miechen had sent it for cleaning and forgotten to have it collected. Stopford said Boris might try to retrieve it.

'Risky,' he said. 'But I quite understand why Boris Vladimirovich is tempted to try. Its sapphire alone would buy a great number of dinners.'

He wouldn't tell me what they'd done with Miechen's treasure.

'What you don't know,' he said, 'you can't inadvertently repeat. But I will say it hasn't been easy. The odd earring or two one can hide, necklaces are harder. Be warned, if you're thinking of transporting anything of value. They're getting wise to coat seams. We've managed to spirit everything away. Whether they'll be worth anything is another matter, but everyone's in the same predicament.'

Miechen was in urgent need of money.

'It's been rather a shock,' he said. 'Everyone's been accustomed to a year's credit at least. But the butcher and the baker have now decided they should be paid, monthly. It'll be cash on delivery next, you'll see.'

I asked him about Miechen's beloved Vladimir tiara.

'Impossible to hide,' he said, 'short of breaking it up and there's no sense doing that just yet. One would need to get to somewhere like Antwerp to sell gems of that quality. But it's in a place of safety, that's all I'll say. I've placed it in the most trustworthy hands I could think of.'

He could only have meant the British Embassy. Perhaps it was already on its way to London in a diplomatic bag. Now of course it seems foolish to have worried about a tiara. When will any of us ever wear such things again? All they're good for is selling off, diamond by diamond, and somehow they're never worth anything like as much as one was once led to believe.

I know nothing about money. Mother said it was a subject discussed only by tradespeople. What does one do when the bank says you have nothing? We used to have money. Where can it all have gone? Cyril doesn't seem to know. He used to sign pieces of paper and settle accounts once a year, but the details were still dealt with by his father's people, even all those years after Uncle Vladimir's death. The steward and the book-keeper. Where are they now that one needs them? Gone south, gone east? Gone to hell, Cyril says. But I do think he might have managed things better. I always thought that was a husband's job.

The von Etters say we're not to worry at all, that we're welcome to stay here for as long as we need, but it's too humiliating for words. I'm afraid Cyril and I quarrel about it, but only in bed. It's bad enough being impoverished house guests without having embarrassing rows as well. The girls are happy, at least. For them it's a long holiday and Daddy's home from the war. They dance about, swinging on his arm, but I'm absolutely furious with him. When a person tells you repeatedly 'Leave this to me,' the very least you expect of them is that they've made certain provisions.

Cyril says, 'I got us out, didn't I? Don't be so ungrateful.'

Ungrateful! If he'd listened to me, we'd be in Crimea now with all our friends and family. At least we'd be warm. We might even be on our way to Cannes. Mother would fix us up with a house. Those beastly Bolsheviks can't get their hands on her money. She has everything safely lodged in Germany.

In the course of one of my rages, I'm afraid I accused Cyril of being an incurable ditherer.

I said, 'You always were. If you hadn't dilly-dallied, if you'd had the guts to declare your love for me, I'd never have married Ernie Hesse.'

And he said, 'As I recall, Ernie Hesse also dilly-dallied, as you put it. Does it ever occur to you that the world isn't waiting to fall at your feet? You're no great beauty, Ducky, never were, and frankly you're not the easiest person to live with. It's a pity you didn't have more brothers, to keep you in your place.'

He didn't mean to be cruel, of course. I know I'm no beauty. And I have become rather shrewish, with all the upheaval and the baby and everything. One says things in haste. One can apologise, but one can never really take them back. It's all right though. We'll survive.

33

It was the last day of April. Cyril said I should stay indoors the next day. There were parades planned, for May Day, and things might run out of control.

I said, 'In that case, don't let the girls hear the word "parade" or they'll be pestering all day to go and watch.'

In Germany they used to keep Walpurgis Night. Not us, but the ordinary people. They'd build great bonfires and stay up all night carousing, so the next day had to be a holiday because everyone's head was thick with drink. But I didn't remember May Day ever being a particular holiday in Russia.

'It's called Labour Day,' Cyril said. 'An international celebration of worker struggle and revolutionary victory. Another bloody excuse for disrupting the day's business.'

It was a glorious, sunny morning. People were gathering at the Marsovo Polye. The Buchanans would have had a ringside seat at the embassy but we, of course, were not invited. From Marsovo Polye it wasn't clear where the marchers would go next. Down Sadovaya to Nevsky Prospekt? Along the embankment past the Winter Palace? Perhaps both. They could go wherever they pleased and no police would oppose them because they were the new police. The People. They were judge and jury too. Nicky's old force had been persuaded to disappear. Boris had seen one of them thrown from the tower of the Lutheran Church. As he said, '*Pour encourager les autres*.'

By the end of April the Tsarskoe Selo house was locked and shuttered.

'Forget it,' Cyril said. 'It's the property of The People now. If we ever get a country place again, it'll be one allocated to us by the government. A wood shed, probably. Shared occupancy.'

I said, 'Do you think it's amusing?'

'I think it's reality.'

'Why are we staying on? Why aren't we getting out while we can?'

'Because it's home. And because Russia may be a better place when all this settles down.'

Glinka Street was beginning to feel rather depleted. When we first lived there, we'd had twenty servants. Miechen insisted that we couldn't manage with fewer than that, though it wasn't a very large house and we didn't give many dinners. When the troubles and the strikes had begun, certain faces had disappeared. I have a feeling they just slipped out occasionally, when something was happening on the streets, and then came home to eat and sleep, but one was nervous of enquiring too deeply. No one ever spoke out or left us in the way Kuzma and Peach had done, but the atmosphere in the house was different. Then, little by little, some faces disappeared for good. Cyril joked that he quite expected to run into some of them in the corridors of the Tauride Palace.

He said, 'But instead of carrying your breakfast tray, darling, they'll have a ministerial portfolio under their arm.'

So by early May the only servants we still had were two maids, nervous little creatures, not much older than Masha, and two doormen, Mefody and Serafim, which was one too many but

Mefody came with the property and would be there till he died. Anna, our cook, had gone, which would have been calamitous once upon a time but not any more. They say every black cloud has a silver lining do we but look for it, and in that instance it was true, because she had taken her mother with her. I was able to venture down to the kitchen without fear of finding the Groaner on her usual stove-side perch. I learned how to warm through dishes Serafim brought in from the *traktir*. We managed well enough.

Cyril came home on May Day evening in a very good humour.

He said, 'Did you see any of the parades?'

I said, 'How could I? You said it would be too dangerous to go out.'

'Yes,' he said, 'so I did. I didn't expect you to listen to me though. Well, you missed a treat. Some of the banners were priceless.'

He asked for writing paper.

'A little Russian test for you,' he said.

He wrote Х Л Е В   В С Е М.

I said, 'Bread for all?'

'Look again,' he said. 'Bread for all is obviously what they intended it to say, but it doesn't.'

I looked and looked.

Masha said, 'I know the answer! Bread is Х Л Е Б, but they've written Х Л Е В. But Daddy, what's Х Л Е В?'

'Х Л Е В,' he said, 'is a cow stall. Well done, Masha. A cow stall for all! Can you believe these people? And they think they're ready to govern. We'll be an international laughing stock. Here's another one.'

Д О Л О Й   Ч Е Р В И! *Doloy chervi.*

Doloy was 'down with, away with'. I'd seen that word often enough since the troubles began. But *chervi* meant nothing to me. Even Masha couldn't fathom it.

'Well,' Cyril said, 'what they're trying to say is "Down with tipping". It's all part of this fair wage campaign. Apparently being left a little gratuity is now considered a patronising insult. Damned if I understand why. So the word they should have used is Ч А Е В Ы Е. Ч Е Р В И are maggots. Which renders the slogan rather comical, don't you think? Down with maggots! I'll drink to that.'

I wasn't really in a position to laugh, seven years in Russia and still stumbling to say quite simple things. And as Kira observed very solemnly, no one likes maggots so getting rid of them was a jolly sensible idea.

Summer arrived in a hurry. It seemed the last of the snow had only just gone and suddenly we were too hot. Between them the humidity and the mosquitoes and this restless baby prevented me from sleeping. I don't remember being so uncomfortable before. One's forties are not the age for bearing children. If Elli had lived I'd most likely be a grandmother by now. Cyril, on the other hand, who was busier than he'd ever been in his life, slept very well, until the night we were jolted from our beds by hammering at the street door. It wasn't yet properly light.

Cyril was awake and on his feet at once. We could hear men's voices, Mefody, I thought, and Serafim and then others.

Cyril said, 'Go to the girls. Lock the door. Don't come out till I say so.'

Then he ran downstairs, still pulling on his dressing gown.

I couldn't lock the girls' door, of course. One doesn't allow a child like Kira the temptation of a key. I pushed a chair against the door and sat on it, trying to hear what was being said down below. I couldn't catch anything, but the tone seemed conversational. I imagine if one is about to be arrested it's done without any niceties. But I couldn't be sure. Everything had changed so quickly. Russians used to be dear people who called me '*Barina*' or '*Matushka*' and bowed when I passed them. Now they're like dogs that have turned and bitten and when a dog has bitten once it can only be a matter of time until it bites again. Cyril's assurances were all very well but the fact remained, the Emperor of All the Russias wasn't free even to walk in his own park.

Kira slept on. Masha had woken but she lay very still. I put my finger to my lips. She slipped out of bed and came to sit on what was left of my lap.

She whispered, 'Have they come to shoot us?'

What a thing for a child to say. She could only have got that idea from Ethel Peach.

We heard the street door slam, and then silence for what seemed an age. Masha's fingernails were digging into my neck. I began to think she was right. If you come in the night and take a man from his home in his dressing gown, you must surely intend to shoot him. I was a convinced widow by the time we heard the door again and then Cyril bounding up the stairs.

He tapped on the door and said, 'All's well. You can come out.'

Kira woke, very cross at first at having missed the excitement. Then she pretended she'd actually been awake through the whole episode. Cyril tried to make light of it. Too much so. I observed that he was trembling, just as he had after the executions at Kronstadt.

'It was just a few Marine Guards,' he said. 'Good lads. They're due back at Kronstadt first thing and their transport's run out of fuel. I was the first person they thought of. You see, Ducky? I have their confidence.'

He'd given them one of our precious canisters of petrol. Good old Grand Duke Cyril. Such a good sort.

He went to his dressing room. I followed him.

I said, 'Masha thought they'd come to shoot us.'

'Silly girl,' he said. 'Where did she get such an idea?'

'I can't imagine. In this country where admirals get shot by their men and the Emperor is under house arrest. Perhaps it's normal now for little girls to think such things.'

'You're upset.'

'I'm not upset. I'm frightened. We should leave. I want to leave.'

He was buttoning his shirt.

'Well,' he said, eventually, 'perhaps we all need a holiday. Let me see what I can do.'

Mist hung over the city all day. I went to St Isaac's, I don't know why. I saw no particular reason God should grant me any protection, but I felt a great compulsion to stand quietly in a sacred place. It calmed me. A priest asked me if I wanted him to hear my confession. I told him I wasn't Orthodox.

'*Anglichanka*,' I said. '*Protestanka*.'

'Pah!' he said, and he gave me such a pitying look.

The canal water looked dead and oily. I saw brother-in-law Boris strolling along the Moika.

'You all right?' he said. 'You look all in.'

I told him about our early morning callers.

I said, 'Cyril seems so sure everything's going to work out. Do you think so?'

He said, 'If I had a wife . . .' But then he stopped. 'Frankly,' he said, 'I don't know what to think. One minute we seemed to be plunging over a sheer cliff. Now we seem to have landed on a ledge. Will it hold? Perhaps it will, as long as Nicky's bundled out of the country to some distant exile. Why do they delay so? All those guards tied up at the Alexander Palace. It makes no sense. As for you, I think you've been an absolute brick, staying here while

Cyril's playing politics. If you went south, took a little break and went to visit Ma, no one would think any the less of you.'

It wasn't other people's opinions that bothered me. Quite a number of people I'd counted as friends had deserted me anyway. It was Cyril. Some days I felt he was terrifically brave, some days I thought he was an utter fool. One thing was always true: there was no hurrying him.

'Like an ox, Cyril Vladimirovich,' Pa once remarked. 'He will plod on till he reaches the end of the furrow.'

I said, 'I was just in St Isaac's. It was so peaceful. All these extraordinary things going on out here, but step inside the cathedral and nothing's changed.'

'True,' Boris said. 'But for how long? This new crowd love taking things to pieces. The monarchy. The Duma. I imagine they just haven't got round to the church yet. They probably will.'

That was the last time I saw Boris, on the Moika, just across from the Yusupovs' closed-up palace. I find my thoughts often begin that way now. The last time this, the last time that.

'Kisses for *les animaux* from Uncle Boris,' he said. 'Take care of yourself, Ducky.'

Cyril came home early.

I said, 'When do we leave?'

He held up his hand. 'Whoa!'

'You promised we'd take a holiday.'

'Yes,' he said. 'And we will. But one doesn't just disappear. One has certain commitments. Now, I have a plan. I'm hoping to bring Kerensky here tomorrow, to see us *en famille*. Nothing showy, Ducky. Just tea and jam will do. And serve it yourself. No maid.'

I said, 'And the purpose of this humble tableau? I'm sure Kerensky hasn't forgotten you're a Grand Duke.'

'The purpose,' he said, 'is to show him that we're reasonable people, living modestly, adjusting to the new regime. The purpose is to get permission to travel, for me to take my poor careworn wife somewhere cooler until her confinement.'

I said, 'So, not to Crimea?'

'No,' he said. 'Not to Crimea. Too many Romanovs down there already, especially Ma and Dowager Minnie. Sooner or later this lot are bound to start worrying that they're plotting a comeback. But no one else has gone to Finland. Haikko would be perfect. Cooler for you and without any complicated family loyalties.'

I very much doubted Cyril would be allowed to travel anywhere no matter how humbly I served tea to Minister Kerensky. The thing to do was to go, not wait for permission. I told Cyril so.

'Please, darling,' he said. 'Let's try to do this correctly. If we run and we're stopped, there's no telling what they'd do. We don't want to end up like Nicky and Sunny. Red Guards on the door. No, Kerensky is a reasonable man. He trusts me. Now I want him to see the private side of me. The family man.'

I said, 'And my role?'

'Act tired and pregnant.'

'I *am* tired and pregnant. Am I allowed to speak?'

'Do I usually muzzle you?'

'And the children? I imagine they're to be in this picture of domesticity?'

He thought for a minute.

'Yes,' he said. 'But just briefly. Perhaps a brief glimpse when he first arrives, but they shouldn't sit with us for tea. There's no telling what Kira might say.'

34

Alexander Fyodorovich Kerensky. Cyril put great store by him.

'The coming man,' he said, although actually Kerensky had already very much arrived, with two hats on his clever head. He held office in the Duma and in the Petrograd Soviet. Cyril predicted he would soon be Minister for War and when that happened there'd be a new offensive, a strong push against Germany before next winter.

I didn't know what time to expect them, or even whether Kerensky would come. I got out our last tin of Huntley and Palmers, then thought better of it, but not before the girls had spied them.

Kira ran about shouting, 'Hurrah! Biscuits! Granny Miechen's coming to tea.'

I said, 'Not Granny Miechen. An important person Daddy needs to talk to. When they arrive, you may come to the drawing room to say Good Day. Then you must go upstairs and play.'

'What important person?' she wanted to know.

'Minister Kerensky.'

'Doesn't he like biscuits?'

I spent the afternoon running between the water closet and the window that had the best view of the street. You may guess where I was when they arrived.

Minister Kerensky is quite personable. He was younger than I'd expected, probably not yet forty. A little starchy, considering these new, informal times we're now supposed to live in, but his manner was pleasant. He has a very fine head of hair.

Kira and Masha came in and did exactly as I'd instructed them, exactly as Cyril had said.

I said, 'Off you run, then.'

Then Cyril, quite infuriatingly, said, 'Oh, darling, let them stay. I'm sure Alexander Fyodorovich won't mind.'

Masha hesitated. She could see I was flustered. But Kira needed no further encouragement to stay. She stationed herself by Kerensky's chair and proceeded to quiz him. Did he have any girls?

'No,' he said, 'I have two boys.'

'What are their names?'

'Gleb and Oleg.'

'Are they older than me?'

'They're eleven and nine. How old are you?'

'Eight years and one month. Do you like biscuits at all?'

'Yes, I do.'

'We have a whole lovely tin of Ginger Nuts in our pantry but Mummy said best not to make too much of a splash.'

So then it was Cyril's turn to worry what Kira would come out with next. Served him right. He sent them to play.

There was no business talked. It was an entirely social call. Kerensky took two cups of tea and two half-spoons of raspberry jam. Everything about him was very precise. We discussed the weather. The Gulf of Finland would be cooler, we agreed, for anyone fortunate enough to be able to get out of the city for a while. We talked about jam. Apricot makes a refreshing change. Strawberry can be difficult. It doesn't always set well. In Tashkent, where he'd lived for some years, the quince jam was very fine. We talked about jam far too much.

Sometimes, as Kerensky turned his head, the light bounced off his spectacles and I couldn't see his eyes. Once, when I could see his eyes, I caught him looking at my wide waistline. I was afraid of him. What was he thinking? There's another pesky Romanov soon to enter the world?

Cyril thought it had all gone very well.

I said, 'How can you possibly judge? He could be playing with you. The man's a complete sphinx.'

'But he's a family man,' he said, 'I'm sure he remembers how hard Petrograd summers are for a woman when she's expecting. He'll see what he can do about a travel permit. He assured me of that, out on the step.'

'Why didn't he just give you permission? How hard could it be?'

'Darling, Kerensky is a lawyer. He likes to follow procedure.'

'And then what? When you get this permit?'

'We'll go to Haikko.'

'And just not come back?'

'Leave this to me.'

'What if he says I can take the girls but you can't go? What if he just says no?'

'For heaven's sake, Ducky.'

That's always Cyril's exasperated cry when he doesn't have an answer to a perfectly sensible question.

For two weeks we heard nothing.

I said, 'Remind him. It might have slipped his mind.'

'No,' he said. 'It wouldn't be appropriate. And anyway, Alexander Fyodorovich doesn't forget things.'

That may have been true, but the Russian way isn't to wait politely and hopefully. The Russian way is to keep asking, even after many refusals, to assume that 'No' was just a slip of the tongue that will eventually be corrected to an exhausted 'Yes'. Cyril can be so terribly English about things. Sometimes you'd never think he was Russian.

I had good days and bad days. When the air was warm and thick with moisture, I felt I couldn't stay in Petrograd another moment, that I should just take the girls and run and to hell with Minister Kerensky. How many times I woke and thought, 'Today,' but then couldn't summon the energy. And when a breeze got up from the west and one could actually breathe, my mood became more positive. Cyril was right. It would be better for us to stay together, for us to go with official sanction. If Kerensky said no, then I'd carry out my threat.

There was little I could do to prepare. The bags I'd first packed back in February were opened and repacked several times but only after the girls were asleep. I couldn't have borne their questions. And what exactly does one pack? A summer holiday is easy to plan for, and so is a winter jaunt, but for the rest of one's life?

I took Bertie Stopford's advice and unpicked the seams where I'd hidden my jewellery. That too could only be done when the children were asleep. I decided the only thing was to capitalise on my interesting condition, wear an extra pair of bloomers and carry as much as I could between the two layers. Miechen had once remarked that Cyril wasn't very generous with jewels, but when one is about to take flight a small collection has its advantages.

Uncle Bimbo called on us. He brought us apricots from the hot-houses at Tsarskoe Selo. I found it quite amazing that they were still functioning, that they hadn't had all their glass panes knocked out.

'No, no,' he said. 'There are some decent sorts out there, keeping things running. Growing things, you know, it always improves a person, I've often noted it. Some of them have become quite devoted to their work. They're not all idiots, those lads. Unlike our Commissar for Posts, Telegraphs and Telephones. I gather your line isn't working either.'

One never knew from hour to hour. Sometimes it worked, sometimes it didn't, but Cyril discouraged me from using the telephone anyway. It was no great loss. There was really no one left in town for me to call.

I wanted to say something to Uncle Bimbo, to give him warning that we might leave, but Cyril had said the best thing was to tell no one. Then in the front hall, just as he was about to put on his hat, Uncle Bimbo said, 'How much longer till your time, Ducky?'

I calculated it was about ten weeks.

He said, 'I hope Cyril Vladimirovich is making suitable arrangements. Living in this madhouse, it can't be good for your nerves.'

I went to say something but he put a finger to his lips.

I said, 'Stay to dinner.'

'Tempted,' he said. 'But I'd best get back before the Commissar for Railways prevents the trains from running. What a shower. Take care of yourself, Ducky, and of those dear girls. And the baby, of course. New life. A wonderful thing.'

Masha asked me why Uncle Bimbo had been so sad.

I said, 'He wasn't.'

'Yes, he was,' she said. 'I watched him from the window when he crossed the street. He was wiping his tears. Perhaps he's lonely.'

Kira said, 'He should get a wife. He was pretty keen on Peach, you know. He used to get pink cheeks when he talked to her. Well, I'm jolly glad he didn't marry her.'

Ethel Peach, who'd bitten the hand that fed her, who'd disappeared from our lives and taken Kuzma with her. She was, I imagined, working her way east, perhaps back to Shanghai where she knew people or just taking any route she could to reach England. But I was wrong. She was still in Petrograd and it was as though, by saying her name, Kira had conjured her up.

35

I was awake and about to get up when they came hammering at the street door. Cyril was shaving. The noise so startled him he cut himself. He went to the door with blood on his neck.

'*Kto vas oopolnamochil?*' I heard him say. 'By whose authority?'

'*Pyetrogradski Sovyet,*' someone said, very confident.

Still Cyril kept them on the step and there were more voices, not threatening, but raised and excited. I went and stood beside him at the open door. I thought the sight of a pregnant woman in a rather shabby dressing gown might lower the temperature.

Cyril said, 'Everything's under control, darling. They've had a wasted journey, as I'm trying to explain to them. I've already agreed in principle to the forfeiture of Crown Properties.'

This was news to me, as I suppose must have been evident from my face. It was Peach's laugh I recognised. She was at the rear of the group with two other women. They were all wearing red headscarves tied factory-worker style.

I said, 'What do you mean, "forfeiture of Crown Properties"? Miechen bought us this house.'

'I know that,' he said. 'It's the Tsarskoe Selo property they should be assessing, not this house.'

'So, send them away.'

Cyril said they wished to come in and assess the size of our rooms. He hadn't recognised Peach.

I said, 'Tell them they may not. This is our home.'

He spoke to me very quietly.

'They have a written order. Darling, you're making things unnecessarily worse. Do go in and leave this to me.'

I said, 'You should be ashamed of yourself, Ethel Peach, disturbing people at this hour of the morning.'

Cyril tried to hush me but I wasn't for hushing.

I said, 'You hardly need to come in here with a measuring tape, upsetting my children. You know this house as well as I do. You lived in it for long enough, warm and very well fed.'

I thought she looked a little embarrassed. Just a very little. I believe I might have shamed her into leaving and taking her friends with her but Cyril was all for humouring them.

'It's a silly mistake,' he said. 'The simplest thing is to let them come in and do what they've been ordered to do. It won't take long. The mistake can be straightened out at a more civilised hour.'

And so my husband allowed a measuring squad of the Petrograd Soviet Housing Allocation Committee to enter my home and run about with yardsticks and stubs of pencil. That was the moment I decided I wouldn't spend another night in that house. With or without Cyril, I was going to leave and take our daughters with me, and as soon as I'd made that decision I experienced a wonderful feeling of calm.

I told Peach she must remain in Cyril's study until the ridiculous exercise was over. I didn't want the children to see her.

'All the same to me,' she said.

'Did Kuzma get you into all this?'

'Get me into it?' she said. 'I didn't need "getting into it". I believe in it.'

I said, 'Believe in what? Throwing policemen off church towers?'

'The Revolution,' she said. 'The new Russia, Ducky.'

Ducky! The absolute cheek of her! And there was my husband running around like a footman, opening doors for the other Revolutionary clowns. 'And this is the dining room.' Anything to oblige.

In spite of my efforts Masha and Kira did see Peach. As the Measuring Party were leaving, the girls came running downstairs and Peach turned to look at them. Masha was bashful, but not Kira.

She said, 'Why do you have that thing on your head? You look like a village woman. Did you marry Kuzma?'

'Marry?' Peach said. 'Nobody gets married any more.'

Kira said, 'I'm going to. You can't come back, you know? We don't need a governess now. I'm going to the Annenschule and then to the Smolny.'

Peach laughed.

'Well, Ducky,' she said, 'how long till you drop the next little parasite? I'm surprised you didn't make a run for it while you could.'

That was the last we saw of her.

Kira said, 'What's a little parasite?'

'Peach was just being rude. She's turned into a very unpleasant person.'

'But what is it?'

'She meant the baby I'm having. But "parasite" isn't a nice word. We don't use it.'

'Are you really going to have a baby?'

'Why else do you think I've grown so fat?'

'I thought it was because you stopped hunting. Can old persons have babies?'

I followed Cyril to his dressing room.

He said, 'I know what you're going to say.'

'Do you?' I said. 'Two of those types were carrying rifles.'

'Just ancient Berdankas,' he said. 'They can't possibly have cartridges for them. We were never in any danger. It was unpleasant, I know, and I'm sorry it happened but it's over.'

I said, 'Yes, Cyril, you're right for once. It's over.'

'They're not entitled to this house.'

'I know that. It belongs to Miechen.'

'They are entitled to the Tsarskoe Selo house. Crown property.'

'They can have it. We don't need it. We're leaving. Today.'

'I hear you,' he said. 'But do stop shouting. Think of the girls. Those people. They're measuring everyone's houses. They weren't picking on us.'

'With Ethel Peach guiding them to our door? Of course not.'

'It's just about living space.'

'I understand. And tomorrow they may decide all we're entitled to is a coffin width. But we won't be here, Cyril. At least I won't and nor will our children. Let them shoot us if they must. A pregnant woman and two little girls. That would make them look good on the world stage.'

He finished dressing in silence. It was only eight o'clock and the heat was already unbearable.

He said, 'As soon as I've spoken to Kerensky, I'll telephone you. I'll say . . . what shall I say? Please send my short boots for new heel irons. That's what I'll say. That will be the signal.'

I said, 'Signal? You're not in some *Boy's Own* story. The signal for what? That Kerensky said yes? That Kerensky said no? And then what?'

'Keep your voice down,' he said. 'And don't be obtuse, Ducky. The signal will mean that you must be absolutely ready to leave.'

'I've been absolutely ready for weeks. And by the way, the telephone isn't working so your signal hardly matters. Do we have a Commissar yet for Carrier Pigeons?'

He slammed the door on his way out. His shaving mishap had bled onto his shirt collar.

All through the morning I kept picking up the handset to see whether I could get a connection. The line was still dead. I longed to go out, to take the children to the Summer Gardens and perhaps happen to bump into someone, *anyone* to talk to and break the awful silence, but I was afraid to leave the house in case Cyril found a way to send news.

Kira spent an hour bouncing on beds to see which mattress gave her the greatest propulsion, then fell into a sweaty sleep. Masha came to me and asked if something horrid was going to happen. She looked so solemn and grown up.

I said, 'Don't worry about this morning. Those people who came here had made a mistake.'

'Oh, I know that,' she said. 'Do you know, one of them said a whole family could live in our bedroom? Which is completely impossible. But why were they so hateful?'

'Were they?'

'Yes. They said we're like a rotten tree. "You lot," they said. "Dead timber. We'll be rid of you, root and branch." What does that mean? And why was Peach with them?'

I told her Peach seemed to have fallen in with a bad crowd.

'Yes,' she said, 'that's what I thought. And, you know, her teeth weren't terribly clean.'

I did wonder, I still do, if the Romanov tree is really so rotten, root and branch as they say, why are those people in such a hurry to be rid of us? They have their new government. Why couldn't we be allowed to retire to a dacha and keep bees? I'm sure Nicky and Sunny would like nothing better. Do they fear us? Are they nervous that some little green Romanov shoot will spring up and take back the throne?

I told Masha we were going away for a little holiday.

'Tonight,' I said. 'But don't say anything to Kira. She'll only get over-excited.'

'Hurrah,' she said. 'And perhaps by the time we come back Emperor Uncle Nicky will have thrown all those horrid people in prison.'

36

Cyril came home just after four. He sent the girls straight to their room.

He said, 'You may come down to the drawing room at five o'clock but not a minute sooner.'

Kira said, 'Is it because I bounced on your bed?'

'No,' he said. 'It's because Mummy and I need peace and quiet.'

He was very tense. He loosened his shirt collar.

'Well, Ducky,' he said. 'This is it. Kerensky has arranged a pass for us for Finland.'

'Tonight?'

'Tonight.'

'Do you think he knows you won't come back?'

'Very likely. He's no fool. Probably relieved to see the back of me. He'll have taken plenty of criticism for working with me. A Romanov will always be a Romanov. Treating with the class enemy and all that. It's a wonder to me he keeps going. He'll never manage to make everyone happy.'

'So we can go quite openly? We have permission.'

'We do. But no sense in making a noisy exit. Better just to slip away, discreetly.'

We were to go in two cars. Cyril first, with the girls and a staff driver. I was to follow an hour later in a British Mission car. It would set off as though taking me to Tsarskoe Selo and then double back to the Finland Station. It all seemed very cloak and dagger. I began to wonder if Cyril really did have Kerensky's blessing.

I said, 'The girls should travel with me.'

'No,' he said. 'Point A, I'm less likely to get challenged if I have children with me, and point B, if I am challenged, my driver is armed. You'll be fine. Any questions, just play the British card. They'll probably offer you an escort to the station.'

He rebuttoned his collar, reached for his coat. He was going out again.

'Won't be long,' he said. 'An hour at most.'

I said, 'But you promised the girls you'd talk to them at five o'clock.'

'No,' he said. 'I told them they can come downstairs at five o'clock. You can put them in the picture. Now I really must be off, darling. Still a few loose ends to attend to.'

I supposed it was La Karsavina he was going to see. I hadn't the energy for another row. But I did watch from the window and he did set off in the direction of the Mariinsky. A farewell fuck? Well, a man has his needs and a wife who looks like matryoshka doll can't hold much attraction.

Kira was beside herself with excitement. She began assembling her most treasured possessions on the drawing-room rug.

'One bag, only,' I kept reminding her. But she sensed my heart wasn't really in it and used my weakness to good account. Masha rather nobly offered her a little space in her own valise but when she raised an objection to accommodating all the Noah's Ark animals, Kira said, 'If you're going to be so mean, Masha Kirillovna, I shall carry them in my drawers, like Mummy's doing with her pearls.'

Cyril returned at six. I will say he's extremely punctual, even in his philandering. The girls were all over him. Kisses, hugs, plans for sea bathing and bicycle rides and shrimping. He went up to change his clothes. I found him standing in the doorway of the yellow guest room.

'Just doing a quick tour,' he said. 'A last look round.'

That undid me. Just a tear or two. It was only a house. Just bricks and tiles.

He put his arms around me.

'Not much longer, darling,' he said. 'Stiff upper lip and so forth. This time tomorrow it'll all be behind us. And who knows, perhaps we'll be back. If this lot make a terrific muddle of things.'

I must say he didn't smell of another woman. Perhaps he hadn't gone to see Karsavina after all. Perhaps he'd just popped out to buy his stomach pills.

I said, 'When you and the girls leave, I won't come down.'

'Absolutely not,' he said. 'Wouldn't be the thing at all. Air of normality. Keep yourself busy. Or rest. That's what you should do. We won't be travelling in comfort, you realise? No Imperial coupé.'

Serafim took the bags down. Then Cyril took the girls. He was all brittle cheerfulness.

Kira said, 'I want Mummy to come with us.'

'Too much luggage,' Cyril said. 'There isn't room for her. Too many dolls.'

She began to wail. 'There's heaps of room. I only brought seven dolls.'

I said, 'The thing is, Kira, I have errands to do before we leave. Far better for you to go ahead with Daddy and Masha and make sure we get good seats.'

'Very well,' she said, 'but that's a different reason altogether. And I certainly didn't bring too many dolls.'

Then I was alone in the house. Serafim and Mefody were in the yard waiting for my car to come. There was nothing left for me to do. I picked up a Pinkerton but I read the same page over and over. I had an urge to go into the street and walk about but my feet were so swollen I could barely squeeze them into my shoes. I saw a stranger in the looking glass. She had the darkest circles under her eyes.

My car was late. I began to fret even before it was late so by the time it truly was late I was sick with nerves. The baby, which had leaped about all afternoon, didn't move. Was it holding its breath? No, unborn babies don't breathe. I could see nothing ahead but calamity. We'd miss our train. Cyril and the girls would be noticed at the station by some rogue faction of Bolsheviks. They'd rip up our permit to travel. 'Kerensky!' they'd say. 'That lukewarm!' Cyril would be shot. Then they'd come for me and when I asked for my children they'd say, 'Children? What children?'

A Grand Duchess isn't often alone, you know? Quite aside from one's friends and relations, there are always maids and footmen and drivers, and all those other souls, cooks and boot boys that keep up a comforting hum of activity even if one rarely sees them. I don't believe Miechen or Mother have been alone for a single moment of their lives. Even Sunny, cooped up at the Alexander Palace, has some of her ladies for company. That poor creature, Vyrubova, is still incarcerated, as far as we know, but Sunny has the comfort of Hendrikova and Isa Buxhoeveden. I suppose they may go with her to England. But I'm quite cut off. I don't know where Mother is. I can't talk to my sisters. Georgie Buchanan isn't permitted to see me. And everyone else has melted away, if not to the south then into the country, keeping quiet, hoping for the best, minding their own business. Gone to ground.

I was in that rather miserable reverie when Serafim called up to me, '*Barina!*' and then I heard a familiar voice say, 'Transport alongside, ma'am.'

37

If I'd been asked, Willie Gerhardi was the very person I'd have chosen to drive me into exile.

'Don't look back,' he said. 'If I may suggest, just get into the motor and look straight ahead. Think of lovely, cool Finland.'

But I had to say something to Serafim. He'd been so loyal when everyone else deserted us. I told him we'd see him in September. October at the latest.

'*Da, Barina!*' he said. 'Octyabrya, wid many mushroom!'

He smiled but there were tears in his eyes.

Gerhardi didn't delay for an instant. He pulled away towards Ekaterinovsky Prospekt and then turned south along Voznesensky.

He said, 'I've been instructed to make a little detour, in case your departure has aroused any interest. I honestly don't think it will have done. Everyone's too hot and tired.'

I asked him if he was staying on.

'Yes,' he said, 'most likely. But my situation's entirely different to yours. We don't get any trouble at the British Mission, quite the opposite actually, and Kerensky seems a reasonable type. However my brother, Victor, wouldn't agree. He thinks Kerensky's a five-minute wonder. Victor predicts he'll be out before long. Then the Bolsheviks will start emptying everyone's pockets. My mother goes along with whatever Victor thinks. So they'll leave. Probably when the weather cools down. Mother would hate to leave any of her furs behind.'

We crossed the Obvodny Canal and followed the embankment past Resurrection Church before we doubled back and began to travel in the right direction. The sky was leaden. No prospect of darkness, just hour after hour of gloaming. I hate the White Nights.

Gerhardi never stopped talking. He meant to keep me diverted. He saw how anxious I was. I will also say that his driving was greatly improved.

'Now here's something you may not have seen,' he said.

We'd just crossed the Fontanka heading towards the Alexander Bridge.

'On your left,' he said. 'Do you see what they've done to the church?'

The outside of St Panteleimon was hung with red flags. You would hardly have known it was a church. Actually, Gerhardi thought it probably wasn't one any longer.

'Churches are on their way out,' he said. 'That's the word. They've probably turned this one into a workers' canteen. Or a Soviet committee room. They do love their committees. And they breed like rabbits. The committees, I mean, not the Bolshies.'

We were nearly there.

He said, 'I don't imagine you've been to the station since recent events. The old Imperial pavilion belongs to the People now so I'll let you down at the front entrance. Just walk in and find your family. Don't worry about your bags. I'll bring them round.'

My feet had swollen even more during our drive. I hobbled into the station, no idea where I was going. I couldn't see Cyril though the place wasn't very crowded. I asked a worker if there was a train leaving for Riihimäki. He shrugged his shoulders but he didn't walk on. He'd caught my accent.

'*Vy, otkooda*?' he asked me. 'Where are you from?'

'*Velikobritanniya*,' I said, and he shook my hand. British was still the thing to be. Then I heard, 'Mummy! There's Mummy!' and Kira came hurtling towards me and threw herself into my arms. When I looked to where she'd come from I saw Cyril and Masha waiting with our bags, but they made no move to join me. In fact Cyril turned his back. His face was quite known in Petrograd, I imagine, even sheltering under the brim of a Montecristo, and he was feeling nervous.

When Willie Gerhardi appeared with my bags, the sight of his British Mission khakis confirmed my '*britanskaya*' credentials. The worker shook his hand too and the three of us stood and smiled at each other idiotically until Willie said, 'Well, I suppose . . .' and our new Bolshevik friend went on his way.

Cyril was tetchy.

He said, 'Why must you chat to people? One never knows who they might be. One never knows who's listening.'

I said, 'I was only playing the British card, as recommended. Did you find our train?'

'Yes and no,' he said. 'A meeting of the rail workers' Soviet was called so our locomotive has been kept on a low fire. They're only now starting to get up steam. It'll be another hour at least before we get away. The girls say they're hungry and I've already dismissed my driver, so perhaps your chappie could go and find them something?'

Gerhardi said there was nothing to be had on the station.

'But give me half an hour,' he said. 'I'll see what I can find.'

'Meanwhile,' Cyril said, 'I suppose we may as well go and appropriate a carriage. There are no baggage porters, needless to say. They're all too busy attending meetings.'

Cyril pushed me from behind and I climbed up so he could hand

309

our luggage to me piece by piece. I felt as though everyone was looking at us. They weren't, of course. Everyone was absorbed in their own little world and we were just another family getting out of the heat of the city for a while.

Kira said, 'This isn't our train. Our train has carpet.'

Masha hissed at her to shut up. A ten-year-old has some understanding of difficult situations, of the need for tact, but an eight-year-old will blunder on and the more you try to silence her, the more insistent she grows.

'This train is disgusting,' she said. 'It smells of poor people.'

It did smell. Of cabbage, I think. It wasn't so very bad.

Masha wondered about beds.

Cyril said, 'No sleeping car this time, Mashenka. We're going to sit up all night. What an adventure, eh!'

She said, 'You mean all the way to Haikko?'

'No, just to Riihimäki.'

'Then what?'

'The von Etters will send a driver for us.'

'How will they know when to send him?'

'I'll send a wire when we get to Kouvola Junction.'

I said, 'You mean you didn't wire them yet? What if they're not at home?'

'As you may recall,' he said, 'I've been somewhat occupied today. Anyway, of course they'll be at home. Where else would they be?'

'Send them a wire now. You have nothing else to do.'

'Ducky,' he said, 'I will contact the von Etters when I judge the moment to be right. Kira's right, there is a frightful smell in here. I should have told your chappie to bring us some Jeyes Fluid.'

I said, 'He's not my chappie, Cyril. He's Second Lieutenant Gerhardi and he's Alf Knox's extremely kind and obliging chappie.'

'Ha!' he said. 'And one of those young lady-charmers, clearly.'

Gerhardi was gone a long time but he did return. He brought cheese and salted cucumbers and sticks of barley sugar.

'No bread, I'm afraid,' he said. 'Mother did have some but she wouldn't let me bring it. She says it isn't fit for humans.'

He'd been to his family home to raid the pantry.

'And a little something for the grown-ups too,' he said.

He'd brought vodka and a pack of cigarettes. We said our good-byes.

'I hope all goes well,' he said. 'I'm sure it will. An anxious time for you, I imagine. Baby due and all that. But perhaps you'll be back, if things settle down. I expect we'll meet again.'

Off he went, and we were left alone.

Cyril said, 'Did he say he got these provisions from his mother? But he's one of Knox's men. He's British.'

'British, Russian. His people have been here for years. They have some kind of factory.'

'You seem to know all about him.'

'I've met him several times. He was often at the Buchanans'. He's a writer.'

'What does that mean?'

'He's writing a play and a novel.'

'Good grief,' Cyril said. 'And yet he seemed like a perfectly regular sort of fellow. One just never knows.'

So, even on the night we fled from our home with no more than we could carry and our hosts not expecting us, I did find something to laugh about. Bookish people made Cyril uneasy, doubly so if they were men. Pa had been just the same. I don't believe either of them ever opened a book after they'd passed their trigonom-etry paper at cadet school. Cyril likes motoring and shooting and identifying naval vessels through a telescope. He likes to belong to clubs where he won't encounter any Willie Gerhardis.

We finally got underway just before ten o'clock. We had the carriage to ourselves. The girls were wide awake with excitement.

Cyril took my hand.

'You all right, old thing?' he said. 'Not liable to give birth en route, are you?'

I said, 'I need to sleep.'

'Yes,' he said, 'you do that. Actually it might make things easier, should there be any hitches. A sleeping woman, in a certain condition. They won't wake you.'

'Do you think there will be hitches?'

'No,' he said. 'But let me put it this way, I'll be a lot happier when we're the other side of Beloostrov.'

Beloostrov was the customs post. But before that we had to get through Terijoki and the border control. The train seemed to proceed at a crawl. Half an hour and we were barely past the mills and the factory chimneys. Kira needed the water closet and so did I.

I said, 'We have to wait until the train stops.'

She whined. 'Why can't we go to Finland in Granny Miechen's coupé? Why did that man bring us cucumbers for our supper? I hate cucumbers. Why can't we go to the dining car?'

Masha said, 'There is no dining car, squirt.'

The train slowed to barely a creak.

'Terijoki,' Cyril said. He checked his papers for the hundredth time and we came to a halt beside a platform. The new guards don't have a uniform. I'm sure they will, before long. A uniform makes such a difference. But for now they come as they are. There was a woman guard in a greasy army greatcoat, in spite of the heat. There was a boy in nothing but an undervest and a pair of wool *reituzi*.

312

They both carried pistols but awkwardly, as though they weren't accustomed to going armed.

Cyril asked for the *noozhni*. The Necessary.

'For my wife,' he said. 'And my children.'

'*Dakoomyenti*,' the woman barked.

It was my cue to appear. When the boy saw my size, he pointed along the platform to the guard room. The woman paid me no attention at all. She was interested in Cyril's permit to travel. As he had explained it to me, Kerensky's signature should remove all barriers. 'But this is Russia,' he'd added, 'so one should take nothing for granted. Some of these types have gone a little power-mad.'

There was no water closet, of course. It was a bucket. Kira said she'd rather die than use it.

'Very well,' I said. 'Die. But do it quickly before the train leaves.'

'I'm telling Daddy,' she said.

But she did use the bucket.

Poor child. It wasn't her fault Miechen had tried to make such a little Grand Duchess of her. It wasn't her fault Emperor Nicky had bungled things so monumentally and put us out of house and home.

Cyril was still being questioned. A third guard had joined the party and was studying Kerensky's permit very closely. His face was impossible to read and so was Cyril's. He said something about me, I don't know what.

'*Moya zhena*,' was all I could make out. 'My wife.'

The guard gestured to me to get back into the train. I felt it was a good sign.

Masha said, 'I can understand why they might stop a person coming *into* Russia. They might be brigands. But why would they stop a person from leaving a country?'

It was a good question.

Terijoki station was silent. It was the middle of the night though you'd never have known it from the sky. Cyril was the last passenger still detained on the platform. Then I heard laughter and he appeared, smiling.

'All in order,' he said. 'Off we go!'

I said, 'What amused them?'

'Guard asked me when you were going to have the baby and I said, "Not tonight, I pray." But I'll tell you what was really funny. That boy? He couldn't read. Hadn't a clue. He was holding Kerensky's letter upside down.'

We rattled on to Vyborg at a good clip. There are fewer factories out there, just small houses, packed together. Perhaps we'll end up living in one. Mother would prevent it if she could, and so would Miechen, but they might be poor too, when the war ends. I don't really understand about money. Only that it can just disappear. I wonder how much those little houses cost.

Masha read to Kira from *Jock of the Bushveld*. Kira was still sulking about the bucket and refused to look at me.

Between Vyborg and Beloostrov, the train crawled again. Cyril's shirt was stained with sweat. He needed a shave. He pushed open the window. Soot came in, but no air. I tried to think of sea breezes. I imagined taking off not just my second pair of drawers but all my underclothes. I imagined walking into the water wearing nothing but my bathing dress. Not even a pair of stockings.

'Here we go,' Cyril said.

He could see we were at last approaching the customs shed. He lit a cigarette.

I said, 'What do you expect?'

'Bags gone through,' he said. 'Coat lining. Boots. I'm sure they have a routine by now.'

He leaned out of the window.

'Place is deserted,' he said.

It was nearly two in the morning. Was it really going to be so easy? My heart was pounding.

'Ah,' he said. 'Hold on. Signs of life.'

Two men were making their way along the platform, stopping at each car.

Cyril said, 'Nobody seems to be getting down. Close your eyes, Ducky. Or look bleary at least.'

I never saw their faces. They sounded agreeable enough.

'*Zhena zhdyot ribyonka?*' I heard one of them say. 'Wife expecting?'

Another voice asked about money. Cyril showed them what he had.

He offered them each a Park Drive.

'*Schastlivava pootee,*' they said. 'Bon voyage.'

We sat in silence while they continued on along the remaining carriages. A wheel tapper passed by and a cock crowed. Then, very, very slowly, the train began to move again.

'So that's that,' Cyril said. 'Couldn't have been easier. The poor buggers just wanted to get back to their cots and sleep. I presume you do have a few gewgaws hidden away?'

I said, 'I'm not prepared to say. One never knows who's listening.'

'Touché,' he said.

'And you? I presume you're carrying more than you showed them?'

'Of course,' he whispered. 'Very useful having a daughter who can't travel with fewer than seven dolls.'

We began to see clapboard dachas and smell pine trees. Kira moved to sit beside me and make her peace.

I said, 'I'm sorry I was cross with you. I know the bucket was horrid.'

'That's all right,' she said. 'One must expect horrid things some-times. There is a war on. I do understand. I am eight and three months practically.'

She put her face close to my belly and bellowed, 'I am your big sister. You must do exactly as I tell you.'

The sky was starting to burn pink and white to the east.

Masha said, 'Are we in Finland yet?'

I said, 'Yes. We've left Russia now.'

And Cyril bit his lip and turned his face to the window.

Epilogue

I was born on August 30th 1917 at Borgo in Finland. My parents, Grand Duke Cyril Vladimirovich and Grand Duchess Victoria Melita, had fled there with my sisters, Masha and Kira, as the Bolsheviks rose to power in Russia. It was hoped to be a temporary arrangement, until Russia enjoyed calmer times. My father thought so, at any rate.

My earliest memories are of Coburg in Bavaria where we settled after the end of the war. The house we lived in had belonged to my maternal grandmother, Granny Edinburgh. I don't remember her. She and my other grandmother both died when I was still very young, robbed of their health, Mummy always said, by war and revolution. Granny Miechen, my father's mother, was German by birth but Russian by adoption. She was apparently all sparkle and gaiety until the Bolsheviks did for her. The notion I have of Granny Edinburgh, who was Russian by birth but German by adoption, is that she must have been dark and heavy, like the furniture that cluttered her house.

My earliest impressions of Father are of a person most often seen from the back, on his way out of the house to the golf course or the motor enthusiasts' club. I've heard it said that a housewife doesn't like to have a man under her feet during the day and Mummy certainly seemed always to be busy. We had very little domestic help.

Mummy looked much older than Father though I believe they were almost exactly the same age. He called her Ducky, she called him Cyril with a soft *c*. The first time I heard a Russian refer to Father as Grand Duke Kirill I thought he'd made a mistake.

I'd say we were a happy family. But when I was about five years old there was a sudden change in our circumstances. Father fell ill, but in a way that was puzzling to a child. He had no visible wounds or rash or fever but he began to look frail and trembled a lot. His golf clubs gathered dust. My sister Masha explained it to me as, 'Daddy's nerves are worn out.' We moved to France, to Brittany, in the hope that the sea air would help him to recover.

St Briac was an idyllic place for a little boy. I was allowed to run about the beach in all weathers and, as hoped, Father began to regain his health, though he became increasingly odd. Instead of filling his days with golf or bridge or motoring jaunts, he commandeered a spare bedroom and spent his time planning to restore the Russian monarchy.

I had no idea what this meant but one day he summoned me to his tiny study, this hub of Romanov operations as he saw it, and tried to explain it to me, carefully drawing everything out on a sheet of shelf paper. He and Mummy were cousins, their shared grandpapa had been Emperor of All the Russias and by rights, Father said, he should now be Emperor. Indeed someday he would be, and in time so would I because I was his only son. At that point I burst into tears, not so much at the prospect of being Emperor, but at the thought that my duties might prevent my playing on the beach.

I remember Father drying my eyes and saying, 'Don't worry, dear boy. It won't be for a few years yet. I'll make sure you're properly prepared.'

I also remember my aunt Missy saying, 'If His Imperial Majesty wants a cup of coffee, I think he might leave off surveying his Empire for five minutes and make it himself. This isn't the Ritz.'

Aunt Missy was the Queen of Romania, another concept that escaped me for years because I thought queens wore crowns and Aunt Missy almost always wore curlers or a straw hat. She often visited us in Brittany and she and Mummy would paint walls and plant vegetables and do all kinds of other un-queenly things. Mummy was always particularly gay when Aunt Missy visited, and Father was always particularly glum.

Our blissful life in France seemed about to end when I was seven and we returned to Coburg. Mummy explained that Coburg was a more fitting residence for the Guardian of the Russian Throne than a seaside cottage in France. Also that Father wished us to commence using our rightful titles. So I became Tsesarevich, Grand Duke Vladimir Kirillovich, Masha became Grand Duchess Marie Kirillovna and Kira became Grand Duchess Kira Kirillovna. Mummy was the Empress Victoria Fyodorovna. Father was always particularly pleased when anyone addressed her correctly.

When my sister Masha married Fritz-Karl in 1925, she became a Princess of Leiningen. Father regarded this as a regrettable step down in the world. He thought a Russian Grand Duchess could have done better for herself. I believe the Leiningens held quite the opposite opinion. I missed Masha terribly when she went away, but before long I was compensated by the news that the rest of us were to move back to Brittany, not just for a holiday but to settle permanently. At the time I imagined, in my childish way, that this had been arranged solely for my happiness. I now understand that Coburg, and Bavaria in general, had begun to regard our presence as an embarrassment. The Communist Party there was a considerable force. If some of them found Father's posturing as Uncrowned Tsar amusing, most of them didn't. I think he was asked, politely, to go elsewhere.

So we returned to Brittany, to St Briac, but not to our old rental. Instead a house was bought, a larger property, in need of some renovation, but reckoned to be potentially more fitting for an Emperor. I don't know how it was all managed. I suspect some family member, better placed than us, took pity and gave us money. I'm sure Aunt Missy helped us when she could. Mummy's jewellery disappeared too, piece by piece, and she painted a little. There was always someone willing to pay for a watercolour by the Empress of Russia.

Father ruled over his 'Empire' from his study next door to the winter kitchen and spent a great deal of the money we didn't have on postage stamps. Being Emperor seemed mainly to involve writing letters. Somehow we survived and I never wanted for anything, but now I look back I can't imagine what we lived on.

Occasionally we were visited by Russian relatives. Uncle Boris, who had settled in Nice, Great Uncle Sandro and Great Aunt Xenia, who lived in Paris. As I grew older I gained the impression that they came more out of fondness for Mummy than to present their credentials at Father's court-in-exile. I think they thought him slightly batty.

There were other relatives spoken of in hushed voices though not, as a rule, if I was known to be within earshot. They needn't have tried to spare me. My sister Kira, never one to mince her words, had already told me the only reason Father had given me the title Tsesarevich was because my predecessor had been shot by the Bolsheviks. Not only him, according to Kira, but his sisters and his parents and his dog. It was the thought of his dog that did for me. I blubbed and Kira got a roasting. Mummy said there were some people, Great Aunt Dowager Empress Minnie for instance, who still hoped Tsesarevich Alexis might be alive, somewhere in the world, and the rest of his family with him. The Dowager Empress was a very old lady and we must be sensible of her feelings. If *she* believed all those people were still living, who were we to cast doubt and speak of them as dead?

My parents were married for more than thirty years and as a child I rarely heard a cross word between them. Mummy humoured Father's Imperial ambitions and ran a comfortable house. Father was affectionate towards her, in his own rather brusque, military way. But when I was in my mid-teens something changed between them. Mummy came home early and unannounced from a visit to Coburg and there was a truly fearful row.

The only words I heard were, 'In our house! In my home! How bloody well dare you!'

I'd never heard Mummy so passionate before. Kira and I speculated.

I thought Father might have burned a hole in a good rug with one of his endless cigarettes. I was a rather innocent fourteen-year-old.

'No, you noodle,' Kira said. 'It's something more serious than that. I'll bet it's a showgirl. I'll bet he was caught with his pants down.'

Then furniture was moved and the green guest room became Mummy's new bedroom.

'See?' Kira said. 'Father has a sweetie. I bet you.'

I don't know. He never seemed like a ladies' man but perhaps one's father never does.

Mummy's journal quite shocked me when I read it, though in a pleasant way. In it I met a person I hardly recognised, much sharper and funnier than the one I'd known. Her face, in repose, always had a tendency to look sad, particularly after the Father Incident, whatever it was. We rarely saw her smile, even when Masha presented her with a steady stream of grandchildren. After a while Kira grew impatient with Mummy's long face and so did

321

Aunt Missy. They felt she should pull herself together and buck up, but I don't think she was capable. She seemed worn out. Perhaps it was all those years of being staunch and optimistic for Father's cause. Aunt Missy used to say, 'Tsar Cyril may keep the Romanov standard flying but Ducky's the engine under that bonnet.'

When I was eighteen, it was arranged that Father would take me on a jaunt to Paris. The official reason for the visit was for me to get some much needed coaching in the Russian language and history. I suspect there were also some extra-curricular activities on the menu, to introduce me to the ways of the world, a plan I scuppered by developing whooping cough almost as soon as we arrived. I was very ill. Mummy had been on her way to Germany where Masha was about to produce child number five, but she was so worried about me she broke her journey and came to Paris. She wouldn't leave my side until she was sure I was over the worst.

Father and I went home as soon as I was well enough to travel, Russian coaching and any other Parisian activities postponed, and Mummy continued on to Würzburg. She was with Masha when the baby was born, another girl, Mechtilde, and she stayed on for the christening. She seemed in no great hurry to come home. Quite soon after the christening Masha sent a wire. It was addressed to Kira. Mummy had suffered some kind of seizure, but she was conscious and showing signs of a good recovery. There was no need to alarm Father but Masha suggested it would cheer Mummy up no end if Kira visited her. Kira set off at once. I wanted to go with her but she insisted that Father's need of me was greater than Mummy's.

'Your job is to stop him worrying,' she said. 'Distract him. Play cards with him. Ask him about Russia. And make sure he doesn't leave cigarettes burning on the arm of his chair.'

Father and I heard nothing for twenty-four hours, then came Kira's telegram. TALK OF RECOVERY TOSH. COME AT ONCE.

It was a hellish journey. Father wouldn't eat or drink or close his eyes for a moment of rest, but neither would he give way to the least display of emotion.

'Only fifty-nine,' he kept saying. 'Strong as an oak, your mother. Kira given to melodrama. Always was.'

Mummy lived on for another three weeks though it was clear to all of us that there could be no recovery. My aunts Sandra and Baby Bee came to see her but Mummy barely acknowledged them. Aunt Missy was her favourite sister. She was the one Mummy would have wanted to be there but day after day Aunt Missy failed to arrive. There was some difficulty over permission for her to travel. I remember saying, 'But she's the Queen of Romania?! Who's to stop her?' and Kira said, '*Was* the Queen of Romania, dear. Cousin Carol wears the crown now and he's as nutty as a Dundee cake.'

By the time Cousin Carol gave his permission and my aunt arrived, Mummy was barely conscious but I'm convinced she knew it was Aunt Missy who was sitting beside her. We were all there when she died. It was very late at night, and the doctor said the end was imminent. They can tell by the way a person breathes. Aunt Missy moved her seat so I could hold Mummy's hand but when Father appeared in the doorway she gave him such a blistering look that he came no closer. He just hovered, not sure what to do with himself. When it was over Mummy looked twenty years younger and Father looked twenty years older.

'Terrible business,' he said. 'Not like Ducky at all. Never sick, hardly ever, all the years I've known her.'

The next morning arrangements were begun for burial in the family mausoleum at Glockenburg. But then at luncheon Aunt Missy said, 'I begin to wonder though if she wouldn't have wanted to be buried at Darmstadt, at Rosenhohe, with Elli.'

And Father said, 'Bury her at Darmstadt? So she'll end up next to Ernie Hesse? Not bloody likely. What a ghastly suggestion.'

I had no idea who those people were. Elli. Ernie Hesse. Kira had to explain to me that Mummy had been married to someone else, long ago. His name was Grand Duke Ernst Ludwig of Hesse and they'd had a child, Elisabeth, Elli, who had died when she was eight. It was the first I knew of any of it but when I'd digested the information Aunt Missy's idea seemed quite a good one. Father would have none of it and prowled around muttering, 'Bloody Ernie Hesse.'

So the funeral went ahead as planned in Coburg where Granny and Grandpa Edinburgh were buried and Mummy's brother too, Uncle Affie. He was someone else I'd never heard of, someone else who was never talked about.

'Consumption,' Father said.

'Shot himself,' Aunt Missy said.

What a family we were for secrets.

We took Father home to St Briac. I was supposed to be going to London, to study or, as Father preferred it, 'to prepare to reign'. Kira had plans too but neither of us felt we should leave him.

'What rot!' he said. 'Perfectly capable. Vast amounts of work to do. I shall hardly notice you're gone.'

Perhaps our staying with him wouldn't have made any difference. Without Mummy he was a boat without a rudder. He lasted just over two years. Each time we saw him he was thinner and frailer, his clothes were grubbier, his ashtray always overflowing. But he was as full of Imperial bluster as ever and Kira's wedding provided him with his last hurrah. She married Lulu Hohenzollern, which in Father's eyes was a vastly superior match to the one Masha had made.

'The great dynasties of Prussia and Romanov united!' he said. 'What a splendid thing.'

324

We didn't have the heart to remind him that the Hohenzollerns were about as washed up as we were.

Father died in 1938, just one day short of his sixty-second birthday. It was assumed by me and my sisters that his body would be taken directly to Coburg for burial but then Uncle Boris intervened and said there must be something done for him in Paris, a memorial service at the very least, so that his loyal subjects might pay their final respects. Uncle Boris was right. Whatever the rest of us thought about Emperor Cyril's dreams, there were plenty of exiled Russians in Paris who believed in him. A *panikhida* was said for him in the cathedral in Rue Daru and I had the alarming experience of being reverenced by crowds of elderly Russians. They made deep bows signifying that they now regarded me as their new Tsar. It seemed a bit rich. I've never set foot in Russia.

Uncle Boris tried to reassure me about my new position. He said there was no need to fire off communiqués as frequently as Father had done. Just an annual newsletter would suffice. Also that perhaps, if times should ever change, if I should live to see the day, it might be a nice gesture to take Father's bones back to Petrograd, to Leningrad as they now call it, though Father never bent his knee to that abomination.

'Back to Mother Russia,' Uncle Boris said. 'I imagine it's what he would have liked. On the other hand, perhaps he wouldn't want to be separated from Ducky. You could take her too. But then, would she have wanted to end up in Russia? Buggered if I know. I leave it up to you, dear boy. You're in charge now.'

Kira said, 'I don't think bones have wishes. They're just bones. And anyway they'll probably be nothing but dust by the time anything changes in Russia. Why must Uncle Boris complicate everything?'

So, as the possibility of taking Father's body home to Russia was as remote then as it is now, we travelled on to Coburg and laid him to rest beside Mummy, in the Edinburgh mausoleum.

I was eighteen when Mummy passed away, twenty when Father died. A bit too old to be considered an orphan but it did point up the disadvantage of being born to aged parents. Now I have a little daughter of my own, I miss my mother more than ever. Everyone should have the pleasure of two grannies, at least for a few years, and my mother would have been a granny with tales to tell, better than anything in a story book.

She and Father left Russia not a moment too soon. The tide was on the turn. Another month, another week, who can say what might have happened to them, and for a long time they had no idea of the fate of those they'd left behind. When the war ended, when trains and letters began to move freely again, their world had disappeared.

VLADIMIR KIRILLOVICH ROMANOV, MADRID, JULY 1954

The Roll Call of
Ducky's Disappeared World

Those executed in Siberia in 1918:

Nicky, Tsar Nicholas II
Sunny, Empress Alexandra
Nastinka Hendrikova, Sunny's lady-in-waiting
The Grand Duchesses Olga, Tatiana, Maria and Anastasia
Alyosha, Tsesarevich Alexis
Dr Genya Botkin
Misha, Grand Duke Michael
Seryozha, Grand Duke Uncle
Grand Duchess Aunt Ella
Vladimir 'Vova' Paley

Those executed in Petrograd in 1919:

Grand Duke Uncle Paul
Uncle Bimbo, Grand Duke Nikolai Mikhailovich
Uncle Gogi, Grand Duke George Mikhailovich

And those who survived in exile:

Grand Duke Great Uncle Nikolasha
Grand Duke Uncle Sandro and Aunt Xenia
Dmitri Pavlovich
Grand Duke Boris Vladimirovich
Dowager Empress Minnie
Miechen, Grand Duchess Marie Pavlovna
Grand Duke Andrei Vladimirovich
Olga Paley
Countess Brasova
Felix and Rina Yusupov
Tanya Botkin and her brother Gleb
Alexander Kerensky
Anna Vyrubova
Isa Buxhoeveden

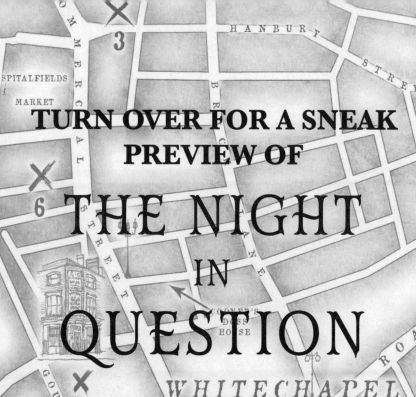

**TURN OVER FOR A SNEAK
PREVIEW OF**

THE NIGHT
IN
QUESTION

THE NEW BOOK FROM

LAURIE GRAHAM

AVAILABLE NOW IN HARDBACK AND EBOOK

I don't powder my face till I've had the ten-minute call. I like to have one last thing to do, something to distract me from the shakes. You can't prevent them, but you can decline to pay them much attention. So I have my little routine. I rub eau de cologne on the back of my neck, then I tie an Indian shawl under my chin to keep the powder off the front of my gown and, once I've started powdering, woe to anyone who tries to strike up a conversation with me.

The young ones are the worst, the girls particularly. They do their turn and then they come off full of bubble and chatter, with never a thought for them that's still waiting to go on. Tittering and squealing. It's like trying to compose yourself in a monkey house. Boys seem to be more circumspect, and the old-timers are like me. We may be depended on for patter and jollity on stage, but just before we go on we require silence. I've often thought theatres should have two dressing places. One for Before and one for After.

So I tie on my shawl and while I'm powdering I make a gargoyle of myself in the looking glass. I don't mind what I see. The passing years are on my side. Not like some. I've seen faded beauties drummed off the stage in tears. If good looks were your ticket, audiences will show you no pity once they've faded. Men don't want to be served mutton when they can get chicken. But if you're a comic it's a different matter. The worse I make myself look, the more they laugh, and it has another advantage: if they happen to see me on the street without my rouge and lamp black they never know me.

The next call comes.

'Miss Allbones to the stage.'

Sometimes you only have one stairway to climb, sometimes you have to walk a country mile. Every venue is different. I've played halls where the only way to reach the stage was to go outside, through puddles and God knows what else and risk catching your death. And I've been lost a few times too, when I first started out in proper theatres, took a wrong turning and nearly missed my cue. But gradually your feet remember even if your brain doesn't. You can go back to a theatre after many years away and trust your feet to convey you safely to the wings.

The wings. Not pleasant places, I will say. They smell of rubber and turpentine and fear. What little space there is is cluttered with ropes and hoses and bad-tempered gas men and lime-boys. And you don't want to get on the wrong side of them. A cross word and they might give you too much light and show you to disadvantage. Or they might extinguish you entirely and leave you in the dark.

But the wings are where you must wait and observe something that can never give you any pleasure: the closing minutes of the act that's gone before you. Say the artiste is being very well received? Then the audience don't want him to finish. He's set the bar high. How can you follow that? On the other hand, if he's dying on his feet he's putting the audience in a bad mood and you'll have the job of winning them back. He can't win. He may be your dearest friend in the world, but not when you're in the wings waiting to go on after him.

Then off he comes, pushing past you, dripping sweat and either beaming like a loon or cursing the day he ever took up the profession.

That's the moment. There can be no turning back, no crying off sick because you've got two ears on your head. The chairman taps his gavel.

'Ladies, gentlemen and . . . lawyers, tonight for your delectation, a magisterial mélange of music and merriment, *pause for good-natured groans*, a banquet of bathos, burlesque and badinage, *wait for it, wait for it*, I give you, *gentle drum roll, if Bones hasn't fallen asleep*, the inimitable, the incomparable lionesse comique, Miss Dot Allbones!'

1

So this is how it all started. It was a Friday the first time she claimed me. I know that because Valentine was waiting for me in a hansom. He had rooms in Dalston at that time but on Fridays he'd usually come home with me for a glass of bubbly and a bite to eat. Any other night of the week I could ask my manager, Monty, if I felt in need of company, but on Fridays Monty has to eat dinner with his mother. It's a Hebrew custom.

I kid him about it. I say, 'Would it really kill you to miss Friday dinner once in a while?'

'No, Dot,' he says, 'but it would likely kill my dear mother.'

The thing was, some nights I was quite happy to go home alone, but some nights I wasn't. I can't explain it. I'm not a silly woman. I don't suffer from the vapours. I can step out onto a stage in front of a thousand faces but coming home to an empty house, in the dark, sometimes it gave me the jitters. When I was a kiddie my brother Albert used to think it a great lark to hide in the ginnel along the back of our house and jump out at me, so perhaps I should blame him.

Now Victoria Park, where I was living, is a superior kind of area, not dangerous like Whitechapel or Wapping. But there was a passageway at the side of the house, with a door leading to the back yard and another set of rooms, and it was as dark as a coal hole round there. I'd have preferred to keep that door bolted but Mr

Earp, the gentleman who lived at the back, used to say it wouldn't be convenient to his callers. I don't think he ever had any callers, but what could I do? He paid his rent and he was entitled to do as he pleased with his door. So, daft as it may sound, I was happier when I had a gentleman to see me home, even if it was only a scaredy cat like Monty Hyams, or a slip of a lad like Valentine. It put my mind at rest.

Sometimes there was no gentleman available. If I was playing second house I might ask, 'Who takes drink with Miss Allbones tonight?' but the old hands would already have had a nip or three from their flask, before, during and after as you might say. They wanted to go home, and the younger ones didn't want to keep company with an old-timer like me. They had their sweethearts to attend to. But Valentine didn't have a sweetheart. He was a bit backward in that respect, or so I thought, so I was always glad to see his name on the playbill. Valentine St John, Genuine Male Soprano, because then I knew I'd have company for Friday night.

We were both playing the Griffin Hall in Shoreditch. I'd been engaged for the last two weeks of June and the reason I was delayed coming out that night was that Jimmy Griffin had commenced arguing about my fee. He said the houses had been very poor, the box was down and we must all be prepared to take a cut.

I said, 'Your houses are poor because you don't hire enough decent supporting turns.'

Jimmy Griffin can be as tight as a duck's arse. Nobody wants to see clog-dancers in this day and age, nor spoon-players. They'd as soon watch rain run down a window pane. People expect value, but I can't carry a show on my own. I'm good but it doesn't matter how good you are if your audience has got the hump by the time you go on.

'Well,' Griffin said, 'I'm afraid I shall have to talk to Monty.'

'Yes,' I told him. 'You do that.'

Valentine had a cab waiting for me at the end of the passage and I was hurrying to get to it when suddenly she appeared in front of me. She gave me quite a fright, stepping out from the shadows like that.

'Is it Dot?' she says. 'Is it Dot as used to be Little Dot? From Wolverhampton?'

I've never glossed over my humble origins. Make a feature of them, is what I say. You must use whatever you've got. But still, she caught me by surprise, speaking of Wolverhampton.

'Yow wouldn't remember me,' she said. 'I used to live across from your house. It's Kate, off Bilston Street.'

I never should have recognised her. What had it been, fifteen years? No, more like twenty. And time hadn't been kind to her. When I think what a corker she used to be. When I was a nipper I'd have given anything to have her curls and her pretty face.

She took off her bonnet.

'Now do yow know me?' she says. And I did. Well, it was more the set of her that was familiar, and her Black Country way of speaking. I've quite lost it myself.

'Never expected to see me again, did you?' she says. 'I'll bet yow didn't even know I was in London.'

Well I hadn't thought of her in years. I asked her how she was, though it was clear from the look of her that she wasn't doing well.

'I see you're going on all right, Dot,' she says. 'I hear you're getting a hundred pounds a week.'

That's the way people talk. A hundred pounds a week, two hundred, even three hundred. They just think of a number and double it. And they never reckon on your outgoings, or the weeks when you have no engagements. There's nothing steady about being an artiste.

I said, 'A hundred a week? You should go on the halls yourself, Kate. You're quite a comic.'

'Oh, Dot,' she says, 'I do wish yow'd lend me sixpence for my bed tonight.'

She said she'd been sleeping at the casual ward in Mile End but she was hoping to get a bed at Cooney's that night. Then I felt badly for her. Nobody lodges at the Casual if they can help it, nor at Cooney's.

I said, 'Is it sixpence for a bed in that rat hole?'

'No,' she says, 'it's fourpence for a single, but if I have another twopence I can get a drop of rum to help me sleep.'

So I gave her a shilling for her honesty and she called down all the blessings of heaven on me.

'Yow'm a good 'un,' she says. 'I've often observed it's the ones with the plainest faces that's got the kindest hearts. God bless you, Dot. Tararabit.'

And off she trudged, down towards Spitalfields Market.

Valentine said, 'Jiminy Christmas, Miss Dot, did you know that woman?'

I said, 'I did. That was Kate. I'll think of her last name presently. She used to pass for a beauty. I used to study her, across the street. Played with her a few times too, before she got too old for playing. And now look what she's come to. Begging for the price of a bed in Cooney's. What a shock. What a come-down.'

He said, 'She wasn't here by chance, then. She'll have seen your name on the playbill and laid in wait for you. You know, I wonder you never thought of changing your name. Spongers are the worst when they know you. They know how to play on your heart strings.'

Valentine changed his name, of course. There surely cannot be a man alive who came into the world as Valentine St John, not in

Wigan at any rate, but Valentine's quite cut-glass these days and I've never managed to get it out of him what name he started out with.

'That person,' he says, 'is dead and buried.'

There was a time, years ago, when I did think of changing my name. I tried Dolly Du Charme for a while, when I was playing the Birmingham theatres, but I found it didn't suit me so I went back to Dot Allbones. People like that, somehow. It sums me up. Our dad used to say, 'I've seen more meat on a horsewhip.'

Valentine said, 'How much did you give her?'

'Only a shilling, poor creature.'

'Too much,' he says. 'You'll be seeing her again. You know what they say. Pay a beggar, keep a beggar. Now, shall we be off? Your cold cuts'll be curling at the edge. And I cannot *abide* warm Bolly.'

Valentine loves his glass of Bollinger. Well so do I and I shall have it as long as I can afford it. There's nothing better after all those hours in a stifling theatre. And he was right about the cold cuts. I had this girl, Olive, who came in daily. I didn't need more than that. She'd come in of an afternoon, flick her duster around, donkey stone the front step once a week. She was a good girl. Clean and quiet, and honest. She never pocketed any of my trinkets. The only problem with Olive was that there was always one last thing she'd omit to do. Like, she'd forget to put the hall runner back after she'd mopped the linoleum, or she'd forget to lay a damp tea cloth over the supper tray to keep everything fresh and dainty till I came home.

I hardly ate a thing that evening. Artistes are generally hungry after a show. It's a well-known phenomenon. It was explained to me once, how it's caused by nerves. You're wound up, tight as a fiddle string before you go on, which saps you without your realising it.

Then you come off and feel like you could eat a ferret with the measles. But that evening I didn't have much of an appetite. Perhaps it was seeing Kate. I think it was.

Valentine said, 'You're not your usual self, Miss Dot.'

I said, 'You know Griffin's talking about cutting wages?'

'Well,' he said, 'let him try. I shall walk out and he'll never engage me no more. I'm booked for Collins's and then the Liverpool Adelphi. I'm on the up and up, so Jimmy Griffin had better not threaten me.'

I didn't like to point out that Collins's Music Hall hardly amounts to being on the up and up.

He said, 'And as for you, he wouldn't dare. You're a star. Griffin wouldn't have a show without you, and he knows it. It's an idle threat. I wouldn't give it another thought.'

One good thing about Valentine is he knows when to apply a bit of soft soap.

I said, 'Anyway, Monty deals with all that side of things. He'll tell him what's what.'

'Quite right,' he said. 'Make Monty Hyams earn his percentage. Miss Dot, I've been thinking.'

'Beginner's luck,' I said.

We had a laugh.

'But seriously,' he said, 'I'm thinking of giving up my digs.'

'I thought you liked it there?'

'I did. But there's a type moved in upstairs and he's not very clean. When he's passed through the front hall there's a horrible whiff. It hangs about for ages. You know me, Miss Dot. I'm very particular about cleanliness. And he has no consideration. I think it's generally known in the house that I'm in the theatre. I work late hours and I must have my sleep, but he's clodhopping about above my head at five in the morning.'

'And then does he go to work?'

'I suppose he does, but he takes his time about it, back and forth, back and forth, and always with his boots on. Well, once I'm awake I can't get back off. I'm a wreck. So I was wondering. About your spare room?'

I'd always kept that room made up in case my brother Albert should think of visiting me, though he never did. It was a handy place to hang my gowns too, my theatricals, not my day wear.

I said, 'It's hardly suitable for a lodger. It's a small room.'

'And I'm a small person,' he said. 'We get along, don't we, you and me? Sometimes I wouldn't even be here. Two weeks and I'll be off to Liverpool. I'd be a phantom lodger.'

Anybody else, I'd have said no at once. I've lived alone too long to be accommodating other people. Sometimes I stay all day in my wrapper, until it's time to go to the theatre.

I said, 'I couldn't allow a lot of hot food brought in. I don't want the smell.'

'Strike me down if I was ever to do more than coddle an egg,' he said.

'And if you required your bits and pieces taken to the wash-house you'd have to come to an agreement with Olive.'

'We'd be company for each other, on a Sunday, say, or when we're between engagements.'

'But only by prior appointment. No coming into the parlour unannounced. I like to take a bath in here on Sunday afternoons.'

'My eyes will be averted.'

'And sometimes I have callers.'

It's only Tom Bullen, but if you're going to take in a paying guest it's as well to have everything on a clear footing from the start.

340

'You'll find me the very soul of discretion,' he said. 'And when you've thought about the rent, be so good as to write the figure down on a little billydoo. Friends shouldn't talk about money. Now, Miss Dot, it's not like you to leave a custard tart.'

'You have it. I've no appetite tonight.'

'Is it Griffin who's upset you? Or seeing that person?'

Kate from Bilston Street. I did keep thinking about her.

I said, 'Anybody can go to the bad, I suppose. Look at Chip Carver.'

'Who's he?'

'Novelty siffleur. Well, he was. Before your time. He was highly successful, though you wouldn't think it to see him now.'

'What happened?'

'Lost all his teeth.'

'That was bad luck. And he had nothing else to fall back on?'

'No, more's the pity. He does a bit of message-carrying nowadays. I see him sometimes, on the street. He keeps very cheerful, considering, but that's my point. A bit of bad luck, a wrong turn here or there. How many misfortunes, how many wrong turns does it take before you end up like Kate, sleeping at Cooney's?'

'A great many,' he said. 'And it's hardly a prospect that should worry you.'

'But you get to forty, Valentine, and you do start to wonder who'll look after you when you're too old to work. When you're alone in the world, like me.'

'You'll never be alone in the world,' he said. 'You'll always have me.'

I said, 'I remember when men used to turn to look at Kate. She was very bonny. And she didn't care what anybody thought of her. I remember when she was the talk of our street.'

'Oh do tell,' he said. So I did.